A Call of Moonhart

The Sundered Deity

David O. Engelstad

Sylphan Media Group

Madison Wisconsin

Sylphan Media Group
PO Box 45454
Madison WI 53744-5454
https://sylphanmediagroup.com/

Publisher's Note: This is a work of fiction. Names, characters, places, and incidents are a product of the author's imagination. Any resemblance to actual people, living or dead, or to businesses, companies, events, institutions, or locales is completely coincidental.

Book Layout © 2016 BookDesignTemplates.com
Cover design by Sanja Gombar, http://bookcoverforyou.com/
Photo of the Author by Dan Myers, Lumi Photography, Madison WI.

A Call of Moonhart / David O. Engelstad. -- 1st ed.
Print edition ISBN 978-0-9985368-1-1

To Stef: My collaborator in so many ways

Contents

Cast of Characters

Moonhart

Aichae, cearnan to Moonhart

Bardán, former shaman to Moonhart.

Corra, hetairan to Moonhart.

Eanna, a hunter.

Feanna, current shaman to Moonhart.

Goban, toolmaker and mate to Sarae.

Grainna, a hunter.

Rhia darSelwe, a hunter.

Sarae darAichae, a hunter who is huntmate to Rhia.

Selwe darSeien, an elder and mother of Rhia.

Siova, ekma to Moonhart.

Sleikin, a provider and age mate to Rhia.

Tien, under shaman to Moonhart.

Tiera, hunt leader for Moonhart.

Lynx

Gaunt, hunt leader.

Hrothar, male hunter.

Kiri, hunter.

Taltaya, both hunter and provider.

Tasso, hunter and cousin to Taltaya.

Treassa, former hunt leader and sister to Taltaya.

White Eagle

Dáiri darFiona, hunt leader, daughter of the ekma.
Fiona, ekma to White Eagle.
Niall darKiri, provider.
Pendal, shaman to White Eagle.

Players

Barrol darBlinna, youngest member of the troupe. Actor, juggler, tumbler.
Beathen durBeglan, singer, juggler.
Beccán, brother of Dughal.
Blinna, the last of the female Players of Bardeelin. Mother of Barrol.
Camran, oldest member of Bardeelin. Actor.
Catha durBreaslain (also darElli), lowlander woman.
Dughal durFortin, leader of Bardeelin.
Fortin, former leader of the troupe and Dughal's father.
Kyna durKellen (also darScothe), lowlander woman.
Oean darJeanna, the playwright of the troupe, actor, singer.
Sionn durGreagir, newest member of Bardeelin. Actor, juggler, singer.

His Own

Broc, member of His Own and formerly betrothed to Kyna.
Cleirach durMiach, also called The Prophet, leader of Kairnaclav.
Fachtnel, leader of His Own in Beldann.
Firchar, member of His Own.
Goodman Tornan, local leader of His Own in Rillsherd. Kyna's father.
Neacal durCleirach, leader of His Own in Bainellen.
Perrin, member of His Own.

Miscellaneous

Barton, stonemason in Lechsede.

Benvi, lowlander woman.

Cassán, keeper of the Old Inn in Bierncarra.

Cedric, stonemason in Lechsede.

Eabr, carrinani in Lechsede.

Edana, innkeeper in Lechsede.

Eimhen, innkeeper in Beldann.

Olchobhar, innkeeper in Lechsede.

Stafan, stonemason in Lechsede.

One

Rhia

May you be favored by Na the Goddess

- Ealdranna curse

I couldn't run fast enough.

Memories nipped at my heels like wolves their prey, sucking the strength from my legs. I focused my attention on the next tree, the next curve on the beaten-dirt trail we followed, the squawks of starlings startled into movement by this silent band of running women. But such distractions lasted a few moments at best. Then the nightmare scenes rose up again and I gasped for breath, stumbled, and urged my legs to greater speed.

Dreams should fade with the light of day, washed into shadows with bright sunlight or held at bay by the arms of a lover. But this was no mere dream: the Goddess Na had reached into our sleep and crushed us to the ground as if our blankets had sprouted roots deep and fast into the soil. None of us could move until She had imparted Her Calling. Into my mind Na had cascaded scenes and sensations, a deluge of memory flooding my will like water submerging stones, each stone a terrible event: wanton slaughter, empty ekarras, nameless perversions from the lowlands creeping ever closer to the crags.

I shook my head and looked up again, again outward away from the rising tide of the Calling. But despite the bright glow of the early season sun, the events She had shouted into my mind with Her whispers fouled my perception of the world like smoke fouls the air, coating what had been vibrant and healthy with an ash of utter, desperate loneliness.

Just after midday, Tiera called a halt. We'd eaten as we could on the run, choking down waybread and pemmican, but even hunters need to stop, regain gasping breaths, and relieve urgent bladders. I almost smiled as I squatted: some things can be counted on when everything else has been uprooted, like eating and pissing.

Our hunthounds flopped themselves to the ground, tongues lolling, resting but alert. I envied them. They saw this morning's run as excitement, another kind of chase and so they waited, looking to us for whatever came next. I looked to my stealna and lied to myself, for a brief moment, that she had the answers, that she knew what lay ahead just like she knew the well-worn paths we ran along. But Tiera's haunted eyes told me she'd only seen enough of the dream to be terrified, not Called. I closed my eyes and leaned against Sarae, my huntmate, finding solace in our shared strength.

"So who is it?" Eanna's unwelcome voice lashed out. "Who has the whole of the Calling?"

"What makes you think tis one of us?" Tiera asked, her voice more calm than I'd have expected. "All of Moonhart dreamed the Calling last night. Perhaps every eknos in the uplands." She gasped, her voice catching. "Could be any."

"It wasn't me!" Eanna sounded as if she'd been accused of something vile.

"No one asked," Sarae said.

"You!" I felt a shadow fall upon me and I opened my eyes. Eanna stood before me, hands on her hips. "Is it you? Tell me!"

"Are you giving up the hunt to become shaman, Eanna?" Sarae asked. "No one else has the right to demand details of a Calling dream." Sarae reached for my hand and squeezed it, then lay back against me, her eyes closed as if that settled the matter. It was a fine hope but a vain one, where Eanna was concerned.

"Why don't you say something?" she demanded of me. "There's no botha for you to run and hide in like a startled chipmunk. Say *something*!"

Cold swept through me, dread and fury both, and I was on my feet and moving towards Eanna without conscious thought. She stepped back from me, her eyes wide. "Don't ask me! I'm no one special to be Called by Na." My voice caught and I stepped back. I looked away from Eanna and whispered: "I'm just a hunter, like you."

"Not like me!" It was Eanna's turn to anger and she reached out and grabbed my tunic, her greater size and strength pulling me off balance. "I wouldn't have missed my shot and made that roe buck suffer. It's not my fault that Na's angry with us. With you!"

I peeled her hands from my tunic and pushed her away. "Do you think I wanted that deer to suffer? The wind blew my shot wrong!"

"Eanna!" Tiera stepped between us. "This Calling has nothing to do with the death of one deer, no matter how clumsy the manner of its killing."

"No? Tiera, you even said at the time that Na wouldn't suffer a hunter treating Her animals so. We're all taught that they provide us food at Her pleasure."

Eanna reached past Tiera's shoulder to point her finger in my face. "*I* dreamt packs of wolves attacking herds of ibex, sleuths of bears, and calls of moonharts, but they didn't eat. They just left the carcasses, bloody and torn, upon a plain to rot in the sun." Eanna choked, then turned away and heaved up the waybread she'd just eaten. Labraitha reached out and gathered Eanna in, holding her as she threw up bile and grief and fear.

"I saw that, too," Tiera said. "But more besides. When the Touch passed I was no shaman, but even I can divine that Na didn't send a Calling to task us for one wayward shot." She looked closely into my eyes and I stood there, silently willing Tiera to forego asking me what I'd seen. I couldn't say. Not yet. "But there's more to tell than even I dreamed. So, let us up and make haste. We'll reach the ekarra tonight. With luck, Feanna will tell us what it means." She reached down and gathered up her pack, the hunthounds jumping up, eager to be away. The rest of us took up our things as determined, if less eager, than our hounds.

Tiera loped off down the path and we, her hunters, fell in line behind her, the hounds ranging out around us. For the rest of the day we ran. By the day's end, fatigue did for me what conscious effort had not and kept the fearful images at bay. I felt un-hunter-like as I longed for nothing less than to be held by my mother amidst the throng of our eknos, a child-like hope that I might set aside, at least for a night, what I'd dreamt and what it meant. With both eagerness and trepidation, we entered the ekarra and hurried towards its center, where all of Moonhart eknos had gathered.

We paused at the top of the shallow bowl that held the Speaker's Mound and the central fire. Surrounding this, each with an unobstructed view, the family fires ranged up the gentle hillsides of the bowl. Those speaking from the Mound could be heard by all in the bowl. Unless, of course, the four hundred families all talked at once, as happened often. As happened then. Shouts went up when those gathered saw us. Hundreds of people lurched to their feet, their voices a-buzz, as if we'd disturbed a hornet's nest.

Tiera led us down to the central fire to where the ekma and other elders of Moonhart waited.

"Good that you're here, Tiera." Siova had been ekma all of my life – more than a score of years – but I hadn't thought of her as old until that evening. The glow of the fire made her hair appear even more gray and the flickering light seemed to leave lines upon her round face. "The other two hunting bands are still out and we hoped we'd have at least one stealnan here." Still, Siova stood tall as if in defiance of her own worry as she pulled the lean and wiry Tiera to a warm embrace and then she reached out and took each of our hands in turn.

When she came to me, she took my hand and scanned my face, searching. I hid a scowl but, sooner than was strictly proper, I pulled my hand out of the ekma's grasp and turned away, anxious to hide what I feared showed all too plainly in my eyes. It would come out soon enough.

"Are any of you hurt or in need of comfort?" Corra, the hetairan, asked from behind the ekma, then smiled an understanding smile. "Or any more comfort than the rest of us?" Her warm, caring eyes looked to each of us in turn, but I avoided her gaze as well, looking instead for my mother.

"Na's Bidden hasn't come forward yet?" Tiera asked.

"No," Siova replied. "She may be from one of the outlying family groups or at one of the seasonal camps, or she might arrive at any moment." Siova stopped and looked back at the other elders of Moonhart. They looked wary, as if they feared further portents. "Unless any of you hold new, as yet unspoken, parts of Na's Calling, Her message is frightening but not immediate."

I pulled Sarae to me and whispered in her ear. "Does she assure us or seek assurance from us?" Amazement shook my voice.

Sarae shrugged, her eyes wide and troubled.

Siova drew herself upright, her generous body an imposing sight. "Visit the shaman soon to tell her your part of the Calling dream. Reunite with your families. When Feanna knows more, we'll gather and discuss."

Goban came up then, as if he'd been waiting for the ekma to be done with us. He pulled Sarae into a close embrace and I smiled at them. The comfort they took from each other gave me some comfort, too. Goban reached out with one hand and I gave it a squeeze. Behind him I saw that the cearnan, Aichae, had stepped down from the

Speaker's mound to welcome her daughter Sarae home. Aichae was an age with my mother and had led the providers for two hands of years.

I looked again for my own mother and didn't see her. She was often gone from the ekarra to trade or travel but, on this night, I'd hoped that I wouldn't be alone in our botha. When Aichae had kissed Sarae I tapped her on the shoulder. "Aichae, where's my mother?"

Aichae reached out to me. "Ah, Rhia. Selwe left with a hand of others some days ago to trade with the sowers."

"Now?" I stilled, the familiar feeling of separation yawning open between me and my eknos.

"The sowers offered and we had furs to trade, so they went. I'm sorry, Rhia." Aichae pulled me into her embrace, pulled me back from the abyss of estrangement that so often gaped at my feet. I clung to her as I hadn't since I was a young girl.

Aichae's long hair tickled my nose. In that way, at least, the mother was unlike the daughter. Sarae never allowed her hair to grow out as much as half an inch but the provider leader's hair fell as a dark cloud upon her shoulders. "I would expect they'll return any day. I'm sure they all felt Na's Calling and will hasten back."

She gave me another squeeze and then held me at arm's length. "With Selwe away, you'll share our fire again, won't you Rhia? I'll set food aside."

How could I tell her that what I wanted most was to escape the din of fear and uncertainty to my botha on the edge of the ekarra? *Ha. Like a startled chipmunk.* "Yes, of course. Thank you."

"Do you wish to call upon Feanna yet tonight? I've no doubt you had a powerful Calling."

At the reminder of Na's Call, I swallowed hard. When I spoke, I heard a childish petulance creep into my voice. "Ah, Aichae. Not you, too."

She gave me her stern look. "Humph. You don't deny it. You'll talk to her soon?"

"Of course. But Tiera's had us running all day and I haven't had a chance to breathe, let alone think. Might I set down my pack and perhaps change my clothes?"

Sarae looked at her mother and then nodded to me. "Go. Stow your gear and get into something clean. Come back soon or I'll come looking for you."

I smiled at her and left them to their reunion. I spent less time than I would have liked washing my arms and face with the water warmed and set aside for that task, and then walked to the botha I shared with my mother while Koudu, my favorite of the hearth-hounds, trotted alongside me. Her tail wagged encouragingly, eager to sooth the spirits of her people upset by the Call. When I entered the botha, Koudu settled down outside beside the door, head on her paws, as if to be there in case of need, as willing to provide solace as a hetairi. The botha felt damp, unused, even though my mother had been gone only a few days. I shivered in the dark, chiding myself for my childish needs and yet her absence unnerved me. Unlike almost everyone in Moonhart – save my mother – I usually enjoyed time spent by myself.

The thick bark that made up the skin of the structure kept out the cold but also much of the light, especially once I let the heavy leather flap close over the entrance. I reached for the shelf that held the collection of small oil lamps, found one by touch, and struck steel to flint and lit the first lamp. I lit the others from that one and set them about the botha and soon enough, their steady flames took the chill from the air.

I changed out of the stiff leather tunic and heavy woolen trews into softer and more comfortable clothing, trying to leave my misgivings on the floor with the discarded stuff. It didn't work. Many days on the hunt followed by the anguished dash home had left me sweaty and tired. I stretched out on the platform, wondering if I might seek the oblivion of sleep, when Sarae slid aside the leather door and came inside.

"Mother says your food is getting cold. Are you coming?"

"Just falling over asleep would be frowned upon?" I sighed. "Or hiding?"

She pulled me to my feet and into a hug. "I know you're not hiding."

"But?"

"But you used to spend every moment you could listening to the stories of the old hunters. You don't do that any more." She let me go and stood back. "It's been noticed."

"But I'm not hiding!" I turned away, fiddling with the lamps as if their flames needed urgent adjustment.

"I know, my love. You're practicing: with your sling or your bow or you're calling the birds. But you do it alone."

"I'm not as good as I need to be. They're expecting – "

"They've always expected too much of you. Now that you're a hunter, even more eyes are on you. I know." She sighed. "It breaks my heart. First the ekma and other elders set you apart with their unfounded expectations and then you retreat even further from the rest of us in trying to fulfill those expectations. You don't have to do that."

"No?" I wanted to believe her but she didn't feel the looks, see the disappointment mirrored on so many faces. I turned back to face her. "Eanna will tell everyone that it was *my* poor hunting, the suffering that *I* caused, that brought about the Call."

"Yes, most like. But no one gives Eanna much credence." Sarae bloomed into that grin that always takes my heart and gives it a shake. "We'll just have to give Eanna another explanation for your long absences." Sarae touched my face and pulled me close for a kiss, soft and urgent.

Her honest, urgent, desire brought a storm of emotions and tears like rain to my eyes. "We've run all day, I'm sweaty and dirty, the Cearnan is expecting us to come and share her fire, and Na has Called us to some as-yet unseen fate. And you want to share pleasure with me? Now?" I laughed and kissed her again. "Do you pester Goban when he's busiest?"

She grinned, a faint dimple creasing her cheek. "He says I find him most attractive when he's doing something else, like tanning leather."

"Ugh. I know." And now it was my turn to wear a sly grin. "We've discussed the matter."

Sarae turned to stare at me, her eyes wide. "No!"

"Oh, yes." I grinned at her. "We've shared many stories since you took him as a mate. Is it true you like him to—"

She stopped my words with a kiss. "Remind me not to take a lover and a mate who are friends."

"Yes, Badger." I'd called her that ever since we were children. She'd argue with me and hold her ground on any point as if she had claws to dig into the soil.

She affected a huge sigh and pouted. "We should go eat. Mother's worried about you. Says you're too thin."

"She's always said that. She waits for me to grow up big and strong like the daughter of her blood." I pulled Sarae into another kiss.

"Now, don't mock the cearnan." Sarae rested her hand on my chest. "If you're not careful, she'll have Goban build a botha that'll fit all three of us, just so she can have you close in case you need feeding." I turned away to seek a robe that I wanted, that my mother often wore on cool nights like this, so early in the Burning season.

Sarae sat herself sideways on my sleeping platform, her feet sticking out over the side. "How about if we go together to see the shaman tomorrow morning?"

I turned to her and she winked at me. I sighed. "Aichae or Siova?"

"Truth be told, while they have traded off giving me Meaningful Glances since I returned, twas Goban who suggested that you may just need a friend to lean on." Her eyes turned all dewy when she mentioned his name and I had to smile.

"As I said, he's a good friend." I turned back to the pile of clothing and hides. "You don't suppose mother took that one bearskin robe with her, do you?" At the sound of rustling, I turned around and Sarae held out the robe to me.

"You mean, the one I've been sitting on?" She rose and took my hand. "Come. I'm hungry."

The crowd around the cearnan's fire near the bottom of the bowl called out to me when we joined them and I began to relax in their welcome. Sarae and I were handed large plates filled with a variety of good things to eat and we sat and ate and listened to everyone talking all around us.

No matter what track their tales took, every story circled back like a sower lost in the deepest woods, to talking about Na's Call. Some spoke of the dream they'd experienced and some spoke of how they weren't ready to talk about their Call. Sarae gasped at each new theme added to the greater Calling, each element of the riddle laid bare. But without the thread that tied all the elements together in order, each story, each dream, amounted to nothing more than the uneasy sense of gathering storm with no shelter in sight. When asked, Sarae refused to speak her dream, saying that the shaman should hear it first. I borrowed that excuse and mollified the Elders by mentioning that Sarae and I would visit the shaman first thing in the morning.

"I look forward to seeing you, Rhia." I hadn't realized that Feanna stood nearby. "Come early, child, and we'll have *te'na* together."

"Certainly, shaman." Sarae squeezed my hand even as Goban spoke up.

"Have you discovered Na's Bidden yet, shaman?"

Feanna frowned and shook her head. "No."

Breaths that had been held escaped from disappointed lips.

"And I doubt I'll know the purpose of Na's Calling until I know whom Na Bids. We have to be patient." The shaman smiled in a way she meant to be reassuring. "Not every Calling is tragic."

Goban shook his head as she walked away. "If she can counsel patience, I suppose I can be patient. My fragment of the dream tells me nothing but that I'm not Na's Bidden." He shivered. "Ai, but that must be a terrible thing: Na Calling you out of a sound sleep and a warm botha."

Aichae had been watching me while Goban spoke. "Goban, Rhia's mother received Na's Bidding, the year before Rhia was born. Does Selwe seem so terrible to you?"

"I'd forgotten that." He gazed at me for a moment. "Rhia, what she was Bid to do?"

I shrugged and set my plate aside. "I'm not sure. She's never said much about it."

Aichae's eyes lingered on my face before she spoke up again. "Selwe not being here, I'll tell the tale in her stead." She stopped and looked deep into the fire. "At least, as much as I know of it, for it's in my heart that the tale is not yet ended."

I shivered and pulled the bearskin robe closer about my shoulders.

"Selwe and I were close when we were young, although not huntmates, Rhia, as you and Sarae are. I'd been out with one of the cearna when a Calling came upon us all. Twas more than halfway through the Gathering season, but the dream showed the leaves heavy and deep green, and the lowland fields golden in the sun. Aye, just as some have seen in this most recent Calling, the dream showed us the lowlands. Then, however, we were shown broken stone buildings and many heard great and sonorous voices speaking. It may have been Na or even An, but we couldn't recall the words once awake, even though we've never forgotten how those words felt. Twas as if the words echoed through our souls."

For some moments, Aichae looked not at us, but deep within the fire as if she sought the sounds, the words of those voices. "When we awoke, the cearnan hurried us back to the ekarra, much like Tiera did to you. The shaman determined, once he heard from all of us, that Selwe had experienced all of the Calling dream." She looked off to the east, away from our fire and the ekarra. "The shaman divined that Na Bid Selwe to travel alone into the lowlands and seek out a particular religious house, built to honor Na the Goddess. But naclavs and honoring the Goddess had fallen into disfavor amongst the sowers long ago and this religious house lay in ruins. She had to find this place and bring back something from it, something that would be of great value to the eknos."

I told myself that it meant nothing that Aichae's gaze fell on me. "Your mother came back with items of great beauty and significance from the naclav, as well as great knowledge of the lowlands from her travels, knowledge that she has added to every year since." She sighed and shuddered. "It must be hard, to be so often separated from the eknos. I don't know that I could do it."

"Did she do as Na had Bid her, then?" Goban looked between Aichae and myself. "Or is that why she keeps going back to the lowlands? Does she still seek something there?"

"She did as she was Bid." But then, in a voice quiet and uncertain, Aichae added: "She must have."

Two

Dughal

As a youth, I remember well the Equinox celebrations. Pa haggled with the merchants that arrived from all over Anacarra while ma visited the grocers. My sister and I sought out the Players. I could envision no life finer nor more romantic than to be one of the Unencumbered, traveling the length and breadth of Anacarra, honored and feted everywhere they went.

- Diary of Kalen dirAila, Mayor of Rillsherd during the reign of Ailnaric I

Bainellen has long been an ill-luck province for me. Fool that I am, I took myself and my troupe of Players there anyway, hurrying south down muddy roads out of Maukellen province in order to arrive in a goodly-sized town before the equinox celebrations. I had thought Rillsherd would suit our needs and we stood just outside the gates to the town proper.

My Players put on their clothes for the entrance spectacle: garish and gaudy, a garden's worth of colors on each sturdy and spangled tunic. The loose clothing allowed for easy movement but the billowing sleeves were cuffed and leggings fitted snugly to the skin so that juggled balls or clubs or knives might not go awry.

Oean rummaged within our wagon and I wondered what instrument he would deem fit for playing us in. Nine years ago I'd coaxed Oean away from his troupe of Unencumbered Musicians and I trust he didn't regret it. He's a fine musician and a magnificent wordsmith, but the troupe he'd been with had asked no more of their word-wright but that he compose the occasional short lyric or bawdy verse. When he sought more he sought me out.

I laughed when on this day he pulled out the Glanellen pipes. He slung the strap over his shoulder, and began to huff and puff into the blowstick to engorge the bladder, causing the pipes to squawk as the drone came up. His nimble fingers flew across the two chanters and brought forth such a happy - and loud - tune as begged to be danced to. Oean's light brown eyes seemed to gleam gold with rapture and his usually-placid features seemed lit as if from within.

"I can't sing to that!" Beathen called out, clapping Oean on the shoulder. Oean shrugged, never missing a trill or an ornament. Beathen drew in a deep breath that swelled a chest that seemed to have been made by the cooper's art, and began to bellow a bawdy song all at odds with the reel that Oean played.

"Enough!"

At my words, Beathen fell to laughing. "So, Dughal. Juggling for me, then?"

I nodded. We all had our jobs within the troupe Bardeelin. Mine own was the task of setting the stage, arranging my players where their talents would best serve the play. Or, as in this case, the spectacle. "You and Sionn trade passes while following Camran on the wagon. Barrol will take tumbling runs between you."

"Ah, that's how it's to be, is it?" Sionn hunched himself over so that he peered at the young Barrol through a fall of long dark hair. "Then it will be knives we'll be throwing," he said in a thick Maukellen accent, so at odds with his normal light Glanellen speech. Sionn's crooked smile blossomed forth as he tossed his hair back. "You'd best be spry, youngling."

Of course, since Barrol was but five years younger than the twenty year old Sionn, Barrol just scoffed. He reached up to tie his blond hair - worn long in imitation of Sionn's - back off of his face. "Aim for Beathen and not me. I'll not get in the way!"

"Good lad," I said. "Sionn, I'll thank you not to perforate our youngest performer. We'll need him for Playing later today."

Sionn affected his most innocent expression. I marveled that he could cultivate such a look given that he and innocence were but scarcely acquainted. His eyes went soft and just a bit wide, and upon his cheek just a hint of his most dangerous dimple showed. "Dughal! You wound me."

"Just don't wound me!" Beathen smoothed his hands down across his well-muscled chest. "This tunic has been mended enough so I'll thank you not to put a hole in it. I wouldn't want to appear unkempt before the fine people of Rillsherd."

Sionn rolled his eyes and turned away, rummaging in one of the compartments beneath our tall wagon. He brought out the juggling knives that were both very shiny and very dull. Oh, the tip could pierce the hand that caught it ill, but the edges were no more sharp than the clubs. With a casual ease, Sionn flipped three of the knives at Beathen, who spun them into a cascade.

Sionn often reminded me of my older brother. Our ages had been much as Barrol and Sionn's were, but alas, Beccán had never gotten much older. He fell victim to the Anwroth when he was but twenty and three. Sometimes my memories of Beccán led me to give Sionn more latitude than I should have. It may be at times that I was unjustly harsh, no doubt for the same reason.

Oean's song continued to spill all around us. Beathen and Sionn began passing the knives back and forth while Barrol stretched and readied himself for tumbling.

"To the top then?" Camran asked.

I turned to the oldest member of Bardeelin. "Up you go. 'From yon lofty perch survey all that would pass before you,'" I quoted from the

Old Poet. "Keep a weather eye out, my old friend. I would compare your assessment with mine own."

"Relax, Dughal." Camran squinted up towards where the sun glowed bright in a cloudless sky. The silver that shot through his once-black hair gleamed in the intense light. "No storms coming our way."

"Optimism?" I asked, projecting astonishment into my voice. "From you, Camran?" I held my hand to his forehead. "Do you fever?"

"I never fever!" He laughed as he hauled himself up to the seat, far above the ground. "No, Dughal, I'm no moonhart to change my hide with the seasons. I just have more fond memories of Bainellen province than you do."

And more dire, too. His long-dead wife Avrea had hailed from Kairill, an important town in this province. As dour as the oldest member of Bardeelin was normally, any thought of Avrea eased his mood and I'd not sour it with mine own misgivings. I nodded and slapped the side of the wagon and we moved into Rillsherd.

Rillsherd teemed with three times its normal numbers as those in the outlying crofts and carrins made their way into town for the Equinox festival and a brief respite from the hard toil of readying the fields for planting. Even expecting that, the size of the crowds surprised me. In the ten years since Bardeelin last played in Rillsherd, it had grown most prosperous. Unlike many areas of Bainellen, Rillsherd seemed to have regained a vitality, a burgeoning growth, despite the repeated reaving of this area by the Anwroth. It looked little like the cross-roads hamlet we'd last played.

With Oean's piping behind me, I strode along the main thoroughfare calling out at every opportunity: "People of Rillsherd! We are Bardeelin, Unencumbered Players of Anacarra! Be entertained! Be amazed! Be edified! We shall perform a play for your delight this very afternoon." Between the noise of the pipes and the two huge horses pulling our distinctive wagon, the milling crowd made way for us – some with smiles and some with frowns. These I'd expected.

I was not prepared for the glares sent our way by the members of His Own.

We'd first met His Own in the north, but this ascetic sect of worshipers of the lonely God were few in Maukellen province. Here in Bainellen they flocked much more thickly. I counted a dozen before we reached the town's center and I began to worry: ascetics seldom see the benefit in diverting entertainment. One of His Own cast me an inscrutable glance and then ran off ahead of us towards the center of town. I began to wonder if I'd chosen the right town to play in.

Throughout all of this, my expression scarce changed, my patter varied as needs be, and the wagon wound through the crooked streets of Rillsherd until we reached the main inn at the center of town: a solid, two story building with a large courtyard surrounded on all three sides by a low gray stone wall. Canvas booths of every description huddled close outside those walls, with merchants selling all manner of goods and services. I noted where a tinker's stall stood so that I might send Sionn there to have some of our properties mended.

The inn itself saw brisk commerce as thirsty farmers took advantage of the inn's ale and food ready to eat. The wagon lumbered by me and I nodded my approval. Sionn walked nearest to the wagon facing forward while casually tossing knives over his shoulder. Beathen, looking both elegant and the epitome of calm nonchalance, caught the knives even as he flung his own at Sionn's back. No one ever seemed to realize that Sionn's gaze stayed focused upon a collection of mirrored pieces affixed to the wagon. Few could pick those out from amongst the bright paint and other gaudy bits adorning our cart, but Sionn used that collection of jumbled mirrors to keep his eyes upon Beathen and the hurtling knives.

Barrol took a fast tumbling run, flipping between the flight of knives and landing beside me with a grand flourish. More gasps and scattered applause erupted and my young scamp bowed low and elegantly, as if to the richest carrinan or carrinanen.

Barrol had been a Player since before his birth, carried upon the stage in his mother's womb. Lona had been the last woman player of Bardeelin, as fine an actor as any I've ever seen. Her performances had made strong men weep and timid lasses fill with resolution. But the edict against female performers had fallen not long after she was delivered of Barrol and she never set foot upon the stage after. A great pity, that.

It was some tribute that Barrol now played many of the roles his mother had performed before him, and I credited him with a studious reading of his mother's notes in the margins of her scripts. I had great hopes that someday he'd play the roles with the same depth of meaning and experience as his mother had in her prime. For now, he was coltish and lanky, with a placid alto voice, long blond hair, and the deep blue eyes of those that hailed from Danellen.

Oean's tune ended. As often happened when he was the sole musician the applause, when it inevitably and enthusiastically came, startled him. He blinked and blushed brightly as he took a hesitant and self-conscious bow.

Beathen dropped the knives at his feet and both he and Sionn turned and bowed, acknowledging the applause. I stepped between them and Sionn gave me a challenging look, his dimple sharp. "You've been practicing," I said sotto voce to Sionn before calling out to the audience: "We welcome you all, for we are Bardeelin, Unencumbered Players of Anacarra. If you enjoyed this merest taste of what we can do, please tell all of your friends to come join us the second hour after noon when we will perform a play for you all."

"Tell your friends to join us," Sionn echoed. "Tell your enemies to try the mussels at the fishmonger's tent." Sionn scrunched up his face and grabbed his nose. "Whew!"

The audience laughed and some of my anxiety ebbed away, for if they laughed at such a well-traveled joke they were well-enough disposed to Players. I bowed once more to those gathered and turned to gather my men around me.

Camran had climbed down from the high seat and stood at my shoulder. "Sionn will have to work in some praises of fishmongers in the play today."

I nodded. "I know. I own he finds as much fun in that as in the insults before."

The crowds dispersed once they were sure there would be nothing more from us for the moment. My men put away their entrance frippery and properties: Oean set the pipes lovingly amidst his extensive collection of instruments while Sionn placed the knives among the equally numerous juggling implements.

The inn took up all of the south side of the courtyard, so I had Camran maneuver the wagon into place on the northern side. Had there been fewer people about, or the promise of fewer for our performance, I'd have had us take the east so as to have the full of the sun and capture all who would come out of the inn. Today, with so many people about, finding an audience wouldn't be the problem that managing it would be. We would be lighted well enough by the sun as it moved west, and furthest from the door so as to not impede the innkeeper in his custom.

Said hosteller had just come out of his establishment and bustled across the courtyard to us, his powerful hands wiping themselves on the once-white towel at his waist. A large man, with a great shock of black hair and a prodigious set of whiskers, he huffed and puffed across the space. I had moved to intercept him when someone took hold of my arm.

The man importuning me wore the same clothing as the rest of His Own I'd met in my travels – black trews surmounted by a black tunic surmounted by a black wide-brimmed hat with a single band of red upon the crown of the hat and at the cuffs of his tunic – but I could tell he was no simple religious. The cloth and cut of his garments was finer, the shoes and hat more delicately buffed, and the way he peered down at me even though we were of a height told me that this man played a far larger role in this town than I'd expected. I caught Camran's eye and he moved towards the innkeeper while I allowed the man at my shoulder to wait but one moment more. I directed Sionn and Barrol to begin their work of converting our tall wagon into our stage. With that effort commenced, I turned my attention to the man beside me. His eyes had narrowed and his mouth pursed so that it disappeared beneath the combined onslaught of beard and mustache.

"Good day to you, my friend. I do apologize for keeping you waiting. It is a task of no little effort to create the proper space for a performance, but we should be ready by this afternoon."

My respectful greeting caused his beard's angry advance to retreat a bit. "Your effort will be for naught without my leave."

For over 500 years, during both the Rici and the Republic, the law has stated that no local power may deny Unencumbered Players their right – and duty – to perform. My interlocutor could not be ignorant of such a fact but he might be willing to challenge it. I knew better than to scorn a leader in his own town, for whatever else he might be, this man was far more important to his neighbors than any troupe of Players.

"By all means...?"

"Goodman Tornan." He gave me his name as if reluctant to part with it. "I am mayor of Rillsherd and a deacon of His Own."

"I am pleased to meet you, Goodman Tornan." I bowed deeply. I judged he knew to a fine degree just how much deference he was owed. "It has been some time since last we played Rillsherd. Any guidance you might have for us would be appreciated. We seek only to fulfill the role that the God of sheaves has ordained for us. As, no doubt, do you yourself."

His mustaches scowled at me for that. Tornan was some dozen years or more my senior. At least, so I judged based on the deepening lines around his hard, blue eyes. He reached up and took hold of the lapels of his tunic and stood up straight as he peered down at me.

"A man who knows his place and seeks to understand what the lonely God has ordained for him may, at last, come to wisdom. So, allow me to instruct you in this: the town of Rillsherd does not appreciate Players or their wanton ways within the town limits."

"Oh?" I frowned, confused. "Then how do you hear news of the other parts of Anacarra? How do your people learn of the glories of our past? Why the Old Poet himself said that Players provide the living chronicle of the times."

Tornan's eyes glittered under his thunderous dark eyebrows. "Be that as it may, the people of Rillsherd are Godly folk."

"There is no conflict, Goodman. We're more than happy to perform a play that is as moral as it is edifying." The set of his jaw told me he was not convinced. "Why, it is well known that – for the simpler folk, you understand, not one such as yourself – words of a most serious nature are most oft heard and remembered when presented as part of a spectacle. Sermons spoken from the Priest's spiral may be righteous indeed, but will they be remembered?"

"And your plays are remembered? They are so much fluff and lies."

For a moment, words failed me. But as he began to turn away, I blurted out: "To be sure, *some* plays are just such fluff, I do confess it." Tornan turned back, smiling as if he'd scored a point upon me. "But the best of the poets and playwrights knew that art should provide usefulness in its delights. Such a one we will present today."

"The playwright? Tell me, who would you play?" Tornan stood, hands upon his lapels, waiting.

I did a quick mental inventory of the plays that we might do for this vexatious man. "We'll present a play by Hereric." I thought, if any playwright could win his approval, it would be the monk turned poet from the darkest days of the Rici.

Tornan seemed to consider this. Finally, he nodded. "Well, Player, I'll give you a chance. It may be true that the rustics from the crofts might remember your message better than mine." He moved closer to me, his smile all of teeth and nothing of mirth. "But woe to you should I judge your message heretical."

"Oh, have no fear, Goodman." I gave a small bow. "It is what I do."

"Hmph. One other thing. While I will grant you your time upon the stage, I'll not have you playing more depraved fare off of it."

He stood impassive but resolute, yet I couldn't for the life of me take his meaning. "I'm sorry. What?"

His nose crinkled in disgust. "Since you affect to not understand me, let me be plain. I won't tolerate any sexual depravity nor any woman or girl importuned by your lusty fellows."

I struggled to keep my mouth from gawping open at his description of us. It wasn't wholly untrue, of course, but rarely so specifically or insultingly applied. I closed my mouth and smiled with reassurance. "I daresay the fellows in my troupe are no more lusty than the next man."

Tornan glared. "I know all the men in this town. I don't know yours and all hear of the licentiousness of Players. It's said that in the western provinces women act like harlots with actors, and I'll not have you thinking to treat the good women of Rillsherd in similar manner."

He was serious! Of course, players had long been sought out as partners in pleasure. In the western provinces, yes, but in the east, too. Until now, if Tornan's attitude reflected the prevailing one. "I assure you, we will importune no one."

"I have your word?"

"My *word*, Goodman." He seemed somewhat mollified if not actually convinced.

Camran arrived at my side even as another black-clad man approached Tornan. Camran shared a glance with me as Tornan's companion shared a whispered word with him. Tornan's eyes grew wide and then narrowed as he looked back at me. He nodded and his fellow ran off. Tornan turned back to us. "We will be here to see what lessons you will present today, Bardeelin." With that, he left us, turning on his heel with no word of leave-taking.

"What a peculiar man." I shook my head as if to shake off the contagion of the man's foul mood and turned to Camran. "He threatened to deny us leave to play!"

Camran stroked his beard, pausing as he considered his words. "He might well have. Our innkeeper told me that Tornan rules over the sacred and secular both. The priest in the Temple Fields is said to look to him and not the Hierarch in Bierncarra."

"These His Own are so strong in the town?"

"In the province. The innkeeper said that all in Bainellen look to this Prophet: priest and plowman both." Camran smiled, the lines around his eyes deepening. "Our friend the innkeeper was much put out by this. I'd wager he feels displaced from what had been his own position in Rillsherd."

"I'd know which way the wind blows, Camran."

"As I am vane, let me tell you then. The innkeeper feared Tornan would forbid us our Playing. In part to demonstrate his strength, in part to discomfit the innkeeper. Except that Tornan is distracted."

My heart began to beat slower and my hands unclenched. "Let us hope he stays distracted and not think to turn his gaze on us again."

We walked towards the wagon. Camran pitched his voice low so that only I could hear amidst the bustle of the inn yard: "It's said aloud that Tornan's eldest daughter died of mischance."

I closed my eyes and took in a deep breath. These were clouds I'd not expected to see in such a fair town on such a faire day. "And what is said in whispers?"

"The darker whispers say that she seduced Tornan's lieutenant, a deacon and family man, and has run off for shame. Others say that she simply bedded some poor crofter, a man not of Tornan's choosing, and has run off to be with him."

I forced a hearty smile on my lips and slapped Camran on the shoulders. "Well, then. We'll not play *The Rape of Sarru.*" The only reaction to my jest was a single grizzled eyebrow arcing upwards. "Keep your eyes and ears open, old friend. With your help, we'll not misstep."

As each had their place in the entrance spectacle, so too did my Players have their roles in preparation of playing. Rillsherd had been, until recently at least, too small to have built an amphitheater. So, my two youngest opened our wagon up to become our stage. A masterpiece of the wainwright's art, the wagon was so cleverly designed that in under thirty minutes we had a proper stage on which to perform wheresoever we might be. Few such wagons still rolled across the Anacarran countryside, but Bardeelin had one and it never failed to impress.

While Sionn and Barrol prepared our stage, Camran arranged with the innkeeper for every manner of things necessary to our performance: for space, for patrons, for notice, for our food and lodging. As has been the custom since the days of the Rici, we wouldn't be charged for our room or board, provided that we told the news of the wider world to all who asked and performed songs, plays, and tales. Had we with us those who didn't perform such as women or servants, then Camran would have set with the innkeeper the fee for their food and lodging. But none such had traveled with Bardeelin since just after Barrol's birth.

Given the cautions of Goodman Tornan, I thought to perform something more somber yet still engaging. I took Camran aside and called out to Oean and Beathen to leave off their tasks of setting out the costumes and properties.

"My conversation with the mayor of this town has convinced me to change today's bill."

"I thought you spoke to one of His Own?" Beathen asked.

"The one and the same," I replied.

"What shall we perform, Dughal?" Oean asked. "A comedy would seem to suit a festival."

Camran shook his head even as Beathen spoke: "Not here. Or at least, not today. Have you not felt the mood?" When Oean had joined Bardeelin, so too had Beathen. They'd made music together, singer and musician, for some near score of years, but he, too, had had reasons to seek out a new troupe. As I'd been in dire need of Players, I hadn't asked what they were. I've not had cause to regret it, for he has a commanding stage presence, a powerful voice, and a deft hand with juggling, in addition to his singing. Beathen tugged at the hem of his tunic as if he sought to smooth the uncertain emotions of the town. "A comedy wouldn't endear us to such as these." He motioned with his head towards the flock of His Own that still roosted in the courtyard.

Sionn and Barrol trotted over to join the conference. "What's afoot?" Sionn asked.

"We're changing the play. We'll perform *The Wayward Son.*"

"Then it's to be a comedy after all?" Oean asked.

"Ah." Camran cleared his throat. "No. We do it as Hereric intended, moral and somber." He paused and sighed. "Alas."

"Exactly." I turned to Oean. "You, the son, are naive and frustrated by desire. Uncertain, unwanted, uncomfortable desire." Oean's eyes narrowed at the thought and after a moment he nodded, his mobile mind already at work fitting the old words to the current mood.

"Barrol," I said, "your young maid is upright, innocent, chaste. Her desires are pure and her actions right."

"Oh!" The exuberant youth nearly bounced upon his feet. "I see, Dughal. Yes. Neither tease nor temptress, but woman wronged by the importunities of her beloved."

He's been talking to Oean. I smiled and clapped him on the shoulder. "You have the right of it."

"Ah, Dughal!" Sionn pouted, his dimple most uncharacteristically missing from his cheek. "The uplander Huntress is so much better played for comedy. Hereric was a stuffy old fool."

I pulled myself upright and gazed upon my headstrong young player. "No doubt. And yet, you'll play the uplander woman as Hereric envisioned her: licentious, venal, cold and deadly. A fine moral lesson to all who see your performance." I turned to Beathen and Camran. "Questions?"

"I don't think so." Beathen tugged at his beard. "It's been some years since we've played *The Wayward Son* in such a fashion." He shrugged. "Since anyone has played it that way, I dare say."

"Then we'll be accounted original for our efforts." I turned to all my Players. "Go. Prepare. Oean will hand out the pages so that you can enact the words anew." I looked up at the sun and then out through the courtyard's gate to the rest of the faire. "We perform in two hours. Be ready."

Three

Rhia

Na sat upon the ground and began to speak. In Her tales are found the wisdom of Ealdranna.

- Eknos story

The sun hadn't risen far into the sky when Sarae scratched upon the botha and slipped inside.

"Good morning, my love," she said in a tone she no doubt intended to be cheerful.

I combined my greeting with a kiss. "How was your reunion with Goban?"

Sarae blushed happily and smiled. "I do believe he missed me. I'm delightfully sore this morning and he walks about very carefully but with a great smile upon his face." Her smile faded and she sat down on my sleeping platform. "I needed him, the pleasure and the distraction. I half expected to have the dream come to us again, although I'm sure Na knows I need no reminder."

I turned away and washed my face and sweat-soaked scalp in the basin: Na had Called to me again in the night, the whole of the dream fresh in my mind. I took a towel and dried myself. "Many people sought distraction and comfort last night." I smiled. "Sound travels."

"The hetairi heal hearts as well as bodies. You could have called on one of them. Telnan has always favored you. I'm sure he would've given you comfort had you asked."

I shook my head. "The company of my own thoughts was all I was fit for."

She rolled her eyes. "Ready?"

"No." Sarae simply took my hand and led me from the botha.

Thick clouds hinted at the possibility of snow later, but for now the morning felt warmer for them as we walked along, Koudu trotting beside us. My botha lay on the outermost edge of the ekarra while the shaman's occupied the very center, and I looked with dream-fresh eyes at my home as we passed through it. Children who had not yet experienced the Touch – and therefore young enough to be spared Na's Calling – played away from the worried glances of their minders; Aichae and her providers met to plan for the next gathering expedition; and others kept busy by fletching arrows, weaving baskets, working leather, and other crafts. The elders sat by the central fire, speaking with each other and whomever else sought them out.

They greeted us but I didn't want to see the looks on their faces. All my life I'd seen them: the looks that said they expected more of me. The looks that I'd somehow disappointed them by being no different than any other child. And then, when I'd undertaken the hunter's rite of passage as I did, suddenly the gazes became more expectant and, consequently, more disappointed. *Thank Na I'd had the good sense not to tell the* whole *tale of that hunt.* Was it a wonder, then, that I held myself apart?

Sarae returned the greetings for both of us. Before we had a chance to announce ourselves, Feanna stepped out of her botha to greet us. Being ten years younger than my mother, she'd never seemed old to me. But this morning she looked as wan as I felt. Her hair had not been rebraided, her eyes seemed haunted and haggard.

"You didn't sleep well, shaman?" Sarae asked.

She shook her head. "No, I'm afraid not. Many came to see me even after the feast last night, and when I did fall asleep, Na's Calling came upon me again. I fear that it will share my bed like an unwelcome lover from now on."

"Please, Na, let that not be true," I said.

Feanna held open the flap to the botha. "Please, come inside. Or, as the morning is fine, do you wish to be outside?"

I shuddered at the thought of the eyes of the whole ekarra watching us. "Inside if you please."

She showed us in and we put aside our heavy outside robes and sat down upon the benches carved directly into the rocky soil and covered in soft hides. Her botha took up more than twice as much space as my own, with room for sleeping platforms and benches for seating a hand or more of people. A small fire pit, smelling of applewood smoke, provided light and heat for a kettle, most of the smoke wafting out through a hole in the top of the botha.

"As promised, I've waited on the *te'na* for you." The shaman paused and looked at Sarae. "You are still drinking the *te'na*? You and Goban will be mated next Singing season, is that right?"

"That's correct, shaman. We should be drinking the *t'ana* when the snows come again."

"When keeping each other warm is a pleasure. Good." Feanna poured the woman's tea out for all three of us. We drank for a few minutes, the grassy and slightly earthy taste doing more to ground me than anything else since I'd returned to the ekarra. "Which of you will begin?"

My guts gripped inside of me, but before I could swallow my tea, Sarae answered, "I will." And yet, for several more moments, Sarae simply sat there turning, turning, turning the earthenware mug in her hands, a sure sign of frustration in my huntmate.

"This is what Na sent to me, and may Skiem take me to the briarwood if I know what it means," Sarae said. "The ekarra spreads out before me but it's empty, no people, no cats or hounds anywhere.

29

When I'm awake I can't see the whole of the ekarra, but in the Calling I see every botha. They lay empty." She shuddered and sipped again. "I turn away because I know that I won't find who I look for there."

Sarae drank down the last of the tea and frowned, setting the mug aside. Feanna filled it with another brew steeping beside the fire and handed it to her. So preoccupied with her memory of the Calling, Sarae didn't even nod her thanks. She took a deep breath and began again. "Within a step, I stand at the furthest reaches of Moonhart territory. But instead of looking back, within the territory, I look outwards. I no longer search or patrol. Now I act as sentry. I wait."

"What direction do you watch?" Feanna asked.

Sarae paused and looked deeply inward. "South. I remember thinking that the sun off to my right is old and weary, about to set below the Crags."

"And what do you wait for?"

Sarae didn't answer at first, but turned instead towards me and reached for my hands. "Rhia. I wait for Rhia to return to me."

The barest twitch of a smile flickered across Feanna's lips. "Your love for your huntmate is so strong that it makes itself felt even in the midst of a Calling dream."

"No," Sarae demurred, "I don't think that's it." But she squeezed my hand. "In any case, I wait. The year is yet young, before the equinox. Then leaves appear, growing to green and filling the trees. Then the year turns old, late in Hunting Season, perhaps as late as after the equinox." Her hand moved to her belly and she smiled at me. "Rhia, I was pregnant!" The smile faded. "But even the stirring of life within me doesn't make me feel whole. I feel as uncertain as if I stood upon a rope bridge in a thunderstorm. Still, I watch and wait, vigilant." She let go of my hand but not my gaze. "I don't know what I stood vigil against, but I knew I mustn't fail."

Feanna nodded when it became clear that Sarae would say no more. Slowly, as if they were afraid I'd bolt like a moonhart calf, they both turned towards me. I drank down the last of the *te'na* and set the mug beside me on the bench, clasping my hands in front of me. I knew, once I spoke my dream, that my life would change irrevocably.

When I looked up, both Sarae and Feanna watched me, their eyes warm with love and concern for me. *My life has already changed. It changed the night Na Called me to do Her Bidding.*

I stood as if to declaim but couldn't pull in a decent breath. I began to pace, forcing air into my lungs, so that I could speak. Ha! So that I wouldn't faint. I had only a step or two in which to move, but I couldn't just sit. At last I began to speak, to shape the dream world into knowable truth.

"Listen, then, and hear the whole of Na's Calling. Aye, I know I hold the whole of the dream, and once I tell it, you'll know it, too. The woods are dark and clouds cover the moon. I begin to run to the south, the roots of the trees tripping me, fallen branches scratching me. I hear Sarae calling for me and I gain confidence knowing that she and the ekarra are safe and will wait for me to return. When I set out, tis dark and I run, although I don't know what I run towards."

"Do you not?" the shaman asked. "Tell us what compels you."

I shook my head. "It's a jumble; not just one thing, shifting in my mind and memory as if I sought a particular pebble in a stream, but the current pushed it from my hand even as I reached for it. When I see light ahead of me, a clearing in the woods, I hope to discover what's drawing me."

I shook my head and stopped. Sarae gazed up at me and nodded and, with her strength, I continued. "It's suddenly brightest day and I'm standing next to a great stone shape that reaches all the way up to the sky. From it's base pours water that cascades over the edge of a great precipice. I watch the water fall and then realize I'm looking out over the nosmoot plains and Moonhart territory is far behind me."

"There's no waterfall there." Sarae's voice trembled with wonder and confusion.

The shaman hushed her. "Tis a dream, child. Let her continue."

"No, there isn't a stream flowing south through the nosmoot plains," I agreed, and sat beside her. "But in the Calling I watch the water flow in a swift and glittering stream through the plain and I smell the heady freshness of it, the life of it, and I know it as the gift of Na.

"Across the plain it flows, but the plain isn't empty. All manner of animals roam there, gathering at the stream side to drink deeply of the blessed waters: elks and bears, ibex and moonharts, lynx and white eagles. And even cougars, falcons, and serpents, the lost eknos."

"Did you feel a kinship to them, Rhia?"

"Yes, shaman, I knew them to be our kin in totem form. They were mine and I was theirs and I longed to go down to the plain and join them. I knelt beside the water where it gushed from the monolith and drank of it, sharing that with those gathered below."

"Was it the time of the nosmoot, Rhia?" Sarae asked. The shaman nodded her approval. We were some years away from the next nosmoot and if that was the gathering I'd dreamed, we'd know when Na wished us to act.

I shook my head. "No. Tis happening even now." They accepted my assertion without demur for such is the knowledge of dreams. I continued: "The creatures share the water, still they hold themselves aloof, one from another, ignoring all the others. Tis peaceful if not at peace, so I look for a way down from the high cliff to join with them. That's when I see, edging ever closer to the milling animals, a pack of wolves."

The shaman hissed. "No eknos has wolf as its totem."

I nodded, drank again to ease the dryness of my throat. "And yet, I feel a kinship with these wolves similar – but not the same, tis true – to that which I feel with every other animal upon the plain." I shivered and stood again. "These wolves, with fur as black as the inside of a cave, have come up from the lowlands." Sarae reached for my hand: she knows how I feel about the lowlands. "The wolves begin to circle the plain. I plead for wings like the white eagles so I can fly down to warn my kin animals that our sisters the wolves have turned on us. I wish to bugle like the elk and alert them all, or grow hooves like the ibex and traverse the scree of the cliff face in scant moments. Despite that none of my pleas are answered, it becomes clear that the nine sets of animals know of the wolves' presence."

"And?" Sarae prompted. "What happens?"

"They do nothing." I stopped my pacing and turned to Feanna. "The wolves attack. Falcons are brought down, and then cougars. Serpents, too, are killed, the wolves eating the hearts from them all. The cast of falcons is no more and then the clutter of cougar are gone, but though the carcasses should be wet and streaming blood from ribs gaping wide, old bones litter the plain. The others don't flee, don't give aid to those being attacked. No. They leave the stream side, put more room between each other, and turn their backs to the wolves."

I slumped down on the bench next to Sarae and Feanna gave me a tisane of sumac, rosemary, and rosehips: dark and sweet. I drank and wished my heart to cease its pounding. "I feel red, ravening eyes upon me and I seek the eyes that sought me. Then I see the greatest of the wolves searching the woods behind me."

"Does this wolf find you?" Feanna asked.

"No." I shook my head. "It's odd. I know that the wolf must find me. Will find me. He doesn't mark me but I mark him: large and lean, eyes intelligent but cold and pitiless. Black fur splashed with red like blood."

I shuddered and Sarae reached for me. "But just then the great wolf's attention slides away from me and the other wolves fall upon the animals of eknos. They scatter the glaring of lynx, and threaten the sloth of bears and the herd of ibex. And the call of moonhart."

Sarae closed her eyes and cursed while Feanna rose up, her fists clenched. She took a deep breath and I waited for her this time. Clearly mine wasn't the only strength being tested.

"When the black wolves first fall upon the moonhart, I rise up off of the ridge as if I'd grown the wings I'd wished for. The nosmoot plains roil as the wolves stalk the edges and the animals run every which way. I force myself to watch the wolves hunt and see few carcasses upon the ground of the uplands, and for that I thank Na's mercy."

"Go on, Rhia," Feanna said when I stopped. "You haven't finished the telling."

I laughed at that, although twas a near thing. My eyes felt hot with tears. "No, there's more. I begin to float upwards, upwards, until the cries of the wounded fade and the stench of blood eases." I wipe at my nose with my sleeve, for the memory is strong. "All of the Crags lie below me, like a knobby spine down the center of Anacarra. I float high above the great escarpment, across the denuded lands that had belonged to Falcon eknos before the sowers broke them so long ago, and then to the eyrie of the White Eagle."

"From such a height, do you note anything else of the world?" Feanna asked. The shaman's expression nearly evoked a smile: such powerful curiosity admixed with a dread of knowing.

"Not that I recall, although when Na offers me the dream again I may see more. No, off to the west, over the edge of the Crag, the lands are indistinct, as if fog or time or distance obscures them. The winds blow me to the east, over the lowlands themselves." I stopped and swallowed hard.

"Rhia doesn't like the lowlands," Sarae told the shaman.

I grasp Sarae's shoulder and squeeze it. "Not so," I say. "Better said, I'm terrified and yet the Calling takes me right over them. Even in the depths of the dream I gasp at the sight and cry out."

"But the people of the lowlands aren't so different from us," the shaman chided me. "Save that they live by the plow and not the hunt. The eknos today once lived in the lowlands."

"I know, shaman. My mother tells me the same. And yet...."

Her eyes grew soft with sudden understanding. "Oh, my poor child. And with your mother always descending to the lowlands, that must be hard for you."

"She's there now." I shook my head. "I don't know how – or why – she does it."

Sarae looked from me to the shaman and back. Finally, she turned to Feanna and asked a question that I'd never been able to bring myself to ask: "It's said that the lowlanders don't know Na's Touch and are, therefore, made mad by their isolation. Is that why they act as they do?"

Feanna shook her head. "Tis true, they don't know Na's Touch. But I don't know that such a lack would make them mad. The children of eknos aren't mad, are they?"

Sarae and I shook our heads, but I still sat down next to my lover and took her hand in mine.

"Come, Rhia. There is more."

"Indeed. The lowlanders may not be mad, I can't say. But Na's Calling shows me creatures in the lowlands, monstrous huge creatures, each one as large as a meadow, a whole valley. Just as each raindrop that falls pools together to make a pond or a lake, so, too these creatures cover the land like a storm. Thousands of pale white claws grasp at the ground, stripping the fields of health. People walk by or even amidst these creatures with no sense of the fearsome wrongness of it!

"I turn away, look back to my beloved uplands, and see those same creatures attacking the very forests of the Crags, the briarwood no longer keeping them at bay. Provider meadows begin to fall under the weight of these creatures, the bright colors and heady life leaching from the uplands, to be replaced by barren white. Even as these creatures grow and grow and grow, theirs is a ravenous hunger never truly sated. They deplete the soils even as they crouch there in their own filth.

"Disease?" Sarae asked. "Tis said that lowlanders crowd so thickly within their 'towns' that terrible maladies spread through them like fires across the tree tops."

I nod. "That may be, although I'm not certain. The Calling shows me a swarm of humanity spread out from crossroads and fords, building after building. Even as the wolves attack the people of eknos, the sowers attack the land, not with swords but with plows."

I drank the last in my mug, though it had grown cold. No matter. No warmth seemed possible as the dream filled even my waking senses. "Does Na truly Call to us?"

Feanna nodded. "I wouldn't be shaman if Na's Touch hadn't left me in communion with Her. What I felt, came from Na. Do you doubt it?"

I shook my head. "I felt Na's presence in my dream, without question. It rang within me like echoes from the time I experienced Her Touch: familiar and frightening both. But Na wasn't alone, for the Calling felt saturated with ... maleness. Masculinity."

"But what would An of the sowers have to do with us?" Sarae asked. I shook my head, for the more I contemplated these feelings, the less I understood.

"Na is only one aspect, Sarae. When our Foremothers still lived in the lowlands, we worshiped the God and Goddess in their joined aspect. It seemed to us then that An and Na strove together. Perhaps that's what Rhia felt."

"Perhaps," I acceded.

"Was that the whole of Na's Calling?" Feanna asked.

"Nearly. I blow south as if on the wind, high above the lowlands, and yet I see them clearly, see the people working in their fields, see the wagons pulled by great beasts on their roads, oxen and horses both. I see their towns and villages and even some great cities that hold more people than live in all of the uplands. I see great festivals that seem to hold little joy or celebration and much of fear and hatred. Even so, they do not see the flood that rises to cover their fields and roads and villages. Water red as blood, red as death, rising from the southeast of Anacarra to overspread the lowlands. Soon, great waves of red topped with white caps crash against the hills and cliffs of the Crags themselves."

I stopped then. Stopped my tale short even though it's believed that to be eknos means to share all, especially when what's shared is from Na: be it hunted animals, gathered food, or Called dreams. But I couldn't force the words from my mouth, the words that would tell of the single moonhart doe, caged and carted south, towards the rising waters and surrounded by threatening men.

For some while, the only sounds in the botha were the crackle of the small fire and Sarae's attempts to muffle her sobs. I gathered Sarae into my arms, seeking to both give comfort and take it. I kissed my huntmate and turned back to the shaman.

"Is there any dream that you've heard that isn't part of my own dream?" I force the words past the catch in my throat

Feanna's face looked troubled. She seemed to search her memories of all those who had shared their dreams with her and I wondered if my omission would be called out. Feanna asked: "Do you feel that the final part of Sarae's dream is an aspect of yours?"

I cleared my throat. "I did feel the passage of time, some months, as I experienced the Calling, before it faded and I awoke. I can't say that I saw Sarae, pregnant and waiting for me." I stroked Sarae's hand. "I can't say that I saw myself returning to Moonhart, not before the year again grows old." *If even then.* "But neither did I dream anything that contradicted her dream."

"It may be that the final part of that was an element of the Calling and it may be that it is from Sarae herself, her love for you amending the Calling to something more ... palatable." Feanna placed her hand on Sarae's shoulder even as she turned to me. "Rhia, why did you not step forward as the one Bidden as soon as you awoke yesterday? Why carry this burden alone as long as you did?"

I shook my head as if I could deny it. "We knew a Calling had been sent. Tiera couldn't have run us any faster if she'd known I was the one Bidden." I shrugged. "Besides, Eanna would've delayed us all to accuse me of hubris."

"But you didn't even tell me!" Sarae grabbed onto me as if afraid I'd disappear that moment. "Why isolate yourself so? It makes no sense."

"I wanted...."

"What, my love?" Sarae, my dear Badger, demanded. "Make me understand."

"You don't think I knew I was the one Bidden? That out of all the eknos, Na Bids me to do whatever it is I must do? Of course I knew! But for just one more day I wanted to be ... ordinary."

Silence. Silence save for the blood pounding in my ears. And then Sarae laughed, unfettered, relieved peals of laughter. Her hands lifted my chin so that I gazed into her eyes.

"No one has ever mistaken you for ordinary, you fool. Save you yourself, most like." Sarae kissed me. "Even your green eyes set you apart!"

"That's not fair! The ekma, the cearnan," I turned and pointed at Feanna, "not even the shaman ever had any reason to think me other than what I am. And yet they've always singled me out."

"It grows wearisome, with all eyes upon you?" Feanna asked.

"I grow weary of my every action being judged by any standard but who I am. I'm no one from a tale."

Sarae touched my hand. "That's good. You're nothing like Delara from the story."

I smiled, wiped my nose. "You're still wrong about the 'Promise' tale."

"Do I have to throw you in the fish pond again?" Sarae asked and then pulled me close. "You're made for extraordinary things, Rhia my love."

I shook my head, sat up straight, and held Sarae's hands tightly. "I'm just me!"

Feanna smiled, but her eyes were sad and her voice replete with something not unlike regret. "Rhia, Na Bids you to serve Her."

At the noontime gathering, Feanna had me stand before everyone and recite the Calling dream again. I stood upon the Speaker's mound, my strained voice still carrying easily up the hill to the hundreds gathered there in utter, compelling silence. At each stage of the telling, I saw recognition spark in people's eyes as I spoke their part of the dream. Recognition and relief well mixed with fear as the whole shape of the dream became clear.

As before, I couldn't speak of the last image in my dream, the solitary moonhart doe. Silence lasted for only a few moments until the shaman stepped to my side. "I have heard the whole of the Calling dream in Rhia's. Is there anyone present who feels that the dream they shared was not to be found within hers?" When no one spoke, Feanna placed a ceramic pendant on a leather thong around my neck and the weight of it felt like a curse. It told all eknos, Moonhart and all others, that I followed Na's Bidding, that I should be given aid and discretion.

The ekma pulled me into her embrace before I could wiggle free, kissing both of my cheeks. "Your mother will be proud, Rhia. We've always known you had a greater destiny to fulfill and I've every confidence that you'll succeed in what Na has Bid you to do."

"Which is what, exactly?" Aichae asked. "And by herself? What is she Bid to do?"

And thus began the arguing. For all that I was to do Na's Bidding, precious few people asked me my opinion on what I was Bid to do. Some decided I was to be a messenger to lead a large party to every eknos in the south. Others felt that I would lead hunters into the lowlands to seek out the black wolves of the Calling. With each declaration that I was Called to command others I shook my head. The Calling had shown no others, I said. But no one listened, save perhaps the shaman who urged patience, that Na had more to show to us.

I feared the shaman was right.

Sarae, at least, gave me no opinions nor asked any of me. She simply declared that she'd be my support in whatever I might be Bid to do. Her quiet and sure words warmed me, but I knew that regardless of Sarae's declarations, I'd be alone in this. I began to set aside things I'd need for my journey even as I told myself that I awaited the shaman's understanding of what I'd been Bid to do.

A hand of days passed. Bands of cearna and stealna returned to the ekarra. Families that usually lived apart from the main body of Moonhart eknos arrived anxious to tell their portions of the Calling dream. With the ekarra swollen with people like a pond with snowmelt, the need to feed the eknos became urgent. The meat we brought in from my kill lasted no more than a single meal. Aichae sent one of the cearna groups out to retrieve the kills cached by the hunting bands, but foods gathered accounted for far more of our meals than meat, so she sent two other cearna groups out to gather what could be found so early in the Burning season.

One group she sent to a provider meadow half a day's walk east of the ekarra and they told the following upon their return: They spent the day gathering the seeds and grains and digging the tubers still left after the long cold months and that night they sat around the fires and talked of the Calling, for few spoke of anything else. Then the stillness of the evening burst open upon the fierce and urgent barking of the harvest-hounds. The cearna rushed with staves in hand to discover the cause of the outcry.

Sleikin had been one of those that had gone with my mother to the lowlands to trade. Now he stumbled up the path towards Moonhart. He was alone.

The cearna hastened with their burden to the ekarra. The ekma came, and the shaman. Someone, Telnan I suppose, sent a runner for me. The cearnan brought Sleikin to the heitairan's botha and Corra covered him with what blankets he could bear. One arm jutted at a wrong angle and bruises so darkened and swelled his face that only one eye would open. Blood matted his scalp and blood darkened his trews and blood stained his tunic above his ribs. But worst of all, the stink of putrefaction oozed from the gash in his side.

Corra realized that they couldn't heal Sleikin, only comfort him in his final hours. She adjusted his blankets and gave him tea laced with pain-easing herbs, and only then did she motion to the shaman. Feanna stepped forward briskly, her usually-easy manner replaced by urgency. She knew she had only a short while to understand what had happened.

"Sorchen is dead," Sleikin said when the shaman squatted by his side. "Killed by the treacherous lowlanders who took the others captive."

"How long ago was this?" Feanna reached out and grasped his uninjured hand.

Sleikin began to shake his head, then blanched and gasped. "I don't know how long it took me to reach you. But it happened the fifth day after we left the ekarra."

"The night of Na's Calling!" Telnan sounded so surprised. For my part, I just wished that Na hadn't delivered Her message in such blunt terms.

The ekma motioned to me and I stepped closer. Sleikin tried to speak, coughed blood, and Corra gave him more to drink until the shaman stopped her. "We need to hear what he can tell us. He'll find the fires too soon as it is."

It went ill with Corra and the hetairi to see anyone suffer so when comfort could be given. When the tightness in him began to relax she nodded.

"Those we met seemed fair enough," Sleikin said, his voice again audible. "Eager for the hides ... and other trade goods ... we'd brought. No different from any other sower." He closed his eyes and drew a deep, gurgling breath. "But then, up rode men. Five men. Hooded. Cloaked. In black cloth. They spoke quietly with the sowers. They shared laughter without mirth. Emissaries from one they call the Prophet. Some holy man from the lowlands. They shared our fire. Our food." He opened his one good eye, his gaze falling on me. "In the night, they fell upon us. With clubs. They killed the dogs first. Seems they meant to take us. Captive."

Sleikin gasped in a horrible bubbling gurgle of a laugh. "Sorchen's head was too soft. Mine too hard. His they split wide open but me they only stunned and I got to my feet despite all. Gave to one his death and ... another will remember me ... to the end ... of his days." His good arm came up and drew a line across his cheek. "Gashed his face." He smiled through blood stained teeth and then he coughed again and blood frothed at his lips.

"What of Selwe?" I asked. "And the others?"

"Taken." I felt Sleikin's bloody hand take hold of my own, but I didn't see it, for all had turned dark. I scarce heard his next words, so hard did the blood pound in my ears. "Bound ... by the black cloaks. Tossed unmoving into the wagon. Me they left for dead. Sorchen was dead in truth." He looked away from me then. "Twas the last I saw. Passed out."

"Black wolves hunting moonhart," the shaman murmured.

"And other eknos?" the ekma asked.

Sleikin had told all he could and the elders left the botha together to discuss what was to be done. They didn't ask me along. I sat with Sleikin for it took him some while to die. Ere he died, he wept for the outrage done to him and I wept with him, for the outrage done to all of us. He cursed with bloody voice and gasping breath the wolves who did this. Telnan gave him more of the tea: stronger and stronger yet. It eased his coughing, eased his raving and his pitiful moans.

Finally, he exhaled a breath that bubbled up and out of him and he did not take another.

I rose up and left, my thoughts ricocheting between the reality of his death and the impossibility of Selwe's abduction. Mother knew more about the lowlanders than any among us. If they could take her, hurt her? What then for the rest of eknos?

Four

Rhia

*The Ealdranna number Nine, each within its own territory upon
the Uplands in the center of Anacarra. Honor them as the Goddess's
own children. Fear them for the same reason.*

- Wisdom of the Divine Nabryht'ric, year 167 of the Rici

Sleikin's body had been washed and he'd been wrapped in coarse
milkweed cloth for the trek to the final step. All of Moonhart eknos
gathered to accompany him on this last journey. I'd been moved
much further forward in the procession than I deserved: I was neither
immediate family nor age mate. We'd shared Na's boon a hand of
times but so had many others and none of them gathered with me at
the front. But as his death seemed to relate directly to Na's Bidding, I
walked with the elders and family.

Not half a mile from the ekarra, the ground falls away suddenly in
a sharp cliff on three sides of a rocky outcrop. The whole of Moonhart
can gather there with the pyre set on a tongue of land thrusting out
from the cliff face. When the winds blow from the west the smoke
and ash float out over the small valley a few hundred feet below. The
final step is a long one.

There is silence as the flames are lit. Silence, the shamans teach, for at the end there is no longer breath for tales to be told. But once the flames of the pyre have caught, after the flames have soared up and the body begins to crumble to ash, then those gathered tell stories.

In ordinary circumstances, the stories would be all about Sleikin and his short life. But now, many stepped forward to tell larger tales: tales of Callings of the past, tales of the Two who left the lowlands over 300 years ago to became the eknos reborn, tales of the dangers the lowlands have always posed to the ealdranna.

"They only seek to reassure themselves, Rhia," Sarae whispered to me. *She knows me so well.*

"Of course."

"Aren't you reassured?" Her grin was forced.

I grimaced and tossed the stick I'd been shredding to the ground. "They tell of 'Kirianna's Flight' and 'The Sower and the Hunter' and 'The Moonhart and the Bear.'"

"All good, triumphant stories."

"Oh, aye. That they are. But what I hear is 'Skiem's Wager' and 'The Dirge of Amarna.' Even 'Hiron's Walk.'"

"Leave the dark and dangerous tales alone, Rhia!" Sarae shivered despite the pyre's intense heat.

But I wasn't the only one thinking dark thoughts. Eanna stood up and I shared a look with Sarae. When Eanna began her tale, Sarae's eyes grew wide and then her mouth clamped down, indignant on my behalf. Me, I wanted to laugh. "Didn't I mention 'Hiron's Walk'?" I asked.

> *The northern wild winds grow still as the southern warm air*
> *returns*
> *Still nothing of haughty Hiron's audacious quest is heard.*
> *Then Burning season begins across the lands, from the*
> *briarwood to the ekarra*

*And thus green grow the provider meadows and in the
    groves leaves appear.*
*But still no Hiron is seen, so the ekma decides to seek him
    out.*
Hunting bands are brought in and bound together in effort
To find the foolish lad and thus his folly to end

> *At once.*
> *His kin they long to see him,*
> *The folk of the ekarra wait.*
> *The hope he's hale grows dim.*
> *Twas time to learn his fate.*

*High in the hills they discovered hope to have ended for the
    boy's return.*
*Upon a slender bough no broader than a single bird might
    settle*
*Perched proud Hiron, his broken body proving his boasts
    foul folly:*
*The sheer-walled crags could not, by his strength alone, be
    climbed.*
*The Moonhart Matriarch still within her deepest forests
    moved*
*And his doom had been determined by the last danger he
    faced.*
*The fabled fruit he had sought through four seasons still
    swung free.*
*He had fallen far short, his promised goal he had failed to
    find.*
The hunters left him there, above the forest tops so high,
His wracked body unburned, his youthful boast unproved.

> *He still*
> *Rests high within that tree*
> *So Moonhart know this tale.*
> *A lesson he will be:*

As you boast so shall you fail.

"That's an ill-omened tale to tell, Eanna." The ekma stood and, with the shaman at her side, approached the pyre.

"No," Eanna insisted. "It's a lesson. You say Rhia is the one Called
—"

"Na says so," Feanna corrected her.

"But even you can't say for what." Eanna turned from them towards where I sat. "Rhia has been silent on this, like on everything else. She didn't even tell us, her hunt mates, that she held the whole of the Calling dream. I asked her and she denied it!"

"She doesn't seem to share things with you." Sarae's laughter almost didn't sound forced. "I wonder why?"

"It's long been thought that Rhia held great promise, a destiny," Siova said.

Eanna bristled at this. Her jaw worked as if she tasted each word before she found the sweetest ones to say. "Not all have thought so, ekma, but perhaps we've been proven wrong now that the shaman tells us that Rhia's Bid by Na. And yet, we saw on this most recent hunt that Rhia has, perhaps, spent too much time listening to her own thoughts and not enough time listening to the elders, the old hunters, and other wise people of Moonhart."

"What are you getting at, child?" the ekma asked.

"Rhia needs guidance. Remember what happened to her on her *stealna kir.* I told the tale I did because there are many lessons to be learned from it. One is, to not reach for what's beyond our grasp. Another may be, don't travel such a path alone."

Then I stood. "You say I've been silent, but I haven't. You just haven't listened to *me!* Those who hold these parts of the dream can testify, I'm Called alone. None have spoken of seeing anyone but me in their dreams." I closed my eyes, seeking the presence of my eknos standing around me. I took a deep breath and opened my eyes. "Do you think I want to be alone in this?"

48

"But you shouldn't be! And you don't have to." Eanna's eyes grew hard and her mouth twisted in distaste. "That's not the eknos way, the ealdranna told us so in their stories." Eanna turned from me to the ekma and shaman. "Send me with her. Or, better perhaps, send our entire band with her, with Tiera to guide us all."

"That's not— "

Tiera stood. "The hunting bands are needed here."

"There are other bands...."

Someone stood up in the back and shouted to be heard: "The cearnan should be amongst the group as well, not just hunters!"

"She's too young to go alone! Select a group by lot," another added. Soon the whole of Moonhart eknos stood and shouted, poor Sleikin's pyre treated as little more than firelight, until the words came too fast and too urgent and became as senseless as the crackle of the flames.

The shaman whispered something to Siova and the ekma nodded, her eyes upon me. She then motioned for the rest of the elders to join them beside the pyre. Despite her protests and continued arguments, Eanna finally agreed to resume her seat. When Feanna held up her hands and the last of the din subsided, she called me to stand beside her. "This is a grievous decision and we must make it in neither haste nor error. Rhia is Bidden by Na, there is no question of that. As she is the daughter of one Called to Na's Bidding herself long ago, many have believed – yes, even feared – that this day would come for Rhia as well. We will hold vigil tonight, listen to our hearts and to what Na may yet have to tell us, some in your dreams and some in our hearts. Tomorrow Moonhart will meet and at sundown we'll give our decision."

The fire burned low just before the waning moon rose in the east. Those of us still gathered departed for our beds. The dogs roused and shook their heavy brindled coats as they left the warmth beside the pyre. Sarae's path parted from mine as she went to spend the remainder of the night with Goban and I continued on alone, save for Koudou padding beside me.

I entered my dark and empty botha, lit a couple of lamps, and reached for my pack. Since even before Sleikin had staggered beaten and broken into the hands of the cearna, I'd been setting aside items I'd need if I were to travel the length of the Uplands. By myself: no hunting bands or groups of cearna, and certainly no Eanna. Like a squirrel when the acorns were plentiful, I'd gathered much more than I could reasonably carry and so I sorted through all the items piled upon my mother's sleeping platform. Some things I must have: fire kit, water skin, knife and hatchet, bow and sling. This early in the Burning season snow still covered much of the ground, and so I packed my long sleeved tunic but the weather would warm and so in went the sleeveless tunic as well. Schirh for running over the snow and my heavy woolen leggings to keep me warm until I could safely set them aside. A light and supple hide to serve as my blanket and while it weighed more than I liked, it weighed far less than the tent I'd considered. Although I had but modest skill with it, I desperately wanted to take my mother's flute, carved years ago by he who was then shaman. But Selwe had taken the flute with her to the lowlands and where ever it was now, it was beyond my grasp.

Not so long after, the door flap eased aside and Sarae let herself in. Her breath caught when she realized my intent. But in only a moment, she settled herself onto my sleeping platform, leaned back and stretched out her legs.

"I thought as much. You won't wait for the elders, will you?"

I shook my head. "No. I'm pulled to the south and I must leave soon. Before morning." I bent again to my task. "I fear I've waited too long already."

"But why alone?"

I loved Sarae very much at that moment. In answer, though, all I could do was shrug.

"Because that's what feels right?" she asked.

I nodded, sat down on the step below her, leaning against her legs. I didn't want to leave, to be alone against what I'd seen in my dream. For a moment I thought about waiting, seeing what the ekma might decree. She'd no doubt send others with me. To aid me.

The clenching of my heart answered that. Aid, perhaps. But it *felt* wrong. "Too many people. Too much noise. Too...." Again, all I could do is shrug. "*I* was the one, the *only* one, Called."

Sarae nodded. "So you leave me with the two hardest tasks."

"Indeed. You have to tell the elders what I've done." I reached up to her hands and clasped them hard. "And you have to wait for me to return."

A single tear escaped her eye. "Hurry back, then, my love. You know I don't wait well."

"Even with Goban to pass the time?"

"He'll make it less onerous, tis true." She looked down at me and let go of my hands. "But you know what this truly means, don't you, Rhia?" I shook my head and a small smile flashed upon her lips. "It means, she-who-is-to-do-Na's-Bidding, that the ekma has been right about you!"

I stopped and the blood rushed from my face. Just as quickly, I felt it rush back and I blushed. "Oh, by Skiem's black wing! You're right!"

Sarae grinned at me. "Well, you did go on your *stealna kir* like one of the Old Ones out of a tale, wearing naught but your skin. It isn't as if five generations have passed since anything like that had been done."

I stuck my tongue out at her. "Oh, that's right," she continued her favorite tune. "It has been five generations since anyone had done that. But it wasn't as if you only used an obsidian blade to bring down that moonhart buck." She paused and I waited: *one, two, three....* "Oh, that's right, you did—"

"Enough!" I grabbed her by her ankles and pulled her towards me. "It's been eight years and you're still envious you didn't think of it first."

"Ha! I've seen the scar on your hide from the moonhart's horn, remember?" She leaned forward and kissed me. For a moment, all I thought of was her touch. After too short a while, Sarae pulled back and reached up, brushing her hand across my cheek and then the back of my neck. I leaned forward and rested my forehead against her own. "Do you go now to fulfill that great promise, Rhia?"

"No! I've never wanted to be special. I'm just... I'm just going as Bid."

"That should do it." Sarae closed her eyes, her hands on my neck and our foreheads touching. After just a moment she looked up at me, her eyes glistening, and said, "We've only been back a few nights after a long hunt. Do you wish me to shave your scalp for you? We don't know when you'll be able to do so again, do we?"

I hated when my hair grew out, so I agreed eagerly. I handed her my best and sharpest knife and fetched hot water from one of the cooking fires. Before long, I sat comfortably on the floor between Sarae's knees, my head covered in soaproot lather. She sat above me on the platform, my knife in her hands. I held onto her legs, her solidity and warmth, and tried to lose myself in the joy of her confident touch.

"Will you go to the place where they were taken," she asked me, "and then follow their trail from there? You'd be in the middle of lowlander territory and they'll be many days ahead of you."

I would've shaken my head but didn't want to get cut. "No, I don't think so. Rescuing my mother is too ... personal for Na to take notice. We've all been in danger before. As Eanna so helpfully reminded us, I nearly died on my *stealna kir* but Na troubled no one's sleep then."

"No, *you* were the one troubling my sleep those nights."

I stroked her leg and continued. "The Calling showed that not only Moonhart are threatened by these 'wolves.' So, I think to follow a different path. Would you listen to my plan and tell me if I'm missing anything?"

Sarae's hand touched my cheek. "Go on, Rhia. I'm listening."

I struggled to gather my thoughts as if they were tender shoots hiding beneath the detritus of blown leaves. "Sleikin, before he died, said that those who took our people were emissaries for someone they called The Prophet."

"Really?"

"Indeed." I blew out a breath, sudden anger scalding me. "And Na laughs at us. For many years, my mother has collected any knowledge she can about this man, this Prophet. At the last nosmoot she paid handsomely for information brought by a hunter of the White Eagle eknos."

Sarae whistled softly, the knife paused its scraping across my skin. "White Eagle never parts cheaply with anything. What did she discover?"

"Little enough, it seemed to me. For the price of that moonhart skin, the one I killed—"

"The dappled one, just turning from black to white?"

"Yes! That very hide, all she learned was that the Prophet had his seat in one of the religious houses called Kairclavan."

"That was worth a moonhart hide?"

"Not to me. Not at the time. But now...? That place lies far to the south of us, just east of White Eagle territory." I took in a deep breath. "I can't tell you how, but I'm certain that my path lies across the uplands, directly south, to White Eagle eknos."

She chuckled. "You've never been able to tell me how you can be so certain of things, like how you approached your *stealna kir*." She sobered and then asked quietly. "Will this allow those who took your mother and the others to escape? The lowlands stretch wide and long from here to White Eagle territory."

I shrugged, for at that moment the thought of my mother abandoned to the mercy of those black-cloaked wolves stopped my breath. The lamps began to gleam and I wiped at my eyes. Sarae reached down and wrapped her arms around me. "I don't know," I said when I could speak again. "It may be that their fate is their own.

But I feel, if I head south and seek what help I can from the eknos along the way, I'll find them again."

"I'm sure any eknos who you meet will give you all aid. Unencumbered, you should be in White Eagle territory in just over two score days. This will work."

"You've always had great faith in me, my love." I squeezed her ankle.

"And you've never let me down." She kissed my ear. "There, your scalp is nice and clean and you again look like a true hunter of Moonhart eknos."

I sluiced the soaproot off of my skin and dried myself. I took my knife back from her and set it next to my pack and then caught her looking off to one side, a puzzled expression upon her face. "What is it, Sarae? Is there anything amiss with the plan?"

"No, but there is one trail I don't follow. Why does your mother seek information about a lowlander religious, one of An's? Has she known that he'd be a threat to the eknos? To her?"

I shook my head. "Although she's never said, I think it has to do with what Na Bid her to do. She may have learned of him, or even met him, in her journey through the lowlands." I thought of her abducted, held. Beaten? Worse? "Well.... It's right that her own hunt for knowledge of this Prophet should lead me to her."

I held out my hands to Sarae and helped her to her feet. "You should go back to Goban. Your handsome mate has been without you most of the last two score days. I'll leave as soon as I finish packing my kit."

"He knows I'm here, and why. In fact, he's told me that I should give you all I can tonight, since you'll be without hearth, home, kith or kin for far too long. He said, 'may the memory of your kisses give her strength to go on until she returns to us, as your kisses always give me the strength to endure until you return to me.'"

Sarae has always brought me joy and a sense of belonging. That Goban - my friend indeed - might offer me such consideration, made me feel well loved, no matter the dissension in the eknos. "He's a poet, that one," I whispered into Sarae's ear. "You tell him he has my many thanks for his kind words, and ... and...."

"Hush." Sarae's kisses smothered the words I sought to say, the farewell I couldn't speak. Our bodies shared a language even when our voices failed, and so that is how we said good-bye.

The morning birds hadn't stirred when I slid from beneath the warm furs of the sleeping platform, and the warm embrace of Sarae's arms. She sat up, took my hands in hers, and offered a final parting kiss. But no more words: we'd said all that was needful. I shouldered my pack, tucked my sling and knife into the belt of my tunic, and left the botha.

The cold Burning Season air filled my lungs as I walked out of the sleeping ekarra, awakening my faithful hearth-hound. I squatted down next to her and gave her a sliver of jerky, scratching a spot just behind her ears. Koudou stood up and would have followed me, but sat when I commanded. Hers were the only eyes to mark my departure. The sliver of the moon provided enough light to see paths I knew as well as I knew myself. I looked to the east and frowned, for the sun was close to rising. Sarae and I had spent more time talking, packing, and pleasuring than I'd intended.

I quickened my steps, glad that my botha lay far from the central fire and the elders. Within a few yards, the woods enveloped the path and I left the ekarra: without permission, without plan, but with Na goading my every step. I began to trot, the long, ground-covering stride that every girl learns if she wishes to be a hunter, the heavy pack settled firmly on my back.

After a hand of days I'd left Moonhart territory and entered that of the Elk eknos. Within their territory lay the nosmoot plains that had featured so prominently in the Calling dream. Twas my plan to run to that plain, for I hoped that the fewer hills would make the way smoother. As well-used as I was to running with a full pack, I'd never done it all alone, nor from sunup to sunset. I stopped and took rests throughout the day, eating rich pemmican and drinking sweet mead. I needed energy and between us, Sarae and I had filled my packs and skins with all that I could carry. Even so, I hungered and my pace slowed.

Would that the paths were as empty as my stomach. Last year's leaves lay under half-melted snow and fallen branches fouled the path, slowing me, scratching me, hindering me. After three days of such arduous running, I slipped and fell sprawling in the icy mud. I gripped the very stones of the path so hard that I nearly cut my hands, my arms shaking with fatigue and anger both.

I hauled myself up and wiped the mud from my trews. I can't do it. I can't run all the way to the Kaircrags without stopping, fool that I am. I need to rest, gather some fresh Burning season greens and maybe snare a rabbit. Only a child would believe that Na Bidding me to Her service would keep me safe from my own foolishness. I can still break my neck alone on an Elk hunting trail – or Lynx or Falcon or White Eagle.

I stopped while the sun still rode high in the sky, built a goodly fire, and set snares for any animal that might seek the first shoots of the Burning season. Before night fell, the distinctive squealing of a dying rabbit woke me from my doze by the fireside. I reset the snare and that night I caught another. I roasted and ate one then and the other the next morning. With the snows not quite gone from most of the paths, the meat on the rabbits had little fat, but it gave my limbs strength and some of my assurance returned. I slept well and deeply, rested into the morning, and left when the sun was high. I lost a day, but I regained my footing and sense of purpose.

More than a hand of days later – aye, closer onto seven days for twas the day of the equinox although I found it easy to lose count – I paused for my midday meal beneath the shadow of an ancient cairn built above the nosmoot plains. These mounds of rock were built, it's often said, by the Old Ones – the Ealdranna – before the earliest of my lowlander foremothers crossed over from Dolun on the Mervanna isthmus. No water pooled below this cairn, and while it was as broad as two women standing abreast, it rose only half again as high as the tallest woman, and not all the way into the sky as in the Calling.

I finished a last bite of dried elk and ate from my pouch of nuts and dried fruit while I wandered around the base of the cairn, running my hands against the unworked stones joined without mortar. Lichen had grown along a few of the edges, but I could find no damage from the weather or from age to mar the near-perfect joins of the rock. It's hard not to think of magic when one sees these monoliths, but the Old Ones had assured us they had no magic.

There are eight cairns scattered throughout the Crags and each eknos had a story to go with the cairn in their territory. Moonhart is the only territory that contains no cairn, but we had our stories to explain even that. Stories are how the Ealdranna taught us to be Eknos.

I turned away from the cairn and looked over the nosmoot plains. No stream plunged the hundreds of feet down to the plain below, and on this day, the plains were empty of all but the animals who made their homes there. No wolves stalked them with cruel intent. I shivered and looked behind me as I had in the Calling dream, but no great black wolf splashed with red like blood stood near to hand. I let my breath out and the sound of my heart pounding in my ears faded enough for me to hear the normal forest sounds. I wiped sweat from my forehead even though the day was cold, and left the cairn to make my way down the cliff.

Once I reached the wide, flat grasslands of the nosmoot, I found I could remove both the heavy schirh from my feet and the woolen trews from my legs. With no trees to provide shade, the plains were free of snow and dry. I could run much more quickly and I began to feel like I might even make up for the slow travel through the woods.

I ran across the eastern edge of that plain. The space was flat and wide and ample to hold the several thousands that would travel there to meet, to trade, to find mates, or to see old friends. Empty now, the plain seemed vast and I felt exposed under the pale, distant blue sky. My goal lay to the south and east and thus I would only stay within the plain for a short while. I contemplated taking advantage of the ease of running across this open space, even if it took me away from my most direct path.

But the weather robbed me of that option. The sky gave way to clouds angry and dark. I read the signs and stopped early, knowing that I didn't want to get caught out on the plain with no wood for a lean-to or a fire. I changed course and dashed off into the forest that had been along my left hand side and up into rocky bluffs. I read blazes that told me of shelter, and followed them up steep hillsides and into a cave, the opening of which faced away from the wind and driving rain that soon began to fall. I tried not to complain about the weather, for such satisfaction is thin gruel. Instead, I thought of an old riddle I'd heard as a child.

> *A bright blue sky beautiful and still*
> *Gives way with graceless speed.*
> *High in the branches is heard a heralding wind.*
> *The wise hunter heeds the warning,*
> *Foregoes the blood-foraging. For with bowstrings wet*
> *She hurries herself down the hart's road,*
> *Close to the ekarra to escape the cold.*
> *Hands empty but heart happy that the*
> *Forests drink their fill. At the fireside*
> *Eknos tell their tales while I travel*
> *Across the crags carrying my burden.*

The storm lasted another full day. I spent most of it sleeping: both avoiding the inclement weather as well as renewing my strength. When the clouds would ease up on their gift-giving long enough for me to venture into the wet world, I used my sling to bring down a few partridge or set the snares for more rabbit. I ate and slept and waited with growing impatience for the storm to pass.

Five

Dughal

The Divine Ricu had it wrong. No one is so vain that she wants to see herself portrayed upon the stage. None of us desire to have our naked selves exposed before all and sundry. But put your actors in paint and long braids, make them cry out in odd voices, make them act perfect fools. The audience will repeat your words as they leave the playhouse, taking the tale with them into their lives, hiding their own nakedness.

- The Bard's letter to Carrinanen Brocan durBrocan

List, all those here gathered, and mark my words.
For to you do I offer my sad tale
Of a wayward son led astray. Sixteen
Years did I teach him his duty. Sixteen
Years did I raise him in honor. But no
Man may keep a son from all harm for the
World is large and full of peril unsought.
Into pain and degradation and death.

Beathen had the right of it. We'd not played *The Wayward Son* as a somber, moral tale for many a year. This play by Hereric, with its uncompromising and unrelenting moralistic tone, could be easily mocked, played broadly to great comedic effect, and we had played it so last we played it. Nonetheless, Beathen performed the opening with the proper degree of frustrated anger at the behavior of his "once fine son / betrayed by his own lusts." Beathen thundered from the center of the stage, his dark beard brushed with chalk to lend him gravity in his role. He filled the stage with his large presence and filled the courtyard with his booming baritone.

Oean crossed the stage in hesitant steps, moving closer to the audience in anguished confusion and then stepping back in certain disdain. A marvelous playwright and an astounding musician, Oean never achieved more than a kind of truce with his acting. But in this play, his discomfort with being on stage served to underscore the uncertainty in the character. He pitched his resonant tenor voice a tad higher and, if it quavered a bit, so much the better.

> *The world is to me a new-found place full*
> *Of strange and wondrous things that my father*
> *Never thought to tell me of: the bold taste*
> *Of wine, the heady desire for women.*
> *Of these and more do I wish to savor.*
> *Yet, so doing, will I lose his favor?*

Oean sighed and sat upon the end of the stage, his head downcast as if in thought or melancholy. When he looked up, the sun fell full upon his face and the light caused his pale brown eyes to glimmer gold.

> *Woe, that my sire to me would give a girl*
> *So chaste. Would that our night might come. I yearn!*
> *Dearest God of the field.... But wait. Should I*
> *Offer up my lamentations to the*
> *Goddess who dwells upon the hills so high?*
> *The God of my Father bids me to wait.*

Oean stood then and sidled to the far edge of the stage to look, not at the audience, but over to where Barrol, dressed as the Beloved, has made "her" entrance. As Barrol moved with ease across the stage, his long blond hair hidden beneath a wig of even longer brown hair that fell unbound to his waist in the fashion of unmarried women, the Son begins musing aloud that, "p'raps / she feels such sweet desire as I."

The dark hair caused Barrol's pale blue eyes to seem to be the biggest feature of his face. He batted his lashes with an innocent coyness that powerfully contrasted the Son's lustful lines, "her" eyes opened wide in sweet innocence at the impetuous importuning of her beloved.

Then came a scene that always brought much laughter when we played it as a farce. For many lines, Oean's Wayward Son would hint at the carnal pleasures of man and woman while Barrol's Beloved would agree most heartily that the married state brought with it pleasures of companionship and shared duty. Hereric was such a master of the chaste innuendo that the scene ran to nearly fifteen minutes wherein never once was the matter plainly said. Both, indeed, grew more and more frustrated at the other until Barrol's lines near the end of the scene.

> *What two may do as man and wife should not*
> *Happen between two such as we may be.*
> *My mother has kept me in all innocence*
> *So that upon the day we wed, my rose*
> *A gift to my husband he may possess.*
> *Be that man who will my flower acquire.*
> *My duty doth outweigh mine own desire.*

Beathen returned to the stage and remonstrated with Oean, comforted Beloved, and sent for The Priest to see if he (I) could salvage the son's honor. Upon mine entrance, I strode out onto the stage and marched across to my mark, my steps bouncing with the flex of the boards beneath my feet and my hands gripped upon my priestly staff.

And my mind gone blank as slate washed by rain.

I crammed down the familiar panic. My lines always hid themselves from my conscious mind and if I sought too hard to capture the words they'd flee like frightened hens. But if I allowed myself to find the ebb and flow of the scene, my mouth would speak the lines when needed. The thought that we had so altered the pitch and pacing of the play as to make it unknown rose up to choke me.

The Priest tried to soothe the youth, turn him from the treacherous path he followed. The words arose from I know not where within my mind or offered to me as a gift of the Goddess, once said to be the patroness of singers and storytellers.

> *We are not as the beasts of the fields, for*
> *We have been shown the right and proper course*
> *By the lonely God.*

In my speech I praise An, the God of sheaves, for showing us, His people of the lowlands, how to tame the cattle and the soil, and entreat the lonely God to guide the Wayward Son back to the righteous path. But my Priest can not restrain him and Oean's Wayward Son rushes off the stage to end the first act.

Camran had a long speech to mark the beginning of the next act. Wise Counsel he was, and he spake to the groundlings about duty. Here, far from the jaded cities, heads nodded approval at the rigid proscriptions laid down by the monk-turned-playwright Hereric. The world Hereric described held little pity for any who chaffed at those proscriptions, for:

> *The stars follow their course around the sun*
> *Never deviating from their allotted*
> *Paths.*

And neither, Camran's Wise Counsel told us, should we. And taking quite a long while to do so.

Beathen and Oean had, in the past, gotten into heated discussions over this passage, taking great delight in parsing minute details. For my part, the nuance of interpretation mattered less than if the presentation earned us sufficient coin to give us leisure to argue such details. As was our right, we'd pass the hat after the performance, and the coins collected would provide answer to the subject under disputation. We had half a year to earn the fee for our Seal, but I knew my men and our talent and had no reason to suspect difficulty.

Our innkeeper strode around the edges of the crowd filling mugs and collecting coppers. His serving girls - no, boys. I realized I hadn't seen girls serving in the inns since we'd entered Bainellen province - slipped in amongst the audience itself, selling nuts and skewered sausages. A line of black-cloaked old men stood fast against the wall of the courtyard to our right. Judging by the dour expressions upon their faces, they seemed unaware that they were at a holiday faire. But for all that, they neither offered disruption nor distraction. Nor, from what I could see, did they seem to lose themselves in the performance until Sionn entered the stage.

Wise Counsel still spoke, but no longer stood alone upon the stage. Sionn had slunk in from the wings. He stood bare legged in a tattered leather tunic padded into an imitation of breasts, with lime in his long hair to fan it out from his head and in his hands he carried a necklace made of bones.

Camran's speech acquired an accompaniment of grumblings and groans, boos and hisses. Usually, Sionn's entrance as the uplander would bring laughter and ridicule. The venom expressed startled even Sionn for a moment. He squinted. He crouched and sidled forward. He bent over and shook his backside at the crowd. The boos increased, but Sionn seemed to take their animosity and use it to shape his portrayal of the uplander woman. They (and Hereric) wanted her to be evil? So be it. Sionn nearly hissed back as he climbed to the top of our wagon as if upon a high hill, squatting there to deliver his lines.

I have no care for the fall of the rain. I spin no thread and wear clothing or not as the whim takes me, knowing the feel of sun and rain both upon my skin. I know men. Aye and women also, either at my own desiring. No priest at the center of his web of green tells me right from wrong. I follow a path of my own devising, not trudging behind the tail of an ox, caught forever between hedgerows.

I watched the audience from the wings, keen on any hint that they found the words to be overwrought or underplayed. Sionn twisted all of his usual charm and sense of good-natured mischief most foully and the audience reacted as we had hoped: they booed and hissed, they muttered to themselves. Sionn continued:

I live a life unbounded and so the weak minded of the lowlands are as much my prey as any boar or partridge. Despite what his priest tells him, to his ruin will I lead this youth, for I am constrained by nothing: no knowledge of the God of sheaves, nay nor morality. I will do whatsoever much damage I may.

The act continued on and, true to her words, Oean's Wayward Son was tempted beyond bearing by the vision of immediate satiation offered by the Uplander. The Son ignored all the admonitions of Wise Counsel, Father, and Priest, flouted the prohibitions against consorting with uplanders, and therefore brought about his own doom. Our Son lost his way indeed, and so too did he lose his verse along with his morals.

Did AnA not deliver to the Ealdranna their high hills? Did not Na set a season for all beasts save those that walk upon two legs instead of four? Are we in the right to twist and tame the earth and beasts instead of emulating them in their free estate?

I'll take to me that which I desire. I'll not wait for a season nor not another day. I've hunted the lowlands for that which will satisfy me and in my Hunter have I found her.

It is said that all uplanders are Touched by the Goddess and are made mad by it. This madness is the reason given that the Two – the people of the old lowland provinces of Aelfallen and Varranellen – left their plows and climbed up the crags, to live the lives the Old Ones taught them. Whatever the truth of that, Sionn's Uplander was mad without a doubt. Diseased. Bestial. When Oean's Wayward Son forsook all that he had known for the forbidden vice of Sionn's Uplander's charms, he, too, went mad.

I understand that there are some playhouses in the Fallow Fields of the capitol city of Bierncarra who enact most explicitly and enthusiastically the scenes of The Son's transgressions against our oldest of taboos. But the text that we have from Hereric shows it not, so neither did we. Just hinting at it often makes men uncomfortable and women blush, but I hoped as written the play wouldn't offend even His Own watching from the courtyard's wall.

The final act began with an ever-widening spiral of madness and despair. That some wag in the centuries after Hereric's death sought to turn such a didactic and deadly tale into a farce I saw as greatest genius, for presented as it had been written, there was little to laugh about.

I spent most of the last act on stage, moving from one troubled soul to the next, never successful in my efforts to offer peace or healing. Wise Counsel spoke to me, but the words were for those gathered. He delivered such a speech that laid bare the souls of the groundlings, admonishing all who heard him to tell the tale of what had transpired so all the lowlands would know of the treachery and threat posed by the uplanders.

One of His Own burst into the courtyard and broke the spell cast by Camran's beautiful, awful words. This black cloak dodged and scurried the width of the courtyard to get through the audience to his fellows by the wall, knocking aside those at the back of the crowd intent upon the stage. Their exclamations of protest quickly quieted into muttered imprecations to their fellows, distracting still more from the play.

After a moment or two conferring, the flock of black-cloaked crows took flight, cleaving their way through my audience without so much as a by-your-leave. And so the damage was done, for the attention was no longer on me and mine, but on His Own.

Sionn saved the play for us then. From his perch upon the roof of our wagon that formed the arch of our stage, he called out to those black cloaks streaming from the courtyard. As the Uplander, Sionn rained abuse down on His Own, wagged his buttocks at them, cackled and spit. And then as the last of them left the yard, Sionn segued seamlessly into the lines of the play that cast similar abuse upon Beathen's Father and the meek Beloved. I quickly smothered my smile as the audience turned their attention again upon us and our performance.

Sionn's speech mocked all that was good and noble in the lowlands. He laughed. He capered upon the arch of the wagon. He prophesied grave doom upon all of Anacarra. The Uplander enticed the Son to climb high upon the arch, and so climb to his doom.

Climb, boy! Climb to where the Old Ones abide beneath the trees and upon the highest crags. Leave behind the ways of the plow and the penning of dumb beasts. Harnessed to the plow is to be harnessed to the land.

Such is no life for humankind. The Goddess has shown the Ealdranna another way, and such I give to you.

Barrol's Beloved, driven mad by The Son's abandonment, gave a perfectly heart-wrenching speech that contained no sense, only the purest grief. Barrol knew grief well, and such was his young skill that tears flowed from his eyes. Nearly from mine as well, as I watched the Beloved kill herself, the prop knife plunged into the straw-breast, the bit of red cloth that hinted at blood spilled, the wail of pain and despair as the Beloved breathed her last.

Hers was but the first death. In short order, Father killed the Uplander only to be killed in his turn by the Wayward Son who then, in the midst of his madness, found sense enough to despair and, in despair, kill himself. Oean's Wayward Son fell to his knees, the same dagger that had taken the life of the Beloved held in his own hands (we had but the one working knife). He cried out his pain and grief. Nothing mad in that final speech and Oean seemed to forget his stage fright as he cried out the lines and plunged the knife into his heart.

When all lay dead upon the stage, I proclaimed their epitaph as the epilogue. I stood amidst the bodies, my staff in my hands, and the words flowed from me, unthought but not unfelt.

> *Unhearing are the ears into which I*
> *Would give counsel. Untasting are the mouths*
> *Into which I would pour my herbs and fine*
> *Tinctures in vain hope of curing his vile*
> *Madness. To these I have no more to give.*
> *But to you, fine people, I will offer*
> *My words: follow the plow, as the lonely*
> *God wills. Be guided by the priests of green*
> *That the spiral path be made straight for you.*
> *With this blessing I now depart this place*
> *May the God of sheaves give to you His grace.*

When the final word rang out into the stillness of the courtyard, I had a moment to hear the distant sounds of the marketplace, the rustle of the breeze stirring the trees. When the applause came, it burst upon us loud enough to frighten the birds from those trees. My Players rose from their deaths and we took our bows while the noise rose even higher. I strode forward to the edge of the stage and bowed once more before holding out my hands.

"Good people of Rillsherd, we thank you for such an enthusiastic response. We hope our tale has been edifying. Please visit us tonight at this fine inn where we will share news of the wider world, spin stories of the Golden days of the Rici, and sing songs to make the most weary soul feel good cheer. We are Bardeelin and we thank you."

I stepped back in between Camran and Beathen and we took a final bow. As we stood, Barrol and Sionn sprinted with the energy of youth to the farthest reaches of the courtyard, hats in hand, to stand most prominently and thank most loudly those who dropped coins inside. Beathen and Oean took the middle distance while Camran and I stood nearest the wagon. I heard many words of praise and a few clinks of good coins dropped into my hat. The goodly sized crowd seemed in a fair mood as they slowly dispersed into the inn while others sought the wider town beyond the courtyard.

When we had collected all that would be collected, my men joined me at the wagon and Camran gathered the coins into our lockbox, counting every silver and copper. When done, he looked up at me and some of my good mood at a good performance evaporated.

"So little as that?" I asked.

"Sionn did not show his dimple enough," Beathen said.

"Or showed his backside too much," Barrol added.

"I can do more tomorrow, Dughal, if you just tell me which of my sides to present that will give us the most coin!" Sionn laughed, his dimple showing to us at least.

Beathen tugged at his beard while he looked out over the town. "We have another day or two here, as long as the festival lasts. Then we have the next town and the next after that, and all Bainellen to walk through. And half a year to do it in."

"It may well take all of that," Camran said. He locked the box and stowed it deep within the hidden compartments of the wagon. "Let us hope that the hosteller is as good a purveyor of food as he is of news. He told me that Bainellen suffers from uneven weather and uncertain leadership." Camran cleared his throat. "The Aric is weak and more concerned with his own comfort than the well-being of the province, or so he said."

"Well, Master Lackcheer." Sionn bounded up from where he'd been leaning against the wagon. "May it never be said that you let a sunny day and a country festival ruin your pessimistic mood!"

"Come, come, Sionn," Oean said. "Remember, the Old Poet said 'the witless may smile at the sun, but the wise man wears a hat.'"

Sionn hunched over and shuffled up close to Oean, his slightly crooked smile twitching at his lips. "How now? Must I of needs call the 'pothecary, that you be catching the lackcheer as well?" With that he screwed his youth's face up into that of an old man and wheezed at Oean: "A dollop of old goat's piss admixed with vinegar will set ye aright!"

"Will that cure our meager take, Wise Old Man?" Camran asked.

"No, good sir, it will not," Sionn admitted, turning back to our oldest Player. And then his eyes gleamed again. "But still I offer to stand you a pint of old goat piss at yon inn. A fairer deal you'll not find, I warrant."

"Enough." I held up my hands. "Seeing as we none of us know the future - save perhaps the Prophet in Kairclavan - we will eat while we can, drink what we may and do our duty to Anacarra." I handed my priestly staff to Beathen. "Go. You each know your roles after the play even if you enact them with less of a will. Close the wagon, stow the costumes, and then we'll go into the inn."

Six

Dughal

As a youth, I remember well the Equinox celebrations. Pa haggled with the merchants that came visiting from all over Anacarra while ma visited the grocers. My sister and I sought out the Players. I could envision no life finer nor more romantic than to be one of the Unencumbered, traveling the length and breadth of Anacarra, honored and feted everywhere they went.

- Diary of Kalen dirAila, Mayor of Rillsherd during the reign of Ailnaric I

The afternoon advanced into early evening while we spent our time within the inn. We weren't idle: custom flowed in and out of the inn all the day long and with each new group of people we told our news anew. We told of a hard Fallow season, with unusual cold and much snow in Maukellen, how traders more often make use of the new route through the uplands in the north of the province, providing a much faster (and more profitable) route to the high quality steel, aromatic cedar, and fine-spun cloth goods of Glanellen province west of the crags. No, we assured our listeners, the eknos, to our knowledge, had not been savagely attacking caravans, but Ricbera, the First of Dennellen province, had raised tariffs to such a degree that the merchants complained much as if they'd been attacked.

We told stories and sang songs as well, and these I did not feel needed to be of the same stiffly upright character as the play this afternoon. Most often, we simply sang what was asked of us. Surely, if Tornan objected to that he should talk to his flock, not to my Players.

I sent my men in shifts to the inn's kitchen for our mid-day meal. With the growth of Rillsherd, I was pleased to find on the menu, not only olives from the south of Bainellen, but creamy cheeses from Glanellen, and hams from Aethellen. After several days on the road the accommodations of Rillsherd were most welcome indeed.

So it was that I felt relaxed and all unguarded. I sat with Camran and the young Barrol at a too-warm table nearest the fire, carrying on a pleasant conversation with the Inn's landlord. The others worked the room as was our duty: Oean and Beathen spoke in earnest conversation with an elder of the town while Sionn told a ribald story to a group of young men gaming in the corner. But all conversation and story telling ceased when Tornan and a dozen of His Own tossed open the door and marched into the room.

I looked about, surprised at the reaction of the men nearest me. Surely the His Own of this town were welcome and even sought after guests. But of those around me, none would look towards the doors – though furtive glances began coming our way. Into the silence I spoke up: "Greetings, Goodman Tornan." I put as much hearty enthusiasm into the greeting as if I stood upon a stage and read from a script. "Would you sit and have a pint with us?"

He frowned, the mustaches and beard coming down so hard around his pursed mouth as to obscure his lips entirely. "You are Dughal durFortin, are you not?"

"I am, Goodman. May the God grant you better remembrance, for we met just this afternoon right out there in the courtyard. If you will recall, you were kind enough to grant us permission to play today and on the morrow. You even offered up your sanction on the play we performed and stayed to watch it. I hope it met with your approval."

He glanced about the room. As a performer myself, I know that look. Tornan sized up the crowd and determined its mood, the better to match his words to those listening. "Your words are false, Player. I gave you no such permission." He turned to the man beside him and said: "You're right. They spread lies and slanders."

"Sir, I protest!" I rose from my seat and Camran rose with me. "We told no lies. If I mistook you, then for that I offer apology, but no deception was intended."

"Nonetheless," returned Tornan, "you have no permission to be here. Players are vagrants, thieves and liars. You will leave before full night. I'll not have you within the walls of the town."

My stomach dropped but I affixed a smile upon my face. "Please, Goodman. I'm sure that we can come to an understanding. Come, sit. I'm sure our innkeeper would be pleased to bring you his best ale to keep your thirst at bay while we discuss what might be done to change your mind."

Barrol eagerly made way, showing the empty seat to the Goodman. I desperately wanted to get Tornan off the "stage" so that he no longer performed the role of stern and uncompromising judge to those here assembled.

"I wish you luck with that, Dughal," our innkeeper sneered. Loudly. "Tornan might share a mug with the Prophet or Neacal, but he's too good to bend an elbow with the likes of either of us."

I don't know if he meant to sting Tornan's pride so as to make him more malleable or if he knew from long acquaintance Tornan's intractable disposition. Regardless, Tornan glared at the hosteller and raised his shoulders. A lifetime on the stage told me that the speech to come would be one to fire up the groundlings. He pitched his voice as if he delivered a sermon from the top of a hill: "There will be no more deceitful playacting or false performance in this town."

"Ah, well." Sionn projected his words from across the room, his voice crammed full of regret and concern. "And so, by proclamation, are all religious services in Rillsherd forbidden."

Gasps from the simple farmers and angry mutterings from His Own met this casually delivered comment. Sionn stepped back as if in surprise, his hand going to his chest. "Oh! You meant *us*. But that can't be right. All know that we tell stories. It's His Own who proclaim truth and yet tell lies about innocent Players."

"You *dare?*" Into the thicket formed by mustache and beard appeared a gaping O from Goodman Tornan's surprised mouth. Then his jaw snapped shut with such force that I fancied I heard the sound from where I stood. His eyebrows moved together and he raised his fist towards Sionn. "I could have you whipped for that insult to the lonely God."

Sionn laughed. "I offered no insult to the lonely God, Goodman. But it's telling that you see no difference between yourself and Him."

"Sionn, you're not helping." My words were too late and too little. Sionn's words, on the other hand, were having a momentous effect.

"Bah!" Sionn picked up his pack. "The Goodman here played us false. Do you truly believe he's here to deal honestly?"

I turned towards this Deacon of His Own. Tornan stood tall as he could, shoulders squared as if ready to do battle, his eyes narrowed. Here was a man who would brook no insolence from one he deemed to be his inferior, and so were we deemed to be. The men with Tornan looked from him to me and back again, some with eyes gleaming in eager anticipation of a fight. "No. I suppose not," I said to Sionn. Then I addressed Tornan. "Since such is your most resolute will, we'll get us gone, and in good time, too." My men needed no more urging. With final gulps of ale and hastily pocketed slabs of cheese and bread, we moved to leave.

"That you will, sirrah. But first you'll pay the innkeeper what you owe for the ale you've drunk, the food you've eaten." I began to protest anew, but my words faltered when I saw just how proud he was to have thought of this method of demeaning us. "Your kind provide nothing to the common good, no meat, no barley, nor no labor. Therefore you'll pay ere you leave."

"Outrage!" Camran shouted. He, at least, had not lost his words in the face of this insult. "We've done our duty as tradition and the laws of Anacarra require. We shared news with all who have asked it of us and provided entertainment in this public house. We *have* earned our meat!"

"Vagabonds and liars. Add theft to your crimes and I'll see you all pilloried."

Another moment and Tornan might decide to do so whether we further provoked him or not. I placed a hand upon Camran's shoulder. "Come, Bardeelin. Let us collect our things and we'll be away. Camran, settle with the innkeeper. There are other places to go where we will be more welcome." I took three strides forward and stood face to face with Tornan. "Rest assured, Goodman. We will tell all the Unencumbered troupes of our treatment here today. When your town is cut off from news of the wider world and your people begin to forget who they are as Anacarrans, then will you rue this day."

My curse on him was met with laughter. "We don't need debauched players to tell us what goes on in Bainellen. His Own travel all about the province. We hear what's meet and right and necessary for us to hear. There's no need for your news and no market for your lies." He leaned down to me as if to share a confidence. "Take heed of *my* advice, Player, and seek another path for earning your meat and drink. If you think this is what the lonely God has in mind for you, then you've been believing your own lies too long."

Utter silence met this statement, the men of the common room either cowed or concurring, I know not which. I shared a look with my men and we exited the inn, the sound of Tornan's mirth echoing in our ears. Tornan would allow us only enough time to stow our gear within the wagon and put our old horses into harness. I feared for the state of our larder and I seethed at the capricious demands of a petty tyrant that would deny us even the time to purchase supplies of food and grain and beer from the market fair.

Camran returned sooner than I'd expected and more mollified than I'd hoped. Despite what His Own had ordered, the innkeeper had taken nothing more than a single copper from us.

"He would've gladly followed tradition and the laws but knew that His Own would inquire as to whether or not he had charged us."

"He treads a narrow path, that one. Finding himself at odds with His Own could imperil his livelihood as well."

Camran huffed. "I begrudge His Own even that copper."

In marked contrast to our entry into Rillsherd, our exit occurred with no fanfare and the only crowds to note our passing was a line of stern-faced His Own. We slunk out onto the road and into the lengthening shadows of the vernal-eve as if we were the vagabonds we'd been accused of being, our walking staves thudding in dull tempo with our steps. We spoke little, mulling over our own thoughts instead of the good mulled Aelfallen wine we might have had as the evening had grown cooler. The road stretched on before us, the temperature dwindling as the sun fell towards the Crags to our west. When the gloom of the Craobac woods pressed in close around us, Oean began to whistle a tune, a mournful music by which to march.

"That Players should have fallen to this!" Camran walked beside me instead of upon the wagon seat: the horses knew enough to follow us. "Not even in the bad days of the Anwroth plague did Players lose their welcome. We didn't even have time to visit the baths." He sighed. "I'm all over sweat and dust."

"They called us liars, Dughal!" Barrol was most indignant. I could see he'd been chewing on that insult since it had been given. "We don't lie. You've told me never to lie or even embellish when telling the news of other places."

"Indeed. And yet His Own seek to begrudge us even that."

"They seek ignorance," Beathen said, speaking up for the first time. He looked up, as if startled that he'd spoken out loud.

"They seek control." Camran hawked and spit on the ground. "Didn't you hear what he said? They tell their own news to one another. They've no need of Players to do it for them."

"They don't tell all the news, I warrant," Sionn said. "Nor to all who'd want to know. They fear us for what we can do."

Beathen laughed. "They may well fear those elements outside of their control. As becomes more clear with each step we take, we are not." He smiled. "But, we annoy them."

"I'm annoyed with walking so far on a night I'd hoped to sleep sound within four walls," I said, weary of the discussion. "We should find a place to stop, and soon." Camran nodded his agreement. He winced as he moved for the cool night air didn't help his old joints any. Nor mine neither, if it came to that. "Next chance, a clearing with room for the cart and the horses, we'll take it."

We walked for near half a league more before we found the spot I wanted. A small stream flowed beside the road and when it turned away I had us follow it. Soon enough, it curled fast away and then back, forming an oxbow wherein we could take our ease, guarded by water on three sides. Grass enough for bedding, for our horses, and the woods close by on the other side of the stream to hide us from the road. We should be out of sight and tolerably comfortable.

The sun had set fully before we set up our camp. Camran built a fire to light our efforts and to prepare our meal, a bit of warmth to offset the cold anger of those in Rillsherd. Camran had great skill in cooking but regardless, this evening's repast tasted long past prime, with hard bread and mutton as long on the hoof as it was long since the day of its cooking. We'd have to stop in the next village and, performance or no, buy supplies.

We shared what we had and settled down to sleep. The weather was none too cold this night before the Equinox, dry for the nonce, with high clouds veiling the moon's fair face in wisps of eldritch lace.

I tried to take comfort in this, find beauty in these wild lands of Anacarra, and relax into sleep. Alas, sleep played false with me. I'd doze and wake, for no reason I could discern, until the moon began to sink and even the frogs had grown still.

Then I realized that even the frogs had grown still. I sat up, my blankets falling about me, and strained my ears to listen for what had brought the frogs to anxious silence. Then I heard it: someone pushed through the underbrush towards our fire. Born a Player, and with a player's imagination, I envisioned black-cloaked ruffians sneaking towards us as we lay helpless. With my heart beating in urgent rhythm, I rose silently and silently I woke my fellows, urging them in wordless signs to take up their staves and be ready. If strife was to find us in the dark, I'd meet it on my feet with a staff in my hand.

But soon, as if I'd imagined it, the woods fell silent. Barrol looked fearful and I did what I could to put the boy at an ease I little felt myself. Camran huddled with Beathen for some minutes before they both approached me. Despite the silence, or because of it, they whispered to me.

"Would His Own track us down in the dead of night?" Barrol asked.

"Does it matter who comes at night in stealth?" Beathen asked. "Rarely does that end well."

I nodded; too many stories attested to the truth of his words. "We should break camp, and quickly lest–" My speech ended unfinished as a figure lurched out of the dark of the woods and splashed through the stream. Before we could react, she staggered into the ruddy glow cast by the last of our firelight. The woman held out her hands to us before toppling to the ground.

I rushed over and fell to my knees beside her. Ah, by the dire Bargain, what harms we do one to another! Even in the dark her sex could be discerned: Not from her hair, for she had none. Not from her clothing, for none of that had she either. She'd run through the uncaring woods bare to the night sky and any man's sight. Thorns and worse had torn her skin and bruises shown clear even in the uneven light from the moon. I blanched to see her hurts.

"Na sent me to you," she whispered in a markedly accented voice.

"Eknos!" Camran hissed. He stepped back and pulled Barrol with him.

I turned back to the woman lying on the ground and winced at the extent of her injuries. *If the Goddess sent you thus, She might have done it without the gash spilling your guts upon the ground.* "Uplander, we're none but humble Players, yet we'll attend your hurts as best we can."

"Yes!" Barrol pulled free from Camran's grasp and stepped forward. "You need rest. We'll keep you safe 'til morning when —"

"Hush, boy," Beathen said gently. "She'll not see another morning."

"Aye," the woman whispered. Her good arm reached up, and grasping my cloak she pulled me closer. Despite all the blood staining her skin and darkening the grass, I doubt I could have resisted her strong grip even had I so desired. I leaned in to better hear her laboring voice. "Players? I've heard of such as you. Tell tales and stories to the sowers of the plains, is that right?"

"In all degrees," I assured her.

"Then hear this tale and tell it ... to all who will listen. We came down from the uplands at the ... invitation of those sowers near to us. We came ... to trade and to pledge peace ... with our neighbors. In trade for our trust we were given pain ... and captivity. See, you, what peace we were given?" Her bloody hands passed across her body, carrying our eyes with her motions. "There are two hands of us ... men and women ... both. We were taken from the crags ... drugged and bound by men ... dressed all in black. We're starved ... beaten ... and forced to lie beneath men who strike us ... before they enter our bodies and curse us ... even as they cast their seed."

She coughed and blood frothed her lips. Gathering her strength, she held up her hand to me and revealed a small flute, made of bone and carved with great skill. "Take this and sing my tale. Know by this that I am a hunter of Moonhart Eknos. Burn my flesh that the course of my life might start anew." Her gaze implored me but I held my tongue, for I knew not what to say. With her last words came her last breath and she died.

Oean knelt next to me and leaned over, sliding his hand across her face to close her eyes. "Farewell, brave hunter." He looked about to say more, but fell silent and shook his head.

I struggled to my feet and turned away from the body, the fire, and my friends. Few are the moments when we know that our lives have just changed irrevocably. As I struggled to catch my breath without losing my dinner, I wished with all my heart that this moment was not one of those.

And by our Seal, it won't be. I turned to face my Players. "Come! We must quit this place, immediately. We must hit our marks with great precision. Scour our campsite as best you can and make sure nothing is left that can point an accusation at us. We must not have ever been here." I looked at the flute in my hand as if I held an angry snake. I opened my pouch and – with no little trepidation – dropped it inside.

Sionn rose from where he knelt at the woman's feet. "Wait!"

I started. "What is it? You have your part."

His face was flushed and he pushed at his hair, unruly from sleep, as if the better to see us. "We must give this brave hunter to her Goddess in flames. As she asked." He looked around at all of us staring at him blankly. "We can't just leave her lying here!"

Camran spit upon the ground, his arms hugging his chest. "Yes! We can. Whatsoever that one was doing in the lowlands it bodes ill, for us and for all of Anacarra."

I looked from Camran to Sionn and shook my head. "I understand your desire, Sionn, but in her death she's dangerous to us as Camran says. Leave her where she lies, for this road is well trod and she'll be found. But no one who comes upon this body should see that she found succor at all. Brush away our footprints, disturb not her blood and leave her naked to the stars." I turned to all my men: Beathen's ashen countenance and Sionn's flushed one, Barrol anxiously moving from side to side while Camran's hands clenched and unclenched, Oean looking more perplexed than anything from where he knelt down next to the body. "Set the stage properly, my friends. Alone and friendless she died, her tale still behind cold lips."

Oean hovered by the body after he'd cleared away any signs of us. I took him by the arm. "Why do you stand here? There's nothing we can do for her and we *must* make haste."

"Yes, Dughal. I heard you."

"So? What would you?"

He looked up at me with a terrible, sad, smile. "She never told us her name."

Only the Goddess knew her name now. "There's nothing we can do about it, Oean. Leave it be. We must make *haste*."

Sionn stood staring down at the cooling corpse while his hands clenched and unclenched. "This isn't right, Dughal. This is foul, a stink that fills the plains. We can't just leave her here!"

I felt my face grow hot with the shame of hearing my conscience calling out to me in Sionn's voice. I shouted it – and Sionn – down: "What would you have us do? We can't save her, can we?"

Sionn glared at me and I wanted to see something other than disgust in his eyes. I swallowed my shame and spoke in my most reasonable tone. "There are six of us, men and boys. Think, Sionn. We should march up to those of His Own so full of themselves that they imprison, rape and murder her kind, and simply ask that they stop?"

Sionn's hands decided upon fists. "Oh, no. Not ask."

"It isn't right that we run," Barrol said.

"You!" I was shouting again. "You know nothing of the world save what you play on stage. Those who would do such as this—"

"This twice forbidden act!" Beathen growled out.

"His Own would delight to find us with such as she." Camran's calm voice undercut the heated shouting. "Then they'd have just cause to see that we shared her fate."

Any further word stayed within his lips for he must have seen the look in my eyes. Torn between fear and rage, I pushed Barrol off to complete the tasks I'd set. Oean stared for another moment, as if memorizing the face of the woman lying dead and naked at our feet. For myself, I dearly wished I'd never seen her nor chosen this spot for our camp. If the Goddess had indeed sent the poor, dead woman to us, then She makes dire sport of our lives.

Seven

Rhia

And the lowest is the sea, for the land sinks below the waves and every year the waves claim more of the land for their own. The next lowest are the lands settled by the children of Aethen, and the Ealdranna will find no welcome there. Above those begin the Crags, which stretch from the Everwhite Mountains in the north to the Mervanna Isthmus in the south. Lowest are the lands of the Serpent, the Falcon, and the Cougar, open and inviting, with much running water. Higher yet are the lands of Elk, Moonhart, and the White Eagle: the earth is rich and the dense forests teem with game. Finally, above all, where the clouds crowd close to nuzzle the Mother and even the trees tire of the climb, are the lands of the Ibex, the Lynx, and the Bear. Harsh places and rugged, the sky is wide and the winds blow. Only the strongest find succor in such places: only such places may succor the strongest.

- From the Book of Beginnings, Fifteenth Chapter

When I turned more east to avoid the storm, I crossed into Lynx territory for the first time. The forests thinned, providing less shelter against the wind and freezing rain that rolled over me during those days. The bones of the Mother showed through the thin soil and the elevation increased. Pines and conifers comprised the bulk of the trees I slept beneath. And down the center of the crags, on the western edge of Lynx territory, an escarpment rose another thousand feet, sheer and harsh, the highest range in the Midcrag.

I knew of no way over the escarpment but I knew that if I drifted too far east, that massive wall of rock would force me to go around it, adding days to my journey. I considered moving even further east, seeking the Lynx main ekarra on the far side of the plains, but that, too, would add days to my journey.

Despite days of solitude, I hesitated. Lynx should know of the Calling, I reminded myself, and know of the danger all the uplands faced. I wondered if Na had Called me to be messenger to all the southern eknos and the thought of it was more daunting than the prospect of running all the way to the Isthmus or being a sole hunter against the wolves stalking eknos. But my heart told me to keep to the west and my feet followed my heart in this.

That night I discovered blazes on trees that told me I approached a Lynx ekarra. I entered a small cluster of empty bothas, sealed up against the weather and I walked into it unchallenged, save by the most curious of the cats. I guessed from the size and location that the ekarra housed cearna when they arrived to harvest the apples and other fruit trees, only now setting bud.

To deny hospitality to anyone, be she from another eknos or even the lowlands, is a powerful taboo. Food and drink provided by the cearna and safe sleep guarded by our hearth-hounds welcomed any visitor to any of the eknos. So it was that I approached the dormant camp and felt welcomed and happy to be once again within familiar surroundings, especially after days of sleeping cold beneath the stars. I chose to stop, refill my pack, use my sling to kill what prey I could, and recover some of my stamina.

I made myself comfortable in a botha, spread my furs upon the sleeping platform and welcomed the warmth bark walls would provide. I might have felt as if I stood within the botha I shared with my mother. The heavy pendant that announced that Na had Bid me to Her service lay between my breasts, bringing with it the memory that the other side of the botha wasn't empty because Selwe was off on some trading expedition. This botha belonged to Lynx eknos and my mother's gear, her bedroll and clothing and even her flute lay scattered along the banks of the river where they'd been attacked.

Those gloomy thoughts pushed me off the sleeping platform and I sought peace outside, next to the fire I'd built using wood that Lynx cearna had set aside for their return. I'd taken some of their beans and herbs for my meal and had cracked the seal on one of their jars of honey water. The mead's bright and sweet taste brought with it the warmth I sought and I drank my fill and then filled the skin I had emptied on my run here.

I'd never been alone in an ekarra before! I'd always had Sarae if we went to a hunting ekarra, or (when I was a girl) Aichae and other cearna when we traveled to any one of the numerous gathering ekarra. No children laughed and I'd never thought to miss that raucous noise! No old men across the way making supper and ribald jokes, only the questioning meows of the cats wondering at the out-of-season arrival of a stranger to their ekarra.

I discovered that night that I had need to borrow somewhat else from the stores the Lynx set by. My *rosblud* came upon me as I lay in the botha and I realized that I'd packed nothing for the bleeding. As I still drank the *te'na* every day, the light flow needed little to capture all of it, nonetheless I couldn't help but feel satisfaction that, in listening to my heart, I'd found this place. Finding the empty ekarra had been providential and after another day of rest I resumed my journey south, cheered on by the earliest chickadees.

Traveling during the Burning season is difficult, made more so by having no companions with me. Rain fell more often than snow, but not that much more often. The days stayed cold enough that I needed to wear my heavy woolen trews even as I sweated with my exertion. Even the thick schirh I wore on my feet came with a cost. Enough snow remained beneath the trees and in the northern lee of hills that I needed the supple soles and high uppers of the schirh to maintain a grip on the ice and slush. But the bare paths, wet with rain and snow melt, made running in them hazardous. The further south I traveled, the more I found I also needed the schirh because of the rocky terrain and my Singing season-tender feet. Alas, soft-soled schirh meant for ice and snow were no match for the increasingly harsh rocks of this part of Midcrag. Seams began to spring and the soles began to shred.

Three days later, further into Lynx territory and more than a full fortnight on my journey, I felt my steps to be shadowed. Is this how the elk feels when he realizes by the sounds of the forest that he may no longer be alone? Do thoughts enter his stolid consciousness that such sounds might mean twas time for him to give himself to our hunters' bows?

I climbed high in a tree barren of leaves and focused all of my senses down the trail behind me. A gentle breeze blowing towards me brought the smell of smoke from a campfire recently put out. I heard bird calls from flocks that had not yet returned to the Crags, and knew that the hunters signaled one another. And I espied the slow stalking of at least two hunters as they stepped up onto rocks or into clearings.

I thought about waiting, about letting them come to me. My heart had led me to the ekarra and now to Lynx hunters as well. We could share food, company, and I could warn them of the dire threat from the lowlands. But then, rarely was I one to take the simplest course.

I laughed aloud as I climbed down from the tree. I strapped my pack and bow securely to my back, checking that nothing was loose or would rattle as I moved. Then I scurried through the woods due south, running in silence. For as long as we traveled in the same direction, I'd play the Moonhart indeed. I wondered how good of trackers these Lynx hunters were.

I varied my routine: I started before sunrise, I stopped later for my midday meal. I left the path for rocky outcropping beneath the pine trees, hopping from boulder to boulder until I'd gone some goodly distance, and then resuming the path to run full out. Or at least as fast as the game trails I followed would allow. A rain shower found me when I'd stopped to make an early camp and I left my small fire behind to smolder in the downpour, picking up my gear to find a different camp after another hour of running. My thoughts, often enough gloomy from the weight of Na's service and my mother's captivity, engaged themselves on this sport of mine. Never before had I sought to think as my prey might, how to evade and yet still travel and eat and sleep.

Admiration for my pursuers grew. When I lost them during the day I'd hear them again as nightfall came. I thought my actions very clever and yet still they kept pace and I wondered: if they were on a hunt indeed, why did they continue to waste time with a lone traveler? And yet, as hunters, they showed formidable skills.

I lay down one night and fell asleep considering how I might best lose the hunters on my trail upon the morrow. No sooner had my eyes closed than I plunged into the Calling dream. The same, yet different. The wolves still attacked and killed, but this time I stood silent. Silent as the wolves harrowed prides of lynx. Shame filled me. I opened my mouth, shouting warnings of danger. No one heard. And then I found myself standing high above the trees. Not floating as in the first dream, but standing upon sharp and painful rocks. And while I could not see them, I knew that the wolves prowled the woods below me and the dream ended in blurry images of death and danger and the final image was of a moonhart doe amidst the carnage.

I awoke before the dawn but sought no more sleep. I readied my camp for departure and then waited for the hunters to find me. I could no longer play this game. I must focus on what I'd been Bid. When they arrived, I'd invite them to share my fire, tell them of Na's Calling and the danger that all eknos face, and then resume my journey.

I used the time as I waited to replenish my supply of *te'na*. I had more than a week's worth of the woman's tea brewed and stored in my drinking skin with enough additional hot water for the hunters to brew more for themselves if they so desired. Hospitality.

Faced with seeing other people for the first time since my quest began, I found myself quite eager to meet them. I tired of the pemmican, dried fruit, and salted meat in my pack. Yes, the occasional squirrel had found his way onto my fire, but if this was a hunting party of the Lynx, then they'd no doubt offer me meat and other supplies to help me fulfil Na's Bidding. If their course also headed south we could spend some days together before our paths must part.

A tall woman, lean and angular in her limbs and movements, strode from the wood to stand before me. The Lynx eksig had been long ago carved into the lean flesh between small breasts but the woad marks that curled and wove across her face and arms were newly painted and bright. The marks showed the reason why I had seen no sign of hunt-hound or other dogs on my trail.

The rest of her hunters stayed hidden so I couldn't know for certain where the other four might be. I smiled up to her. "The water's hot if you wish to brew your own *te'na*. I'd offer you some waybread or jerky if you haven't already broken your fast."

Her eyebrows arched in surprise and she squatted down next to the fire. "What do you do here, Moonhart?"

She spoke softly, pleasantly. I swallowed a mouthful of tea and said: "Tis a long tale, that, but one that you should hear. All of you." I showed her my open and empty hands in greeting. "I'm Rhia darSelwe. Please, call your hunters out, share tea and what little I have to offer, and I'll tell you of the Calling Moonhart received."

"A Calling!?" Her intense eyes widened as she spotted the pendant in the neck of my tunic. "Indeed, so I see." She stood up and motioned for me to do the same. "We've no time for your tale now, Moonhart.

Yours is not the only sacred quest and we must be on with ours. Come with us and tell me your tale while we travel."

"What?" I shook my head. "But you need to hear this. All eknos are affected by Na's Calling!"

"Yes, I'm sure, Moonhart. You must tell it to us, of course, but not at this moment. So ready yourself to come with us. Come. Make haste!" She reached for my arm and, unthinking, I stood at her urging.

She whistled, long and low, and a woman a few years younger than myself stepped out from the woods behind me. She, too, had been marked with woad on her face, chest, and arms, giving credence to the claim of a sacred hunt. "Kiri, take up the pack of the Moonhart hunter. She's to come with us until we stop for the night."

"I've given you my name, Lynx. I'm Rhia darSelwe of Moonhart eknos!" She smiled at me as if I'd made some sort of joke and then motioned for Kiri to carry out her instructions. "What? Stop! Listen to what I say and then I'll move on. My path doesn't run with yours, Lynx."

"Are you sure?" She set her hand on my shoulder, a very companionable gesture. "Are you certain? Does your Calling dream contain the image of this dell, this meeting?"

I looked at her and at Kiri. I looked around the clearing in which I stood and my little fire. "Well...." I hesitated, the most recent Calling fresh in my mind. "I know I'm to tell you...."

For a moment, the woman seemed to look deep inside herself: she became very still, her eyes closed. Then she smiled and I felt as if the sun came out. "Ah! I see. Might it be that Na's Bidding and the tragedies my eknos have suffered are pieces of a whole? What Na Bids for you and our quest lie together for some time. Yes, I'm certain of it."

I had no such certainty. The Lynx hunter's grip on my shoulder grew strong and she turned me away from Kiri and towards her. "Young hunter, I must insist." She motioned to Kiri and said: "Do as you're told, Kiri."

I heard Kiri begin to pack up my things. I pulled away. *This isn't right!* "I'll stow my own gear, if you please." I snatched at my pack. Kiri's eyes grew wide and she froze like a startled rabbit.

I was jerked backwards by the powerful grip on my arm, thin fingers digging into my flesh. *This Lynx hunter thinks she has authority over me, despite I'm Moonhart and doing as Na bids!* Even as it rankled, I spread on the innocent and reassuring smile heretofore reserved for my own ekma and handed Kiri my pack: "Of course, if you'd prefer to pack for me, I would remember the kindness."

"Don't take this amiss, Moonhart," the tall woman said, turning me again to face her. "I tell you simply that our time is short. You've already cost us so many days tracking you—"

"Tracking me like prey does not mean I am prey."

She paused and looked around, her hands hard on my wrists so that when she closed her eyes as if she listened intently to something only she heard, I still couldn't break free. "By Skiem's foul breath, I see it now."

Despite myself I asked: "What? What's wrong?"

She sighed, motioned to Kiri, and took my pack from her. "Every day we're away from our eknos brings them closer to destruction and dissolution. But maybe, just maybe, I believe I see how, with your help, all can be made right again." She took from my belt my knife and sling and gave them to Kiri (who already had my bow upon her back), strapped the pack to my back, and then turned me around and gave me an ungentle push towards the path. "We must make haste. Kiri, cover the fire and then catch up." And off we went, heading east instead of south.

Kiri caught up with us just a few minutes later. She handed me the jerky I'd set aside for my breakfast and then fell into step behind me with the leader afore. She may very well have been on her first hunt, so young was she. Freckles splashed across her nose and beneath her wide-set, brown eyes. I don't blame her, nor any of the others, for what transpired. But neither do I remember those first few days with any joy.

Because of what she did later, this hunt leader of Lynx is now Nameless. I'll call her Gaunt and that's the only name she'll be remembered by. Gaunt was at least twenty years my senior. By Kiri's actions, twas clear that she held Gaunt in some awe and would no more question her commands than she'd argue with the storm clouds. With the determination of one who is young and unsure of herself, Kiri borrowed Gaunt's certainty and urged me forward whenever I might slow my steps.

I chewed my jerky and my thoughts, although the tough meat proved more palatable. *They take me away from my course! And at a pace that would make the hedgehog seem frenetic.* If she meant to take us around the escarpment, my mother, Grainna and the others, couldn't pay the price of that delay.

By the time we paused at midday, we'd covered a scant three miles when the day before I'd covered thrice that in the same amount of time. Gaunt wouldn't talk to me and wouldn't allow Kiri to either. Gaunt barely gave me enough time to squat to relieve myself and take a drink of water before we were off again: hurrying along only to move slowly through the woods until we stopped not long before sunset.

Gaunt sat me down beside a boulder and bid me stay in such a tone of voice that I thought myself more hunthound than Moonhart. I feared what might happen should I disobey. She set Kiri to stand near me and then strode off to speak to the others as they entered the campsite.

A huge bear of a man strode into the camp, carrying a staff nearly as tall as himself. A man! On a ceremonial hunt! At first, I thought him of Ibex eknos, for the only eksig I espied was the one that encircled his right biceps. But the faint lines of the Lynx eksig did mark his chest, nearly obscured by thick hair. That hair grew in an unbroken line all the way up to his cheekbones. His newly-shaved scalp had burned to a fine pink, a shining dome arising abruptly out of the forest of hair on his face.

To women Na had given the honor and duty to shed blood for their eknos: in menstruation, in childbirth, and in the hunt. Men simply don't understand what it means to give blood in order to provide life. I searched my thoughts for any tale or proverb that hinted at such a precedent.

Another oddity: a woman a few years older than my mother entered into the camp, carrying a bow with a comfortable grace that spoke of the long practice of the hunter. And yet she wore her hair long, the black mane generously silvered and falling in a queue to the small of her back. At her side strode a young woman who shared enough features of face and body with the long-haired woman that it came as no surprise when I later learned they were kin. The younger had a hand of years or more on me and her easy competence spoke of a full and seasoned hunter.

Gaunt gathered those three together and spoke in low and earnest tones to them for some while. The man, for his part, couldn't look away from me. "Is she our guest then?" His voice boomed as big as his chest.

Gaunt glanced at me and smiled. "Of course, Hrothar. What else would she be? I'm sure once we share our tales she'll see that I'm right, that we're meant to share a path for at least a little while." She walked over and squatted down next to me. "Until we have a time to tell such tales, you'll do us the honor of accepting our hospitality, won't you?"

Her intense brown eyes captured mine and I found myself nodding. Quick introductions were made as if I were a guest indeed, but I stayed well to the side as the Lynx hunters made camp and cooked dinner. Hrothar spent much of his time with the hunter, Tasso. Each sought to teach the other, it becoming clear that Hrothar had heretofore been a cearna of some rank but seeming eager to learn the ways of the hunter. Some while later, Taltaya – the long haired woman – handed me a bowl filled with a stew of roasted young rabbit, some roots and greens, along with a chunk of hard journey bread. I ate with great hunger, despite the easy walk we'd had that day. The Lynx hunters ate in awkward silence, with many meaningful glances between them. My presence discomfited them but no one seemed eager to challenge Gaunt.

So after the food was eaten, I tried again to reach her. "We follow the wrong trail, you and I," I said to Gaunt. "Why do you detain me?"

Gaunt set her plate aside and turned. "You're our guest, Rhia! And you're right: dinner has been eaten, tis time for tales to be told. The last few years have been hard for Lynx. In these dangerous times, and with the very survival of our eknos riding on our success, I won't take any chances." She stopped and frowned in sadness and confusion, sharing this woebegone look with her hunters. "Please, tell us your tale. Perhaps that'll help me discover what path we must follow."

I reached up and touched the pendant where it lay within my tunic. The early Burning season sun had already set and I shivered as a cold breeze blew across the campsite. "The tale is not a pleasant one," I said and then gave them a rueful smile. "Although, I suppose Na trusts us to find the pleasant things in Her creation on our own. It's the dangers She Calls to our attention."

"A Call!" Taltaya rose from where she sat, her hand on Hrothar's shoulder. Kiri nodded, her gaze intent upon Gaunt, while Tasso's eyes narrowed as she focused upon me.

I took in a deep breath and told them the bare outlines of the Calling dream: the wolves, the dangers to all eknos, the rising tide lapping against the crags. I even told them that I saw dead lynx in my dream, torn apart by the wolves. "With Sleikin's death, we saw Na's Calling made manifest. The sowers had taken some of our people captive and killed two others. I'm Bid south, both to warn those as I can, and to see if any rescue might be made."

Gaunt's fierce gaze captured mine. She near rose from her seat by the fireside. "Ah! That must be it. I'm sure that what Na Bids you to do is entwined with what we are about." And then she shrugged and turned towards Tasso. "Though I do wonder that a Calling so important would come to but a single eknos, or be left to a single young hunter."

My cheeks burned as I remembered slipping from the ekarra before dawn. "What do you do here? You all wear sacred marks and sigils seeking Na's support in your quest. And yet, you interfere with mine. What's so dire that you ignore your obligations to those Na Bids to Her service?"

"Interfere? Oh, no! While I don't hear Her words well enough to be called shaman, still in my deepest thoughts and dreams She does speak to me. I knew that you had to come with us as soon as I saw you, for our quests lie together. Rhia, you accuse me of interfering with you, of detaining you, but if I've been over-forceful in persuading you to come with us, I assure you I sought no more than to prevent your youthful folly." She stood up, pausing for a moment with her eyes closed, and then she turned to me and sighed.

"Lynx eknos has suffered great hurts in the last few years, Moonhart. Two years ago we ventured down to the borderlands in the east, land claimed by sowers but we know to be ours by right. Our hunters took a few bison and were on their way back when they were attacked. The lowlanders killed two before our hunters drove them off. When we attempted to retaliate for that insult, a stealnan died and two of our strongest cearnan died as well."

She sighed and shook her head. "Our ekma is old and wanders in her thoughts. She gave us no clear direction. Gellae – my sister – was to have been the ekma after her and had been trained, but she was lost in another terrible hunting mishap. Lynx fractured then. Many families moved away from the ekarra to make a go on their own." She fell silent and turned away again, her back to the fire and her hands to her face.

"Tragedy does seem to be stalking Lynx."

Gaunt said nothing and Tasso spoke up, her voice hardly rising above the crackle of the flames. "A hunt went out just after Na's night, again down to the borderlands for bison. They were short handed, but.... I ... we of the Third band, were late in returning to the ekarra. The First band didn't know we'd had a successful hunt, they only saw that the meat was nearly gone in the ekarra. They chose a hunt that should have provided great gain with few hands and less risk: there's a steep cliff there and they would drive bison over it. But—"

Gaunt turned back then, but her voice was curt, her words clipped. "No, let me. I was there, after all. Twas gravest misfortune, Moonhart. Rains had made the footing treacherous, the skies dark and our surroundings indistinct. The bison spooked early, charged at us instead of away." She shrugged and fell silent again.

I heard sniffling and turned to see Taltaya wipe tears from her eyes. Tasso reached out and gathered Taltaya into a close embrace and I realized that the taciturn Tasso cried as well. I looked about and Hrothar took pity on my confusion. "Gellae was not the only one lost," he told me, his usually booming voice held to a low rumble. "Treassa, stealnan on that hunt, also died. She was both sister to Taltaya and mother to Tasso here. Tis a great loss to kith and kin both."

"I'm so sorry." Tears that I'd not shed for my mother and Sleikin threatened my eyes now.

Hrothar nodded continued the tale. He motioned to Gaunt as he said: "Herself was terribly wounded in the accident and only after several days was she able to make it back to the ekarra to give us the awful news. Now we have no strong ekma, the shaman has fallen silent, the hetairi are without comfort. Lynx may well pull apart if we don't succeed."

Gaunt seemed to gather her strength and she patted Hrothar on the shoulder as she picked up the tail of the tale. "It came to me in a dream - no, I don't say twas a Calling - that Lynx needed to know, to see, that it's spirit was whole. Even though it would take almost all of our remaining hunters from the woods, we must undertake a Totem hunt. With Her words in my ear, I selected these disparate members for this special band and chose our path, the one that crossed your own."

As she spoke, she moved to stand behind each of the hunters in turn. "Kiri, so young that she had scarce wiped the woad of the *stealna kir* from her skin when she painted it back on for me. Hrothar had come down from the Ciscrag near on thirty years ago to be with his mate Kel. He's done so well to learn the ways of Lynx that no one remembers his birth in Ibex eknos. I heard his voice in my dream and feel that Na bid me to include him, both as cearnan and as a representative of the other eknos. Tasso, despite mourning the loss of her mother, is here from the Third band. And even though it's been many years since Taltaya last walked the woods as a hunter, she still knows the forests intimately. Until called on through dire need to again be a hunter of the Second band, she'd been among the cearnan who fetched meat cached by hunters back to the ekarra."

I felt my guts clench around the food in my belly. "That's a terrible tale. And you? Surely you were chosen leader for a reason."

She looked at me sharply but then a smile touched her lips. "Yes, of course. Myself, I used to be part of the First band and can hear Na, so you see how we are all represented on this hunt."

I nodded. "Aye, I do see that. But what I don't see is how I am a part of this. You've heard my tale. My way lies south. Will you let me go?'"

She frowned and closed her eyes for a moment. When she opened them she looked at me but her words were for the other members of the group. "I now believe that Na sent us here to find, not a lynx to be captured for our eknos, but a Moonhart. You, Rhia. I think now that we came to find you, that your path lies with us, and that you will be the salvation of Lynx eknos. You must trust in my greater understanding. You come with us."

"Whether I will or no?"

"You will come with us."

"But what role do I serve?"

"You will come with us."

Eight

Rhia

Don't offer to wager against Na. You just might win.

- Ealdranna proverb

I followed where Gaunt led for the next few days. All my life, I'd followed my own path, enduring much criticism to do so: my living apart from my age mates, my *stealna kir*, my actions in response to Na's Calling. But in this, with Na's Bidding pushing me from behind and Gaunt's imposing will pulling me forward, I set aside my own misgivings. With great effort, constantly renewed, I attempted in those first few days to do what my ekma had long sought of me: to listen and obey, more like Sarae than myself.

There was little enough to listen to during the day. Gaunt spoke seldom to me and the others hunted as we hiked, walking several hundred yards to one side of the path or the other in search of small game for the pot, barely glimpsed through the forest. Gaunt walked well ahead but she placed Kiri directly behind me, not letting her participate in the hunts. Kiri took no notice of this slight. "Wouldn't you rather be hunting than keeping me ... company?" I asked.

"Oh, that's all right," Kiri said, a blush burnishing her freckles. "I'd be more like to scare the rabbits away, I walk so loudly through the woods. But I'll practice walking silently upon the path, and make our stealna proud of me." Her earnest desire to please brought me up short and for some while I simply pondered the sway that Gaunt had over young Kiri.

Isolated though I was as we walked, in the camp of a morning or evening, the others felt no compunction to keep me apart and I listened closely then. Sarae would have been proud. Or amazed. They fed me well, they spoke openly and kindly with me. Taltaya's and Hrothar's manner towards me shifted constantly: sometimes they chided me as they would any young hunter ignorant of their forests. Sometimes they deferred to me as one honored as Na's favorite. Sometimes we laughed as equals and friends. Hrothar, especially, loved to laugh and jape. But often, as my sides ached from laughter, Gaunt would appear. She'd ask if she'd missed one of his funny Ibex tales, or had that been one of Kel's anecdotes, and at that, Hrothar's laughter would fall away.

Or Taltaya would be showing me the features of the land we passed through, where the caches were placed or where streams and other water sources were to be found, and Gaunt would arrive and inquire after the pain in Taltaya's shoulder.

Or Kiri, innocent Kiri, asking me for stories of hunting in Moonhart territory, her hazel eyes hesitant to meet my own, her shyness palpable, and Gaunt would send her off on a needless errand.

Tasso spoke rarely to me but as the days went on I realized that she spoke hardly at all to anyone. I couldn't tell if that was because of her grief or a taciturn nature.

At first, I thought little of it: each hunting band has their own way of merging strong personalities into a single purpose, and those ways weren't always kind. Eanna came to mind. But an avarice gleamed in Gaunt's eyes when she looked at me and I saw no purpose in reminding each of the hunters of their differences or past failures when, as stealna, she should seek to build them up.

By the third day we followed a curve in the rocky hillside to our south and began a course that was at least half as much south as it was east. Although I moved a step or two closer to my goal, I still chaffed at the delay and I realized that they were taking me directly to the high escarpment. The sheer purple-gray cliffs rose above us in the distance, directly athwart the path. The sight of them so close, and so opposite to my own desires, brought me up short. I'd tried acting as I thought Sarae would and that had brought me to the escarpment. Now I'd try acting more like my ekma.

I halted in the path causing Kiri to collide with me.

"Rhia? What's wrong?" she asked.

I answered, but my words were for Gaunt, some few dozen feet further up the path. "You're going the wrong way!" Blackbirds rose from the trees off to our left with squawks of alarm at the sudden sound of a loud human voice. As we'd climbed, the forest changed from deciduous to conifer, a warm blanket of needles soothing the rocky path beneath my feet, the smell of pine resin sharp in the air. "For three days I've followed you. I've done as you asked, followed where you led. But nothing you've done or said or shown convinces me that our paths lie together."

Gaunt had stopped in mid stride, nearly falling over from the surprise of my voice echoing from the trees. "Hush, Moonhart. We go the course I set and you go with us. It's been decided."

"No. I'm done. I've tried your path and it doesn't suit me, especially if you plan on going all the way around the escarpment. No, you go your path and I will go mine." I turned to Kiri who listened with mouth agape and eyes wide. "Kiri, please give me my weapons."

"Kiri, stop." Gaunt reached out for me but I turned aside so that she missed. She grew red in the face and her eyes narrowed. For a moment, her gaze turned cold and her lip curled. I stood up taller, my heart beating hard in my chest and sweat starting on my palms, shocked at the violence I glimpsed in her manner. But then her true emotions were pushed aside, smothered like a fire covered by turf. "We've had this discussion, Moonhart. I don't know why you insist on bringing it up again. We had agreed—"

"I know. And I tried to follow you. But with every step to the east my heart quails within me. It isn't right and I know it. I'm Called elsewhere: my path lies to the south. I can't help you."

She shook her head, pity at my foolishness clear on her face. "Come, Moonhart. You're young, you can't possibly understand all that I do. You *can* help Lynx, Rhia. I'm sure of it." She opened her hands and moved slowly to stand next to me. She put her arm around my shoulder and, with surprising strength, moved me down the path and away from Kiri. "And the other eknos, of course. I must ask you to trust me. I've been hearing Na whisper since my first bout with the Touch and I do know what's best. I believe you are vital to what Lynx needs to survive, Moonhart. I'll not let you just walk away."

I thought about pushing her arm off of me, then thought two can coat words with honey so as to mask the bitter taste. "It isn't a question of trust. I can hear that you believe your words to be true. It's a matter of trusting myself."

She smiled as if I'd made a joke. "But didn't you decide to hie off on your own? And you trust that's the best way to fulfill Na's Bidding?" She shook her head and shame rose in me.

I straightened. "Yes. It was to me that Na Spoke and so I was the one who decided how best to do as I was Bid."

Gaunt turned me to face her, so that her back was to Kiri still up the path and out of earshot. "That is convenient, isn't it? You tell us of a Calling, but is it truth or only a tale you tell yourself? I can only imagine what might be the truth: cowardice in the hunt, perhaps? Since that's too painful, you might tell yourself a tale to cover your shame. If Na had truly Bid you to such momentous service, would your ekma or shaman let you be here alone? Think how that looks to the others." During the whole of this speech, the sadness never left her eyes, the resignation never left the stoop of her shoulders.

We don't lie, eknos one to another. It's too hard, for each of us is so attuned to the emotions of others that knowing truth and speaking false shudders between us like a fly struggling in a web.

I gasped at her accusation. "I'm no Skiem to do such a thing! I do as Na Bids me. Listen and know that I speak the truth."

She smiled but her eyes glinted cold. "As you say," she replied, her voice such as one would use to placate an unruly child. "But we must be sure. Anyone who would profane Na's Bidding must be stopped, wouldn't you agree? No decision should be made lightly since the penalty for such blasphemy is severe. Do you remember what the penalty would be?"

Then I shook her arm from my shoulder but managed to keep my voice as conversational as her own. "'Tis the same penalty imposed on any who'd impede one whom Na has Bid to Her service. Death."

Gaunt's startled laugh rang out in the woods. "I must say I'm surprised. I would've never guessed that moonhart does have horns!" She stopped laughing and gazed at me, less sanguine but more appraising than before. When she spoke, her voice was low and cold and very, very clear. "I'm the only person left who can save Lynx eknos. Don't ever forget that, my lonely Moonhart doe, for I assure you: they don't." She motioned with her head to indicate the rest of the hunters.

Gaunt straightened and smiled, patting my shoulder again. "Now let us continue on our way. We'll come to the escarpment in due time and then you'll see that I'm right." Her hand slipped down to my elbow and gripped me hard as she motioned for Kiri to come up to us. Gaunt glanced down at my feet. "Oh, dear, Moonhart. You didn't plan for your trek very well, did you? Those schirh were never meant to be worn this far south in the Midcrag. They've become no more than scraps tied to your feet." Her intense gaze locked onto my own. "Pity. Your feet will bleed soon."

Gaunt turned away and continued on up the path as Kiri reached me. "Rhia, are you all right? Have you two come to an understanding?"

I shook my head. "No." I sighed. "I don't understand any of this." I turned to Kiri and put my arm across her shoulder. Where Gaunt had done it in manipulation and mockery, I did it for the simple need of companionship. "Beware of her, young Kiri. I.... Just beware."

She started to ask questions but, with a final squeeze, I turned to follow Gaunt.

At our next rest break, I sat with my back against a large, sturdy oak, glad that I still had on my leggings and wishing for a pair of the schoh such as worn by Lynx. Where my schirh are supple and made to grip on snow and ice, the schoh are hard, made for walking upon the sharp exposed rocks of the Midcrag. Gaunt was right about one thing. My schirh were nearly destroyed by the path we trod, and my Singing-season soft feet had begun to chafe and blister.

Kiri motioned for me to stay where I sat, and for the first time I saw uncertainty in her eyes. I shook my head to warn her away. She smiled. "Don't worry, Rhia. It'll be fine."

She rose smoothly to her feet and walked to where Gaunt sat, some ten paces from me. Kiri stood about my height, perhaps an inch or two more, but from where Gaunt sat upon a boulder, she didn't have to look very high up at her. I saw Kiri shake her head and I saw her motions become more animated. And then she stopped, both moving and speaking, while Gaunt simply stared at her, some of the easy-natured mien dropping away. Kiri squared her shoulders and spoke again. Gaunt stood and swung in one motion, striking Kiri on the cheek with the back of her hand, a cuff such as a parent might give an unruly child, aimed more at domination and authority than pain or hurt.

Kiri's hand went to her reddening cheek. Gaunt pointed at me and then sat back upon the boulder. "Get back to her, you stupid kit!" Kiri staggered back to my side, her eyes streaming.

"Are you all right?" I asked. "Did she hurt you?"

Kiri took her hand away from her cheek and sat up. "No, of course not. She wouldn't ever hurt any of us," she said, even as a tear rolled down her bright red cheek. "No, obviously I spoke out of turn. She was right to chastise me. How else will I learn how to be a great hunter?" She rebuffed any further attempts to speak with her. Soon enough we continued on our way.

As if Gaunt had brought on the pain by her mention of it, throughout that day and the next I felt blisters on my feet appear, spread, and then burst; the soles of my schirh thin and tear, the seams surrender. By the morning of the fifth day of my captivity by Lynx eknos, I left the remains of my schirh behind and hoped that the usual callus on my feet would form quickly.

We walked until dusk in order to reach the escarpment, camping in a dell of large boulders on two sides with a sheer cliff wall being the third. When I rose from my bedroll in the gray light of an early twilight, I found myself standing before a set of stone stairs cut into that sheer cliff. Stairs so old that the center of the steps bowed slightly from the weight of thousands of feet. Or hundreds of years. My feet, with neither schoh nor soles hardened by a Hunting season of running, were bruised, torn, bleeding. I stared at the steep, harsh stairs with dread. How was I to climb those?

I've run the woods since I first stood upon my feet. When on the hunt, I've carried full-grown moonhart carcasses upon my back for miles. Yet a single morning climbing the cliffs of the Midcrag and my very breath escaped me. After the first hour of treading those stairs, my hips, thighs, and buttocks voiced a fine harmony of distress to accompany the torment singing from my feet. I resolved not to show my pain but I slowed just so I could move without limping, without crouching over to place my hands on my thighs and gasp for elusive breaths.

Twice, Kiri took pity on me, calling out to Gaunt for a rest before our usual time. I didn't wait for Gaunt to accede, I simply collapsed upon the nearest boulder, easing the strain from my feet and legs, working my lungs as best I could. The air felt thin and weak and with that I knew we'd gained higher ground than ever I'd climbed before. The third time Kiri called out to Gaunt, she came back to see what was the matter. She glanced down at my bleeding feet and shook her head. "Yes, you see. I was right. You weren't well prepared to do Na's Bidding, were you Moonhart? If you were Bid, of course. Good thing we found you when we did. Your feet must hurt you terribly." She turned away and called out to the others to begin again. I struggled to stand upon my gashed and bruised feet and started up behind her.

I'd begun to fear I could climb no further. A red haze blurred my sight and the very air eluded my loud, laboring breath, always fulfillment just out of reach. When the stairs opened out onto the top of the escarpment, I collapsed sprawling upon the ground, too tired and winded to pull meat from my pack or water from my pouch. Kiri hunkered down near, her worried gaze upon me. She looked from Gaunt to me and back again, indecision plain on her features. Finally, she reached around into her pack and set a tightly wrapped package of pemmican in my hand. "Eat, Rhia. Rest." The dried meat and rich fat mixed with tart fruit pumped energy into my body as I devoured it. So intent on eating, I didn't notice Kiri had gone.

With fresh strength filling my belly, I chanced to look around. And caught my gasping breath. I could see for miles. I saw only the tops of my beloved forests as they stretched to the horizon all around this bare plateau, the even brown canopy dusted with the pale green of early leaves high at the tops, now far below me. My spirits rose somewhat in that I had some hope that route over the escarpment might bring me more swiftly south than the path I had intended through the trackless woods to the west. However, instead of smooth stone steps under my feet, a rocky and narrow trail wound between larger outcrops of granite well into the distance.

I drank deeply of what water I had left, uncertain if there would be any spring at this high elevation. There were so many things about the wider world that, not only didn't I know, I'd never thought to even wonder about! All my life I'd spent my days beneath the trees of the great uplands forest. No more. The wind whistled unhindered along the naked escarpment, blowing grit full in my face. As the day wore on I began to feel exposed: the horizon too far distant and the sky too pale a blue. The sun arched high overhead, bearing down on me in Her full force, unmoderated by branches or leaves. I should have felt cooler in the face of the mountain breezes, less enervated from the heat, but I felt as if a fever burned on my face and no amount of wind would cool it.

For two days we trudged across the plateau high above my longed-for forests. Springs did dot the escarpment, but few and far between. Taltaya and Hrothar did what they could with dried meat and withered berries for our meals and Kiri tried to keep my spirits up. It took all my concentration to walk without limping; to focus on the very, very distant horizon instead of the far-too close pain in my feet. Small, sharp-edged stones littered the path and my abused feet began to bleed once more. In the morning of that second day, when taking a turn around a particularly large boulder that had shunted the path aside, I stepped right upon the edge of just such a stone. A cry escaped my lips all unlooked for, and I staggered up against the boulder, my foot in my hands, my thumbs pressed hard against the cut now welling blood.

"You hadn't planned for your trek so well, had you Moonhart?" Taltaya said. "Not all trails are as smooth as those in your woods."

I pointed to where Gaunt walked far ahead of us. "She says the same. But unless you forget," I gasped, in pain and for breath, "I'm not the one leading us on this path. My way would've taken me through the valleys west of here."

After calling to Gaunt to stop, Taltaya hunkered down in front of me and took my wounded feet in her hands. "It wouldn't have mattered much. The trails throughout Lynx show the bones of the Mother through them, even in the deepest forest. Your feet might not have been quite so cut up, but neither would you have gone uninjured."

"What is it? Why do we stop?" Gaunt had come back to us and she gazed down at me. "Ah. You're asking for help, Moonhart?"

"You knew she suffered? Why didn't you say something?" Taltaya demanded. "What were you thinking taking this path and not providing proper footwear for her?"

"*Most* hunters don't wish to be coddled, Taltaya."

Taltaya drew in a deep breath and then turned away from Gaunt. She let go of my foot but motioned for me to stay seated. "I have balm and some herbs in my pack. And, if I am not mistaken, a pair of schoh that should fit you. I would guess that my foot is larger than yours, but by the time I've added the poultice and balm to the soles of your feet, they should fit well enough."

"Thank you, Taltaya," Gaunt said. "I'm sure, having yourself been so grievously injured in your time, that you're best suited to take care of our Moonhart companion. But please be quick about it. I hope to be at the Cave of the Arch before nightfall."

While Taltaya wrapped my feet in a sweet-smelling poultice, I drank the last from my waterskin. Hrothar, who had stopped to see what we were about, handed me his own.

"Don't worry, little doe. Drink deep," he told me. "We camp tonight at the edge of the escarpment where a fine cold spring flows fresh all year round. Your body is unused to these heights and you exert yourself harder than you might otherwise. You need both the food and the drink."

"Thank you." After I drank I handed the skin back to him. "Did you find it difficult, adapting to these heights?"

He laughed. "This little bump? Why, tisn't even a foothill in the Ciscrag. I could tell you—"

Gaunt strode back, interrupting Hrothar's story. "Are you finished yet? The day grows late."

"Yes," Taltaya said as she stood. "Rhia here can now continue."

"Very good." Gaunt turned away, whistling the signal to begin again. The schoh she had given me were an older, well-worn pair and might have been comfortable for her but they were not crafted as my own schirh had been. They didn't rise above the ankle but were laced tightly over the foot. I felt blisters begin across the tops of my feet within a handful of minutes while the poultice squished and pricked against the bottoms.

I own I felt far less pain than I had when my bare feet trod the rocky path, but that only gave me enough energy to chew over other thoughts. I'd done what I could to treat Gaunt as I treated my own stealnan. But Tiera treated each member of her band as worthy of respect, and so we all respected her. Gaunt rarely opened her mouth except to chide and chastise. In this way, I'll admit, she treated me no differently than any other in her band. Not that such seemed a benefit.

The longer we walked, the more I became convinced I could walk no further. With each step along the narrow and rough trail, I simply focused on the next large boulder athwart the path in the same way that I would've focused on the next large tree had we been within my beloved forest. The day had turned gray, both with my inability to concentrate as well as the thickening high clouds. At first, I greeted the hiding of that wrong-blue sky, but then felt like to smother from the close weight of the heavy clouds that dropped rain on us from time to time, adding slipping and falling to my list of trials. After a short scramble up a particularly steep hill, before me stood a long sandstone bridge slick and shiny with rainfall, carved from the ruddy rock by a swift stream flowing below it and the ever present wind above.

"Ah, Moonhart! I think that nowhere within your eknos do you have something so wondrous as this." Gaunt reached back and pulled me forward, onto the wet surface of the bridge. Since I could scarcely feel my feet I could hardly trust my footing and I shuffled my steps across that span of rock, a dozen yards or more, terrified that my pain-numbed feet would betray me to my death. Gaunt, smiling, walked behind me as if on the forest floor, commenting on the marvels of the bridge and the spiritual history of the place. I heard scarce a word of it.

At the other side of the bridge, the land sloped down into a steeply sided glen with a large cave at one end, all of a piece with the rock from which the bridge had been carved. Here we camped, the light of our fire flickering off of bridge above us and the cave walls behind us. We dined on fresh-caught ptarmigan and I drank my fill from the spring that rose clear and cold right next to our campsite. But despite a day cold with chill rain, my skin felt hot and my face flushed. I sat well back from the fire and hoped the breeze would cool me.

Later, Taltaya removed my schoh to replace the poultice. She frowned at the burst and raw blisters oozing across the tops of my feet. "Oh! Rhia, I'm sorry. I hadn't realized that this would happen. Why didn't you say anything?"

I laughed. I shouldn't have, for she was being kind, but her words struck me as particularly absurd that night. Such was my mood that it seemed to me that the sparks from the firelight joined in the laughter as they floated above the camp.

She startled and then looked up at me, a rueful smile curling one edge of her mouth. "Ah, no doubt you're correct. My apologies. Let me see what I can do for this on the morrow." She rubbed a balm on my feet, top and bottom, but did not wrap them. "Let the skin breathe of the cool night air. It may be a few days before you have to put schoh on again, as we may be here for a bit." She patted my shoulder and we shared a moment of silence, the snap of the fire echoing in that dell, the sparks climbing up past that magnificent arch. Taltaya asked: "Rhia, do you know the story of this place?"

I shook my head. "We've no such places in Moonhart territory nor did I find anything like it in Elk, although I only crossed a portion of Elk nearest the nosmoot and, well I'm sure you all know that territory...." I realized I'd begun to babble and abruptly shut my mouth. I may not have been acting much like my ekma at the moment, but neither did I feel entirely like myself.

Taltaya didn't seem to notice anything amiss, but simply nodded. "The Old Ones knew this place as sacred. It's said that it was in this glen that the Eknos came into being."

Moonhart has our own sacred places and our own stories. Eknos have stories for everything: it's how the Ealdranna taught us to be Eknos. Looking about me, I felt my soul expand outward, encompassing the fire and people and rock and even the whole massive escarpment. It would not have surprised me if, at that moment, Na Herself strode across the stone bridge to share our fire.

Gaunt stood and came over to where I sat and squatted down in front of me. "At one time all eknos gathered in this place and learned – together – to take care of the forests. I hear the echoes of Na's voice here still. I hear Her telling the original ekmas to protect all of these lands, from Ciscrag to Midcrag to Kaircrag." She shook her head, sorrow in her downcast eyes. "By turning your back on Lynx you are turning your back on Na's Bidding."

I shook my head to clear it of the easy sound of her voice, the over-warm heat from the fire, and the languor from a too-big meal after all the hard exertion of the past few days. What had felt so clear to me before no longer had the clarity of purpose. "I'm not! I'm here, aren't I? Despite you haven't told me what, other than sharing the Calling dream, that I might do!"

"What *do* you want from Rhia?" Taltaya asked. "We've heard her tale. We're warned against the Sowers, as if we had further need of that. Have you heard Na speak? What does She say?"

Gaunt stood up and moved towards the fire, and then slowly turned so as to look at each of us in turn. "Yes," she said. "I see. I've been remiss. When I can see something so clearly I forget that none of you has my understanding." Gaunt paced back and forth for a few moments, and then stopped, her profile to me, and closed her eyes. I saw her jaw work a few times as if she chewed on what she might say to us to explain her inner visions. "I've never claimed that my understanding of Na's wishes was complete. I feared we wasted precious days chasing down a Moonhart when our intention had been to hunt a lynx. But then, when Rhia joined us, I felt certain twas the right thing, despite Rhia's protestations to the contrary. *She* was our purpose. We needed to hear Na's Calling and I know now that, with Rhia, I – we – will effect the salvation of Lynx eknos."

"How?" Tasso asked. Throughout the discussion, she'd sat beyond the reach of the fire's light, polishing the wood of her bow.

Gaunt wrapped her arms about herself and shook her head, eyes filled with confusion and even pain. "I don't know! You know I don't hear Her as well as I would wish." She sat down as if defeated, her breath heaving. Then she looked up, wiped a tear from her eye. "We must ask Na for guidance. Here, in this sacred spot. We'll begin preparations on the morrow for a vision quest. With all of us here, including our Moonhart friend – Na's favorite – Her will should become clear."

I shook my head. "The Calling showed me threats to the uplands, to all of us. It showed me the harrowing and capture of people of the crags, and I believe that it showed me that I was Bid to rescue those who've been captured by the lowlanders."

Gaunt strode to me again, hunkering down and taking my chin in her hands. She peered deeply into my eyes, searching for I know not what. Suddenly she smiled. "Yes, I believe you are right." She released me and stood up. "If we can not say with one voice after a vision quest that we all share that your way goes with ours, then we'll let you resume your trek south, your packs filled with what we can spare you."

"But?" I asked.

"But, if Na shows us your Bidding and our quest will succeed together or fail if we part, then I'm sure you'll agree to come with us."

She left no room for another answer, but walked from the fire's side.

My sleep.... I don't remember if I slept that night, or if I did, what rest I may have gained. Dream fragments followed me into waking and hallucinations followed into my dreams. At some point, not long before the sky began to gleam with the first hints of gray, I knew what was happening to me. Na's Touch! My emotions soared with my fever and fell like a spark on the wind.

I breathed a prayer of thanks to Na for putting me in the path of this party of Lynx hunters. Despite we all endure the Touch after we first join in pleasure with another, it's hard on the body and spirit both. Not everyone suffers the Touch more than once and I hadn't, not since the first time. In my planning and packing for my journey, never did I consider that I might be alone in the wilderness with the Touch upon me! It would have been my death.

I pulled the blankets up tight beneath my chin and tried to slow my racing breath. Not every one's second bout of Na's Touch is as bad as her first. If I began to hallucinate while I walked, or the euphoria or physical sensations became too intense.... I rolled over, curled onto my side as I turned my thoughts away from what might happen to me if I again suffered the degree of arousal that I did the first time I experienced Na's Touch. A lover would usually care for the sexual aspect but I had no lover here. No, nor anyone I trusted.

Dawn broke in earnest and I pushed aside my blankets and carefully eased myself to my feet. Dawn colors glowed bright and fervid across the eastern sky under the bellies of rolling clouds. I found myself fascinated by the subtle change in the sky as the sun's rise continued. I might have stood there as morning flowed into day and back into night but I roused when I felt a cool touch upon my fevered skin.

"What ails you, Moonhart?"

For a moment I thought twas Selwe asking me. But then Na's Touch withdrew a bit and I smiled at Taltaya. I focused hard on the kind brown eyes that looked down on me. "It would seem that Na has chosen to Touch me in order to add some excitement to what she Bids me to do."

Her fingers moved up my wrist to find the point where the pulse beat below the skin. Then she felt the heat of my forehead and sighed. "You are, indeed, Na's Favorite, aren't you?"

At that, giggling burst forth. I hadn't giggled since I was a mere girl, well before the *stealna kir.* "I've had Na take note of me twice then in little more than a score of days. I'd rather she turned Her attention elsewhere."

"Come and sit down, Rhia." Taltaya kept her voice quiet and calm, as if she would soothe a frightened child. Tasso helped me back to my bedroll as Taltaya poured a packet of some dark and pungent herb into my half-full skin containing the last of my *te'na.* "This should help. It will sharpen the focus and add strength to the limbs. Are you hallucinating?" Before I answered she handed me a square of waybread, baked hard but full of nuts, fruits, and greens.

"No," I shook my head and then choked back a sob. "Not yet." Then, my words a whisper, "Not much."

"Does this happen often to you?" Taltaya asked.

Again I shook my head. The herbed *te'na* had already begun to help for I could actually answer her question seriously. "I'd hoped I'd be one who went all of her life and only experience Na's Touch but the once. Once was enough. My fever spiked high and hot, and yet I couldn't lie still abed but tossed restless and would wander about. I spent much of my time talking to the hearth hounds." Taltaya clutched my hand in sympathy and I squeezed it before I continued. "As soon as my fever abated, came the passions. My body hovered just on the wrong side of relief for nigh on three days, quivering and excited and aching. Dearest Na, I longed, I needed, I reached and reached, but nothing."

I shuddered. "I hadn't known what my wishes would grant. Once I finally crested that peak, I started to climax again and again." I sighed. "And again and again and again and...." I stopped before threatened mirth bubbled up and out. "I must've reached climax a hundred times in a span of a few days but nothing brought me succor." Tears crested in my eyes, covering the mirth as quickly as a cloud would cover the sun.

Taltaya's eyes wide, regarded me differently. "The first time for me was not so dramatic, less fever but it sounds like equal restlessness. My sister Treassa took great sport with me, for I spoke as if my soul encompassed all of creation and I answered her questions so solemnly and earnestly that it seemed Na Herself whispered in my ear. My family wondered if I might become shaman after that." She sighed. "But I no longer hear Na in my thoughts even though I've had bouts with Na's Touch nigh on a dozen times since then, teaching me to carry this herb with me, for I never know when the Touch might come again. Each time is different but never as intense as the first, never did it keep me from a hunt." She fell silent and looked back at someone I couldn't see. She sat up straight and tossed her long braid behind her back. "For as long as I was a hunter, that is. Let's hope this time is less intense for you as well."

I nodded. "If not, I don't know if I'll survive. Then, I couldn't be sated no matter what my lover did for me. Now, with no lover here, I may very well go mad."

They left me there to break my fast with the waybread and went to discuss the situation with Gaunt. She came rushing over while the others trailed behind her. Again she squatted before me and took my chin brusquely in her hands to peer into my eyes. They closed, briefly, a sigh of resignation escaping. "But we must have the quest!"

"Rhia will have visions soon enough, that seems plain," Taltaya said. "And that can't happen here. There's water, sure, but little in the way of shelter or food."

"There's a hunting ekarra at the foot of the escarpment," Tasso said.

"Aye, and well-stocked I'll have you know," Hrothar added.

Kiri stepped forward and held out her hand. "Come, Rhia. Let's gather your things."

I put the last of the food in my mouth and took Kiri's hand to help me to my feet. Gaunt just shook her head and then rose and prepared to break camp. Before long we left the sacred spot, following a path that led beneath the sandstone bridge and out again onto the escarpment. Within the hour we stood at the top of a deep notch in the cliff face.

I remember the first part of the descent vividly, for I was so taken with the careful craft of the stairway itself I could scarce move my feet for the wonder of it. The stairs cut into the cliff face were fitted and wedged in such a way that a stable path wandered through the talus slope. I'm sure that, unless someone looked up while we were on the path itself, no one from below would be able to see the route up the hillside, for the stairs were made from the very scree we walked through and were no wider than the width of a small woman. I could walk upright and forward, but Kiri, with her wider hips and legs, often had to sidle sideways.

I found that the herb in my *te'na* did help me focus. Traversing the path required extreme care to place each foot on the prepared stone and not the loose scree. At some point the clouds parted, the sun shone down hot and cruel, and I found the sparks struck from the stone by the sun floating up to my eyes, winking and smiling at me. We crept down a notch in the escarpment, sheer cliffs to our backs and to either side, while far below, lovely forests covered the land for nearly 100 miles, before falling away to the unseen lowlands beyond. At times I caught glimpses as of reflected light twinkling and my mind created the fantasy that I could see clear across Bainellen province to the coast some 300 miles to the east. I squinted, hoping to see the slow creep of a wooden cart, hauled behind those great beasts called horses, carrying my mother and others of eknos. But all I managed was to lean too far out over the sheer cliff face until Kiri pulled me back.

It began to seem that we climbed between the stony legs of some giant, tickling her rocky vulva with our feet and hands and I realized that pleasure had begun to grow deep in my belly. Each step moved me closer to an elusive climax but at such an incremental pace I could walk a thousand miles and still not reach relief. But it distracted me and on that path, distractions could kill.

Kiri began to sing a song behind me, a round such as hunters sing on the march to keep rhythm with their pace. It pulled my mind back to the path, the beat of the song matching the slow beat of my footsteps down the cliff side. Great hawks of sunlight swooped down to investigate my descent, huge shadow ibex scampered about alongside me, made up of the dark shade cast by the huge boulders filling the expanse we traversed, and yet the song kept me anchored to the path itself.

I remember the stairs. I remember my feet upon the stairs. I remember the song and the blazing sunlight. I remember friendly hands holding my waterskin so I could drink the potent mixture within, further focusing my thoughts on each footstep to the exclusion of nearly everything else. And I remember the feeling of pleasure growing between my legs, in my belly, in the rubbing of each hard nipple against the leather of my tunic. I remember neither the end of the path nor anything else for days afterward.

Nine

Dughal

The forces of Cathair'naric, called Clan Killer, drove the Ealdranna before him, all the way through the Kaircrags to the Midcrags, halting at the foot of the Midcrag escarpment. Ealdranna fled up the cliffs like goats and used the heights to their advantage, raining down much destruction. However, after some hand of days when the men of Cathair'naric could neither climb the cliffs nor retreat under the trees because of the deadly accuracy of the Ealdranna, and they had grown hungry, cold, and without hope, the attacks suddenly ceased. The Clan Killer sent men up to the cliff top as well as to the forests around them and found no sign of the Ealdranna. Cathair'naric left the uplands then and returned to Bierncarra where he caused a great celebration to be held, commemorating his defeat of the Ealdranna who were heard from no more.

- The Book of the Anarics

My Players trudged through the dark Craobac Woods that night in silence. No one talked, no one sang, no one even muttered a muffled curse to pierce the darkness of either wood or mood. I don't pretend to know what thoughts mimed in the minds of my comrades. I only know that mine own wove such a macabre dance that, despite my weariness, I felt it a comfort to face those painful sights while awake and not in the depths of my dreams.

I doubted any of the others fared better. I expected complaints about the wet, the cold, my decisions, our destination. Instead, we walked for many hours with not a protest or gripe. *Ach, and isn't that a worry? That this lot would miss an opportunity to complain chills my marrow.*

My intention had been to stop at daybreak but the cold, dank mists and the insistent drizzle settled in, so heavy that I couldn't tell whether the sun had risen or not. After some while the drizzle turned to rain and we just kept walking. My thighs ached from lifting feet caked heavy with mud, the back of my neck sharp with cold above my collar but below my hat, and my breath labored in my lungs before blowing steaming into the chill air.

"I'm sodden," Beathen announced suddenly, long after the sun should have risen.

His sudden speech startled me. The cart rolled to a stop and the men stopped, too. Mist clung to Beathen's beard and beaded his tunic. He lifted a foot to gaze at the muddy mess clinging to the bottom of his boot, sighed, set his foot down and straightened his shoulders. I expected him to look my way but he didn't.

"Indeed. So are we all."

"Do we stop, Dughal?" Barrol asked me. "The horses ... this is hard. On them." His damp blonde hair clung darkly to his forehead. He took off his hat and swept away the wet tendrils before setting it back on.

"So it is, lad," I answered.

"By the lonely God's balls, Dughal! Where would you have us stop?" Sionn glared at me as if the heavy mist had been a burden I'd laid on him especial. I couldn't meet his eyes. Instead, I watched as one fat drop collected on the brim of his hat and then tumbled towards the ground, lost in the misty twilight before it landed. I sighed, then coughed.

Camran's bones must ache in this weather. "What are your thoughts, my old friend?"

Camran glanced at the horses and our cart and then down the road as far as he could see. "For my part," he said, his words rolling out with slow and conscious deliberation, "I'd rather keep walking. If we stop, we camp cold and wet. If we walk, we walk cold and wet, but we have movement to keep us warm."

"Or at least, warm-*er*," Oean amended.

"Indeed," Camran agreed. "If we stop every couple of hours to rest and graze the horses, we could walk until the mist lifts or we reach a town."

"While I would not as a rule prefer walking sodden and sloshing to the next town, at least this rain will most likely erase whatever marks we may have left behind." Oean said. "With luck, in this continued bad weather no one – save ourselves, more's the pity – will travel. We'll have time and distance between us and that unfortunate uplander woman."

A few heads nodded at Oean's words but none of them looked at me. "Yes. There is that," I murmured.

"*Do* we stop at the next town, Dughal?" Camran asked.

"We must, but only to buy supplies. Having been so warmed by our welcome in Rillsherd, we'll turn on the first road west, towards the city of Lechsede. It doesn't surprise me that these crows flock in the rural towns but I'd be quite surprised if they've yet to find roosts in a trading town like Lechsede. We will spend some days preparing plays and properties and I'd rather they be spent in a city than someplace where His Own may have more sway." No one responded to my statement. "These thoughts sit ill with you?"

Camran turned away and shrugged his shoulders inside his cloak. "These country roads will turn to muck soon enough —"

"A few leagues back, I think," Sionn grumbled.

"— and the larger roads are better for travel. But the road west brings us closer to the uplands and that gives me pause."

"If what's on the crags stays there, then I take greatest comfort from it," I said.

"But it doesn't, does it, Dughal? Uplanders trade in Lechsede just like everyone else." Camran paused and rubbed his eyes. "I would live the rest of my days content should I never see another uplander woman."

"Really?" Oean shivered and bowed his head down, water spilling from his hat's brim like tears. "I'll see her forever in my dreams, as is."

Barrol nodded, his eyes wide. I suspect the moisture on his face was not all rain. I wanted to reach out to him and to the others, but found I could not cross the new-built gulf between us.

I squared my shoulders to better carry that burden of my guilt even as my regretful heart labored in my chest. I'd misjudged the antipathy His Own had towards Players and that lost us our place in Rillsherd. I'd further been shocked to find that men who call themselves holy would perpetuate such violence upon the body of the poor uplander huntress. I'd thought that kind of violence didn't exist outside of tales of Cathair'naric's pogroms against the eknos centuries ago. I felt the continued existence of Bardeelin perched with weak and shaky legs atop a swaying rope spanning between past and the future. We would walk that slackrope. I vowed Bardeelin would not fail while I led it, but couldn't say whether my vow was to the lonely God or the banished Goddess.

In the afternoon, the fog lifted and the sun broke free of clouds to shine watery beams upon us. That simple gleam of light lifted my spirits after the cold mists of the morning. But before I could even utter words of thanks, rushing clouds banked the sun's fire once again. My unspoken prayer came out as a sigh, as rain began to fall from the quenching clouds. Alas, we no longer had trees to break the fall of the drops or shield us from the wind.

Some hours later, rain a steady and insistent patter upon the fields, we came to a crossroads. Should we stay on the southern route, we'd enter the plains of Bainellen province, an area of great fertility with much of the smoothly sloping land under the plow. Those great plains fed the entire eastern side of the crags. If we went east, we'd hew closer to the coast, but also add a great distance to our trek, and we had only the half year before we needed to be in Bierncarra far to the west.

West would take us to Lechsede, the trading center of Bainellen province. Goods and grains from the south flowed to that city enroute to Maukellen province in the north, and east towards the ocean along the Rill that flowed from the Crags all the way to the sea. People from every province stopped there throughout the year. We could rest, get the repairs we couldn't get in Rillsherd, and perhaps even recover a bit from the shocks we'd taken.

Before I could announce my decision, the sodden splashing of hoofs sounded out behind us. I turned to see a flock of raven-cloaked His Own descending upon us from the direction of Craobac Wood. I looked at my men and they looked at me. The slightest shake of my head and they took up positions around the wagon. Players used to be held in such esteem that no one in Anacarra would think to attack us. But since the Rici fell and the Seven Provinces became Five, even Players had learned to protect our own. I would not be unready to meet the violence we'd learned His Own capable of.

Barrol jumped atop the wagon and positioned himself at the rear while Camran sat on the bench at the front, the reins to our horses gripped tightly in his old hands. Beathen stood next to the horses on the road side and I stood at the rear of the wagon down from him. Oean stood behind me on the field side at the back and Sionn stood across from Beathen at the horse's heads. Between the four of us we could see all points around our cart. Each of us knew how to use our staffs for more than just leaning upon, and a man who can juggle half a dozen knives at once can do else with knives as well when the need arises. We took our places around the wagon as smoothly as any much-played scene upon the stage and I trusted His Own wouldn't notice the defensive nature of the positions taken.

"Greetings, Goodmen. How are you this fine day?"

"You call this fine, Player?" One of the men nearest me scowled. "I'm soaked through."

"Then the grains and grasses that are the blessing of this land will drink their fill. Not all the days the God has given to the world are to our benefit alone." I smiled a humble smile. "Or so the priests have told me."

"You are a learnéd man," said another.

This one had red piping around the brim of his hat and the hem of his cuffs and cloak. But it was his manner more than his garment that convinced me that he had command over the others and I turned my attention on him. A strong looking man with a powerful jaw and a close trimmed black beard, he sat his tall horse well and easily, seemingly inured to the inclement weather. "I'm a Player, Goodman," I answered him.

That earned me a handful of scowls from various men in the group but the leader of this band smiled a mirthless smile instead. "Are you, indeed?" he replied. "I am Neacal durCleirach. We've been searching this road for an escaped prisoner. Have you seen anyone about?"

I could only trust that my histrions were playing their roles as they should. I was glad that young Barrol and hot-headed Sionn had the bulk of our wagon betwixt them and this suspicious band. Despite the nauseated twist in my guts, my years of performance made of my face a mask.

"We were in Rillsherd most recently, Goodman Neacal, and no one told us of any escaped prisoner. We've been on the road since, hoping to walk out of the rain." I took off my felt hat and twisted the water out of it. "You can see our success in that!"

Some half of the scowls had turned, if not to smiles, than at least to no more than a wary caution. One man, with a scarce-healed scar marring the left side of his face, laughed a bit too loud, the laughter turning into a giggle until he thrust a fist in his mouth.

The glance Neacal gave the laughing man surprised me. Instead of glaring at the interruption or even concern over such an odd reaction, Neacal smiled beatifically, as if the man were a new-born who had taken his first steps. His fellows surrounded the giggling man, moving him off and away from our sight.

Neacal nodded and turned back to me. "Keep you an eye to your purse and to your lives," he said. "The prisoner is dangerous. A killer, being taken to punishment in Kairclavan. If you see aught that is amiss, be sure to tell one of His Own you may meet in the Inns or towns along this road." He paused for a moment, idly scratching at his stomach.

"You're most kind to show such concern for both our purses and our safety, Goodman. I thank you for it."

His smile grew wider then and he leaned down as if to give me personal advice. "Do you? Then pay heed and I'll bring you another warning. You and your kind are not wanted in Bainellen. Perhaps there are those in Lechsede that will still listen to your japes and profanation of the God's words, but even there those who've not yet come to the lonely God grow fewer. Should you stray south into the heart of Bainellen Province, then tell no tales and play no plays, for the holy will silence you."

He rose up in his stirrups and I became nothing more than a bit character in a speech played to his own men. "Players may be learnéd – well I know who you are, Dughal durFortin, and I knew Bardeelin troupe of old – but what you do is hateful to the God. I'll have none of it in my province. I admit, in the sordid days of my youth I laughed at your indecent shows and bawdy songs. But then I met the Prophet and learned that the God grows angry at the heresies growing like weeds in the field. There is one Truth, and His Own spread it throughout this province, and soon all of Anacarra. Know your place, Player, and know that the God has numbered your days."

125

"He has numbered all of our days," Beathen said, moving from his position at the head of the cart a step or two towards Neacal. All eyes moved to Beathen as he continued his quiet speech, projected to reach even the mumbling rider in the back. "At one time it was considered the height of hubris to think that aught we might do could change the count of days the God has given us, for death and life are balanced. To remind us that to be born means to die is to tell us nothing." Beathen then swept a low bow, just a whisper short of mocking. "Or so *I* have learned."

Neacal looked fit to return salvo for salvo when I spoke up. Perhaps I shouldn't have, but I'd been walking for uncounted hours in weather so unpleasant that the beasts of the field knew enough to take shelter from it. I was tired, wet, cold, and hungry. Even so, my tone was one of respectful correction, same as I would for any patron who ignored our ancient rights.

"We're Unencumbered Players, Goodman Neacal. You have flattered us in saying that you know of Bardeelin. Then you should know our seal was granted to us by the glorious Aililnaric and wise Aelfanaricu themselves during the days of the Rici near on 700 years ago. In all that time, the Bardeelin have traveled the width and breadth of Anacarra, telling tales and playing plays and giving news. We tell the truth of what we see and hear so that all the people may know what happens in the greater world, from the lowliest crofter to the greatest Aric. It's not for *you* to deny us what is both our right and our duty."

I spread my hands, showing him I meant no disrespect. "We're under protection and owe obligation to no one but the First Among Five. Only he may revoke our rights to travel unencumbered or our obligation to provide entertainment and information to all who ask it of us."

"You dare?" Neacal asked in a tone more of wonder than anger. "You may be learnéd, Dughal, but I would not say you're wise."

I laughed, my mirth nearly as manic as the hot-eyed rider at the back of Neacal's troop. I thought with chagrin of my actions at the death of the uplander and since. "No one in my troupe would disagree with you, I think. But let us not have enmity between us, Goodman Neacal. I will pledge you this: we'll force no one to listen, nor perform that which offends. We will perform only history plays or mystery plays, that the populace may find wisdom by the hearing of Anacarra's glorious past and may find enlightenment in the hearing of the ways of the lonely God. None of the bawdy shows and songs of your youth will we perform while in Bainellen. You can't, in law, object to that, Goodman!"

I had seen such an expression as crossed Neacal's face but once before. He had no doubt that he would win in the end, but until then he'd enjoy the game between us.

"Can't I? Why, of course not. You argue so learnédly."

I vowed to commit his inflection to memory, for being able to take such an innocent word and make of it a contemptible insult is a feat that few of the best players can achieve.

He continued. "See that you follow your words with your deeds. Play no play that is obscene or profanes the God. No plays of the Goddess, no songs of wantonness or licentiousness. Your seal does not grant you license to offend and my duty is to see that you and yours suffer should you do so." Neacal's lips twitched upward in a seeming smile. "Do we understand one another?"

"Indeed, Goodman Neacal. I believe we do."

He called over his shoulder to his men and I hurriedly stepped back off the road as they thundered past, splashing mud. Beathen and Sionn at either corner scurried to take what shelter the wagon provided from the falling filth. I could but bow my head as the muck rained down on me.

I gathered my men together off of the road on the hard springy turf. "This changes nothing. We proceed to Lechsede." I wiped at the filth marring my tunic. Alas, it only smeared. "Camran, do we have money enough to house us all, sufficient food and warm beds, even if we don't play for a handful of days?"

"Why shouldn't we play?" Barrol asked. I motioned for him to be silent and turned to Camran.

Camran looked from Barrol to me and cleared his throat. "Our funds will be adequate, but only just. The Equinox just past brings very strongly to mind that the next Equinox we are to come before the First, offering him our fee to renew that Seal you used to shield us from Neacal. Will half a year be enough to keep body and soul together and earn sufficient for that?"

"Especially performing only dour history plays and dry religious shows," Beathen commented.

Oean blushed. "I'll do my best to craft them into something both edifying and dour-less."

"If our welcome in Rillsherd is any indication, then Bainellen will prove not at all to our purpose," Sionn said.

"I just hope that ... that ... the *misfortune*," Barrol whispered, "is no omen for the next equinox."

I raised an admonishing finger to Barrol. "Enough of that talk." To the others I said: "In Lechsede, the great markets don't rely on any holy day for commerce. Yet look at us. The paint is flaking, the props are breaking, and we walk about nearly threadbare. Even the words fall to dust in our mouths, despite dear Oean's best efforts. I say we spend the next tenday or more putting on a more pleasing mien."

"Indeed, Dughal." Beathen looked down at his mud splattered tunic. "I tire of being taken for vagabond."

"Repair all? Properties, cart, costumes, clothing?" Camran asked.

"All." I reached out and took Camran by the shoulder. "My friend, you take great care with our coin—"

"He pinches the coppers till they well nigh scream," Sionn said.

I pointedly ignored Sionn's comment. "– and I thank you for it."

Camran snorted. "Most oft by being a spendthrift seeming bent on emptying the coffers of coins as quickly as we earn them."

"We do ourselves no favors to seem as disreputable as His Own would make us out to be. We should do all that we can to be worthy of the duty and honor that comes with being Unencumbered Players of Anacarra. It's a narrow path we tread and we need no winds of ill-will pushing us from it."

"So we go to Lechsede, Dughal?" Barrol asked.

"Indeed, my boy, and we go as Players should. Heads held high, a song on our lips, ready to entertain any and all. While repairs are made to the cart and properties, while clothes are cleaned or made anew, while Oean reworks old stories fit for both His Own and the plain folk of the plains, we share the news as Players should."

"Not all news, I warrant," Sionn muttered behind me.

"You'd tell that tale?" I asked, my mouth dry and my stomach clenched in fear. I just managed to keep my voice steady as I'd heard my father berate Players before me. "Truly? Momentous news, that's true. The fine people of Lechsede would no doubt flock to hear it."

I stood up tall, my shoulders back as I glared down at Sionn. "If they believed you, that is. Pray, tell me good Player, how you would impart the news that people of eknos are being taken from their homes, beaten, stripped. Even raped, in defiance of tradition and both religious and secular law? How will you describe finding such a one left for dead and point the finger at the most holy His Own? Those men of the lonely God have the reputation of being harsh in their asceticism and honorable. Can you – a stranger, a vagabond, a rogue to their way of thinking – tell a tale that accuses the most pious and righteous His Own of violating the oldest of our religious laws and not be thrown out of town?"

"Or worse, be laughed at," Camran added.

"Can you tell a tale," I continued, swallowing against fear and gorge both, "such that those in the surrounding countryside – obedient to His Own – would feel the same disgust you do? How would you tell this tale to give that poor, unnamed woman back her humanity in the face of those who have so brutally taken it from her?"

Oean interrupted: "Did any of you mark that Neacal would not own that his escaped prisoner was a woman?"

I could see from the surprised looks that no one had. In truth I'd missed it as well. *Leave it to the wordsmith to note how others bent words.*

"Mark it well," Oean continued. "It would be a most grave peril, knowing that His Own couple with eknos."

"Rape, you mean, word-wright," Sionn said. "And murder."

I clapped Sionn on the shoulder and smiled, striving to diffuse his frustration. "All you say is true. But we've been threatened twice already by His Own. You tell the tale that we all wish we could tell and none of us will see the solstice, let alone the next equinox."

I turned to the rest, gathering them in closer. "Listen. While my father was alive, he might have seen another way clear of this mess. I can only ride the currents as I perceive them, and I perceive that we must forget that we ever saw the uplander woman in those woods."

Sionn spat and others growled in protest. I shouted: "Here me! Bardeelin is *my* troupe, for the Seal was granted to me by Oeric of Aethellen, First of Anacarra. By the oaths you all offered freely to me, I command you: tell no one what passed in the woods that night. You may walk with your head down Sionn, wrapped stoutly in your certainty, but I have no such garment to keep me warm. I see storms ahead for us and I'm doing what I can to see that we weather them."

Barrol nodded, but he's just a boy, easily cowed. He's known no other authority than mine since the day he first climbed upon the boards. Beathen didn't nod but looked away. He had his own reasons for not wanting undue attention drawn to us. Camran nodded to me, catching and holding my glance: he knew the risks we faced, for he had faced them for many years as my father's man. Sionn, fists planted firm upon his hips, took in deep breath to argue further. But at Oean's touch upon his shoulder, Sionn deflated, words unsaid. For the moment.

I pushed my hat back down on my head and took up my walking staff from where it leaned against the wagon. "Come, my doughty Players. It gets no drier standing here. Let us proceed on to Lechsede and hope to find welcome." We turned westward and I own my heart beat a little easier.

Ten

Epistle the First

26th Nabryhtian, In Rillsherd

To Cleirach, Prophet and Voice of the Lonely God and most Honored leader of His Own, I send you greetings and much love.

I should tell you right off that your plans proceed well. I've just come south from the border of Maukellen and every day I see your Vision made real. Finias and myself spread the Word of the Lonely God as you have given it to us. Finias' priestly rank provides us entrance into the Temples and my place in the brotherhood opens the doors of the clavans to us. I watch as Finias stands at the center of the Spirals and, with the Might of the Lonely God flowing through him, preaches to all those gathered – local farmers, townsmen, and priests alike – the Truth as you have shown it to us and I Know that the will of the Lonely God is being made manifest. I feel my consciousness expand to encompass all those gathered and I feel even your Touch upon my soul.

It is Glorious.

On those days, when I can feel the bulk of the Stolid and Evil world begin to shift back onto the path of Righteousness, that's when I feel most connected to you and to all of Anacarra. My Old Affliction bothers me not at all and I see no challenge to the future you have Seen for us. Rillsherd is the perfect Example: the Deacon of that place – a man named Tornan – holds sway over matters both spiritual and temporal, just as you've said it must be in order for Anacarra to again be Right with the God of Sheaves. In Rillsherd I see the Future and it gives me Hope.

Tornan acted very well in regard to a troupe of Unencumbered Players that have blundered into Bainellen. Despite that his own heart was in turmoil, Tornan effectively Banished the Players from Rillsherd, sending them on their way with his curses their only payment.

Poor Tornan. My admiration for him only grew once I knew what torment he suffers. His eldest daughter, dissatisfied with Broc durKinnan as her father's choice of husband for her, most shamelessly seduced one of the deacons of the town. Her father's own friend! She must have thought that her young and unspoilt Flesh would be enough to tempt the man away from his lawful wife and children. Beautiful she was, indeed, for I had seen her just some months past.

But her Lustful ways were not enough to turn the deacon from his duty. There's no question that he suffered a severe lapse in judgment by letting himself fall to the temptations of the young harlot. He willingly paid his fine and stood his Penance in the marketplace before returning, Chastened, to his marriage. When the daughter's guilt was made manifest by the cessation of her courses and the swelling of her belly, her father began the heart-wrenching, yet necessary, steps of declaring her Dead and arranging her confinement in the Fallow Fields.

This was a full Tenday before the Players arrived in town, otherwise I'd suspect them of enabling her actual disappearance. Most likely she chose Death in truth in the forest to Shame in the brothels of the Fallow Fields. And so even in this is the Will of the Lonely God revealed.

For his actions, I commend Tornan to you, good my Master. He acted in a most Righteous and steadfast way despite the attempts of his daughter to Shame him. I have taken it upon myself to reward him with the use of one of the captives and a supply of the Herb. I'm pleased to say, that as I write this, the first stages of the Blessing are upon him. We'll soon have another strong and steadfast man among our ranks.

But, my ancari'ni, it's been many days since I've been in your Presence. Those days when I feel the power of your Word moving the people I feel the estrangement deeply. When I am with you, the path upon which we have set our feet seems most clear and all is illuminated to my sight. Alas, when I am on my own, I find that doubts cast shadows across my way and I worry that I'm not ready for the task you've set me.

For every Gain we make, the evils of the world take from us. Just outside of Rillsherd and with no sanction from me, Broc, in his despair over the death of Tornan's daughter, took it upon himself to show one of the eknos females the "will of God." O how ruinous is the Licentiousness of women! Two men brought low by a willful woman acting out her Lustful ways. I am grieved to report that, in Broc's case, the results were far more dire than even those of the deacon in Rillsherd.

The female so wounded Broc in her escape that he has since died of his wounds. Regardless, since he had taken what rightfully belonged to you for use at your discretion, I had his corpse castrated and his body left unburied in Craobac Wood. I believe the remaining members of our brotherhood will resist the temptations of the flesh regarding the bestial sexuality of the captured eknos and remember the long-honored prohibition against wanton fornication in the future.

As for the female, we still seek her within the forest. Although, given the rough use Broc put her to before she fought back, I strongly suspect that what we search for is her carcass. When I came upon the

Players – for I knew that they must've passed through the woods at about the time the captive made her escape – I questioned them as to what they had seen. My master, it does not profit one to show any Kindness to the fallen. Despite I kept the questioning of them to a cursory level, still their answers were most Impertinent, as one expects from Players. Without explicit instruction from you, I hesitate to violate the ancient code that protects the Unencumbered. By the laws as they now stand, there's little I can see to do (although I have some thoughts on the matter). It galls me that such men are able to roam about at will, capturing people's thoughts and imaginations, distracting them from the dangers of the world and beguiling them with pretty lies. But I let them pass, despite their speech which bordered on the blasphemous. To be fair, I would be Astonished if they had discovered or aided the eknos female in any way. They may lie excellent well but in this I trust my instincts. They know nothing.

Ah, I sense your thoughts, my beloved master. Do not despair over me, your humble servant. I'll find the Strength to prove myself equal to the task you've set me. I admit, it's hard some days, when I'm face to face with the inequities of the world and yet far from your countenance. When you're near, I feel the Power of your Vision and know the Truth of your words. I'll strive to hear those words in the silence of my Heart and, in that way, find my Purpose again.

The nine current captives are piteous creatures, my master. It amazes me that you're able to so ascertain the God's Will that you understood what role these upland savages have in our Deliverance. So far from being Blessed themselves, these creatures fight and curse most angrily at even the gentlest use of their bodies. I marvel at the Mystery that is the Lonely God's plan. That the use of these eknos should ignite the spark of the Divine within those among us destined to be Blessed is truly amazing to me.

I have dispatched Finias to Lechsede in the hopes that he can raise enough of the Righteous in such a Fallen and Corrupt place that we may yet gain more eknos captives from among those that come down to trade. If the Fires that come to cleanse such a place happen to destroy a certain troupe of Players that have gone in that direction, well, such is the Will of the God of Plows.

I've been very Pleased with Finias. During the Fallow season, he had captured a hand of uplanders when they foolishly came down to hunt bison in the Briarwood. Over the course of some days, Finias suborned one of them (told her some lie about ransoming the others) and there is some expectation that she will return with others in "trade." If so, Finias will add those to the numbers he takes from Lechsede. We should have two cartloads of eknos before very long, my dear ancari'ni, ready to further the Will of the Lonely God, as you have Seen it.

Your most devoted Friend and humble Servant,

Neacal durCleirach

Eleven

Dughal

Acknowledged receipt of the following:

3 bushels eating apples from Maukellen

15 bushels cider apples from Maukellen

25 bushels hard wheat from Bainellen

6 moonhart and 5 elk hides from eknos (Elk clan)

9 sides beef, salted, from Danellen

Hundredweight pig iron from Glanellen

5 tuns wine, assorted grades and vintages, from Aethellen

- Signed for on this day, the 43rd of Yffian, by House Steward Artor durArtor, for Carrinanen Eabr

Rillsherd may have grown since I'd been there last but it was still just a rural farming town. Lechsede was a city proper, the largest we'd seen since coming into the eastern provinces and the full flow of Tilling Season commerce swarmed into the city when we approached a hand of days later. We passed the original walls half a day before we entered the city itself, for Lechsede had suffered greatly when the Anwroth first swept across land. In these generations since it hadn't recovered to the grandeur of those bygone days.

On the eastern approach, a new temple grew on a hill outside of the current city's boundary, with much land given over to the worship of the God in His fields. We left our cart at the bottom of the hill and walked the spiral towards the center, the varied plots we passed along the way showed the tender care bestowed upon them by the priest. At the center of the spiral, below the arbor spread for worshipers, we offered up prayers of better fortune for ourselves in the year to come. I've no doubt that some of my men prayed for the poor woman of eknos dead in the woods. I touched her flute in my belt pouch like a talisman and added my own prayer for her.

Pennants slapped in the breeze off of Varran Lake that lay to the north of the city, stretching their designs before us as we entered the city proper. Despite our mood and our bedraggled state, I had us once again put on our entrance display. We wore what still passed as our finery and streamers fluttered from poles mounted on our cart. I sang out our names and reputation as we strode beneath the gates. Sionn and Barrol juggled as they walked, tossing knives and clubs with a practiced recklessness that caused those by whom we passed no little concern. Camran guided the cart with a keen eye to the kinds of obstacles that could distract either men or horses. Walking sedately behind the cart, Beathen sang to Oean's accompaniment on a whistle. In such a town, commissions would come from the carrinans, so I sought to showcase our two fine musicians.

One would be hard pressed to find a road that would own to the description "straight" for any but the shortest of stretches in Lechsede. We wound through the town singing and juggling, taking note of the most prosperous areas and the most rough. As Players we'd spend time in both, for all citizens have love of theater and a desire for news of the Five provinces.

When Bardeelin had been a much more prosperous troupe – during the Rici we comprised a score of players both men and women, three wagons, a dozen horses or mules, as well as servants, spouses, and children – we'd have sought out the largest of inns to provide rooms for all of us. This troupe had not had that problem for a hundred years. I sought instead a quiet inn that would provide us the privacy to rest and repair ourselves and our props. Somewhere convenient to the amphitheater built long ago, in the fortunate days before plague decimated the lowlands, and in continuous use since.

Closer to the docks than the bright mansion of the local carrinanen, we found an inn that looked near as threadbare as we ourselves. I stood upon the cracked cobbles of the courtyard and took in the clean, yet tattered, thatch of the roof of the inn and smiled. "We're here."

I ignored the open exclamation of surprise from Barrol. The boy had been in Lechsede before, but as it had been within his mother's womb, I don't fault him for not remembering that this was just the sort of inn we visited last time. It astonished me to realize that of the proud troupe that had made Lechsede our own some fifteen years before, only Camran and myself remained. Proud Fortin and my charming brother Beccán, both long in their graves, the others settled into new lives as farmers or merchants. As Fortin's heir, I hoped I might do as much to make Lechsede love, respect, and patronize Bardeelin despite our reduced circumstances. I sighed, stood myself up tall, and turned to give my orders.

Camran and Barrol I dispatched to the hosteller to inquire after lodging for an extended stay. I assigned Sionn and Beathen the task of searching out an audience for us and to call on the keepers of the amphitheater to see that it was not already bespoke. Finally, I turned to Oean.

"Yours may well be the most demanding task these next few days, my friend."

He nodded his head. "I fear the same thing. It's no mean feat to so reforge the old plays that they're both known and new at the same time. If they were of my own crafting, that would be one thing. For long, I've had a wonderful idea on how to change *The Last Days of*

Aelf'anaricu into something so much more uplifting than we do it now —"

"It would please me to let you follow in the footsteps of the Old Poet, for of all playwrights living, I think you alone could match him. But such is not the path we tread. We need two plays, one a tragic historical and one a comedic pastoral for the city folk who expect such things. And yet it should not be so, well...." *How can one "mend" a pastoral comedy that – to a one – celebrates the Goddess in the guise of affection and carnal love?*

Oean laughed as if he heard my thoughts. "Have no fear, Dughal. I'll so recast the story of Arminaric, fifth of that name, that his death will be seen as the mirror of our fallen age. For the comedy, I thought that the *Tale of Immin and Aelfwynne* could be smelted again such that the dross is whole lifted away, leaving a moral and funny tale. Indeed, I think I can craft it such that those who would demand of us mystery plays, would see a fine and holy allegory. How say you to that?"

"You do both of those things and it's possible that Bardeelin may not only survive, but thrive."

I'd chosen this inn based on its proximity to those things we needed most: sempsters, wainwrights, tinsmiths, and a measure of isolation for Oean. The bustle of trades and guild people gave us more visibility and would make the repairs we needed easier to come by if we could trade service for service. But at the moment, I set all that aside, for what I most needed – what we all needed – were the baths.

Most towns of any size have communal baths, for cleanliness pleases the God (or so the priests tell us) and towns take pride in the facilities they provide to farmers, carrin, and carrinanen alike. Among ourselves, we'd oft make decisions as to which town to overnight in based on the baths. In this part of Lechsede, these baths were as hard worked as the tradesmen who frequented them. The vestibule showed cracked and peeling paint from the heat and steam, with no fresh coat for many a year. The steam room no longer worked properly, although the soak room provided sufficient hot water and the drains all worked in the rinse room.

Properly refreshed, we all began upon the roles I'd assigned. For the next two hands of days, Oean sat in the common room drinking well-watered wine and cursing at any commotion. I assured our kindly innkeeper Edana – for a woman had ownership of the inn for the first time since we'd crossed into Bainellen – that there was no need to tread carefully but to do as she and her staff always did. Oean claimed that the noise distracted him but if that were true he could write in our rooms, for one had a southward facing window and a table with even legs. Yet Oean thrived in the common room. I don't know if it was the distractions themselves or his ability to unleash his frustrations at his art upon those nearby that cleared the rocks from his pen's plow.

Beathen and Barrol both took turns creating fair copy and actor's copies from the whole new-writ plays as soon as Oean had completed them. Camran found for us wainwrights who agreed to repaint and repair our cart, negotiating down the price to a few coins, free entrance to our shows, and a visit by us to their own inn to perform just for them. Beathen sought out sempsters who would create new garments for all of us. Most of our costumes Beathen himself kept in good repair but our everyday clothes as well as those fripperies and fineries we wore upon entering a town had grown thin with long and hard use. Barrol, especially, had outgrown most of his clothes and the cast offs from the others looked hard used already. We saved those garments that still had some life in them for use as costumes or Barrol's rough clothes for as long as they would fit him.

For my part, during the first few days I pored over our stock of plays, as well-worn as our old clothing. Bardeelin had some two score plays that could be performed by our present, reduced troupe, and I sorted them out according to how well I thought they would be accepted in the changed climate of Bainellen. While Oean re-made the two full five-act plays that would be the centerpieces of our performances with the carrinanen and the amphitheater, I selected those that would be the staple of the inns and courtyards, the short one- to three-act plays which could easily be performed thrice in a day.

Some were so well known that they existed as no more than a title and cast list upon a single page of parchment, the most famous or telling lines written upon the back. Some few were so old that I doubt even Fortin had roused them from their slumber in the belly of our wagon and out into the daylight, archaic lines written out in an ancient hand. Some of those, recopied and with a few changes, would actually serve best, having been written during the age of the Divine Ricu or, like our performance in Rillsherd, written by monks such as Hereric. I wouldn't want to play them for long, but my Player's heart began to rise at the challenge of making such ancient words live for this troubled age. Having winnowed our stock, I set before Oean the stack that he would need to review and rewrite, and escaped before his shocked silence gave way to inventive and erudite curses.

While Oean wrote I wandered the town, talking with any and all who would spare me five minutes. I extolled the virtues of the plays we would present in a few day's time while failing to mention that the plays were neither fully written nor rehearsed. I attended worship in the temple both at daybreak and dusk, for temples are fine places to make acquaintance with people from all ranks, trades, and callings.

I visited carrinanen Eabr in his manor. He held the courts and the wharfs both and I eagerly sought his patronage. A good report of our skills and our conduct from him to the Aric of the province could only help to smooth our way in Bainellen. At least, insofar that the Aric still had any say or control of the province. Given what I'd seen in Rillsherd, I could not be sure such was the case. After visiting Eabr, his carrins and carrinans sought me out at our inn, bringing new custom to our hosteller.

In the nights I sat in the common room of our modest inn and taught myself how to play a highland flute made of bone. Camran scowled at me when he saw me playing it. How could I explain to him? Though fear crushed my chest so tight I could scarce find the breath to blow into it, playing her flute scourged my soul, reminding me of the danger that waited for us if we strayed from the course I'd set.

One of the carrinans wished to engage our performance. This was not unusual and several of the carrinans of the city had already bespoken our time. But, as he was patron of the goldsmiths, he requested that we perform, not at his manse, but in the courtyard of the Hammer and Tongs, a large and prosperous inn of the jeweler's district. Oean, Sionn, and I then sought out the inn in question, to inform its keeper of the carrinan's request and to arrange a time most convenient.

A large group of men crowded the court when we arrived, with one set off-loading large barrels from a series of carts while another set stacked bricks within two large wagons. Despite our errand, I nearly turned away when I realized that overseeing all of the activity were two members of His Own, their black cloaks and hats like cold shadows on the fine Tilling season sun.

Oean must have seen my hesitation. "If we flee before every group of His Own, we will become players of the uplands, for the presence of His Own spread—"

"Like contagion," Sionn muttered.

Oean smiled. "That is, I think, apt." He turned back to me. "A fine actor once said, 'We're Unencumbered Players. Our seal was granted to us by the glorious Aililnaric and wise Aelfanaricu themselves. It's not for His Own to deny us what is both our right and our duty.'" Oean set his hand on my shoulder. "Remember yourself, my friend."

I shook my head and chuckled, clasping his hand. "That's most unfair of you, wordwright, giving mine own words back to me!"

Nonetheless, I nodded and stood a bit taller, squaring my shoulders and striding forward as if with full and righteous purpose. The seeming will suffice until certainty is restored. "Greetings Goodman! How fare you this day?"

Dressed as they are, as alike in their somber blacks as crows on a fence, the mistake is easily made that every member of His Own is like every other. After Rillsherd, I expected the worst and braced myself for it. Instead, I got a genuine smile and a pat on the back.

"Players! Marvelous! I was telling Goodman Firchar just the other day how grand it would be to meet histrions while on our journey and I had hoped Lechsede would provide the opportunity. I'm Goodman Perrin."

The man so calling himself stood a bit shorter than I, a few years on the other side of fifty, once-blond hair gone mostly gray, with pale eyes bright in a face wrinkled from much time in the sun. I shook the proffered hand although I felt a bit as if I'd been walking against a stiff wind whose gusting had suddenly dropped away. "Well met, Goodman Perrin. We're both in luck." I did my best to hide my surprise. "Oean here was just telling me how wonderful it would be to meet Goodmen such as yourself who understand the importance of Players to Anacarra."

"Splendid. Would you join me and Goodman Firchar tonight at table here at the inn? You can tell us the matter and the venue of your next performance." He stopped as if something had just occurred to him. "You do sing, yes?"

I affirmed we had splendid singers in the troupe.

"I'm so glad. I'd be most indebted to you if you'd sing for us tonight. Goodman Firchar worries that singing is of the Goddess. Thus does he appease the God by singing in a most disagreeable manner." He beamed at me, called me well met, and went back to overseeing the work of shipping barrels of ale into the inn.

"It looks as if we'll be hard pressed to drink this inn dry!" Sionn said in covetous appreciation.

"Can even this large an inn finish off so many barrels before they spoilt?" Oean asked. I wondered much the same, but no answer was then to be found as we continued inside to search out the innkeeper, a man by the name of Olchobhar.

We gathered the whole troupe and at sunset we made our way back to the jeweler's district, entering the common room of the Hammer and Tongs, singing and laughing. Our astonishment at finding the common room close to full was nothing to the astonishment on the face of Goodman Firchar at seeing our entrance and hearing our song.

"I told you," hissed Goodman Firchar. "Players are degenerate. They can hardly help themselves. Why I've heard—"

We were not to discover whatever it was that Firchar had heard, for my new friend Perrin held up a hand, cutting off Firchar's complaints as quickly as sight of him had cut off our song. Firchar, perhaps half of Perrin's age, had perhaps only slightly more than half Perrin's weight. I wondered that he sat to dinner at all, for his hard brown eyes glared at me from a lean and ascetic face, all sharp edges and harsh angles.

"It's good to see you again, Dughal," Perrin said. "Please join us."

"Why, it would be our pleasure." I sketched a small bow. Firchar glared at his companion but moved down the bench nonetheless, giving us room. My Players seated ourselves at the table, large enough for the eight of us to sit with only a bit of knocking of elbows. I placed Camran next to Firchar, for I had no doubt Camran would meet even the Void of all Good with reticence and resigned cheer. I placed myself next to Perrin. He clasped my hand again and poured me ale from his own pitcher.

After only moments, the innkeeper Olchobhar sent his boys out with food enough for all. Trenchers of good dark bread quickly filled with a hot stew of mutton and the last of the Fallow season vegetables and was just as quickly eaten. We welcomed especially the chilled beer until we had our first taste. I'd never tasted the like. Pale in hue and quite bitter, the foam head had already disappeared even before I brought the mug to my lips. I was hard pressed to keep a pleasant expression on my face for both Olchobhar and Firchar stared at me most intently while I drank. I nodded my thanks and quickly took another bite of food.

When the fine food had taken the hard edge off of all our appetites, Firchar looked down the table and back up, meeting my eyes at the end. "What was that song you sang as you entered the room?" Only the least wary would have missed the bite of steel in the soft question.

"Why, a hymn, Goodman," I replied, happy that it had, indeed, been so. "You've not heard it before? It's praises the God for shelter and good cheer."

"Excellent!" Perrin said. "I would hear it again after we finish our meal, if you'd be so kind. And more besides." I agreed readily enough but did notice that Firchar seemed only reluctantly resigned to his comrade's request. I suspected he would retire early. He surprised me, then, by asking something of us himself.

"What news have you?" Firchar asked. "You've come down from the north, yes? We've come from the south and I, for one, would like to know what goes on ahead of us."

A fair request and within our duties, too. While dinner went on I told him what news I could: Oeric's decision to step down from his position as First of Aethellen province come the next Equinox; of Elias, First of Glanellen, marrying the daughter of a prominent house in the old Varranellen province; of a feud between carrinanen in Dennellen that affected trade in the province. Of the movements of His Own and eknos, I said nothing. Better to leave something out than to tell an untruth.

Later, I mentioned the many barrels of beer we'd seen unloaded and the strange dark bricks that had filled the temporarily empty wagons. Goodman Firchar's eyes grew wide and then narrowed in suspicion. "Have you not been told of the Prophet's decree?"

"Indeed, we have not." Misgivings nudged the fine food within my belly. Goodman Firchar looked to his partner.

"You need not defer to me, Firchar. This is not a matter of doctrine. My added years add nothing to this new tale."

Firchar quickly warmed to his subject, his long, lean hands gesticulating with every point. "For the last several years, the harvests in Bainellen have varied all across the province. Great abundance in one place is matched by great hardship a scant few leagues away. For some areas no rain falls for months at a time, drying the wheat in the fields. In others, too much rain rots the grains on stem and in storage. Whole barns, spoilt from floor to roof, unfit for human or animal."

"Yes, we've heard horrific tales that spoke of fearsome weather in Maukellen and the coast here, but so far have not experienced it ourselves," Beathen remarked.

"Three years ago or more this blight started. An evil in the land, I tell you."

"But I don't understand what that has to do with beer," Camran asked.

"The Prophet, may he be forever blessed by the God of sheaves, saw in a vision a remedy to these hardships. Plant much barley and after harvest, malt it and form it into bricks for drying. Local wheat would do for bread but should that fail, there would still be beer."

"Beer lasts longer than bread and can be transported further," Oean said, half to himself. "And might be shared more equitably. Ingenious."

"Is that what we saw being loaded onto the wagons outside?" I asked. "Bricks of barley?"

"Even so," he affirmed. "Truly, as you say. Ingenious. A brilliant, inspired idea. The Prophet is a great man, don't you think?" No wordsmith he, but his unadorned speech made the tale all that more surprising. He leaned against the table between us, his hands clasped before him. As he spoke, his eyebrows (the thickest part of the man) covered the ridge of his brow like two hedges lining a walkway. "The lonely God blesses the enterprise, I can tell you. Nary a brick has been lost to mold or mildew, to rot or rats. All bricks, without exception, are shipped by His Own to the nearest Naclav or Clavan where our brothers or sisters make of the malt the beer that is even now gracing this table. We then ship the brew back out to inns such as this one. In the next several days, other hostellers, farmers, even carrins, and carrinans will come and be supplied with barrels of beer as befit their station."

Such a wonder! *His Own are so well organized that they can accomplish such a scheme?* "And those areas which have seen harvests fail partake of the beer regardless. Is that right?"

"Yes! The God has seen fit to provide the Prophet with the means to eliminate want, helping those who starve and thirst. A single remedy to two problems and the whole of Bainellen call him blesséd. Isn't that remarkable?"

Remarkable could well be one description. I didn't know whether to be impressed by the Prophet's care and benefit to the poorest amongst us or be concerned that this self-same Prophet now controlled the bulk of grain produced by the breadbasket of Anacarra. His rapid rise from obscure monk to his hands guiding and guarding the wealth of Bainellen province had been less than ten years.

My earnest companion had continued on, oblivious to my preoccupation, detailing the logistics of the barley bricks for beer scheme. I own the success seems to have saved many lives as the droughts and floods continued in Bainellen. Soon, more of Anacarra would be brought into this plan, for the troubles assailing Bainellen impacted all of the country. When the breadbasket fell empty, those who depended upon it grow hungry.

Twelve

Dughal

Papa allowed me to stay up late last night, for he had hired a troupe of Players who styled themselves Siodaric's Pride to perform for his guests. The servitors set the tables into a horseshoe shape and we all sat on the outside so the Players could have the middle. Papa spent a fortune on candles, lamps, and even torches so that we could all see.

The Players juggled and sang and they put on such a wonderful play! Mama says it was written in the long ago by a man now simply called The Poet. While I don't pretend I understood half of the matter, nonetheless I found myself most amazed. The words, the action, the passion! Oh, yes, passion. I think if papa had remembered the story of the lovers in that play he'd have sent me to bed early.

I miss you ever so much, Avrea. When do you think our father' will allow us to see each other again? I'm not sure mine plans to travel to Kairill even again this year. See if your papa Breaslain will send you to me for the Equinox celebration.

- Letter from Kirra durBroun to Avrea durBreaslain, 12 Yffian 951

After a tenday spent writing, learning, and rehearsing the amended plays, we were finally ready for our first performance. Oean accomplished a remarkable feat of writing, even as the rest of us succeeded in a similarly remarkable feat of memorizing. His subtle changes to the old stories challenged us to remember old and new alike. The *Tale of Immin and Aelfwynne* had fallen out of favor some years ago, as these things do. Despite those years, the old words sprouted like weeds amidst Oean's new-sown seeds whenever I attempted to say my lines. Neither Sionn nor Barrol had any such difficulties, having never encountered the play before in any form. They simply had to memorize an entire five act play anew.

On the other hand, we had performed the play of Arminaric's plight – an untimely death that signaled the end of the Golden Age of Anacarra – just the last Fallow season. Oean tossed out whole scenes and replaced them with new-made ones. His remarkable accomplishment required equal effort from the rest of us in order to make the seams unseen.

And the rest: ah, what I had done to Oean and my troupe. The full plays took most of our attention for they'd bring in the highest fees. But we needed those shorter one- or three-act plays that would be performed on the cart and in the courtyards. The wainwrights desired a holy mystery play. The goldsmiths wished for an historical. The coopers wanted comedy and the brewers desired bawdy. We drew from this new crop and not one of us didn't feel anxiety as each play went on with lines unsure and stagings uncertain. I tested our mettle then, for we learned the full plays even as we performed the short ones.

On this day we'd stage the full five acts of *The Tale of Immin and Aelfwynne* upon the cart in the courtyard of our inn. In just a few days we'd perform these plays both for the carrinanen and in the amphitheater and our performance needed polish. The only way to do that was before an audience.

I paced behind the cart in ill-concealed anxiety, but the rest of my players took no notice. Each followed his own path towards the state of mind needed to tread the boards. Sionn stood in place, eyes closed and arms moving about as he imagined the performance he was about to give. Camran sat quietly and looked out over the gathering crowd. Barrol bent and stretched and burned off his youthful anxiety with swinging arms and running in place. Oean sorted our properties placed back stage while Beathen made a nuisance of himself checking that our costumes were presentable.

For this, our inaugural presentation, we had invited the sempsters, the wainwrights, the tinsmiths, and any other group to whom we'd promised payment in performance. Those groups came, and more besides, with the small courtyard filled to overflowing. Men and some women and girls perched on the stone wall surrounding the inn and the space before our wagon crowded with people shoulder to shoulder. The hosteller had her boys and even her stable girls out selling skewered meats and hot pies to any and all takers. From what I could see, her business was brisk.

Good. They came to enjoy themselves and had brought coin enough to spend. That day the gathered groundlings loved the pastoral comedy, laughing at all the right moments and cheering when Barrol (playing Aelfwynne) and Sionn (as Immin) finally met for a chaste embrace. Catcalls from the walls told me that our emendations had not been missed, for the more knowledgeable had expected something more earnest in the ending. Nonetheless, I felt that – rough though our performance had been – we'd given much joy and laughter this afternoon. When we gathered again at the cart after passing the hat, I found much to reassure me that my decision to come to Lechsede had been the correct one.

The next day we staged *Arminaric V* upon our cart in the afternoon, for that night we were to play it before Eabr and his important guests, all the worthies in the town. Again, I strode across the boards at my entrance, my first lines hiding from my mind like naughty children. Just as we had the day before, we acquitted ourselves well. The bloody finale of the play ended in thunderous silence before changing to enthusiastic applause. I smiled, proud of my players.

Ah, that I might have remembered that feeling for longer than the space of an afternoon! That night when we played *Arminaric* at the manor itself we showed ourselves to be ill-lettered fools. In the second act, Oean forgot his own words and began the original scene. I strove to wrench the flow back into its new-laid bed, with only middling success. Sionn forgot whole lines for the first time since just after joining our troupe and, in truth, my performance was far from my best.

Players exist to entertain and inform the people of Anacarra. So for doing that which we were meant to do, we do not charge a fee when we play in an inn's courtyard. We may pass the hat, but nimble fellows can easily enough pass the hat by. Innkeepers earn back whatever we may cost them in room and board by the increased custom that our presence inevitably brings. A few days hence, when we played in Lechsede's public amphitheater, we would charge an entrance fee, with some portion of those receipts going to the maintenance of those permanent venues. In some instances, we come off the worse for using those stone-seated arenas, but I had hopes after our first show that Lechsede would welcome us.

But when the great carrinanen or the lesser carrinans or carrins have us to their homes to perform in private for them and theirs, we are paid an agreed-upon fee, with half in advance and half upon the completion of the performance. So it was that as we were to take our leave, the carrinanen Eabr arrived with a servant to bestow upon us the second half of our fee. So disgusted was I by our playing I made to return it.

"Carri'ni Eabr, please. We haven't, by right, earned our full fee. Our performance ... lacked."

"Nonsense," Carrinanen Eabr replied. "I found it pleasing. Most edifying."

It would seem that the faults in our playing glared most brightly to those who knew where to look. Despite my disgust with myself and my Players, I think I impressed him by my actions. I'd not intended to make a show as if in humility but he took it as such and actually increased our fee. I didn't demur but silently vowed we would better earn our keep at the next performance.

"He *increased* the fee?" Camran asked.

"Indeed." I handed him the purse.

"Maybe we weren't as bad as we thought," Barrol said. He flinched and came near to bolting when I, Camran, Beathen, and Oean all growled at him and cursed him for a child.

"We were worse," Beathen said.

"I couldn't remember the lines, and I wrote the curséd things!"

"Use your wits," Camran said told Barrol. "That our performance was bad is plain to us. It should have been plain to that fool of a carrinanen."

I sighed. "But it wasn't. While I'll take the fee, that we didn't fully earn it shames me. Have the great become so parochial and uncouth that they can no longer appreciate the art they spend their money on?" I rubbed at the scar on my thumb and then shoved my hands into my belt. "No matter," I declared. "If the great landowners are ignorant that doesn't mean I'm unlettered. Sleep well, tonight, lads. Tomorrow we run through both shows before we perform them again."

No groans but only nods met my words. We had our pride.

Two days later we performed our first show in Lechsede's large arena. Legend has it that stories of AnA had been told to rapt audiences from that spot since the first of Aethen's children had plowed the fertile lands around Varren Lake. The natural depression had been enlarged and deepened over the centuries: terraces carved out of the hillside, paved with great cut stones, and benches raised from shaped blocks.

Providing seating for thousands, the terraces encircled the open area at the bottom on three sides. Behind the stage, a long low building had been built. And rebuilt, from time to time: in the ancient days, when this space was but a low spot beside a hill, the structure had been a simple enclosure of canvas and sticks, set up to provide actors their exits and entrances. To this day, despite the building was made of mortared bricks with a copper roof long weathered to green, it was still called "the tent."

In the days of the Rici, the city had flowed out and around the amphitheater, but after the Anwroth the city had contracted, leaving the amphitheater some distance outside the new walls. Despite that, the citizens of Lechsede thought little of trekking out to the arena, whether for the performance of yearly ritual plays staged by townsfolk or whenever Unencumbered Players came through the district. We found the venue in fine condition and set about walking through our plays in quick order, adapting to the larger space.

That afternoon, I stood within the tent and watched as the arena began to fill. Oean tapped me upon the shoulder and pointed to a space one third of the way up from the bottom and right in the center. "It looks as if our new-found friend Perrin has, indeed, come to see us perform."

I nodded even as Sionn spoke up behind us. "Too bad he didn't come tomorrow to see the *Tale of Immin and Aelfwynne*." He laughed at our expressions. "No? Not one for a tale of unrequited love and great passions?"

"He chose aright," Oean said. "I believe that our performance of *Arminaric the Fifth* will suit him – and his companion Firchar – much better."

"Indeed," I replied. "It's a wonder that he could even persuade that dour His Own to set foot in the amphitheater."

Our first performance went better than I could have hoped. We used the large space to its best advantage, even climbing up upon the tent to provide a greater sense of danger for when the wounded

Arminaric staggered and collapsed in death. The applause was properly muted after such a play and my men shucked their cloaks and raced to their positions to accept what coins we might.

I stood at the edge of the stage and waited as the Goodmen came down to speak with me. "How did you like the play?"

Goodman Firchar scowled and began to speak but Goodman Perrin interrupted him. "Why, it was splendid. Edifying. Most pleasing to the God, I must say."

"Must you?" argued Firchar. He turned to me, his bony finger jabbing in time to his words. "You mock the God's creation with your false seeming. *I'm* sure the God frowns. These shows are but distractions! The God of Harvests is to be found in the future, not the past—"

"Indeed, so say the scrolls." Perrin's eyes glinted with amusement.

"So says the Prophet!"

"I daresay that's where he first read them." Perrin turned to me, the amused glint turned hard. "I don't doubt that you're likely to find the opinion of my friend here to be the more prevalent one in the province. However, even he can't deny that your play was orthodox."

I looked to Firchar and got a curt, unwilling nod. I bowed to him as if Id just received the greatest praise. "I thank you. Usually, our aim is to please those who attend our shows. But today I'll accept not being heretical as the height of success."

"You'll find much of Bainellen to be a barren place for players," Goodman Firchar said with unconcealed delight. "As it should be. If you take my advice, you'll let your Seal lapse. Devote yourselves to honest work."

Much might I say the same to you, you carrion crow. I trust my face did not show my thoughts, but should I open my mouth, my tongue might well give those thoughts voice.

"We leave tomorrow," Perrin said. "We have off-loaded all the barrels we brought and took on as many barley bricks as we can carry. It's back to the naclav for us."

"Do you intend to stay in Lechsede long?" Firchar asked me.

I felt my eyebrow rise in surprise that he'd leave off the lecturing for simple conversation. "Why yes. We have no immediate plans to travel."

He nodded, his eyes not meeting mine. Perrin clasped my hand and wished me well. I returned his well wishes and turned away to rejoin my men.

Over the next tenday, rarely did we see even a quarter of the theater unfilled, and then only on a day of rain. Even Camran confessed his pleasure at our profits.

"At this rate, should we play until Growing season we may well earn back what you've already spent on clothes and gilding for the cart!"

I smiled, for he exaggerated. At least somewhat. The next day we'd play for a carrin who hoped to impress his carrinan and I felt sure that between our fee and his desire to be seen as a man of means, our finances would soon regain the level they had enjoyed before we entered Bainellen.

But even beyond the costs, the men grew less wary, less anxious with each passing day. The simple food arrived without fail, we had clean straw beds instead of damp hard ground, and the folk of the town sought out our company. Few of us had reason to pay a single copper though we drank all the night long.

It's a truth I'd long ago discovered about myself, but it seems true for most Players: unless we're plying our craft, until we are before an audience who eagerly awaits our efforts, we feel at a loss. We're Players and only when we play do we find ourselves. So relaxed had we become that Oean laughed – out loud – in the public room of the tavern. Beathen sang as he went about his day. Barrol lost the confused tension in his eyes and began to look his tender years instead of much older. Sionn flirted playfully with the innkeeper's daughter and the innkeeper herself in more seriousness. Why, even Camran nearly smiled. Once.

Lechsede felt much more like one of the western cities and not at all like what we'd experienced in Rillsherd or even in the towns of Maukellen. We were hailed and greeted and feted by commoner and carrinan alike. We visited near to every Inn and public house in Lechsede, telling tales and news to all found therein.

For all that I talked, however, I listened far more to what others said. What I heard disturbed me. I'd spent my life walking the length of Anacarra, on either side of the upland crags and fronting both seas, and never before had I heard such tales told to me by the traders in Lechsede. Stories so bloody and macabre that had I dared to present them to an audience, me and mine would have been jeered from the stage. It was as if the worst of the history plays had come alive again.

To hear it told, strife walked abroad in Anacarra. From tradesmen I heard of attacks by the eknos upon merchants who dared to use the passes that had been carved from the Crags: the Falcon Way just south of Lechsede and the Serpent's Way to the north. In taverns I heard of the gathering threat that was the eknos, massing in forces not seen since the time of the Clan Killer. In all of them, I heard tell of the ravages that eknos visited upon the innocents of Anacarra, yet never did I hear anything like the tale I could have told of a lone woman beaten, raped, and left to die in the forest.

Something sat ill with me. The tales were *too much* akin to an old play, as if a player misremembered the matter and only told the goriest parts. We had passed through the Serpent's Way not less than a year ago and traveled the length of Maukellen and had neither seen nor heard any such strife. So I returned to the newly fashioned temple to seek a more sober source of information. In truth, I sought the hypaethral sanctuary in hopes of taking comfort within the wide spirals of plants, herbs and flowers laid out with neat and inviting precision. Instead, I heard more horrors: attacks upon religious houses, naclav and clavan both, with the attackers dressed as eknos.

I dropped the flower I'd been holding to my nose and looked closely at the old priest. "'Dressed as'? You doubt they were, in truth, uplanders?"

He laughed with bitter mirth. "No uplander would care enough! Our God means nothing to them save as the stuff of songs to be sung around a campfire. When those religious houses were attacked, no one was killed and nothing of import was taken. But books – books! – were burned. Whole libraries set ablaze." He hacked and spit upon the ground in his disgust at such a thing.

The old priest took me by the arm and we walked the Spirals for some while, but the well-ordered rows of new-green plants no longer had the power to calm my heart. "In my youth I met and befriended an old man of the eknos," he told me. "A good man for all he was a primitive. Pendal his name was, if I remember aright. We spent a hand of days sharing tales by the fire, for he'd undertaken a pilgrimage of sorts into the lowlands, seeking to learn about how we lived. He found it most amusing when I had to take out a book in order to recite to him my favorite poems." The old man shook his head. "Perhaps it's nothing to you, who have whole histories memorized, but in those days I had ready access to my books. I'd well memorized where my favorite passages lay between the pages if not the very words themselves!" He stopped his walk and turned to face the crags far distant. "Pendal told me something I hadn't known, for in my callous youth I'd thought more about the God than I had about those who lived in the God's lands. He told me uplanders are illiterate, their tales told – always – from memory. So, my well-read Player, would the uplanders care enough to burn books that they don't care enough to read?"

He left me there, his thoughts adding their weight to mine own. These attacks upon the people of the lowlands, be they real or rumor only, brought with them talk of reprisals against the uplanders. Fear bred anger in the youths of the town. The merest excuse could set them ablaze.

We'd been in Lechsede for more than a score of days and performing the new-worked plays for a tenday at least. After a performance of the *Tale* we retired to the common room of an inn to eat and drink and share tales, songs, and good cheer. My men sat scattered throughout the room, mostly doing their duties. I doubted that Sionn's earnest conversation with a red-haired young woman had much to do with the politics of Maukellen province, but what did it matter? So long as he did not displease her, I saw no harm in it. There are many ways in which Players earn the good will of the populace and Sionn's new-found friend seemed much in favor of his attentions. Beathen, too, I realized, had met someone. I looked about the room, but saw no frowns, no sign that any other was concerned regarding Beathen's true intentions. None, that is, save the man to whom Beathen's attention was directed.

I trusted Beathen to be discreet as necessary and in that I was not mistaken: Beathen showed discretion sufficient for the western provinces. Alas, we were not in the west, and the young man he was with knew no discretion at all.

The next morning, three of my five men joined me at breakfast. Only Sionn and Beathen did not appear and we all shared smiles and earnestly hoped that both men had found and given pleasure the night before in hearty abundance. When Sionn strode into the inn yard some hours later – late for rehearsal – he accepted the good natured ridicule and ribaldry the others tossed his way. But when Beathen had still not returned and we were to perform but another hour hence, my well wishing turned to something else.

"Oean? You were closest to Beathen and that young man last night. Do you know where they might have gone?"

"I think I overheard the man say he lived in the stonemasons quarter."

"You go," I said to him. I closed my eyes, a dark sense of foreboding clasping my heart. Opening my eyes again, I clasped Oean on the shoulder. "Find him. Bring Sionn with you in case there's trouble."

Oean nodded and, grim of face and demeanor, both he and Sionn left at a run.

Thirteen

Rhia

And so Na left them there beside the stream. Then did the first Ealdranna, the Old Ones before the Old Ones who instructed the Two, celebrate the gifts that Na had given them. They gathered food and ate from the meadows. They hunted game in the woods and caught fish in the stream and built their bothas upon its bank. And they shared pleasure, one with another. In their delight of one another, so did Na delight in them, and one final gift did She give them. She Touched each of the Ealdranna, bestowing her Blessing, but Na's Touch is dire. Many of the Ealdranna fevered, some raved, and all found the pleasures of the flesh to be multiplied within them.

Just as the moon waxes and wanes, so too did the power of Na's Touch moderate within them, but it never passed away. A few of the Ealdranna continued to hear Na's Words within them and to sense the spiritual tides around them all, and they became shaman. A few continued to find fulfillment in the comfort of the flesh and to sense the tides of the body, and these became hetairi. But all felt the emotional tides that surged and sang between eknos. So did the bonds of eknos grow strong.

- Story of the coming of the Ealdranna as told by Moonhart Eknos

I came to myself lying warm beneath many blankets. Some memories of the last few days came back to me. Or rather, some memories of the day some days past: The march across the high escarpment, the campsite below the arch. Waking to a dawn that shuddered and sparkled and all but spoke my name. I remembered beginning the trek down the cliff face. I couldn't remember reaching the bottom.

I lay naked save for the Calling talisman heavy between my breasts. The rest of my clothing lay folded upon a boulder only a few feet away. I slowly stretched my arms and legs, shocked at the heavy lethargy suffusing my limbs. Dried sweat and other fluids made my skin sticky and, just as the first time, Na's Touch left me with sore breasts, chafed nipples, and my lifros so chapped and tender that I drew my legs hard together in a futile attempt to muffle the pain. Even so, within I felt a satiated emptiness. Whatever pressure had built within me from Na's Touch had somehow found release, and with that I knew that the worst of Na's Touch had passed.

Four poles supported a mesh of pine branches as a roof to keep away the worst of whatever weather we'd endured while I tossed in the throes of my illness. It also provided a measure of privacy. We all endured Na's Touch – many of us more than once – but that didn't mean we wished to share what we went through in the full sight of everyone.

I hadn't been long awake (or perhaps had waked and dozed unknowing) when Taltaya and Kiri came over and squatted down next to me. "You're better?" Taltaya asked.

I nodded. "Better." I struggled to sit up, managing even though my breath came in harsh gasps. "But not yet recovered." I hesitated for a moment before asking: "Was it bad?"

Kiri gave me a playful smile. "Not so bad at first. You seemed to enjoy your hallucinations very much. On the second day you began to dance and sing for us."

I winced. "Oh, please tell me you jest. I danced?" I covered my face in my hands. "I'm not known for my dancing."

"I daresay you will be now!" Taltaya laughed, but I heard no mock in her voice. She squeezed my hand and motioned towards the other woman. "Kiri sat with you for much of the last few days."

"Thank you, Kiri," I replied.

Kiri smiled again. "You're most welcome, Rhia." She sighed and reached out to touch my shoulder. "You were beautiful. Na's Touch brought a glow to your eyes and joy to your lips and your euphoria made me quite envious. I've never experienced Na's Touch since my first time and you make me wish it had been otherwise." She then blanched and adjusted the blanket upon me. "Until the passions came in earnest, that is. You worried us then."

I reached out and clasped Kiri's hand. "I'm sorry for that. But I seem to have made it through to the other side."

"And all on your own. Or nearly so," Taltaya said. "Who's Sarae?"

Whether remnant of Na's Touch or not, the mere mention of her name brought my breath catching in my chest and a echo of feeling in my loins. "She's my huntmate."

Taltaya and Kiri shared a look and a fond smile before Taltaya said: "While you hallucinated, you carried on a very lengthy conversation with Sarae. I can't tell you what the conversation was about, for you spoke low and mumbled, but you took great pleasure in it. Twas the only time you ever reached climax. I'm glad that you had your lover with you, at least in your visions."

I smiled and sighed. "She cared for me during my first bout of Na's Touch as well."

Gaunt then strode into view. "Kiri? Come. I need assistance." She gave not so much as a glance in my direction.

"Of course." Kiri stood to leave.

Taltaya reached out and laid a hand on the young woman's arm. "Would you send Hrothar over? I'm sure Rhia needs to feel clean nearly as much as she needs to eat and drink."

"Again, Kiri," I said. "You have my gratitude. You did very well."

Kiri blushed, bobbed her head once and left. The thought of being clean pushed aside much of my remaining fog. Taltaya moved away the last of the blankets and my bare, fever-seared skin drank in the delicious coolness of the morning air. Hrothar arrived with steaming cloths and a drinking skin slung over his shoulder. The cloths he handed to Taltaya, the skin he handed to me.

"Ah, there now," he said. "Those grass-green eyes see us and not somewhat else." His smile broke out, like a sunrise through the trees of his full black beard even as he placed his fists on his hips and gave me mock glare. "I'm not used to being overlooked, I'll have you know."

I returned that smile and thanked him for the water skin before drinking deep. More *te'na* suffused with that herb and this time, sweetened. I drank off half the contents in one go.

"Do you want help to bathe?" Taltaya asked.

I began to shake my head but realized that my arms had already grown weak and shaky just from holding the drink skin up. "If you'd help me out of the bed, I'd appreciate it."

Together, Taltaya and Hrothar helped me to my feet. But I then took a hesitant step and nearly ended up back on the ground.

"Like a new born fawn you are!" Hrothar lifted me and stood me up next to Taltaya. At first, I tried to bathe myself. I relied on them to stand, but soon had to give up on that, too. It took all I had to remain upright while Hrothar and Taltaya washed my skin clean.

At one point, Taltaya looked up at me, concern in her brown eyes. "How did you get this scar, Rhia?" Her fingers traced the ridge of jagged flesh that ran high up on my ribs, from below my right breast nearly to my back.

The effort to speak distracted me from the effort to stand, another kindness that I owed her. "Ah, well. Therein lies a tale. The moonhart buck I took," I said with gasping breath. "On my *stealna kir.* Thought it fit I should remember ... his sacrifice."

"An antler cut you so?" I nodded. "But surely your tunic would've protected you. Well bruised, no question, but not scarred."

"Had I been wearing a tunic ... you surely would've been ... correct. But the woad markings I wore ... instead ... did little to keep my skin intact."

"Such an injury could have killed you!"

At the concern in her eyes, I reached out and touched her shoulder, the one I'd seen her favor. "Or, worse, it might have ... kept me ... from being a hunter."

"Alive is better." Taltaya's words left no room for debate. "You've lost muscle in your fever, but no doubt, at full strength, you can send an arrow far and run nearly as fast. Those, with cunning, make a good hunter. Not flawless skin."

I glanced at Hrothar and nearly laughed at his expression. "Better that I ... had as much fur on ... my hide as you!"

"Indeed, little doe," he agreed. "I've not heard of someone going on their *stealna kir* as one of the ealdranna had in a hand of generations. Twould seem you have courage."

"Or foolhardiness," I replied.

"The two are oft the closest of companions," he agreed.

I shook my head. "Foolish. Vain. It set me apart." I looked to him. "I think you know ... something about being set ... apart."

"Aye, fawn," Hrothar said. "That I do."

"There you are, Rhia. You're now clean. Would you put your tunic on or sleep again for the while?" Taltaya asked.

"My tunic, please. I'd come out and greet all of you." She handed me my tunic and I struggled into it, my breath coming hard and my muscles shaking with the effort. Once dressed – but before I could even manage the trews – I decided to lay down, for just a moment to catch my breath, before going out to the fireside. I fell into a deep and dreamless sleep, and didn't wake for several hours.

The day I'd seen begin with my return to myself after the travail of Na's Touch had come near to ending when I awoke again. I looked around the empty lean-to, spotted my trews and wondered if I had enough strength to pull them on by myself. But my sleep as well as the sweetened tea seemed to have restored more of my strength. I slowly pushed aside the blankets and rose, albeit unsteadily, to my feet. I shuffled as far as the flat boulder upon which both trews and schoh had been placed and took them up. I counted it a victory that I managed to not fall upon my backside but actually sit upon the rock. After a deep breath or two I succeeded in covering legs and feet both.

The days of fevered sleep – my impromptu dancing notwithstanding – had allowed much of the worst damage to my feet to heal. I found that Taltaya had also altered the schoh such that they fit better and I could walk with little pain or discomfort out to the fire at the center of the hunting ekarra. Not quickly I daresay, but unassisted, and for that I felt an inordinate pride.

"Rhia! Good to see you. Ah! Easy there." Hrothar's assistance saved me from tumbling into the fire instead of sitting by it. That dimmed my pride a bit. But the warm smiles from Taltaya and Kiri made me feel welcome indeed. Even Tasso inclined her head in greeting.

They handed me a plate filled with meat from a roasted partridge already off the bone. A goodly quantity of grains that had been stored in the ekarra had been boiled with herbs and early greens filled the rest of the plate. The conversation flowed around me, but they left me to my meal. I feared I was in a race: finish my meal to give me strength before what little strength I had ran out.

"I see you haven't regained much stamina, Rhia," Gaunt said.

I felt my face grow hot. "No," I admitted. "Not yet. But I heal quickly. I suppose caring for me delayed your vision quest. I apologize."

Gaunt waved away my apology. "While Kiri stayed with you, others hunted. I meditated on Na's wishes." She shrugged. "We weren't idle."

The evening settled in as all such evenings do. Kiri sang, her voice pretty but timid while Tasso played a flute. The breathy quality of the wooden flute matching Kiri's voice well. Hrothar and Gaunt exchanged wild tales, each one more unlikely than the last. Taltaya told a story and her voice came near to lulling me to sleep.

"Rhia, you're excused tonight," Gaunt said. "Besides, we much enjoyed your recent dancing. You would be hard pressed to improve upon that!"

My face grew hot and I tried to think of how to respond. Taltaya looked away from Gaunt while Kiri glanced at me and then smiled in reassurance, despite the blush on her face. Not even Hrothar laughed at Gaunt's jibe.

I thought of my mother's quiet dignity and tried to answer as she might. "If I brought a smile to you, then I'm glad. Small recompense for the inconvenience I've caused."

Hrothar took up another song and the moment passed. I shifted about, trying to get comfortable. My limbs felt limp, my body ached, my leather tunic rubbed painfully against my chapped nipples, and the rich food gurgled within my belly. Hrothar noticed my fidgeting and inclined his head in invitation. I leaned my shoulder against the broad and muscled expanse of his back. Soon enough, my eyelids grew heavy and the quiet chatter around me faded away.

I awoke just before dawn back in the lean-to, stripped and comfortable beneath the soft blankets. But noises from the direction of the ekarra got me up and dressed. When I reached the ekarra's firepit, I asked Gaunt what was happening.

She turned a serious face to me even as she set her hand upon my shoulder. "We'll hold the ritual. I'd hoped that you'd be part of it, but you're hardly recovered from Na's Touch. Yet we must begin now."

"Might I help with the preparations, at least? You can decide later if I'm to play a role."

She scratched at her chin. "Aye, that's one path." She nodded. "Alright then. You aren't strong yet and once day has risen fully we'll fast until tomorrow sunset. First, go and eat. Then you can assist Taltaya. She's seeking and mixing the herbs for the honeywine. Her shoulder allows her that, at least."

I walked – slowly to be sure, but much more steadily than even the day before – over to the fire and found a bowl. I ladled some of the porridge into it and sat upon a boulder to eat. The porridge warmed me for the morning was chilly with the sun not yet risen. Sweet with honey, rich with fruit and nuts, my hunger returned ravenous despite the large meal of the night before. I'd nearly finished my second helping when Taltaya strode into view, a bag slung over one shoulder.

"Might I help?" I asked her when she neared the fire.

"Of course, Rhia." She reached out and touched my forehead. "How do you feel today?"

I assured her I felt well and after I'd cleaned my bowl, together we prepared the mixture for the mead. The dried seed pods of this plant, the roots of that one, the leaves of another, we crushed or mashed or shredded and spread out to dry. I had to keep asking how she wanted each prepared, for such a large variety of sacred plants I hadn't seen. With great patience, she explained and I think, despite that, together we accomplished the task faster.

"I'm surprised your cearnan was willing to give you back to the hunters," I told her as we finished. "You're a good teacher and I've met few with your knowledge of the sacred plants."

Taltaya's eyes widened and she bent again to her task. "She wasn't pleased about it but any of us would do what we must to see that Lynx survives."

"Even unto pulling a bow against the pain in your shoulder. You're brave, Taltaya of Lynx."

She glanced over to where Gaunt strode amongst the other hunters, commenting, criticizing, and then turning to look dreamily into space instead of helping with any task. "Not all think so. My shoulder is an impediment to my ability to be a true hunter."

"Those aren't your own words, I think. Let me ask you this. Will I ever be as tall as you?"

She grinned. "No, little Moonhart. I suspect you've achieved your full growth."

I nodded. "I think so, too. Will I ever be as strong as Hrothar?"

She laughed at the conceit. "No one is as strong as Hrothar save Hrothar himself."

"Just so. Strong in both spirit and body, I'd say. So, am I an impediment to a hunting band because I'm not as tall as you nor as strong as Hrothar?"

"Of course not! You have other skills. Why, the fact that you eluded us for days shows you have woodsense aplenty."

"Then why is it, Taltaya, both cearna and stealna of Lynx eknos, that you're an impediment because you can't pull a bow as well as you used to? I imagine you still manage better than Kiri does, and I mean that as no disrespect to our young friend. She simply doesn't have your experience."

Taltaya sat back on her heels and stared at me, her task forgotten in her hands for the moment. Then she shook her head and together we worked in silence until the task was finished. At the end my muscles shook and my breath came fast. Taltaya said nothing, simply allocated the more rigorous tasks to herself. Gaunt felt no compunction against expressing her disgust at my weakness: "You tremble like a newly-birthed fawn, Moonhart. Tis too soon for you to fast and take a full part in the ritual."

I nodded, for at that moment the thought of fasting for the next two days made my stomach clench. The fever and the duration of Na's Touch meant I'd eaten little for days and my body needed food more than anything – save sleep – if I was to get my strength back.

"Rhia, I think you have a role in our ritual, but not directly. Or will have, perhaps." Gaunt frowned. "That doesn't make much sense, does it? I'm not sure I can explain what I'm feeling very well. Your presence among us is what we need to decide upon. You've been

Bidden and now you've been Touched. I can't imagine but that you don't need to breathe Na's Breath nor drink honey wine to commune with Her!"

I nodded, suppressing a shudder. "Aye. I wish I could be a part of your ritual since it so directly touches on what I'm Bid to do. But I don't have the strength. I'd only be a distraction." I frowned when Gaunt's expression supplied the "again" that I hadn't voiced.

Gaunt nodded and put her hand on my head, stroking the stubble on my scalp as if to bring attention to it. "We'll start at midday, so take some stores from the ekarra and a quantity of water, and then go back to your lean-to. It's far enough from the bothas and firepit that you shouldn't be a distraction to us." She peered down at me. "Rest, Moonhart. Depending on what we learn in our vision quest, we may need to travel, and quickly. You don't want to slow us down further, do you?"

I assured her I didn't and she left. Taltaya watched her, her expression guarded. She turned to me and thanked me for my help. "Do you need me to bring anything to your lean-to?"

"Water would be good. She's right, I don't have my strength yet."

"You shouldn't come to the fire, I think, once the ritual is started, but it would be good for you to begin moving about. Perhaps you could hunt some small game. You need meat to regain your stamina and muscle lost to the fever. You might even hunt something larger for the feast that will follow our fasting, if you feel up to it."

We carried provisions and water to my lean-to. She even tasked Hrothar to bring some of their wood so that I could have a small fire and then she brought me the last of the porridge. With the sun fully up they wouldn't be eating it. "It'd be a shame to waste."

I stood on the edge of the small glen in which they'd built the lean-to and watched the preparations. Hrothar and Tasso brought enormous amounts of wood, for the bonfire would burn until sunset the next day. Kiri and Taltaya scoured the land at the foot of the escarpment for a certain plant that, when burned, helped to bring about visions and communication with Na, especially when combined with the herbs I'd helped prepare, already mulling in the mead.

I shivered. I'd had enough communing with Na recently. They had several hours of preparations ahead of them and I'd already exhausted my strength. I lay down and fell asleep almost immediately. But this time I didn't sleep the day away. I awoke in only a few hours, feeling refreshed and hungry. The porridge was cold but I ate the last of it anyway, two full bowls and then some. I walked slowly to the nearby stream and scoured the leather bag with good sand and clean water. Then, with the sun high and hot and the banks of the stream thick with trees to block any wind, I stripped down – rested for a moment or two to catch my breath after even that little exertion – and then waded into the cold water.

The soak felt good and for the next few hours I alternately bathed and warmed myself on the bank, more turtle than moonhart at that point. After a brief nap, I even had enough stamina to shave my head again. The memory of Sarae's hands on my scalp brought a smile to my lips and an echoing tingle from deep within. *You had indeed been with me during Na's Touch.*

As the sun moved towards the west, but before it fell behind the bulk of the escarpment, I dressed again and made my slow way back to my camp, to find Gaunt glaring at me as I walked up.

"Where have you been, Moonhart?"

"Staying out of your way, Lynx. Is there a problem?"

She seemed to recollect herself. "No, no problem. I don't want anything unaccounted for."

"I wish you all luck." I sat down with a sigh. "I'll not disturb you. I'll do what I can to build my strength back. When I get up to move about, I'll stay to the east of your fire and south of the stream. Will that do?"

"Aye, Moonhart." Already she looked distracted. "Fine." With that she left me and in less than an hour, with the last of the sun's rays coming over the edge of the escarpment, I heard their ritual begin.

Their chants sounded far different from those of Moonhart but I imagined that they served much the same purpose: calling on Na to aid them in their quest, calming the mind and opening the participants to what might be encountered in the night, in the mead, in the smoke.

After some while I became restless. With my body recovering, my old habits began to reassert themselves and I had never been one to sit and wait with any good grace. I took my sling and went to hunt rabbits in the gathering twilight and soon had a pair roasting on the fire, smeared with fresh herbs and oil. The wind had shifted so that it blew directly south, taking their smoke and the scent of my roasting meat away from all of us, neither bothering the other. I ate the last of the coneys by the orange glow of fading embers and the silver glow of the quarter moon sinking towards the escarpment. Sleep came upon me soon afterward, the fire banked, the blankets heaped upon me against the cool night air.

I don't say that twas a Calling dream that came after I fell asleep. I can't say what it was, in all truth, but I think that, having undergone Na's Touch amongst these people of another eknos, I'd become more attuned to this small band. I have no other explanation.

Suffice to say that, sometime in the dark of night, between when the moon set and before the sun rose, I joined the Lynx hunters at their fire, playing a role in their ritual just as Gaunt had foretold. Not in body, no, for mine slept still and deep beneath my lean-to. I'm not willing to say I dreamed of them at their fire, for I've never dreamt warmth flicker over me from spectral flames or coughed at dreamy smoke of Mother's Breath billowing into the air. The sensations felt too hard for a dream and yet too dull for reality. For a time I hovered in between.

I wondered at what had brought me to their ceremonial fire. I feared Gaunt's rebuke for interrupting them but she didn't notice me.

Nor did anyone. I relaxed and felt the wonder of the ritual wash over me. I, who've had Na reach into my life too many times, felt great admiration for those reaching out to Her in their need. My love for them grew. It felt as if my arms wrapped themselves around each and every one of them and I held them to my heart.

Kiri opened herself to me immediately, seeking assurance and praise, all-too aware of how much she had to learn as an inexperienced hunter of her fractured eknos. In Taltaya I found a different sort of uncertainty: the fear of skills lost, the searing pain from the plunging fall that shattered her shoulder years before. Tasso focused on the flames and the smoke and the hole inside of her left by her mother Treassa's death in the last hunt, a hole that would not close. I nearly lost myself within Hrothar, so great is his capacity for love and joy and laughter. Equal, alas, to his capacity for despair and heartsickness.

Having shared such intimacy with the others of this band and experienced their desires for this hunt and their eknos, I reached out to Gaunt prepared to find within her a similar pride of purpose. Instead, I found madness and horror.

I wanted to bolt then, flee her mind and the communion. But I couldn't. I went stock still and quiet within her mind, like a rabbit held motionless beneath the hawk's shadow. Gaunt didn't seem to notice me or even those around her, so intent was she on her inward torment. Unlike the others, the nature of the ritual isn't what had opened those doors to the past, I saw that immediately. She lived these memories every waking hour and every dreaming one, too, the thoughts and emotions well worn and almost comforting in their familiar horror.

No longer did Gaunt even need a thread to tie the images all together. They were all of a piece in her mind: that last fateful hunt; the capture by lowlander men dressed all in black; pain, captivity, starvation, arms and legs held in the painful metal bands lowlanders called shackles. I see the lost hunters including Gellae and Treassa.

And some poor cearnan, but Gaunt had never bothered to learn his name. Each in turn are thrown naked to the floor, the women on their backs, the man on his belly, their arms and legs pulled wide. The black cloaks shackle them to rings set in the floor for just that purpose. Each, in turn are.... We have no word for it in the uplands other than violation. Abomination. There was no sharing, nor any pleasure, given or taken. The lowlanders do have a word for it: rape. Gaunt is made to watch and then her turn comes and she, too, is shackled to the floor and she, too, is brutalized. Violated. *Raped.*

The sequence of images repeats and repeats again, a living nightmare that Gaunt inflicts upon herself in guilt and fear. Suddenly, a new scene emerges. She hears the sobbing of those behind her and I feel the echoes of pain in her body from the beatings and the shackles and the rapes. A round face comes into view, the small eyes peering dispassionately into her own and the man sits back and more of the room suddenly comes into view. Gaunt sits on a "chair" before a "table" scattered with "parchment" (unfamiliar words for heavy furniture and useless items). The man smiles at her and then pulls a tie from his long hair and shakes his head, spending a few moments tying his hair back again before he speaks. And a deal is struck, Gaunt is released, but the others are held as surety for future behavior, redeemable in kind.

I fled Gaunt's mind and the communion of those beseeching Na for Her aid of the Lynx eknos. With a start and a gasp I awoke by the embers of my own fire just as the sun climbed above the horizon.

For some while, I huddled beneath my blankets, wet with sweat and cold with fear. What I had seen inside Gaunt's mind horrified me. Incredible. *Dangerous.* I got to my feet, determined to go to the fire and expose Gaunt and her murderous intent. But I'd no more than pulled on my trews before I stopped. "Incredible," indeed. Who'd believe such a tale? How could I have walked among their dreams? Gaunt would deny it, of course, and I'd seem still mad from Na's Touch.

I paced my little fireside, uncertain. If I challenged Gaunt, I might be able to shatter the calm she wore like a mask. But I might not. If I interrupted their ritual, no one would thank me for it, and especially not with the news I brought. I thought of claiming a Calling dream and saying that I saw the images sent by Na. It might have even true, but twas far enough from truth that the blasphemy of it sent me shuddering. The ritual might have drawn me in but I couldn't claim authority nor knowledge other than my own. All would know me for a liar, else.

I began to pack. I hadn't yet recovered my strength after my ordeal, but I'd eaten and slept and would have a full day's light to make my escape. They wouldn't know me gone until sunset at the earliest and after two days of fasting they'd need to eat, drink, and rest before seeking me, probably the next morning. By then I might be either safely away or safely hidden.

Yet, even that little effort had me laying down again to catch my breath before I might escape. I told myself I gathered my strength for what was to come but the truth was, Na had more to show me.

As soon as I slipped into sleep, a true Calling dream came upon me: bound to sleep, unable to rise or awake or cry out, the images carried me along with a clarity mortals never have under the open sky. From a great height I see the nosmoot lands to the north and west. I seek for and find the great escarpment, the steep stairway up the western face of it and then the sandstone arch. From there I find the stairway down it, the crotch of rock and the path below it that I never saw with my conscious mind. Finally, I see five people sitting around a smoky fire amidst a hunting ekarra. A sixth person sleeps beneath a lean-to and I know myself. Then the images become doubled, as if two things happen at once. I can no longer tell one from the other: a moonhart doe, a pride of lynx, hunting wolves, a cage, a wagon. The lynx scatter and are safe from the ravaging wolves! No, wait: one lies dead beneath a moonhart's hooves. Ah, me, they're all dead, crushed in the jaws of the black wolves and it's the moonhart that's fled. Oh!

The wolves surround the moonhart and the cage is made ready, the lynx are nowhere to be seen. Not a cage, or yet an open cage, not even bars to protect the doe from those who hurl stones and knives.

Across it all, every one of the images of death, is the soft patter of a Burning season rainfall and I awake with dew wet on my face. I tell myself it was dew.

I spent all of that day in indecision. Not wondering if I should flee, because the images Na had shown to me proved the folly of that course, but wondering how I might accomplish what Na had tasked me with. I paced my little campsite. I walked to the river and swam in it and paced the river bank. While the sun dappled the river and the breeze blew warm from the south, I forced myself to lie still and listen for the voice of Na.

If leaves have a language, I did not learn it.

What I did learn was that being quiet and still may bring its own reward. Perhaps it was sent of a purpose by Na, or perhaps the early Burning season shoots were best along the river bank. But in either case, while I lay there pondering my own fate, a large boar, one tusk broken and jagged, came rooting up through the loaming. I had nothing with me but a simple knife, long bladed and kept sharp, but for a boar, all bristle-haired and fierce, I would have far preferred to be twenty yards back and with two or three arrows to hand. I looked to my skin, already scarred and still damp for I'd just come from a swim and hadn't put my tunic back on. No woad markings but despite that, not so much different from my *stealna kir* not so long ago.

Ah, if Eanna could only see me now! No doubt she'd chide me for leaving my bow behind.

I waited until the boar wandered behind a rise, out of sight and then I crept up the bank and next to a storm-downed tree, its roots levered up out of the sandy soil to form a wall nearly as tall as myself. If I needed to get away from a wounded boar, I could use that for safety. I turned attention to my prey, silently slipping my knife from its sheath.

Long minutes passed. The breeze dried my skin, blowing the musky scent of the animal towards me. Slowly, he rooted around and moved closer. Finally, he was close enough that I could leap, strike, and leap again to safety.

His outraged snort shattered the stillness of the wood, followed swiftly by the heavy thud of him flinging himself after me, only to run into the gnarled roots of the upended tree. But even Eanna would've been forced to admit that this time, my strike was sure. The heavy animal staggered and fell, the spurting blood from his severed artery slowing to a trickle. Only then did I approach and give him the final release.

"Through your sacrifice of blood, you bring life to Eknos." I said to the boar. "I thank you."

My strength was not enough to carry him even as far as my camp. I did bring rope and hauled the boar into the air, so that the blood would drain and I could dress him. When sunset fell, I bought the fatigued but content Hrothar with me and he carried the meat back with him to the ekarra. Lynx and their one Moonhart would feast that night.

Gaunt seemed calmer. Perhaps the decision she'd made had eased her mind, even though what I knew she intended would have filled most of us with guilt and shame. But as they all talked of the visions seen in the fire and smoke, she spoke as the rest of them did. I could sense no duplicity in her as she told of the need for me to continue with them, of her vision of Na whispering for us all to travel to the edge of the Uplands where we'd find what we were destined to find.

We can't lie, one eknos to another. But there are truths in stories. Even if we don't believe that Bear spoke to Moonhart, or that Na danced with Skiem across the sky, the larger truth binds eknos together. Gaunt believed her own tale so strongly that it had the feel of truth. It wasn't true, she was wrong, and yet the connections between us didn't resonate with deceit.

I had to turn her from the path she trod, the one she carried us all down. If I didn't succeed before we left the uplands, Gaunt meant to turn me and all the others over to the black-cloaks, the wolves of Na's Calling, in exchange for her sister.

Fourteen

Dughal

AnA, the twinnéd Godhead, joins dark to light, land to sky, water to fire, female to male. And so does the world continue in balance, each owing to the other, all needing all.

An brings forth fruit when seeds are planted in season, for this is the boon He grants. Na brings all together in pleasure without regard to season, such is Her gift to us.

- The Third Sacred Scroll, verses 15-18

"Beathen was taken alright," Sionn said when he and Oean returned an hour later. "Seems our friend Firchar expressed an opinion to his superiors that Lechsede teemed with sin."

"That one had an opinion not provided to him by the Prophet?" Camran asked.

"This has what to do with Beathen?" Barrol asked.

"These black crows have begun flocking to Lechsede," Oean replied. "We saw them in the Stonemason's quarter, preaching against 'clannish' behavior."

"Surely not," I protested. "Sharing pleasure has never been offensive when no offense is given. The lad seemed willing enough when I espied them last night."

"I don't understand," Barrol said. "How can sharing pleasure be wrong?"

Good lad. I spoke plainly. "You're right, Barrol. Sharing pleasure is never wrong, should all involved enthusiastically assent."

"These black hearts don't see it that way," Sionn said. "They call such pleasure 'unnatural' and 'evil in the sight of the lonely God.' There are some amongst the stonemasons that heard the words and decided to act upon them, in hopes, I imagine, of impressing the crows."

"Surely Beathen didn't fondle the man in the common room!" I protested. "How came they to seize him?"

Sionn grimaced. "The young man bragged of his dalliance with the handsome player and was overheard. The young man was followed and both he and Beathen are taken."

"Two grown men, held captive? For sharing pleasure?" The concept violated everything the Priests say from within the Spiral. "If this is true, then the world has turned cruel indeed."

"Crueler than a woman raped and murdered and left in the woods?" Sionn demanded. He stood unflinching before my shocked gaze and Camran's scowl.

Even as I admired his courage, I damned it and my fury grew cold. "Yes," I answered, my voice low and hard. "More cruel and more perverse. Rape and murder have always been wrong, but sharing pleasure with a willing and enthusiastic partner used to be a way mortals might come close to divinity. Some call it sharing the Goddess's gift, no?"

I sighed and asked of no one: "Has the world grown so twisted and cruel? How has this Prophet taken such power that upon his word alone he might decree one kind of loving as proper and another as evil?"

"Did you find where Beathen's being held?" Camran asked of Sionn and Oean. "What do they want with him?"

The image of the torn and bloody body of the uplander woman came unbidden to my mind. I closed my eyes and swallowed hard against the fear and gorge rising in my chest.

Oean shook his head. "That we didn't find out. I fear the worst."

"Dughal!" Sionn rounded on me. "You must think of something!"

I turned away from the earnest faces of my companions, some frightened and some angry, but all resolute. A resolution that I didn't share. I could see no act in such a place and such a way that would keep us from ruin. My father wouldn't have found himself in such a predicament, I'm sure, and a single glance towards Camran convinced me he thought so as well. My fear for Beathen settled upon me like a cloak, heavy as if despair were rain.

But. My father was dead these long years passed and it fell upon these weak shoulders to carry the load or be crushed beneath it. I may fail, but by the God and Goddess both, I would not fail to try.

I stood tall and turned again to my Players, squaring my shoulders to the effort ahead. "It would seem so."

I paced for a few moments up and down the aisle of the inn's common room, my men ranged about me. As if we prepared for a performance, I thought, each of us facing the threat in our own way. Sionn stood in place with his eyes closed and breathing deeply as his fists clenched and released. Camran stood at the window, peering intently out into the gathering gloom, alert to any approach. Oean busied himself with bringing in food and mugs of beer, setting a table with a goodly feast, while Barrol – who had never had occasion to fight someone in anger – stretched and limbered himself. I'd never seen such intensity in the boy. No, near enough in age to be called a young man. Scared, no doubt (as were the rest of us), but determined to bring his friend home no matter what.

As was I.

I stopped my pacing and called my men around me. "Well, lads, I don't like the script we've been given to follow this day. No, not at all."

"Need no crows taking one of our own to tell us that, Dughal," Sionn muttered. "What we need to know is what to do about the parts we're forced to play."

"Why, let me ask the wordsmith, here. Oean," I said, turning to himself, "if you come across a word or line or scene you dislike, what is your first thought?"

Oean frowned, opened his mouth and then closed it again. A smile began to dawn upon his face and he said: "Why, I change it, Dughal. That's what I do."

"And that's what we'll do. We haven't played yet in the stonemasons quarter, have we?"

"No, Dughal," Camran answered. "We had a date set for early next week."

"Then few will know us on sight. Fewer still if we dress ourselves for the part."

Sionn, his fists clenched again, asked, "And what parts will those be?" I could see the thought in Sionn's eyes: doubt. Well, let him think what he may. I've set the proper stage for my players all of my adult life. I just hoped I could set this one, too.

"Come, my friends. Let us eat. And while we do so, I'll tell you about a play to perform extemporaneously."

Some hours later, with full dark upon the city, we split into three groups to make our way to the stonemason's quarter and the tavern from which Beathen had been taken. We had ransacked our stores for the right costumes, for only Sionn and Oean would perform the role of Themselves. Camran and Barrol would be the traveling Old Man and his Grand Niece, and I the Merchant.

Most times, Bardeelin perform set plays upon set stages. Plays old and well-known or plays new wrought and innovative. But there are times when we as Players perform what was known from old as Streetshow. A word, a suggestion, the barest idea and Players would take the seed and grow a story from it. We had our story set for us with only the ending still to change.

Camran and Barrol went in first, simple travelers seeking a place to eat before they continue on. It wouldn't be noticed, for the stonemasons have always been a rich quarter and their inns and taverns known for good custom. I'd go in second and act unknown and unknowing of the others' presence. Later, only after they had time to scout quietly about the quarter for ought we needed to know, would Oean and Sionn reappear in the tavern, brashly approaching the same men as they had before to demand Beathen's release. If we three had played our parts well, their entrance would be the spark set to tinder.

"Cover your ears, lass," Camran told his "niece." "You shouldn't have to hear such things said." Barrol sank down upon his stool, the very picture of innocence offended. Camran turned to the man nearest him and stood close, his staff clenched in mottled hands that appeared to shake with age. *Not so close, old friend,* I thought. *He'll see the flecks of chalk coloring your dark beard gray!*

The man Camran approached stepped back, a look of surprise on his face. He stood a foot again taller than Camran and at least that much wider in the shoulders, the dust from his trade bringing his hair and tunic to a gray that nearly matched Camran's own. "Now, old gaffer, I said nothing! Why do you challenge me?"

"Nothing! If I had wanted her to hear such things about Players I would've taken her to the inns nearest the amphitheater! We'd heard the stonemasons were honorable, stolid and solid as the stone they work. But no! We are subjected to such language as this!"

The big man held out his hands in a placating gesture. He sought no trouble and looked thoroughly perplexed as to the source of Camran's ire. I'd come in but a moment or two before, taken a mug and sat down across the room from Camran, with my back against a wall. My entrance being his cue, Camran had begun his scene.

Before the stonemason could say another word, one of His Own, his hat and cloak off in the heat of the tavern, stood and strode towards the affronted pair. Murmurs and movement accompanied this, pulling back and giving him a path to stride right up to Camran. "Good old man," said the crow, "I am Finias. I'd hate to think that such a one as this," and he pointed to the stonemason, "might so disrespect the lonely God and your advanced years by offering you insult."

Camran turned to the His Own as if welcoming a long-sought ally. "I would not say he offered insult, as such. But his language! Boasting to his comrades of some Player caught with another man, or so I heard. Disgusting!"

"I said naught of any Player!" the stonemason cried. "Did I, Cedric?" The man next to him shook his head, but a flush had sprung up on his cheeks. *Ah, that one knows something.* I exaggerated my movements – just enough – focusing my attention upon that conversation in such a way that so, too, did my companions. I trusted that this Finias, unknowing, would play his part well.

Finias had been shaking his head. "Ah, grandfather, I fear you have come upon this inn at a bad time. I'm assured by these good men present that what went on last night – the disgusting act of which you heard – is not, in the main, how men such as these comport themselves. And yet, it did happen, did it not, Barton?"

Low-voiced growls from my companions followed the question as they glared at Finias. The goodman stood of middling height, with long hair, and slim of shoulder and limb. His face had the drawn look of one who fasted more than he ate but his clear eyes flicked towards my corner of the room when the murmurs broke out.

"Good old man," he said to Camran, "believe me when I say that your outrage is shared. The great Cleirach in Kairclavan has been saddened by the decline of morals in Lechsede. His bosom

186

companion, Neacal, sent me here to do all within my power to bring about spiritual uplift and cleanse Lechsede of dangerous elements and outside influences."

The man next to me snorted and turned away, disgust writ plain on his face. "You laugh, man?" Finias cried. "In this very inn, last night, such an outside influence bent towards corrupting one of your own. Do you deny it?"

My companion turned back towards Finias, took another drink and set his mug down most firmly upon the table. "I've known Stafan all my life, Goodman. A great carver, an artist. If corruption be the introduction of aught which does not belong, then no corruption took place."

Finias' mouth dropped open and he stepped towards us. "Blasphemy! As the Prophet Cleirach says, 'A man does not lie down with a man as if with a woman—!'"

"Ach! Goodman, please." Camran's shout distracted Finias, pulled him back away from me and the men around me. *Good, Camran. This Finias is easily pricked. We need more fuel before this fire will burn to our advantage.* I turned back to my erstwhile companions. *These are a bit too sober, I believe.* I ordered another round for all of us.

While Camran remonstrated with both Barton the stonemason and Finias of His Own, I turned to the men nearest, suddenly much more well disposed towards me than before, thanks to some of the inn's best ale (I'd made sure that it wouldn't be the ale brought by His Own). "Have the ...?" I began to ask. Then I closed my mouth and shook my head.

"What is it, friend?" my companion asked me. "Say what's on your mind."

I smiled and raised my mug. "Ah, you call me friend and I value the sentiment. My thought was not worthy of one so called. I will toast your health and leave it at that."

He slapped me upon the back and leaned in towards me. "Despite what yon religious might think, we are civilized men here. Ask your question and we'll answer as we may. Or not, but we won't take offense, will we lads?"

Seeing the heads shake about me, I put on a hesitant expression, as if I sought for the right words. "I thank you, for I admit to a curiosity. I've recently traveled from Maukellen. There's a magnificent building there, the Urdan of the Aric, said to have been built at the fall of the Rici by stonemasons from Lechsede. That's part of why I'm here, to see the inheritors of such a distinguished past and tradition."

The men around me looked very pleased with themselves, chests puffing out with pride and their mugs raised to each other in salute. "And so I wonder," I continued, "why it is such men would allow this ascetic to chastise them in their own inn. Have the long years stolen all pride from the Lechsede masons?"

The smiles turned to scowls in a trice, the promised forbearance put to severe test. "I wouldn't have you think such of us, *friend*." The title sounded a bit forced, but still sincere. I spread my hands and shook my head.

"Oh, I have offended you. Please, accept my apologies along with another round." Suiting action to words I signaled the serving boy to refill all the mugs.

Mollified, my companion frowned, but not at me. "In truth, I can see why you'd say such a thing. No, we've our pride still, but these are hard times in Bainellen. Drought when there isn't flood, hunger in some of the smaller towns and hamlets, and rumors of strife throughout the land. Building is down and many of the trades, masons among them, face an uncertain future. Some – you can understand this, surely – turn to the religious for answers. Thus, such a one as *him*—"

Ah, such a delicious blend of restrained anger, respectful wariness, and contempt in his voice as he nodded towards Finias!

"—is welcomed into our inn and his counsel listened to."

"By some, at least," said another, scowling into his mug.

"And he cautions against outsiders influencing the masons?" I asked.

"In part, yes."

"But...?" I looked to each of my companions in turn, confusion writ across my face.

"Yes?"

"But isn't *he* an outsider?"

Few words met my question but the expression on their faces grew more thoughtful as they drank and looked at where the diminutive Finias remonstrated with Barton and Cedric. I watched their faces for the moment when comprehension changed over to anger. *Timing, Dughal. Too soon a push and the effort is wasted. Too late and it is for naught.*

I touched my companion's arm, turning his attention back to me. "I think I'll be going," I said. "Feels more like a wake in here tonight and I was seeking more merriment." I rose, opened my purse and began to take my gold and silver coins from the table.

"No, please, stay," I was asked. The five of them signaled for my mug to be filled again and I allowed myself to be persuaded. "You are right, though," my companion agreed. "We are not at our most lively. The events of last night, well...."

I judged it right that I say nothing, but I sent one eyebrow upwards in question. Like most people, when upset by events, they find solace in talking about them, to any who might listen. I suspect that these men had been speaking of little else to one another since the morning and they were ready for another set of ears to pour their confusion into.

"You see," he said, motioning me closer. "There are Players in Lechsede and one of our fellows, Stafan, sought them out. He's a great artisan, as I said just now to *that* fellow, and he loves plays and Players nearly as much as he loves the stone. One of the Players, a big bear of a man, came back with Stafan to our tavern last night. Pleasant enough fellow, we all said so." To this, the men around me nodded in the affirmative. *Good man, Beathen. Glad am I that you comport yourself well. Right before you are taken in 'unnatural' acts.* My companion locked his eyes upon mine. "Be clear on this, friend. Stafan brought him here because he knew we'd protect him as we might. Stafan's a kind man and he has the true artist's way with the stone. We know that his appetites don't follow the same path as most. But we don't care!"

Heads nodded all around. "'Na brings all together in pleasure without regard to season,' say the sacred scrolls," offered one man.

"One less fellow sparking with the women," said another.

"We all follow the path that the lonely God set for us, be it well trodden or no. Or so I believe," finished up my companion.

I heard a snort and looked up, to find a scowling Finias standing all too close by. "You dare quote the lies of the Goddess, mason?" He shook his head, a great sadness on him. "Cleirach has told us the future, and it is glorious. But to get there, we have to get right with the lonely God, and that includes following the *true* path. If you valued your friend as you said, you should have kept him from listening to that vile Player."

"Ah, is that how it's to be?!" I heard a shout from across the room and looked up to see Sionn and Oean standing next to Cedric and Barton. "Sure, and now I see it clear. Tell the Goodman here that it's all the fault of the Player. No one knows him, no one will stand up for the stranger." Sionn, affecting a mien far younger than is his want, wiped make-believe tears of frustration from his eyes. "But I tell you this, Beathen is a good man and true. I've known him all my life and never would he have forced someone unwilling."

"Unwilling or no, he should lose his seed spear for plowing the wrong field! Such acts are an abomination in the sight of the lonely God!"

"Since when?" Oean's quiet voice, projected with great precision, cut through the murmurs in the tavern. "Have new holy scrolls been found? Have the old ones been rewritten by the God and Goddess?

Which scroll and verse ranks one expression of love over another? Tell me, for I desire to become learnéd."

Finias turned from us to this new challenge. He puffed himself up, a farcical sight in other circumstances, surrounded as he was by men who hauled and carved blocks of stone all day. "New scrolls found? No. Written! Cleirach is the Voice of the lonely God, prophet and seer. And what he has written condemns such unnatural acts."

"Just because something is written doesn't make it Truth." Oean shrugged. "I've written thousands of words. Might I claim divinity?"

I would have to look through our store of stage paints to see if I could somehow mix the very evocative shade of purple suffusing Finias' face. "Blasphemy!"

Noting that both Camran and Barrol had made their exit, I turned to my new companions. "Is it up to this Cleirach in far away Kairclavan to chastise the stonemasons in Lechsede? Threaten one of your own? With *mutilation*?"

Suddenly there were three groups in that tavern, each one yelling at the other two. My companions and their like-minded friends harassed Finias and his group as outsiders, agitators, violent, and scurrilous. Finias and his friends threatened that the wrath of the lonely God would smite them all for heretics. And Barton and Cedric, along with more level-headed masons, strove to come between the other two groups and put out the emotional fires me and mine had lit.

"Smite me yourself, you scrawny lackstones!" shouted one man, who then picked up the very startled Finias and hurled him at the other His Own, who were good enough to break his fall. Some of the masons who had come to believe what Finias preached – or at least believed that His Own had grown powerful enough to be feared – surged to their feet in his defense.

Soon enough, the two groups would come to more earnest blows. In the melee I rose, held tightly to the wall, and made my way to the entrance. I saw Sionn grasp Cedric's tunic before being pushed aside with some quick words. I slipped outside and to the spot wherein we'd agreed to meet, finding Camran and Barrol there already.

"What, by the Bargain, is going on in there?" Camran demanded.

"Change, I believe. And not for the better."

My statement was accompanied by the sound of splintering wood. I flinched and Camran said: "We may have pushed a bit too hard, Dughal."

"Say rather, we underestimated the amount of tinder before we lit our spark. I think that this conflagration would have come some time."

Camran nodded, but sighed all the same. "Ah, but that we were the ones to bring it."

From out of the Tavern, Cedric came, followed by Sionn and Oean. Barton, too, came out, but he scurried off quickly in another direction. When they neared, Sionn said: "We did it, Dughal. They'll release Beathen to us."

I turned to Cedric. "When?"

Cedric looked at me and my companions. Barrol took off his wig and winked at him and Cedric sighed. "This is an ugly mess Player, and no mistake. You need to leave Lechsede."

"Not without my man."

Barton appeared then, bringing Beathen with him. My men called out just as a loud shout erupted from within the tavern.

"Good even, Dughal," Beathen said over the din.

"Good even, Beathen. You missed rehearsal."

"Believe me, Dughal, I do not plan on making a habit of it."

I left off any rejoinder as two men in black cloaks ran out of the tavern and past us.

"That bodes ill," Sionn said. "Should I go after them?"

Camran scoffed. "To what purpose, you fool?"

"You've no need to follow His Own," Cedric said. I realized as soon as I heard his quiet words, that no ruckus came from the tavern to drown him out. "They'll be after you, soon enough."

"What are you saying?" Oean demanded.

"Don't you feel it?" He looked about him at the darkened city and then shivered as if the night had grown cold. "The very stones shift beneath our feet. These His Own seek to carve all men into something of their own shaping." He hawked and spat. "After what happened here last night," he grimaced and looked, not at Beathen but at the rest of us, "and tonight, you and yours will be no more than the dross left after their making." Cedric looked tired, his words not meant to threaten but to warn. "Get you gone, and soon. Since His Own arrived a few days ago, they've been preaching against Players, uplanders, outsiders. They've even said trade would improve, as soon as we 'get right with the God' by 'cleansing' Lechsede."

"Starting with us?" Camran asked.

Cedric nodded. "But not ending there, I fear. There are a few uplanders staying outside of town this time of year, trading furs for finished cloth and metal before the bulk of Lechsede's trade becomes foodstuff."

"More eknos deaths, then," Sionn told Camran. I couldn't tell if Cedric heard or no.

"He'd blame poor trade on Players and Uplanders? And you believe him?" Oean asked.

Cedric shrugged, his words noncommittal. "It doesn't matter, now does it? Those who hire me and mine to build their houses and their shops may believe and to not be seen to believe keeps trade from me."

As if summoned by his words, a group of some dozen men, dressed all in black, rushed past us. Cedric shook his head and turned away and followed His Own into the tavern. For the second time this season we must leave a city in disgrace to spend a cold and unquiet night on the road.

"Barrol!" He started and turned towards me. "Run to our inn and get the horses from the stable. Roust the stable girls if you must. Go!" He sped off into the night.

"Sionn, run as well and begin to gather our things from the rooms. Oean, seek out our innkeeper and settle up with her. We'll be there as soon as may be." *Two old men and one injured.* I'd noted as soon as he'd come out with Barton that Beathen moved carefully, stiffly. In the flickering yellow light of the street lamps, I saw the bruises on Beathen's face and noted how he held his left hand close to his body. "You're hurt?"

"Yes. Pleasure paid for by pain. I believe I begin to see a trait of His Own, don't you think?"

Shouts arose from the tavern and more breaking of wood and glass. Us three rushed after the younger men as best we could. We arrived in the courtyard just as Barrol entered with our wagon, the horses blowing and snorting at the late rousing from comfortable stalls. Sionn came down with packs and satchels, dumped them to the cobbles, and then ran back for another armload. Our innkeeper began slamming home her shutters even as Oean joined us in the yard and, as soon as our wagon rattled out onto the street, she closed and barred the gates behind us.

With that we left the city in silence as melancholy as our noisy entrance had been joyful. I'd accomplished a few of my aims, yes. Both cart and clothing were new, clean, and repaired. New-fashioned plays had been met with approval and we could add them to our store from which to draw even in the countryside. But our coffers weighed far less than I'd like and again His Own had turned what had been satisfying accomplishment into shameful retreat.

I considered how I might rectify the wrongs done, to us and soon to the innocent uplanders who, all unknowing, stood in the path of bigotry and hatred. For me and mine, I was glad to walk away with as few hurts as we had. But the injustice of it all galled me. *Bah, my impotence shames me more.*

Sionn and Oean came up to me as we progressed through the strangely hushed city. "Dughal! Which of us goes to warn the uplanders?" Sionn whispered.

"Which? Why none, of course," Camran replied before I could even shape a response. "We're escaping with our lives. Beg the God's indulgence for no more. Our journey out into this dark and dangerous night will be all we can manage."

Oean glared at Camran and took hold of my arm in entreaty. "Listen, Dughal. Through our agency, if not our choice, we've put innocent people at risk. We must warn them. One of us can move along the lake shore to the eknos' encampment, warn them and join with the rest of us as we leave by the northwestern gate. How say you?"

"Are you mad?" Camran demanded.

"Peace, old friend," I asked.

He turned on me. "You won't allow this recklessness, will you?"

I sighed. "No. Of course not." Sionn began to speak and I held up my hand. "Any of us would be seen, noticed, and the rest of us would find the way closed and our escape denied. Such a thought does you credit but it could kill us all."

Oean shook his head. "Think you so little of your players' skill? I can change clothes and countenance both, affect a manner like our friend Cedric back there in order to pass the gates. Few would question me and none would take me for anything but another merchantman intent upon an errand outside the walls."

"Absolutely not." I shook my arm free of his grasp and stepped around him. "We exit this stage, our play is done here, and the audience has turned ugly." I walked forward wondering, for a second, if I'd lost them. But then the clop of the horses' hooves behind me on the cobbles and the creak of wagon wheels told me that my players followed me still. I set my features and my feet upon the path and led us through the too, too empty streets.

After some while I glanced back but the cart followed behind me with my men ranging around it in their usual defensive positions with one change: Beathen joined Camran atop the wagon and Barrol walked to my left, the other two at the back. I thought over Oean's scheme but knew such a plan would only put me and mine to a risk I wouldn't hazard. What if we lost all? For what, some tattooed savages unwittingly in harms way? No, it pained me that the uplanders would suffer in the rage sparked by our actions, despite it was none of my intent. Our perch was precarious enough and I'd chance no further throws of the dice.

We were yet some twenty minutes from the northwest gate when we heard a tumult behind us. Our trek had put the temple and its precincts further away with each step, but still we heard the noise, the angry bestial voices raised in such a shout of hatred that the hairs stood upon my neck. "Make haste, Bardeelin," I told them and increased my pace.

We exited through the northwest gates and walked until we passed the walls of the old city before stopping to assess. Walking all night held little charm but neither did a sleepless and anxious night in a dark-made camp so close to a town in riot. I doubted that the riot would spill beyond the city itself: riots, like fires, need fuel, but after having misjudged how close the city had been to riot in the first place, I no longer felt certain of anything. That's when I discovered Oean wasn't with us.

"Where is he?" Barrol cast his eyes down and away from me but I assumed he wouldn't have been told in any case. Beathen and Sionn both assumed their most placid expressions, gazing at me in wide-eyed innocence while my ire grew. Camran swore and spat onto the road.

"Well?" I rounded on the innocent conspirators. "By your expression you know nothing more than that Oean stepped aside to piss against a tree, is that right?"

Sionn opened his mouth to speak before Beathen elbowed him in the ribs. Before Sionn could present the lie, I heard a commotion and Oean stepped from behind the cart and walked over to me. "Were you looking for me, Dughal? Forgive me. I had to piss."

I looked him up and down. His clothes were his own and yet the way they were tied and worn suggested another costume entirely. He returned my scrutiny with a gaze that welcomed challenge and a smug certainty of success. I sighed. "Did the eknos hear your warning, then?"

"Why, Dughal," he exclaimed. "I'm sure I don't know what you mean. I've been following behind the cart in my usual position."

"Of course." For a moment I wondered what good challenging Oean might bring. I'd lost their respect already. At that moment I sighed, suddenly too tired to care. "We rest here for ten minutes and then push on. Take some food and water, for we may well walk the night. I've no desire to be near Lechsede come daybreak."

I heard murmured assents and turned away from them to walk off the track. I sought solitude in the dark night but before I got out of earshot I heard Oean murmur to his fellows: "That rabble will find naught but an empty stage on which to enact their murderous dumb-show."

Fifteen

Rhia

A hunter's life is blood: the blood of the beasts taken in the hunt, the rosblud until she deems the time right to mate, and then the blood spilt in childbirth. And the blood of enemies, whenever they should threaten.

- Ealdranna Proverb

By the time the fire over which the boar had roasted died away the air had turned cold and I sought warmth and comfort beneath the furs and blankets. When the light of dawn obscured the stars like ash over coals, crawling out from under the furs proved surprisingly difficult. But, with the larks singing their greetings to the sun, I rose up with renewed purpose.

The hunt began.

I'd gotten up, rolled the furs and blankets, filled my pack, and dismantled the lean-to by the time Gaunt herself arrived to check on my progress. "Ah, Moonhart. Good to see that you're not always late to awake."

I forced a smile upon my face as I replied: "Not while on the hunt, stealna, although I do admit to the pleasures of late mornings when in the ekarra."

Her expression froze and then she smiled in return. "A commendable attitude, Rhia. We leave shortly."

"I'm ready now." I shouldered my pack and smiled again as I stepped beside her and we walked to the ekarra, Gaunt casting sideways glances in my direction which I chose to ignore. I set my pack down next to some others and bent to help Taltaya, who sorted through her packets of healing and cooking herbs and powders. Gaunt turned from us and strode away.

"How are you this morning, Taltaya?" I asked.

"Ready to be moving on. You look well."

"Well enough," I replied. "Ready to do my part as best I can."

"As do we all." We both stood up and I held the pack while Taltaya shrugged and worked her shoulder loose.

Gaunt returned just then. "No time for your aches and pains, Taltaya. We must leave."

She took the pack from me and slung it over her shoulder with no evident pain. "I'm ready. Are you?" and she strode between the bothas towards the path.

We fell into line behind her. Gaunt rushed to take the lead and set the pace, a hurried scamper that she soon had to moderate. We walked the trail beside the stream, following its course – more or less – as the stream meandered to the east and north. I gritted my teeth at the fact that I went in nearly the direct opposite direction of Na's Calling, but you have to go where the hunt takes you. Today my hunt took me where ever Gaunt roamed.

Taltaya walked second on the path and Tasso third, while I fell in place between Kiri and Hrothar who strode along at his ease in the final place. An hour or so after we'd began I slowed down to let him catch up.

"We don't hunt as we go today?"

"No, lass, you did that for us yesterday. We've the last of the boar meat and so can move towards our goal."

The clouds that had arrived with the dawn decided to drop their rains while we walked. Unlike the cold-but-gentle rains we'd encountered up on the escarpment, thick, fat drops began to fall, splatting onto the young leaves above us. The rains came in earnest soon enough, and the few new leaves couldn't keep it from us. The cold rain brought shivers with it as it landed upon my bare scalp and ran down the back of my neck. Despite the cold, leaving the trews in my pack had been a good decision, for it meant I had only my tunic wet and chill against my skin, instead of the leggings hampering my movements. We stopped for a few minutes rest after a couple of hours walking, refilled water skins at the stream and relieved ourselves into the woods away from the path.

Kiri came and sat next to Hrothar and me. Since I'd awoken from my fever it seemed I couldn't eat enough, but chewing on a bit of pemmican, the rich fat exploding in my mouth and filling my belly, stilled the rumbling that seemed seldom to cease.

"I envy you, Hrothar," I said.

"Oh? Why's that lass? You wish you had a thick pelt like mine?" He grinned suddenly, the forest of hair on his face quaking into a smile. "It seems that you've a habit of hunting in naught but your skin, stealna of the Moonhart. I've seen your hide, young one, and would suggest you take care. Its been damaged enough."

"I wish I'd undertaken my *stealna kir* as you had," Kiri exclaimed. "I'd never even thought it possible, that the old tales spoke of greater times." She quieted and looked at her hands. "But, obviously, I wasn't good enough. What ever made you think of such a dangerous plan?"

Kiri, more than most, had suffered from Gaunt's callous comments and cruel treatment. We couldn't be more different, she and I. Her mother, her ekma, even her age mates, had all thought her over-reaching, that she lacked the skills and the drive needed to be a hunter. At every turn she was expected to fail. Why, even *she'd* expected to fail!

The realization struck me like a blow to the stomach.

"You've seen the scar, Kiri. Wasn't just dangerous, twas foolish."

She shrugged. "With that scar, no one will ever be able to forget your bravery. I wager that, afterward, no one ever doubted you'd be a great hunter!"

I laughed. I know I shouldn't have but Eanna's derision of me the day we received the Calling dream was so at odds with Kiri's youthful imagination!

Kiri's open expression closed down with nearly an audible snap and I reached out to lay my hand on her arm, trying to reassure her. "I'm sorry," I said. "But, in truth, while there were many in my eknos that predicted great things for me – seemingly since before my birth – there were even more who believed that my *stealna kir* a fluke, that I tried to distract everyone from my poor skills by brave posturing."

"But that can't be! There's no way to cheat on such a hunt!" she exclaimed.

Hrothar laughed. "Especially wearing nothing but woad. No place to hide a convenient bow, now is there?"

I shook my head. "Even when the shaman declared me the one Bid, still Eanna and others in my eknos sought to 'prove' to the eknos that I simply wasn't good enough, not the right person. Kiri, I'm not the smartest woman or the strongest hunter and Na's Bidding may only mean that I can be spared, safely taken from my eknos with no lasting harm done to Moonhart. But what I do have is one woman who believes in me, my huntmate Sarae." I shrugged and popped the last bite of pemmican in my mouth. "She encourages me to do, to follow my heart, to trust in myself. Tis a gift I cherish, especially here, far from home."

None of us had heard Gaunt come up. "Why, Moonhart! I would've thought that the speech of a hetairi. You spoke so ... movingly." The look on her face hardened and her nostrils contracted as if she smelled something spoiled. "By Na, you prattle on." She turned away and called over her shoulder: "Tis time we moved. I wish to reach the Glen by nightfall."

On the other side of the Glen we walked towards, lay the bison plateau where Gaunt meant to give me to the black cloaks in exchange for her sister. I wondered if, even now, Sowers dressed all in black waited for us.

Late in the day, the trail came back to run right next to the stream and we followed both it and the stream into a kind of valley. Where we walked stayed nearly flat but the hills around us rose higher and came closer. When Gaunt called the halt for the day, we camped beside the stream between sheer rock walls that rose up high on either side, a bow shot apart. "Tomorrow we'll walk for some few miles and the walls will get closer until we're walking in the stream itself," Taltaya told me. "At the end of this defile is a waterfall and a path down."

"And that brings us down to the bison plateau?"

She nodded. "The northernmost edge of it, yes."

"You haven't forgotten all you'd learned of our territory, then." Gaunt smiled down at where Taltaya sat, preparing the fire. "That's good. Can you still find the path down?"

"Of course."

"Excellent. Take your bow and leave an hour ahead of us on the morrow. I'd like to have fresh meat waiting for us when we get below the falls. I suspect that the animals have grown less wary in this area. You should be able to get close enough to use *your* bow."

Taltaya began to bristle at the implied insult but she chanced to glance at me. After taking a deep breath, she let it out with a smile. "I'd take great pleasure hunting tomorrow. Thank you."

Gaunt's expression was so encouraging that it bordered on mockery. Perhaps she thought Taltaya too cowed to have heard the insult. She didn't see that Taltaya had shed the insult like her skin shed the rain.

Taltaya spoke up once more. "I'd like to take Kiri with me, if I may. The experience will serve her well."

"As long as the kit doesn't spoil your hunt, do what you will," Gaunt said over her shoulder, already walking off to the far edge of the camp. There she sat with her back to the fire, composed as if in meditation.

I clapped Taltaya on the shoulder and she went over to Kiri to discuss plans for the morrow. The walk had been easy enough, and my recovery far enough progressed, that I had strength left over to help with basic camp chores. As the rain still fell, I worked with Tasso to build three basic lean-tos. Kiri and Hrothar gathered what dry wood could be found and began the fire, while Taltaya began preparations for the evening meal.

Gaunt stayed where she sat.

A let up in the rain allowed us all to sit around the fire and get both a little warmer and a little drier while we ate our meal: boar meat in a stew with roots, early greens, and late berries. As soon as the meal was done, Gaunt excused herself and went beyond the fire's light, and there she sat for the rest of the evening, retiring to bed well after the rest of us had sought our blankets.

As we sat around the fire, our conversation happened in low tones as if we didn't wish to disturb Gaunt's meditations. As such, I'm sure she didn't hear Kiri's excited words or Taltaya's steady instruction. Kiri was full hunter, no question, but the turmoil in Lynx had stolen from her many opportunities to learn and she sought them all now. Taltaya seemed to be just as eager to teach. Hrothar told me and Tasso stories. Tasso, I'm sure, had heard them all before, but as they were Lynx tales, I reveled in what they told me of this eknos that wasn't my own. Hrothar's stories spoke of the order of things, how Lynx was the first eknos and contained the most sacred spot, the sandstone arch. He told tales of brave ekmas and strong stealnans and clever cearnans.

When my turn came for story telling, I grinned. "You wouldn't find my stories so laudatory, I fear."

"Why is that, Rhia?" Tasso asked, her voice carrying a quiet intensity across the fire light.

"Moonhart is ... well. Let's just say our leaders are more likely to be an obstacle in a story rather than its hero."

"Such as...?" Hrothar laughed at my expression. "No, little fawn. You'll not get out of a tale that easily."

"Then let me defer," I said. "Tomorrow I'll share a tale and then you can judge what kind of eknos Moonhart is."

They nodded and I sought my bed, but despite the fatigue of a day's hike, sleep didn't come soon. I couldn't help but worry that I'd tempted Na with my pledge. If Gaunt has her way, I may not be free at the end of the day to tell any tale at all.

"It won't be that easy, you know." I'd closed the distance between Gaunt and myself as we'd traveled. All morning, she'd stayed just out of earshot and I had less than an hour before we reached the falls at the end of the Glen, and the path down to the plateau. I couldn't be certain what awaited me there, but I was certain that Gaunt meant it to be the end of my time with Lynx.

We continued to follow the stream and the rain continued to fall. The hills beside us had become vertical walls, a scant twenty yards apart, steep and sheer for fifteen feet. The rain had muted the colors of the stone, but not the textures: layers of purple and dun colored rock, some layers fine as sand, some mottled with large round stones, some flaking into layers and chips. I would've loved to have spent time examining them more closely, but I had to focus on Gaunt.

"What won't be easy, Moonhart?" She sounded as weary as if I'd been pestering her with questions for hours. She did pause and allow me to catch up to where she walked some ten paces ahead of me.

I moved athwart her path and a trick of the terrain had brought me to nearly her height. I looked her in the eyes. "Turning me over to the black cloaks."

Gaunt's eyes narrowed for a moment, although not in fear. Consideration, perhaps. "Is that what you think I'm doing?"

"I'm sorry for what happened to you. Those are terrors and indignities that no one should have to endure."

I turned and began walking further down the path, leaving Gaunt to catch up with me. "You speak of things you can't possibly know."

I laughed and touched the Calling medallion bouncing against my chest. "Of my own? You're very right. What I don't understand is why you kept it a secret from your eknos. The hetairi at least, would've given you relief from your pain."

"There's no pain, Moonhart. You speak—"

"The truth, Lynx, unlike you. You've been very careful until this moment, but that was a lie." I walked a few more paces, wondering how to get passed her self-deception. I'd been drawn too far from my own quest in these last hands of days, but Gaunt could still be saved if she turned from the path she trod.

"The hetairi are leaderless. The hetairan died during the Singing season and no one has been selected to take his place. The ekma, upon hearing word of Gellae's ... loss, retired to her botha and is rarely seen." Gaunt reached out and pulled me to a halt. "Don't you see, Moonhart? There are no leaders left."

"So, you stood up to do what you could. That's commendable!" I took the smile from my face and asked: "At what point did you decide to do what the black cloaks asked of you? Was it when your ekma deserted you, or was it when I crossed your path?"

She laughed then, her eyes bright. "I do hear Na speak, you know. You can hear the truth of that, at least. When we saw signs of your passing through Lynx territory, it annoyed me. It was a distraction that we could ill afford. But then I realized that Na sent you to me for this purpose! Don't you see?"

I shook my head and moved a bit further down the stream side path, only to realize that I'd misjudged either our position that morning or our pace. Not a bow shot ahead, the placid stream fell out of the Glen to disappear towards the plateau below. Just before the falls, the Glen widened out into a small bowl, the walls pulled back another few feet, and the height of the walls lowered as well, reminding me somewhat of being next to the Speakers mound in Moonhart ekarra. I wondered if words would travel as well to the tops of the cliffs as they do to the furthest reaches of the cooking fires. With nothing for it, I turned and faced Gaunt.

"Tell me what *you* see."

She glanced up the stream, but Tasso and Hrothar were well out of range of either sight or sound, especially in the thrum of the rain. "Na's Calling shows you the damage the sowers are wreaking on our lands. Your mother, my sister, Tasso's mother: all caught up in forces too large for any one eknos to face."

"I'm sorry that my warning came too late."

Gaunt waved that comment aside. "You came in good time, Moonhart. I'd made my decision, persuaded the eknos to my way of thinking. They're waiting for me to return. I thought it was symbolic only, a worthless Lynx pelt to show that we were still united enough to overcome the changing winds."

"Do you think now that it wouldn't have worked?" I'd moved around so that my back was no longer at that plunge down to the plain below and, indeed, had moved several paces back upstream, away from the noise of the waterfall. Gaunt didn't see Taltaya and Kiri who now stood upon the cliff above the waterfall. Kiri made to raise her hand and call out, but Taltaya stilled her by making a hunter's sign that meant: *Quiet! Prey sighted.*

"I don't know, but it doesn't matter. For instead of capturing a lynx we captured a Moonhart and that was much better. You were Bid to find the captured eknos. I'm taking you there faster, despite all your moaning and complaining of me going the wrong way."

"You mean to turn me over to the black cloaks." I didn't ask a question, but Gaunt nodded, a smile on her face.

"The sowers know nothing of the hunt or honor, but only of barter and trade. I'll trade you to them, get Gellae back and fulfill Na's Bidding, all at the same time. Gellae will take her place as the ekma and I'll be stealnan. Together, we'll make Lynx so strong that the sowers will never threaten us again."

"We've had this discussion before," I reminded her. "The penalty for interfering with Na's Bidding is severe and immediate."

"You are thick, aren't you? Obviously, Na is relying on me to bring about Her desires. I'm *delivering* you to those who're taking uplanders! Isn't that the fulfillment of Na's Bidding?"

"No!" There was a moment, just the briefest moment, when I saw the image of a moonhart doe surrounded by wolves and I wondered if she were right. Then that part of me, long seared by the power of the Calling dream, rose up in horror. "I'm to raise the eknos and rescue those captured, not become one of them!"

Gaunt hawked and spat. "Ridiculous. A stupid moonhart doe, alone, is going to rescue anyone? You have *no idea* what it means to be in their hands. There *is* no escape, save by death."

"Then Gellae is already dead."

"No— !"

"And you commit their evil for them. Are you going to give them only me? Or have you been so callous towards Kiri and Taltaya because it's easier to betray those you think unworthy?"

For a moment, doubt entered Gaunt's eyes. I don't know what she might have said at that moment, because up from the path beside the falls, stepped a man. A lowlander dressed in black.

"You're late, eknos," the man said. Gaunt spun around to face him. "Finias our master sent me to collect our prizes."

"No! I'm not ready yet." Gaunt strode towards the man. "We were to meet below the falls. I sent two to you already."

"Liar. No one came down to us." The man took off his hat and wiped rain from his face. Upon one cheek he had a scar that looked not to be more than a few score days healing, angry and jagged. He put his hat back on and stood tall, glaring at Gaunt. "We've waited a tenday or more passed the agreed upon time and I don't want Finias angry with me." He grinned, a most unpleasant sight. "I can only imagine what he'll do to show *you* his displeasure."

Gaunt turned to me, hate and terror in equal measure showing in her eyes. "She fell ill. It wasn't my fault."

He stopped and looked beyond Gaunt to me. "What? Only the one?"

"No! You can have five, one more than promised. This one here, she's a Favorite of Na. Finias will be well pleased with her, I'm sure. And there's the two I already sent down to you—"

"Liar." The black cloak strode over to Gaunt. A part of me marveled at the way he walked: there were the two of us and he all alone, and yet he strode that stream side seemingly with no fear of disobedience, let alone resistance. He grabbed Gaunt's arm. "Why stop at five when I can bring six? If there are any more."

Gaunt shook free of him and stepped back. "That's not the trade we agreed upon! You'd free Gellae in exchange. There she is!" Gaunt pointed at me. "Na Favors her! She's far more important than my sister. Take her and give me Gellae."

I'll never forget the look of shock on the man's face. You'd think that Gaunt had spoken in the language of the Gods or sprouted wings. With an effort he composed himself, his eyes narrowing as he pointed his finger at Gaunt. "You've forgotten several important lessons, my little uplander molly. The first is that you aren't the one to give commands."

We never learned what the second might have been. Taltaya rose up from the top of the cliff and launched a shaft. I heard a dull, wet thwock of a damp bowstring, followed by the whir of an arrow through the air. It sang as the metal tip struck sparks from the rock wall just behind the man's shoulder. He shouted in alarm but before he could cry out a second time, Kiri loosed her own arrow. This one flew true, sinking deep into the Black Cloak's chest. He staggered back, clutching at the wood sprouting from his sternum, before he tripped over rocks in the stream and tumbled, over the falls and out of sight.

Gaunt watched the death of her lowlander confederate and then spun towards me. "No! You've ruined everything. We need Gellae and now you've killed her!"

I shook my head. "Your grief has made you mad. Gellae, if not already dead, is certainly not on the plains below. Most like, she and the others are south, with my mother." I looked up to Taltaya, still on the cliff's top. "Keep your bow drawn, if you please," I called up to her. "She may have more friends climbing up from the plains below."

Kiri found a slope slightly less steep, slung her bow across her shoulder, and scrambled down to the stream side to join me. "Rhia! What do we do with her?" Kiri's breath came short after her reckless charge down the hillside.

I sought a response to that question, but ultimately it wasn't mine to answer. "She should be bound and taken to your ekarra, to be judged."

"By Skiem's foul breath, you'll not! I can still make it right, don't you see? You and that kit next to you, in exchange for Gellae. We *need* her!"

I shook my head. "It's over. Drop your knife and step over here."

I shouldn't have mentioned the knife, for she suddenly snatched it into her hand. "No!"

I've spilled the blood of prey to bring life to my eknos and some day I may spill my own blood to bring life to a child. It's the way of things. Hunters are also called upon to shed another's blood in defense of kith or kin, but even so, the thought of facing Gaunt's knife in anger set a hard knot in my guts.

I charged towards Gaunt, my sling unwrapped from my hands. I'd intended on using it to garrote her, immobilize her, so that we might take her prisoner. She didn't share my aims, standing ready for me. My momentum pushed her off balance, but she didn't fall.

Kiri wasn't behind me. When Gaunt pulled her knife, Kiri had run back up stream, shouting for Tasso and Hrothar to hurry. The two of us might have captured Gaunt, but instead, she regained her balance and rounded on me, knife ready.

I kept my sling in my left hand as I drew my knife with my right. The treacherous footing slowed me and Gaunt's terrible smile mocked me. She'd backed up a pace until her feet were right next to the swift stream. I leapt for her. My feet found purchase on the sharp ridges of the rocks themselves. I came in high and she brought her knife up, taking the feint. At the last moment, I landed and sank low, sweeping her front leg out from under her. Her arms flailed as if they would find purchase in the air while I bent back my leg and struck out at her planted foot. I felt a satisfying thud and she yelped in pain before going down into the stream.

I jumped up and back, watching to see how well she got out of the water. Thinking I was far enough back, I chanced a look up, blinking away the rain drops. Taltaya tried for a shot at Gaunt herself but the angle was too low for her. She signaled that she was coming back down and disappeared from the cliff top.

Gaunt heaved herself up and charged at me, shouting curses. Her long legs gave her great speed and she closed quickly. Her knife flashed in the watery gray light and I jumped back. The blade sliced the front of my tunic across my belly. She swung again. I let the knife go by and then followed it with my foot, kicking her wrist even as she reached the arc of her swing, tensing to slash again. My kick knocked the knife from her hand. In counter, she used the momentum I'd just given her to spin around. Her foot struck me in my midriff. With a *whoof,* I went down, the pain exploding throughout my guts, the air driven from my lungs.

I tried to take the momentum and roll with it, but the large rocks of the stream side stopped that. I slammed into one and gasped, the hard pain in my lower back echoing the one in my guts. Sprawled there, on my backside, my legs spread, I suddenly felt like some parody of a lover waiting for her tryst to begin. I laughed at the image in my head, the sound of which caused Gaunt to falter.

My hand found a loose stone and I flung it high, intentionally missing close by her head. She flinched away from the rock, towards me. I surged to my feet, grabbed her tunic and used her own strength and speed against her. I threw her face down into the steam.

"It's over," I said when she had spluttered to the surface. "Why do you continue to fight?"

"My eknos is at stake, Moonhart." Her attention turned towards Kiri, now at my side. "You betray your stealna? You and that stay-at-home Taltaya. Gellae is worth the lot of you and I *will* have her back."

"Why?" Kiri asked. "You're stealna! The ekma trusted you with our sacred hunt." Kiri wiped at the woad on her cheeks. Or perhaps it was at the tears streaming there. "Why would you even think to parley with the sowers?"

Gaunt began to walk slowly out of the creek and we let her, keeping her downstream and closer to the falls. Solid land suited all of us, I think, no matter what happened next. "Why?" she asked, incredulous. "You're so young, Kiri. Perhaps you haven't seen, but Taltaya has no excuse. The lowlanders are winning. The Ealdranna grow fewer every year. Every nosmoot another family fails to show up. Falcon is gone from our southern border and the lowlanders now surround us on three sides, with only the frivolous Moonhart to our north. We need a strong leader to replace our ailing ekma. Gellae was meant to be ekma!" She was shouting now. "She wasn't meant to be beaten and shackled by hulking, soil-stained sowers. Used by them until she begged them to stop. Begged! Gellae, the strongest woman I know, whimpering in pain at their feet."

"Twas terrible. Inhuman," I agreed. I slipped my knife back into my belt. "And yet, you'd send us to that self-same fate?"

The far-away look left Gaunt's eyes. She focused intently on me and raised her knife again. "Without doubt, if twould bring Gellae back."

"It won't. Surely you know that now." Taltaya joined us at that moment, her bow drawn and an arrow pointing at Gaunt. "It's over now. Drop your knife."

"No! You three won't stop me. Na whispers to me. I know I'm right."

A shout came from behind us as Hrothar and Tasso ran up.

"What's this then?" Hrothar yelled.

"She brought us here to give Rhia to the sowers," Taltaya explained. "And us. I only heard parts of it, but it seems the hunting accident that took Treassa and Gellae twere no accident. Those who took Rhia's mother also captured her, Treassa, and Gellae."

Tasso strode forward to stand in front of Gaunt, blocking Taltaya's shot. "That can't be true. My mother would've fought them."

"Oh, she did," Gaunt told her. "Twas a sight to behold." Tasso blanched and stumbled back. Gaunt, ignoring me, pleaded with the others. "But there was an accident, that's all true. Sowers, trying to make a foray into Lynx territory, spooked the bison and they charged early. It distracted us and the sowers took us unawares." She smiled, brief, fleeting, sad. "We fought then, make no mistake, but in the end four of us were taken."

"And you escaped?" Hrothar asked.

"Not escaped," I said. "Freed, for the purpose of bringing more eknos to the sowers. Us. In exchange for her sister, she was told."

"You'd mock Na's own Calling? I offer you the resolution to your Bidding, and you threaten me with harm for it?" She turned away from me, disgust evident in the curl of her lip. She looked at the rest of our band and her nose crinkled as if she smelled offal. "You, all of you, owe it to Lynx to trade yourselves for Gellae. She who would be ekma of your eknos is worth your sacrifice. Why, what are any of you compared with Gellae? A broken hunter who won't even shave her head, a young kit too stupid to think for herself, and a man who'd mock true hunters by shaving his head when he's naught but a cearnan raised over high."

But then a look came across Gaunt's face as she turned to Tasso. "But you," she pleaded. "You are a true hunter. Perhaps, adding you to these others, they'll release Treassa as well as Gellae, a stealnan as well as our ekma back to us."

The faces of my companions ranged from shock, to shame, to pity. I shook my head and softened my voice as I spoke to Gaunt again. "We'll bring you, to the hetairan, the healers. It's over now. I don't think you even realize your actions towards me were abomination. I hear that you believe what you're saying, and for that we'll treat you gently. But you're no longer stealnan and need to give over your knife."

She looked to either side of me as if assessing her chances. "It's over. You see that, surely!" She stood a bit taller and flipped her knife into the muck of the stream side. I stepped passed the knife and felt Kiri following right behind me. She placed a length of leather into my hand and I motioned for Gaunt to hold out her wrists. She complied, slowly, raising her hands before her, her shoulders slumped.

I didn't look at her feet. I thought her beaten. As I got close, she lifted her front foot and used it to flip mud directly into my face. Her hands, already up as I'd asked, grabbed me by the tunic and threw me behind her. I landed hard, the breath knocked from my lungs. When the blackness cleared – no more than a second later – I heaved myself upright. Before I could scramble to my feet, Gaunt had grabbed her knife and plunged it into Kiri's belly.

Taltaya's cry echoed from the walls of the glen, obscuring the sound of her bow as it sent an arrow through Gaunt's neck. She staggered back with the blow and landed just at my feet, splashing into the waters of the brook.

The falls foamed red with the blood for some time afterward.

Kiri still lived. Blood streaked her teeth and lips with each labored breath. I knelt at her side. "I'm so sorry. I should've been more ready. I should've stopped her. I'm sorry."

Taltaya knelt down on the other side of Kiri while Tasso and Hrothar stood nearby. Tasso looked shocked and angry, while Hrothar's tears vanished into the forest of his beard. "Shush, Rhia," Taltaya said. "This wound is laid to treachery not through any fault of yours."

"This death, rather." Kiri's voice gurgled in her throat and we both leaned closer to hear.

"Not if I can help it," I began to say. Her gaze, the eyes shot through with pain and determination, stopped me.

"You can't," Kiri whispered. "But please, don't burn my body with hers."

"It shall be as you wish," Taltaya said. "Find your course in peace, Hunter. When called upon, you shed blood for your eknos, even your own, as a hunter should. Your shot was true."

"Rhia?"

"Yes, Kiri?"

"You'll find them. I've no doubt of it."

I nodded and then stood, leaving Kiri and Taltaya to say their good byes, followed by Hrothar and Tasso. I left Gaunt's body where it lay, her staring eyes already glazed, the arrow fletching towards the sky as if she were pinned to the ground. I looked over the edge of the falls, the constant crash of water noticeable again. It cascaded onto the rocks below, now threaded through with Gaunt's blood.

Tasso rose from beside Kiri's lifeless form and strode purposefully over to where I stood.

"Tell me," she demanded.

"Should we—"

Tasso shook her head. Hrothar and Taltaya joined us and Taltaya spoke. "We need to know the story in full, so we can tell it to others."

I nodded. "You're right. Here, now, where you can judge truly that Kiri's sacrifice may have saved Lynx." I looked up to Hrothar. "I promised you a story, my friend. Moonhart tales are often of how the least of us rise up above ekmas. Or stealnan."

I strode over to where Gaunt lay and looked down at her. Her bowels and bladder had let loose, her eyes had glazed. I pointed at her. "She had thought that I'd play some part in your ritual and it seems that I did. I joined you at your fire, although not in body." I held up my hand at Tasso's exclamation. "No, I don't know how it happened and I assure you, it hadn't been my intent. I'd had enough of rituals and Na playing with my life. But as I slept, I found myself in communion with you, hearing your thoughts. And I heard hers, as well." I told them of the horror infecting Gaunt's memories and of the terrible decision she'd made when she encountered my tracks in the woods far west of here. "The proof of my words is in the body of the black cloak that Kiri killed."

"I'm ashamed that my first shot missed, Rhia." Taltaya's hands twisted against the wood of the bow and she would not meet my eyes.

"It's a lesson I don't always remember so well, but we should always hunt at least in pairs." Eanna's accusations as well as how I'd behaved on this morning's "hunt" both came to mind. "You had Kiri by your side, so when your first shot missed, hers found the mark. As it should be." I drew her attention to Gaunt's body. "And your next shot saved my life."

"But not Kiri's." Taltaya eyes sought out the small form of her friend.

"As you told me, take not that death to yourself, but place that burden where it belongs."

"This is wondrous strange," Tasso whispered. She left us then and went to the edge of the falls and peered down, looking for confirmation I guessed. Then her shout had us running to her side. The water beside us plunged some thirty yards straight down into a pool around ten feet across before flowing out between hills that grew smaller in the distance until they faded into a plain about two hundred yards away. On that plain we saw three figures, dressed all in black, riding their horses at great speed away from us.

"There will be no questioning them," Tasso said. "On those horses of theirs, we could never hope to catch up."

"And you can be sure they'll not linger long in Lynx," Hrothar added.

"We should descend," Taltaya said. "We have much to do this evening, for Kiri deserves her pyre and her vigil."

I nodded, but pointed to Gaunt's body. "What about her?"

"I'll waste neither time nor wood on burning such as her," Taltaya said. "Let the vultures feast." We stripped her body, tossing the soiled tunic far to the side, putting her knife into her pack and Taltaya put the pack over her shoulder. Tasso and Taltaya carried the body up onto the rocks some goodly distance from the water, for we had no desire to poison the fresh flow. We left her laid out, unclothed and unmourned, upon the rocks as a ready feast for the carrion eaters.

Hrothar offered to carry Kiri's body by himself, even though the path ran steep and twisty for about 30 yards, slick from the rain. He made it without error but not without effort and the rest of us followed him as if in procession, carrying Kiri's gear, Gaunt's, and Hrothar's as if in offering. We found the body of the black cloak floating in the pool below the falls where his black-hearted companions had left him. I pulled the arrow from his chest before we threw his body onto the rocks far from the stream.

The creek flowed much higher and faster at other times of the year, for the flood plain of the stream was nearly 50 yards across and plenty of driftwood lay scattered about those shores. Out of that wood Tasso and I built Kiri's pyre while Taltaya and Hrothar washed her body free of blood and soil, and then brought it to rest on the pile of wood. She looked so young lying there. I placed the arrow, her arrow, in her hands and thanked her again for her true aim and courage. The rain had stopped just as we had lit the pyre and it was as if the flames brought with them warmer Gathering season weather. All through the night the temperature rose. *Kiri, you gave us a fine night for your vigil.*

We held silence as the flames were lit, thinking our thoughts. Mine, I'm ashamed to say, most often were about the need for me to do as Na Bid me. It had been some two score days or more since I left Sarae asleep in my botha. *But I've made friends with these hunters of Lynx. Can I leave them so precipitously? And yet, I sit vigil beside one who gave her life to set me free.* My thoughts whirled round and round even as the stars circled across the sky above.

The flames burned hot and soon the tales began. But, alas, Kiri's short life gave too few tales to tell. Tasso was the first to tell a story of the penalty paid for betraying the eknos. Then Hrothar. Then, as if to remind herself that she acted in justice, Taltaya. "No crime is greater."

The sun had risen high before we had light at the stream side below the falls. I took back my bow and Taltaya gave me some food from Kiri's pack, a tunic to replace the one Gaunt had cut as we fought, a second water skin, and a large supply of well-crafted arrows, all of which I accepted gratefully. She then took from Gaunt's pack a beautiful fire kit, contrived and fashioned in a most ingenious way. I tossed out the flint, for it was of poor quality, but decided to use the piece of iron. Taltaya also consolidated as much of the pemmican as she could and gave it all to me.

"What does this mean?" I asked.

"You need to go. Leave the stream and strike out due south, across this valley and up the hills beyond. It's more on your route than the way we'll take."

"But, you want me to leave?"

"We never should have taken you with us, Rhia," she said quietly. "I trusted Gaunt."

"We all did, little fawn," Hrothar added. "I thought sure she heard Na's Voice tell her true and heard no falseness in her words."

"None of us did." Tasso sighed and shook her head. "I trusted her for Gellae's sake, for my mothers, and now it feels as if I've lost them all over again." She gathered me into an embrace, so startling me that I held her back. "Take the pemmican, take whatever else you might have use for, and may Na grant wings to your feet."

Tasso turned away and I looked to Taltaya who nodded. "We'll be fine. You need to resume Na's Bidding."

I embraced Taltaya and then Hrothar, adjusted the pack upon my back, heavier now with the gifts from Lynx eknos. Taking a deep breath I set out, running as I would in my own forests: barefoot and barelegged, my sleeveless tunic covering me as I needed to be covered and yet leaving me free to move as I might. I understand that the lowlanders always cover themselves from head to foot, no matter the weather or the need. I realized that I would soon learn truth from fable.

Sixteen

Epistle the Second

42ⁿᵈ Nabryhtian, Near Beldann

To Cleirach durMiach, Prophet and Voice of the Lonely God, and my great good Friend, I send you greetings and my deepest love.

I've spent the last tenday just north of Beldann, the guest of a carrinanen who seeks your favor, ancari'ni. While he does set a fine table, trust that I've spent my time wisely and well. I've embarked upon a Project that I believe will negate any harmful influence that the presence of Players have posed to the good folk of Bainellen. Should it come to pass as I've planned, these Players will become more than even they can imagine. Wish me luck, my friend, and the Blessings of the God of the Plow, as I set my pen to parchment in labor for the God.

First, I wish to follow up on the one small matter mentioned in my last missive: we've found the body of the uplander female who had escaped. She was yet within the Craobac Woods and, although the area has seen some days of rain, we saw no prints or tracks in her vicinity. I believe she died alone in the woods like the creature of the wilds that she was, wounded unto Death by Broc's ungentle handling. Any word she might have spread regarding our Plans died with her.

While I have great hopes of success for my own Endeavor, I must report that Finias has suffered a Disappointment. He *was* able to raise the city of Lechsede to our cause, completely winning over the Priest there as well as the populace. The Citizens of Lechsede showed great Love to our Finias and rose up at his command, joining our ranks in great numbers! I had hoped that the Players might have been taken in this uprising, but no matter. As it will allow my own Endeavor to proceed, I'm not displeased that the Players escaped.

Alas, there is chaff amidst the wheat. For some reason, no Eknos were found outside the walls of Lechsede. I'd hoped to secure more captives, especially since the other Scheme that Finias had embarked upon during the last Fallow season has come to a ruinous conclusion. The men he dispatched to bring in the additional eknos captives coming down to hunt, met with some resistance. One of our men died and the eknos escaped. Poor Finias. He suffered great Mortification at this setback. If, in your Visions, you see some solace for your faithful servant, please send him word.

I've done my part, sending him out on missions while I Write. He's brought me word of something amazing. Ancari'ni, I Felt your presence with me as Finias gave his report. The power of our Bond is strong, and I laughed to hear Finias speak, for I knew you heard his words through me. Your Voice is being heard! All around us, everywhere that Finias travels, there are those who seek to find favor with You and the God of Sheaves. Through them, we've discovered many Wantons and Harlots, their carnal natures an abomination to all Good folk, and Witches practicing unnatural and loathsome Powers. All will be used in the furtherance of the Lonely God's most Blessed designs.

Tomorrow, we shall leave this place for Beldann itself. The Goodman in charge of that area is an old man by the name of Fachtnel and he believes strongly in the orthodoxy as you have taught it. He has reported to me of his tireless Struggles to turn his charges from their iniquity. He's constantly at odds with the local hosteller, but I think that to be a lost cause. Not all will be able to see your Vision for what it is. I plan on giving to Fachtnel one of the captives to use for his service but, given his advanced age, I don't know if he'll be able to perform as necessary or survive the Trials that the Blessing brings. It will be as the God wills.

So that's the news, my Friend. As I move closer to Kairclavan I feel your Spirit and Love ever more deeply. It pleases me to know that the Fellowship you've gathered around you is so strong and so united in their Love for you. My band here grows ever closer, as more among us experience the Blessings that your Vision has Revealed to us. The doubts that I expressed in my earlier letters fade as I travel closer to you. The certainty of our Cause grows more sure within my heart. You know the Truth of my words, even at this far remove. Give me your Blessing, ancari'ni, as I give you Mine, humble though it is.

We shall be some days in Beldan before riding to Kairill. I trust that I shall have put all in Motion such that the spectacle planned for Kairill will prove to be a Glorious Success. You'll be able to see the flames from your mountaintop!

Yours, in the Peace and Love of the God of the Plow,

Neacal durCleirach

Seventeen

Dughal

"I swear by the twinned Godhead to pledge my allegiance to Bardeelin, greatest of all Troupes, renouncing all other pledges made heretofore. From this day forth I shall be Unencumbered from hearth, home, city or province. Instead, I am beholden to all of Anacarra in the body of the ~~Anarie~~ First Among Five.

I pledge my troth to the Leader and Principle of the Players, to follow ~~her or~~ his lead in all things regarding my time among this Company. I shall hold to my heart the Company in all things: the secrets of the Players and Servants as well as the Plays, Tales, Stories, Songs, and other Properties as shall be held by Bardeelin at the time of my oath or any which shall come after.

Upon pain of death I take this vow, so help me ~~Na, the patroness of Players and~~ An, the God of good works."

- Bardeelin Oath

We'd left Lechsede behind several days before, playing to small hamlets and market towns as we traveled south. But now, we raced a kind of nightfall although the day had just begun, walking in a gloom thick as mud. When the sky began to lighten I allowed my heart a moment of hope.

"Ah, here it comes." Camran nodded towards the crags in the far distance.

"No!" I protested. "I'll not look at the onsweeping rain."

"Looking away doesn't change what is." As if Beathen's words provided the God His cue, the first fat drops fell plunk onto the wood of the cart and fell cold against my cheek. I sighed, swung my cloak over my shoulders, and pulled my hat down tight.

"No sponge plucked from the briny deep ever held more water than my clothes." Oean's voice carried despite the wind. "When do we stop, Dughal? We've walked now for a day and a night in rain, cold, and mud, on roads gutted and gullied by too many storms."

I nodded and then realized that all of us walked heads down and face first into the pelting rain. My tunic clung to me in a most annoying fashion, pressed hard against my shivering body so that it chaffed me most uncomfortably unless I constantly pulled and tugged at it. "Yes. I know," I said aloud. "We risk ourselves, our horses, and our wagon if we push on through this mud and these terrible roads. If we find the town, we'll stop and hope for an end to rain and slop."

"Any thought when we might get to Beldann?" Barrol's tired voice showed his eagerness.

"I shall give you a very accurate answer to that," Beathen said.

"Oh?" I asked, astounded.

"In truth. As soon I espy the damn town!"

His jape yielded a few laughs. I smiled, but no more. My bones ached too much. We ate our lunch cold and on foot, hoping to make the town before what little light the clouds left us departed for the night. Late in the afternoon we rounded the base of a small hill, the road taking us west into the teeth of the rain and, yes by the God, sleet! As we topped the next rise, to the south and east of us, we espied the misty town of Beldann.

Beathen said in most conversational tone: "We should be in Beldann before night."

The feeble jest still sufficed to raise our spirits. I considered entering Beldann as we'd done at Rillsherd and Lechsede and many small hamlets in between: singing, juggling, tumbling, and crying out our presence to all who might hear us. And yet, the weather would keep folk indoors and we'd perform for scant few. The rain would risk our instruments and the mud would risk our joints should feet slip during a tumbling pass.

But in truth, none of that decided me. We'd played in worse and gathered a crowd regardless. No, our recent misfortunes weighted down my heart even more than the mud of the road weighted down my boots. Even correct decisions can torment a person and my spirits felt as black as the muck on my feet.

Camran climbed upon our cart but I told the others to simply take positions. And thus, in silence, with neither show nor singing, tumbling nor laughter, we approached the gates of Beldann, only to find them barred to us.

"Turn yourselves around and be gone," said Beldann's gate guard. "There be no space for such as you within."

"Such as we?" Sionn asked.

"Such as you! Lying vagabond Players. The town Deacons won't have the folk confused."

I sighed. "Then see us not as Players but simply as travelers seeking respite from the rain. We'll stay just the one night. To any folk who ask it of us, we'll tell what news we have, news from merchants and traders and farmers and even Arics. We'll leave once the torrents have abated." I motioned to the bedraggled state of me and mine. "I doubt that any one who saw us now would be confused into thinking that Players lead seductive lives." I finished my statement and began to move forward. The guard stepped in front of me, stopping my passage.

A tall, black-cloaked man, his beard gone to gray and lines around his eyes (*none from laughing, I warrant!*) stepped out of the hut set aside for those watching the roads. I turned to him at once, of course. No question in my mind who gave the orders.

"Do you dispute our decision?" he asked. Once his voice might have been powerful but age had stolen its resonance. It came out wheedling and thin, barely cutting through the rain.

I bowed to him, granting him a respect he'd denied me and mine despite my great desire that the only courtesy he should receive would be a warning before I kicked his skinny shanks. "No, Goodman. Not at all." I smiled my most disarming smile. "I've been to Beldann many times in the past and know the good folk of this town to be resolute in their proclamations. I also know that their hospitality is the envy of the province and they have never, in my memory, turned away cold and hungry men who had coin enough to remedy both conditions and a willingness to spend it."

The black-clad man looked down at me. A slight smile touched the edges of his mouth. "Then it's my great pleasure, sirrah, to give you an experience unmatched in your memory. Step another foot into this town and we'll send you to the stocks. For we are, indeed, resolute."

Sionn bristled and Oean began to argue. I held up my hand and, for a wonder, they both fell silent and fell back. I stared at the member of His Own who stood at ease despite the rain; the cold rain that had for two days soaked through my cloak and hat, leaving me miserable and wet. But not so wet that the fire of my frustration might not spark.

"In whose name do you deny Unencumbered Players access to this town?"

"In the names of His Own, the Prophet, and the lonely God Himself!"

Ach, he borrows an authority he doesn't rightly possess. "Ah. You claim, then, to follow the way of the God?" I peered at him as if the rain obscured the coal-black cloak he wore.

"Of course!"

"Oh! Not the Goddess, perhaps?" Beathen, behind me, drew in a sharp breath.

"Do you accuse me of bedding men, sirrah?" He stepped forward, his arthritic hands clenched into claw-like fists. His anger flared so hot I feared the rain would steam. The gate guard looked from one of us to the other, but I knew which way he'd jump should it come to that.

I held up my open hands and assumed my most innocent and innocently wronged expression. "What? Why no, of course not! Who am I to make such a claim against you? Goodness, Goodman. Whatever would make you think such a thing? No, I ask only because it is said that when the God first visited the upland eknos in the youth of the world, the Ealdranna turned Him away, spurned Him, preferring their own Goddess. Or so it is written."

Oean stepped forward then. He turned to me and spoke as if we simply discussed an obscure scene in a forgotten play, snug within warm walls with a cup between us instead of standing with cold feet in the clinging mud. "But, Dughal. Isn't it also said that later, when the Goddess denied the eknos game because of their foolishness, and they grew hungry and remorseful, the God Himself extended welcome to the Old Ones without hesitation, providing them with good things to eat that came of the ground?"

"Why, yes, Oean. My point exactly." I turned back to the obstinate man standing between me and dry sheets, hot mulled wine, and roast meats. "Therefore, it's said that to follow the God – and follow Him truly – is to be hospitable and welcoming to all who knock at your door. That's why I asked, you see."

I heard laughter behind me but not from any of my troupe. Turning around, I started to see the troop of horsemen led by Goodman Neacal. The wind and the pelting of the rain against my hat had obscured the soft sounds of horses' hooves against the turf, allowing him to come so close.

"Most excellent, Player," Goodman Neacal called to me. "Well played indeed." He rode up and confronted me with that self-same admiration that had shown on his face at our first meeting. We played a game, he and I. It didn't bode well for me or mine, I knew that immediately. *No doubt, his sense of fair play wouldn't allow him to lose.*

"Well met, Goodman Neacal," I answered. "Do you intend to rest here this evening?"

"Indeed we do."

"Pity," I said. "For it seems there's no room in this town. I can only imagine that the one inn has burned down and all the barns are filled with those flooded off of their lands by this cursèd rain. I've been told there's no room for even my small troupe."

"Nonsense." Neacal turned to the bitter old man. "Goodman Fachtnel, unbar the gates. These men are my especial guests this evening."

"You'll vouch for their behavior?" I revised my opinion of Goodman Fachtnel at that. His hatred was stronger than his habit of obedience.

"Indeed, although there's no need for worry. I'm sure the *women* of Beldann have nothing to fear from this troupe of players." He turned from the glowering Goodman Fachtnel and motioned for us to precede him through the gates. "Please be so good to tell the innkeeper - Eimhen is his name – that he should show you Players all *due* courtesy. I'll be along shortly, once I've seen my men well situated."

I nodded my thanks, the rain dripping off the brim of my hat as I did so, and turned towards the wagon. "Oh, one more thing, Dughal," Neacal said. I turned and he fixed his gaze upon me and said, a half-smile twitching at his lips: "We found the escaped prisoner."

Fachtnel glared at Neacal, his surprise clear. "What escaped prisoner?"

"Did you?" I ignored Fachtnel just as Neacal did, as well as Sionn's gasp. I hoped Barrol wasn't not-looking too obviously. "Surely, that's good news, is it not?"

"You must have passed within twenty yards of the body."

"Say rather, we must have passed the spot where the body came to lay," Oean said. "I'm sure if there was a dead body so close to the road, we would have seen it."

"Would you?" Neacal asked.

My men all nodded, innocence dripping off of us like rain.

"Of course, Goodman," I replied. "Is there anything more? Else I'll tell the innkeeper that you're coming." With that, I turned again and motioned to my men to move forward. I shook my head. *How masterful! Provide us with an act of kindness, all out of character, and then when we reel from that, slip in something about that poor woman to see how we'll react!* None of His Own had ever held out their hand save that they expected it to be filled in due course or were preparing to strike you with it.

We trundled through the gates ere they were fully opened and I trust none of them, not even Barrol, gave Goodman Fachtnel as much as a second glance. When we were but a stone's throw from the inn I gathered my men around me and said: "See to it that we seek no warmth hotter than a meal in the common room while we're in Beldann. You heard Goodman Neacal. His Own would be happy to use the least transgression to revoke our right to play in Bainellen province. There will be no plowing in this town, no matter how willing the woman – or man – may seem."

Sionn began to argue and even Oean complained. Beathen's quiet voice stopped them both. "'Seem' Dughal? What do you suspect?"

Camran spoke up for the first time. "He suspects that the righteous His Own would not be above forcing some poor soul into our path just to see if we'd stumble to tumble."

Those fine and wise words sufficed to silence even Sionn's grumbling.

The innkeeper bustled into the yard at our approach, wiping his hands onto an apron strapped across his ample middle. He glared up at the clouds dropping rain onto his bald pate before turning to greet us. "Players! The God of sheaves has seen fit to bless us, He has. This weather has kept many folk fast within the walls and they grow bored. You'll play for us, yes?"

I shook my head. "We're told at the gates that there's to be no playing nor telling of tales." I own I felt encouraged by his dejected looked. Not all shunned Players as rogues and vagabonds.

"Damn Fachtnel for a stiff-necked old fool," muttered our good host. Since he spoke to himself I pretended not to hear.

"We'd welcome two rooms for the night and food brought to them," I told him. "We've money to pay for all of it and would share news as is our ancient duty even if we can't do more to entertain your stranded guests."

He nodded, a gleam of calculation in his eyes. "Hmm, yes. That's well. I have room enough for you and yours. And if I ask for a tale or two, well then, who's to deny me in my own inn?"

I smiled, warmed indeed by his love for our craft, but shook my head nonetheless. "I was also to bear a message to you which I fear will answer your kindly intended question. Goodman Neacal is behind us, settling his men. He also seeks a room this night."

Poor Eimhen's face fell as if into a drain, sliding in a moment from open and friendly to pinched and wary. "You're friends with Goodman Neacal?"

Sionn snorted. "I would that we were better strangers."

I glared at Sionn while Oean shook his head. "I believe our impertinence to your gate guard amused him. It's on his orders that we're allowed into your town and his word to you that we've brought. No more."

Eimhen nodded. "Sure and that would be like Neacal. For one bound to the God of Order, he delights in setting people against one another." Eimhen suddenly straightened up and rubbed rain from his head. "Ach, but I'm a poor host. While I blather out here in the rain, you get even more cold and wet."

"Not sure that's possible," Barrol whispered to Sionn as Eimhen escorted us inside.

"Give those poor beasts warm oat mash and a good rub down," Eimhen instructed the stable girls. "And you, boys. Show these men to the rooms at the far end."

We dropped off our gear before we made use of the clean but simple common baths, luxuriating in the steam and heat before I led all the men back to our rooms. I took Camran with me to the common room, leaving the others safe from temptation or mischief. The two of us would suffice to tell the hosteller we're ready for our food and to take it back with us.

Eimhen sent the serving boys with a tureen of stew thick with meat and last year's roots as well as a tray of trencher bread already sliced. Camran took up a pair of pitchers of the thin abbey ale while another boy followed with a tray of dented pewter mugs. I counted out the silver required, grumbling as I did so of a Player's need to pay when he had tales to tell and songs to sing.

I began to turn away. "One moment, Dughal durFortin!"

I made sure a smile masked my face before turning to Goodman Neacal. He beckoned to me and I'd no choice but to join him and Goodman Fachtnel at a table in the common room. With luck, I could beg off with tales of my supper growing colder and scarcer in the rooms above.

I should have wished for better luck.

"I've been speaking to Goodman Fachtnel here," Neacal began before I'd scarcely set my seat to the bench. As he'd not yet asked any question of me I simply raised an eyebrow and waited. Patience is a trait a Player must learn early and practice often. "Indeed, I've convinced him that he may have perhaps been o'er hasty in demanding no songs, tales, nor plays from your troupe. I've spoken to him at some length of the renown of Bardeelin throughout the land."

"I'm flattered, Goodman," I said when his pause grew long.

"Are you?" Neacal smiled and I grew worried: true mirth sparkled those deep green eyes. "Do you agree to it, I would have your troupe perform a play for us during our stay here in Beldann. An edifying one for the people of this humble town."

I bowed my head, hoping that the movement would hide my no-doubt pale features from his gaze. "We'd be honored, Goodman."

"Would you?"

I began to much dislike that trait of his. "Indeed," I assured him with an assurance I didn't feel. "We've an old mystery play new worked that just the other day we performed for Goodmen Perrin and Firchar. They both gave us their compliments on the skill of our performance."

"Did they?" Neacal turned to Fachtnel. "Do you see, Goodman? Renowned! Just as I said." Neacal turned to gaze at me as if savoring the moment. "But of course you'll not be performing *that* play."

"No?" I asked. "What would you have us do, Goodman? We've several plays that I think will suit your ... temperament —"

He waved his hand and I fell silent. The smile on his face grew yet wider as he reached into a pack at his side and pulled forth a pile of parchment and placed them on the table before me.

"You'll perform *this* play, Dughal, and in no more than three days' time. I've entitled it *Nabryhtric's Heir*, a play of great weight and spiritual import. If you please us in your performance, we'll allow you to travel Bainellen province. Performing this play."

"That's absurd!" I blurted out before my roiling emotions came under control. "Never has Anaric nor priest, no nor seer neither, asked anything of us but that we do our duty. By what right do you make such a demand?"

Neacal feigned an expression of surprise. "Demand? Why Dughal, we offer you a.... What's the word, Fachtnel?" He snapped his fingers. "Ah, yes. A commission."

"Commissions are paid," I retorted. *A wrong move.*

Fachtnel growled. "You should care for your soul more than your purse!"

"No, Fachtnel. Dughal is right in this. I told you that he is a learnéd man." Neacal pushed the pile of parchment slowly across the table at me. I didn't move, although I felt as if I were being threatened by a serpent. "On my word of your good performance, Cleirach might even be persuaded to relax his stance on Players. Should you prove useful, of course."

I sat up straight and pulled my shoulders back. "We're Players, Neacal. We're not a tool to be wielded like a pickax."

"Nothing so blunt, I grant you." He sat back on the bench and scratched at his belly. "But tools you are nonetheless and one that can be used for the greater good." He frowned at my sound of angry denial. "Dughal, I'm surprised. Perhaps you aren't so learnéd as you believe. You, and all the Players ever granted Seal, have *never* been anything more than tools. When the Anarics wished for the Rici to be strong, Players roamed the lands telling stories of the Glorious Rici. When the Rici shattered into the Seven, why then you performed plays of pastoral life, keeping the people on the land so the great landowners might remain great."

I shook my head, but the denial was as much for me as for them. "You're confused, Neacal. You have placed the cart before the horse. Players perform the plays and tell the tales that will see us fed and make us welcomed. If people want to hear about the glories of the Rici, well then, that's what we'll play for them. If they wish to hear a tale of pastoral simplicity, why then that's what we tell them. Our audiences form us as much as we inform our audience."

"How quaintly naive!" Neacal laughed while I held my tongue. He leaned across the table, all at his ease as if he were to impart a friendly secret. "No matter, Dughal. You'll learn this play and perform it well." He leaned back, at his ease. "The God wills it."

"Does He?" With a deep breath, I pushed aside my anger, the ache from the cold not assuaged by the hot baths, the emptiness of hunger that roiled my belly. None of that mattered – could matter – in this. "Bah. You have no right—"

Neacal's words, spoken softly but with precision, cut through my bluster. "I have the simple right of might, Dughal,"

Fachtnel snickered, an ugly sound filled with spiteful glee. "Perhaps you forget how many men Neacal has with him."

Neacal leaned back, a nonchalant wave of the hand. "Fachtnel's quite right, of course. If you fail to act, or don't act to our liking, then you'll be retained here in Beldann by the men I have with me. Bardeelin will simply disappear, it's lies and wicked words disappearing with it."

Fachtnel hawked and spat on the floor. "I doubt many would mourn the passing."

"Is that how you follow the God, then?" I tossed out words like a drowning man flails his arms. "Do you tread such a narrow path that a Player's words might push you from it? What could mere Players say or do that would turn the people of this town or even the meanest hamlet from the course that *you* set for them?"

My anger propped me up against the cold glare of his gaze. No more jokes, no more false fire warmed his countenance. He leaned forward, fists clenched on the table top. He kept his voice low, and all the more menacing for that. "Listen well, O learnéd player. Neither you nor your words mean aught to me, save as a Tool to be used for the glory of Cleirach and the lonely God. Neither you nor your words provide even the merest threat to the efforts I and my master take to turn Anacarra onto the path destined it by the lonely God. But you may be used to hasten us along that path. You and yours have always been tools wielded by those in power. For 700 years you've done as the powers wanted, whether you kenned that or not. "

Neacal stood up and Fachtnel with him. "Rejoice, Dughal durFortin. I've given you a gift. You're now a tool to the hand of the good God, a tool to be shaped by the Prophet and wielded by me. Perform the play as written and you can continue to be what you've always been. Decline, or fail to perform well, and like any tool insufficient to the task you'll be broken and tossed aside."

Back in the room, I sat for some while and tried to eat, but the food had long grown cold and I pushed it aside. "We've been given a commission," I announced. My Players began to chatter in expectation, but when I didn't say further, they all fell silent.

"Which of our plays are we to perform, Dughal?" Oean asked.

Here it comes. "None of them."

"I don't understand," Beathen said.

"Nor I," Sionn added. "What play are we to play if we play none of our plays?"

I looked down at my hands. "We are to play *his* play."

Thence came all of the self-same arguments I'd put forth. I let them run. I stood up and pushed open the shutters to the room. Despite days on the open road and soaked by the chill rain, I suddenly needed fresh air to clear the black miasma from my thoughts. Below our rooms, one of His Own paced slowly back and forth on the street. Across the way, not in the stable but in another building a few doors down, a knot of His Own gathered, their black cloaks darker even than the night around them. Darker than their hearts.

"Are you listening?" Sionn grabbed my arm and I turned to face him, face his righteous indignation twisting his handsome features. No dimple graced his cheek tonight, but his countenance carried staunch pride in its place. "We're all decided, Dughal. We're not day laborers building a wall to their design."

Are we not? I shook my head, despair threatening to drown me. "I like this no more than you. I made all the same arguments."

Sionn pushed away from me, standing tall and pulling his tunic down straight. His voice was almost calm as he declared: "If you won't tell them no, then I will."

I took hold of his shoulders. "You fool, listen to me! We'll be imprisoned if we don't agree. It's not worth the risk."

He shook loose. "Some things are worth risk, Dughal. We won't do it."

"We have no choice!"

Sionn stepped up to me, his face close to mine own so that I could clearly see the disgust written on it. "Of course. You never see any choice, do you Dughal? No choice but to run from His own in every village. No choice but to let those who would beat us leave without a fight. No choice but to leave that poor —"

I punched him in the guts. "No choice but to save Bardeelin!"

The blow stopped his mouth but opened his rage. Sionn jumped me and we struggled, falling to the floor of the room. Drowning indeed, this time I flailed my arms, striking Sionn several times even as his blows landed on me: my face, my jaw, my ribs. Beathen pulled Sionn from me and Camran pulled me from Sionn and as I stood I felt blood trickle from my nose.

"You are released!" My voice started as a shout but I regained some control, although I couldn't keep the grief at this betrayal from my words. "I hold you no longer to your oath to the Bardeelin." I turned away, wiping away the blood. "Now get you gone from my sight."

Camran stepped around to face me with Beathen coming up behind him. I didn't hear the other two but since I also heard no footsteps to the door, I assumed they supported Sionn. "You don't mean that, Dughal!" Camran said.

"Do I not? He's never had the temperament to be part of Bardeelin." I gagged and turned to the window, spitting out a gob of blood and snot. "He's seldom been pleased in me as his master. At every turn he questions my decisions, he argues my judgments of plays to perform and even the blocking of the scenes." The blood flowed freely from my nose and my breath heaved in my chest. Rage and a profound feeling of betrayal did battle in my heart. Yes, that and fear, too, just as Sionn had accused me of.

"Like any colt, he tests you. Wants to know that you are worthy to be his master."

I ignored such an obviously false characterization. "I've shown him enough that he can take up with one of the other Unencumbered or even settle into a city with a playhouse. I'll give him – and any other who questions me on this – a purse and my curse to be gone from my sight!"

After a moment of tense silence, I heard the sounds of men leaving the room. I could see Camran at my shoulder but, after just a moment, I feared it was we two who were the only members of a proud and ancient troupe left. I turned my back to the window and leaned against the sill, my rage burned away and the ashes wet with despair.

"I trust you'll give fair portion to all who would leave Bardeelin," I said. "Though it will mean the end of us, for just us two could not earn enough playing *that* to retain our Seal." I picked up and flung the despised pages against the wall and watched the parchment flutter to the bed. My chest burned with sobs I would not utter, although I suspected that the moisture on my face was not all blood from the fight.

"Don't be an ass, Dughal," Camran said. He pushed me down onto the bed and leaned against the desk across from it. He shook his head as he looked me over. "No one is leaving and no one is released. You no more want to do *that*," he said with the exact inflection I had used, "than does Sionn. He simply said what you wanted to, but could not. He'll cool down, as you must. In the morning we'll begin work."

"Of course they've left, you old fool. What proud Player would fall so low as to perform at the beck of His Own? Not I, I assure you."

Again, he shook his head. "Your father used to tell me that winds blow for a day or mayhap a tenday. But winds from the north turn southerly again."

"When my father held the Seal, never did he have to face a gale such as His Own."

"No? Then it's good that we have Fortin's son leading us in these times, for I grant you, he is more flexible than Fortin ever was."

I snorted at that and winced, the act causing the blood to run anew from my nose.

"I'm sure Oean could tell you from this troupe's own records similar storms we've faced and survived." Camran handed me a towel to staunch the new blood.

"By doing our masters' bidding, no doubt."

"What do you mean?"

My heart pounded near to breaking in my chest. "Neacal said that Players have ever been used thus."

"And you fear he is right."

I laughed, although there was no mirth in it. "I know he is."

"Then know one other thing, Dughal. The days of the Rici are gone. The rule of the Five is weak. And Players such as we still exist while these others have all faded away."

"Cold comfort. We were the 49th Unencumbered troupe and there were as many again granted Seal after us as before. Playhouses or amphitheaters thrived in every city of note." The blood had stopped and I threw the towel to the floor. "Now? There are few playhouses left in all the land with permanent companies and a dozen Unencumbered troupes still trudging the circuit of Anacarra. At some point, every one of those four score and more troupes faced that which destroyed them."

Camran had no answer to this and so we sat not speaking, listening to the sounds of the storm and the flutter of the parchment pages blown by the wind from the open window.

Only five players were needed and I asked Sionn if he wished to be held out. He clenched his jaw but didn't speak, simply shaking his head even as he snatched his pages from my hand. I held Barrol back instead then, since the play called for no women and the youngest role was not given an age. Sionn played that. I divided as I could, but it seemed that Neacal had crafted it with us in mind. An older man, two in middle age and two younger, and so the parts were handed out. After breakfast we sat in one of our rooms and read through the parts aloud, in the company of all the other roles.

I wished to weep.

Oean would be the first to admit that when a wordsmith sits down to smelt the history of Anacarra into tale or a play, he concentrates on the story more so than the history. Players live to entertain and instruct and while there have been many fascinating and exciting periods in the ore that makes up Anacarra's past, the playing of them requires much refinement: one event is folded into another, one character comes from an alloy of two or more people. All done in the interest of telling a good story, of putting on a remarkable play.

Even so, I've never considered presenting a tale so at odds with what the records of history teach us. Until Neacal "commissioned" me to perform *Nabryhtric's Heir.*

"The matter of it, Dughal!" Beathen lectured. "Pedantry and propaganda or else outright lies! We know history as well as any who haven't lived through it, and I tell you this tale is false, from first entrance to final exit."

"I know."

"How is it false?" Barrol asked.

"Not a period much covered in the repertoire," Camran said.

"And for good reason." Beathen turned to Barrol. "Nabryhtric, when he came to the High Seat in Bierncarra, claimed that, not only was he the new Anaric, he was descended from the lonely God Himself. Divine, he said he was, and to be worshiped along with the God in His fields."

Barrol turned Oean as he took up the tale. "For all they claimed kinship with the God, the era of the 'Divine' Anarics is one of the most besieged and beset in Anacarra's history. Unsettled weather for a hundred years, failing crops, earthquakes in the north and tsunami in the south."

Beathen nodded. "For all of that, they claimed that only the presence of the 'divine' on the throne would save Anacarrans from suffering. They conscripted tens of thousands in order to build massive monuments, to themselves as well as the God. Crops that did grow rotted in the fields for want of workers to harvest them."

Barrol looked from one to another of us. "But that's not what Neacal wrote!"

Camran laughed and shook his head. "Well, the last Nabryhtric did relinquish the throne before he was ready!"

"He was murdered, by a common crofter!" Beathen spat on the floor. "Not taken up bodily into the sun."

"How am I to stage that scene upon our cart?" I asked, but nobody had a suggestion.

Now it was Oean's turn to complain as he spluttered incoherently. "The words, Dughal!" he growled. "Doggerel! Base and plain and as musical as a fall of rocks!"

Sionn waived a sheaf of parchment in the air. "This is.... Dughal, *my* verses are better crafted and more mellifluous than this."

"Oh, I don't know," Beathen said. "I've read your verses."

Sionn shook his head, his eyes wide. "I'm serious. List, then, and hear what we're to proclaim from our stage:

> *Nabryhtric's heir am I*
> *To a golden crown. Gold fine*
> *As the sun up in the sky.*
> *The God's sun, in God's time."*

"Was that supposed to rhyme?" Oean asked.

Camran counted on his fingers and looked up, bewildered. "How many beats per line was that?"

"Which line?" Sionn asked, getting a rueful chuckle out of Beathen while the pained expression upon Oean's face never wavered.

"Oh, by the Bargain." I cradled my head in my hands.

"The shape of it, Dughal!" Camran twisted up on his seat. "Plodding from scene to scene while maintaining no tension, no drama. Predictable plot leading to an absurd conclusion."

I shrugged my shoulders. "I'll give Neacal this much: he's seen plays performed enough that he managed to form a basic, three act structure." My voice fell and I spoke more to myself than the others. "I think I can put that on the stage."

"I don't know how you can say it is predictable." Beathen took the pages from Sionn's hands. "Nothing in history matches what this man wrote! I never knew what would come next."

"He borrowed more than structure, Dughal," Oean said. "Within those pages I heard lines from at least half a dozen famous plays, taken up whole or in part and set down amongst his own. No wonder it seems predictable, Camran. You kept thinking you recognized the play!"

I couldn't tell if that was a sob or a laugh coming from Camran. Or myself, for that matter.

I let them talk over the lunch Eimhen brought to our rooms and then, when the dishes fell empty and they fell silent, I looked from one of them to the other. Each, without fail, sighed, nodded, picked up his copy, and walked from the room to practice his lines in private, committing the atrocious, lying, ponderous doggerel to memory. I sighed as well, spread my pages before me on the table, and commenced to learn my role.

Eighteen

Rhia

45 Aililnaian, Year 675 of the Rici

Tomorrow, upon the Solstice, the Ealdranna will come down from the Uplands to take me and mine onto the crags. I've had word from Terra in Varranellen of the same, that all is in motion. The day we've anticipated for so long is nearly upon us!

It will be hard to give up all we know. Give up the plow and the seasons of the land, the sheep and cattle, bread and wine and beer. The horses! I'll miss my horse, I think, most of all. But the Rici has fallen into corruption, abjuring the Balance. Soon, there will be nothing left. Better to give it all than to have it taken away.

My people understand that, in sacrificing the herds and the ways of sowing, they're tossing aside everything that they have known. Yet there are celebrations in nearly every town and hamlet and croft, all of those who have partaken of the pleasure that Na has for us.

- Mara darMara, Onetime prefect of Aelfallen province, then Ekma of Elk Eknos

I passed through the valley of Kiri's pyre quickly for, despite my night-long vigil, I felt invigorated. My feet fairly flew across the open spaces. I slept for an hour at mid-day and another hour in the late afternoon, renewing my strength in order to keep moving far into the evening. I picked up a sizable trail and followed it nearly due south for the rest of the day, until I came upon a gathering ekarra, stocked with firewood and other supplies for the cearnan to manage the water-grass that grew in the nearby lake.

I resumed my journey before the late-season sun had resumed his place in the sky. For most of the day I moved well and surely through the forests of Lynx eknos. The trail I'd followed the day before veered towards the west. Ahead of me, two buttes rose up, bare and rocky, out of the surrounding forest. I passed between them and espied a further line of high bluffs to my right.

I followed alongside the base of those high hills, running for many days and some three score miles. The forests became thicker, less maintained than those to the north. I saw plenty of apple and cherry trees thick with flowers and walnut and chestnut trees. All deliberate trees which meant I often found gathering ekarras to sleep in, but little food ready this early in the year.

For the most part, the brush was no higher than my thigh, but it had been some years since Lynx had set fire to these woods to keep them clear of debris and undergrowth. Burnflowers sprouted across the hillside, thick with buds that wouldn't open until the forest burned. With Lynx in such disarray, unless Na took pity and sent lightning to fire the forest, those flowers would never open. I realized how fortunate Moonhart is in her ekma (bemused though she'd be to hear me admit it) and our cearnan. The problems with Lynx did not begin with the sowers. Such neglect of their forests!

Despite the high hills to my right side, the ground began to slope more and more sharply away, as if the lowlands encroached upon the Crags at this point. My way became slower and slower as even the game trails disappeared and the undergrowth grew thick and tangled. I swatted at more and more gnats and flies and flicked too many ticks from my bare arms and legs. The moist, thick debris on the forest floor bred such nuisances, regularly burned away from settled lands. Thorny plants grew sharp and stubborn and I changed course to even further west. I realized I traveled the briarwood, the part of the forest that bordered lowlander territories. The unkempt forest, choked with thorns and dead fall, and (as I discovered by stepping on them) shards of broken pottery and other sharp debris, served as a barrier to curious lowlanders. Alas, it proved itself a barrier to me as well. I put my breeches and the schoh back on, fuming at the delay.

After two days of this I'd gone barely twenty more miles and I feared that, should this be the condition of the uplands that used to be Falcon territory, I could very well find myself lost in the trackless forest, scratched a thousand times by the thorny bushes and trees, and without a hope of ever catching up to my mother's captors (if hope even yet remained).

I pushed on up a hillside, seeing brighter light through the trees ahead and I stumbled out of the woods and saw, not more unkempt forest as I'd dreaded, but a treeless plain stretching for miles ahead of me. My fears fell far short faced with reality. The tended woodlands of Falcon Territory were no more. Instead of tall trees giving shelter to all within, I saw fields of grass stretching out of sight before me and to either side.

I had entered sower territory.

Fear knotted my guts, and like a moonhart spotted by a hunter, I froze, dread locking the muscles of my legs, my breath. A realization that I stood exposed upon a hillside in sower territory changed my stillness to flight. I scrambled back into the woods behind me and threw myself upon the ground in the thickness of the brush. When my heart had slowed and my breath returned to something close to normal, I ventured to look up and around. Before long, I began to move, skirting the open edges of the fields until I could clamber up a high outcropping.

From there, hidden from below, I could see all there was to see in these open fields. The wide skies above me reminded me uncomfortably of my trek along the escarpment and the treeless waste brought back all the terror of my Calling dream and the fears of my youth, listening to my mother's tales of the lowlands. I waited for night to fall and my courage to return before I attempted those open spaces.

Open, but not empty. Flocks of small puffy beasts ranged these open fields. Children, too young for their *stealna kir* if they'd been eknos, stood watch while dogs ran amidst those flocks of small, awkward things. Short and round as an allium in seed and of one of two colors: a deep brown of ripe walnuts or a dirty white like birch bark. As much as I appreciated my pair of woolen trews and my hood that kept my head warm excellent well when the snow flew, I'd never before seen the creature from which the wool came.

Fascinating. I lay upon my rock, flat to the warmed surface, and peered into the distance, watching. The children and dogs I understood well enough: the dogs minded the sheep and the children minded the dogs. The flocks ranged across denuded hillsides, feeding on the great swathes of grass where trees used to stand. Bleating at nothing, scurrying whenever the dogs came near, the sheep huddled together in a great dirty mass, out in the open, exposed to every kind of predator.

But safe for all that, as another curiosity met my sight. Walls. Great collections of field stones piled one atop the other like a cairn but in long straight lines, dividing the land from itself. No walls had sprung up to divide the forest from these new lowlands. Four footed hunters would gorge themselves on these stupid creatures, were it not for the dogs.

The warm sun bore down on me where I lay, it's warmth tempered by the wind that swept across what had once been forested land. Now, the grass bowed down to the wind, looking very much like waves. The *wrongness* of it all struck through me. Thousands of eknos had once called this land home, once walked beneath towering trees. A few remnants of forest lay scattered about the plains that stretched before me, huddling as if in fear of the lowlander's axes.

I forced my breathing to quiet, my heart to slow, my fists to unclench. My rage at the sowers pushed aside my fear of the lowlands. While a part of me hoped that I might encounter lowlanders upon my trek across these lands, I realized that I couldn't save my mother or the other captives if I stopped to fight a battle long since lost.

Once darkness fell, I slipped down from my perch and slunk out into the fields, keeping one of the stone walls on my left hand. I'd seen nothing on the right-hand side of this line and thought it prudent to avoid those noisy flocks. I began to run, felt the easing of my fear in the simple act of flight. I found running to be more challenging through the tall grass than it had been through the cleared forest floor. But I soon found a rhythm and, with such a straight line laid out for me, covered a great distance that night. I discovered that first field, while extensive, consisted mostly of just one valley. The hillsides, once I reached them some few miles distant, had kept their covering of trees, and I slipped beneath those sheltering arms with relief.

A short-lived relief. With no gatherers to tend them, these forests were as thick and unkempt as anything created of a purpose by eknos to keep sowers at bay. I struggled for an hour to pass through this small strip of woods and was distressed to realize that, until I made it through the old Falcon lands, I would want to avoid the trees except at daybreak. Another reason as well to keep to the fields made itself plain once I stepped beneath the branches. Even the light of the full moon – more than enough to guide me across the fields – could not penetrate enough for me to pick my way through the tangled mess of brush and branches.

Afterward, I avoided those sad, strangled, forests. Only when dawn approached did I appreciate the thick canopy limiting the bright sunlight to dusky shadows. This I did for two nights.

The third night had grown old and my long, loping stride had carried me a great distance over the old Falcon territory. Coming to the end of a field, I leapt a wall only to land right in the midst of a flock of sheep! These had been sheared, stripped to the skin so that only their gangly bleating remained. Twas only by the noise that I realized they were the same creatures as the big fluffy things I'd seen from afar.

They scattered, crying to wake Na. Or shepherds. *Or dogs.* I veered away from the flock, thumping hard enough into the stone wall that I lost my breath. Ere I recovered it, the terrified noise of the sheep had alerted the dogs.

I grabbed one of the smaller sheep (no hunter should waste such an opportunity), snapped its neck to stop both its noise and its struggles, and hopped over the stone fence, putting the wall between me and the onrushing hounds. I didn't bother to crouch behind the wall, trusting the dark and my speed. I fast left the tumult far behind, even with one dead lamb tucked beneath my arm.

I passed two more stretches of woods before stopping deep within one to light my fire. At first I feared that the smoke and the smell of cooking meat would alert any with eyes to see that an interloper ranged their fields. But my fortunes had so improved since my time with Lynx that the clear, warm weather of the past few days gave over to low clouds and scudding rain even as I lit my fire. The rain and fog covered the smoke from the fire, now needed to keep me warm as well as cook my meat, and the rain discouraged pursuit. I ate well and slept better: the young sheep had the most distinctive and pleasant flavor and I gorged myself that morning. When I awoke, red beams from the setting sun struck the retreating bellies of rain clouds: a clear night for running. *Lynx took so much time from me!* I hurriedly ate the last of the lamb and left nothing to go in my pack, burying the bones along with the ashes of my fire.

I'd reached what I thought must be the middle of Falcon Territory sometime that night. The fields had changed over from grasslands to those bare of all save for the remains of last year's crops, showing even rows of broken stems. My feet had wings, then. I made the most of the tilled fields: free of plants save for the earliest Gathering season shoots, free of rocks save those piled into rows, free of trees except for copses left of a purpose, and with hard packed paths separating one field from another. I covered a prodigious distance that night.

With my goal so close to me, I pushed on well past the time I should have stopped and hidden myself. I'd noted the change over from pasture to planting but I didn't think through what it meant. Something arcane, I assumed, that only sowers would understand, not realizing the change meant something for me as well.

As my feet took me deeper into Falcon territory, my mind took my thoughts deeper into the tales of that eknos. The story had made my heart pound in fear as a young girl. The Falcon Ealdranna had, in the misty past, settled the boundary between the Midcrag and the Kaircrag. The spine of the Uplands fell in that spot, sinking so far down that the lowest part could scarce be differentiated from the lowlands themselves. But then Aethen led his people out of Dolun and, slowly, the sowers of old moved north, clearing the land, tending their herds and sowing their seeds. For centuries, the Ealdranna were strong enough and the sowers few enough that the lowlanders could but impotently covet the great valley that split the Crags.

My hands gripped into fists as I remembered the story, the fear of the child replaced by the righteous rage of the Hunter. A hand of generations before my own birth, the sowers – with murder and terror and wanton destruction – shattered and scattered Falcon eknos. They cut the uplands in twain, denuded the hillsides to graze their sheep and uprooted the turf of the valley to sow their crops, destroying the provider meadows and replacing them with row upon row of sameness. At the lowest point ran a road over which they would cart goods between the west coast of Anacarra and the east. And alongside this new road they planted their houses as well as their crops.

I ran down these hills, my thoughts on the distant past, getting closer and closer to the lowest point, as if I approached a desiccated riverbed. Instead, I approached land long ago put under the plow. The gently undulating hills of this part of Falcon territory suited the farmers well, who had left their villages early that morning with their heavy oxen pulling their awful plows.

I dived down to lie behind the nearest rock wall. The rest of the fields contained nothing but the broken shafts of last years grains. The road was wider than I was tall, bounded between a pair of rutted tracks that ran parallel to one another. To my right, came oxen pulling a wagon, the wheels matched to the ruts. I needed to find shelter and quickly.

A stand of the old forest hunkered down within sight of the road, a good two bow shots away. I burst from cover: up and over the fence, across the road and over the next fence. Thence came a race for the trees. I'd hoped that with the sun to my left and the sowers to my right, they might not see me in the glare of the early morning. I wasn't so fortunate. I heard shouts behind me but they sounded more of surprise than fear or anger. Like a moonhart with the scent of the hunt in her nose, I raced for the safety of the trees. I swerved once or twice at random, hoping that should any arrow be lofting its way towards me, I might give it reason to miss.

Of course, I'd been safer than any deer surprised by cearnan in the uplands: no farmer is allowed to carry a weapon. Would that I had known that then!

Another night passed and I again found flocks of sheep and fewer fields being made ready for sowing. Far ahead of me copious amounts of dark smoke towered high into the sky, betoken of a large burning in progress. It made my heart glad. Before the end of the next night I entered a wood and didn't see the other side. I slept, then, until the dawn and began again to travel by day. Before noon, the thorns and thickets of the briarwood had given way to hickory and chestnut, to glades growing with dark green grasses. The smell of smoke grew stronger with each step and ash like snow drifted down to me when the wind shifted.

Blazes marked up high on some trees led me to the pathway through the forest. By middle afternoon of that day, I came upon the site of the burning. Trees still stood, of course, for the purpose of the burn was to tame the undergrowth, now no more than ash on the ground or a few black and twisted sticks reaching up to the sky. The trail I walked grew uncomfortably warm under my bare feet and I gratefully put on Taltaya's schoh once again.

I knew that those who burned wouldn't be far away. I made no attempt to conceal myself or my eknos, my left arm bare to show my eksig. The blazed trail brought me to a stream and I took off my schoh to walk in its cool sandy bed instead of the hot and smoky ground.

While in this stream I found the hungry edge of the fire. The flames danced high, eagerly devouring the dry brush and scorching the very air in my lungs. I moved to the middle of the stream, dropped down into the lowest point, low enough that I might be fully submerged, and swam for some while to get past the most active of the flames and heat, passing beyond the fire zone into uncharred woods.

I came upon a young man, one of the cearnan of White Eagle eknos, with his back to me. He stirred clumps of ashes with a long pole so as to prevent a resurgence of the flames, nonetheless, he must have heard my steps because he began to speak to me as if I were one of the cearnan. "What's the matter, Ferna? Thirsty again?"

"I could use a drink," I said, laughter in my voice.

He spun around, his long staff held tight before him. "Who are you?"

I opened my empty hands and smiled warmly. "I would speak with your ekma."

Cocking his head to one side as if to see me better, he then pursed his lips and whistled, the sharp noise echoing between the trees. This brought the rest of the cearnan to his side, their voices questioning, questions that only increased as they saw me.

These cearnan of White Eagle were, in nearly equal parts, excited by the novelty of my coming among them and wary about what it might mean. They noted my eksig and seemed curious that one of Moonhart had come so far south so early in the season, but held their questions out of courtesy. For all that I'd sought them out, I closely observed each of them, their movements, seeking to learn without asking if I faced any kind of danger from my fellow eknos.

I tried not to let any of my caution show upon my face, and I greeted them all warmly. But then I repeated my request, apologizing for my haste. The young man I'd first met offered to lead me to the ekma.

"I'm Niall darKiro." He reminded me somewhat of Sarae's Goban: deep brown eyes with such full graceful lashes. He had darker hair than Goban, black as dusk under the trees. Niall showed a great calmness, a serenity of movement as he took my hands in greeting.

"I'm Rhia darSelwe," I replied, lost for a moment in those soft eyes. I'd been alone for a long time. I turned away from him, as if adjusting my pack. "May we go? I've traveled a very long way and my travels are not half done."

"Of course," Niall replied. He took up a small pack and then handed me a water skin. "But you did say you were thirsty."

I smiled and nodded, drinking deep of the tepid water. I stopped before emptying the skin, but Niall urged me to continue. "We're not far from the ekarra. Drink your fill."

Not an hour later, Niall escorted me into the ekarra of White Eagle. My presence caused quite a stir, but if they wished me harm, they were being much more circumspect about it than even Gaunt had. Niall brought me to the center of the ekarra and, finding a young lad who shared his graceful looks, sent him in search of the ekma.

"I'll wait with you, if you don't mind." When I smiled my assent, he asked, "Are you hungry? Still thirsty? If you've come all the way from Moonhart territory, you may be tired of trail food."

I smiled, but tensed inside. His manner touched me and confused me. What did it say of me that his very courtesy put my hackles up? I sought to relax, reminding myself that Niall in no ways resembled Gaunt. "I am still thirsty," I admitted.

He tilted his head just a bit as he looked at me. "Since you've had water, might I get you something to drink that I doubt any Moonhart has tasted?"

"If you wish."

He grinned and began to trot away. "I'll be right back."

I sat in the center of the ekarra on a clean and tightly woven grass mat, forcing my breathing to stay slow and my muscles to unclench. As I put effort into simply relaxing, I realized a bone deep weariness made me feel hollow inside. Only my anxious shell kept me sitting upright. The terror of my mother's capture sat unresolved in my belly, now wrapped in memories of my own flight and plight. *If all of White Eagle treats me as kindly as Niall, I don't know what my reaction might be. I have no strength left for weapons but I somehow doubt that weeping would be an appropriate response!*

Niall returned, holding a beautifully carved wooden cup filled with a creamy liquid swirling as he handed it to me. "You look as if you've gone long without comfort. Please, drink," he said. "This is milk from the hickory nuts that grow in our woods, sweetened and wholesome."

I raised the cup to my lips and let the merest hint settle on my lip and then licked it off. "Oh!" I exclaimed and took a deeper drink. The creamy texture filled my mouth, the deep woodsy taste of the nuts promising that the drink would satisfy my hunger as much as my thirst. I felt revitalized with each sip, the sweet liquid spreading energy into that hollow core of weariness. Struggling between savoring the rich taste and filling the void in my belly, the contents of the cup disappeared quickly.

"I'm glad you enjoyed it," Niall said, a smile upon his lips.

"I've never tasted the like."

He looked up and we saw the ekma striding towards us, led by the young boy Niall had sent to find her. Niall stood up and reached his hand down to me. I set the cup aside and stood as well, smoothing my tunic and brushed my hand over the stubble on my head. I greeted the ekma with as much grace and honor as I possessed.

"I give you greetings, Ekma of White Eagle, from the Ekma of Moonhart and from myself, Rhia darSelwe."

"Greetings to you and yours, Rhia darSelwe. I am Fiona darMara, Ekma of White Eagle." She looked me up and down. Her face showed little by way of emotion, but did I just see a hint of smile in her eyes? "I see in you a tale worth the hearing. Is there a message for me as ekma? Or can you tell your tale to all the eknos?"

As we spoke, a small crowd now gathered when they had given me and Niall space before. A tall woman stood behind and to the ekma's right hand, her head shaved for the hunt. She might have been my mother's age or perhaps a bit younger, with strong lines around her mouth and also around eyes the color of river stones. *Here is one who likes to laugh.* But it wasn't her good humor I noted, but the tunic made of a dappled moonhart hide, just turning from black to white.

"My words should be heard by all, ekma," I replied. "But questions I have as well, particularly for the woman to your right." I pointed out the woman in the moonhart tunic.

The ekma's eyes narrowed. "What questions do you have for my daughter Dáiri?"

Before I could speak (since I was unsure how to start first with my questions without telling all the tale) she waved me silent. "No, young Moonhart, forgive me. That's a story knot that can't be untied but from one end or the other." She pulled herself up, her decision made.

"Niall, take her to Kaaran's old botha and then show her where she can bathe, if she wishes. Then let her rest before we eat. Time enough for questions after courtesy has been observed."

At Niall's nod of acceptance, the ekma turned back to me. "You must have been many days on your journey, and yet you manage to arrive here on an auspicious day. The hunters have returned, with a brace of elk and tales of lowlanders. Ah, yes. Your reaction gives me a hint of your story to come. Well, go. Rest. The time for telling tales will be after we've eaten."

With that, she turned from me, beckoning several of the eknos to wait upon her. I allowed Niall to take me to the botha set aside for me, where I stowed my gear. Then Niall led me to a deep pool by an otherwise fast-moving stream.

"Oh, lovely!" Most ekarra set aside places for bathing and washing, but never had I seen one so perfect. I stripped off my leather tunic – shiny with wear and stained from sweat and dirt, the tear from Gaunt's knife now frayed – and waded in. The chill water raised pebbleflesh across my skin. I nevertheless plunged below, to rise spluttering and gasping at the delicious cold that roused my every sense, before I found a spot to stand up out of the river, the water swirling around my legs.

Niall tossed me the soaproot.

"How long have you been traveling?" he asked. I noticed his eyes grow wide as he noticed the Calling medallion between my breasts, but he refrained from asking anything about that.

"I'm not sure." I began to work the soaproot into a lather. "Which season is this?"

He tilted his head, peering at me closely. "It's not yet a tenday into the Gathering Season."

"So late?" I sighed and began to lather the stubble on my head. "I left Moonhart a full three hands of days before the equinox and have been traveling since, save for a bit of delay in Lynx territory. Some three score days." I caught myself and frowned. *How long would it take sowers to traverse their land with Eknos prisoners? Would they run in secret or in the open? And would they stop to gather more eknos as we would stop to gather food from the forest? Was I already too late to save my mother?*

I rinsed off the soaproot residue by diving deep into the pool again. When I emerged, I hesitated, and then took the soaproot once more. "It's been a long time since I've felt really clean." The admission brought heat to my cheeks.

"Take your time, Rhia." Niall's black hair had been tied into a braid and he reached back to shake it out. "If I'm acting as your escort and host, I've no other duties. I'd rather be watching you than searching a just-burned forest for embers." He leaned back against a tree and stretched out his legs, closing his eyes, the long lashes settling onto his cheek.

I began to laugh and then stopped. "Watching me?" I demanded. "Am I a prisoner then?"

"A what?" He sat up at that and if I've ever read expressions aright, I knew his was one of surprise and incomprehension. "Why would you think yourself a prisoner?" He looked back north, as if trying to see the obstacles I'd encountered since leaving Moonhart. "What happened to you?"

I felt embarrassment again and turned away. "Forgive me. I meant no offense." I bowed my head and took in a deep breath. "It's been a very long trail. I'll tell it all, I promise you. I'm sorry."

"It's as if the Tale of Siova World Tracker has come alive," he whispered.

At that, I did laugh, and laughed the harder when Niall's pale skin gleamed ruddy. "Aye, alive and covered in lather." I dove deep, scrubbed the last of the soaproot out of my hair and skin. When I surfaced, the blush that had covered Niall's face had faded somewhat.

"Do you wish to shave your scalp?" he asked.

Ah, Goddess. I did. It itched with the tendays' of growth and I hate it when the hair comes back in. But I shook my head and emerged from the stream to put on my cleanest tunic: Kiri's, beloved for that but ill-fitting. "Thank you, no." He seemed to expect more of an explanation, but I couldn't give him one. *For as long as I have traveled, my journey is far from done. How could I tell him that, in the next few days, I might not want to look quite so much as an Uplander hunter?*

We walked back to the ekarra. Once I'd assured him that I had no other need than for sleep, he left me alone, saying he'd be at hand if needed. After he left, I saw no other take his place outside my door and I chided myself for letting Gaunt's duplicity color my thoughts of White Eagle. I laid down. Despite my anxiety, I slept and knew nothing until Niall touched my arm to awaken me.

"The feast is ready. Come, Rhia. Eat and be refreshed."

Nineteen

Rhia

Weary of the world and the wide-open spaces

Siova knelt

Beside the fire and sighed.

To be at home at last

She wept forsaking pride

And cursing her own past.

- Eknos poem, "Tale of Siova World Tracker"

The feast did more than feed my body. The easy laughter, the high spirits, the evident good health refreshed me in ways that even the food could not. In some amazement, I realized that what I felt was *relaxed*, the first I'd felt that way in threescore days. But among people who seemed very much like my own eknos, I could only feel the familiar tug of kinship and warmth and respond to it.

Familiar, but different too. While White Eagle treated me as I'd expect Moonhart to treat any guest, *I* was that guest. Not since I'd returned from my *stealna kir* had I been the one so honored.

White Eagle arranged the cooking fires at the center of the ekarra exactly opposite to how tis done at Moonhart. Instead of the wide center bowl, with the ekma and the main fire at the bottom, here the main fire was the highest point of a sloping ridge that ended with a high cliff at the ekma's back. All the family groups sat below the ekma on the one side, but I realized the rock wall would serve a similar purpose in that sounds would carry well, even to the lowest fire.

We sat in different groups and I tried to discern what brought the groups together. Mostly families, I gathered, for Dáiri sat with her mother and apart from the other hunters. Two other couples sat there as well, one young man with his new mate and another young woman with shaved head who were introduced to me as Dáiri's children. Niall introduced me to his mother and father (while pointedly ignoring his younger brother's ever more frantic attempts to get his attention). He explained to them that, as my guide, he'd been invited to sit with me up at the main fire. An unfamiliar place was made for Niall and me and we sat down near to the ekma herself.

The White Eagle Ekma presided over the feast. The Hunters presented to her the roast elk that the cearna had prepared and she carved it and served it. So, too, the grains and greens and other gathered things, she distributed them to all who came to her. In Moonhart, the food flowed from below to all and not from the ekma to the rest of us.

Dáiri and her children sat close by her mother and their kinship was apparent. The ekma had seen threescore years come and go, Dáiri at least two thirds that many. The ekma had, no doubt, hunted in her youth, for I could see in her large, strong body the echoes of a more active past. Now she looked both strong and comforting. I couldn't see if Dáiri had begun to go gray for she still hunted, but the ekma's hair fell in a long braid down her back, gleaming and white as a moonhart in the Singing season. Both shared those beautiful lines laughing from their eyes and mouths, both had a look of confident strength.

This close to the sowers, surrounded on all sides by the lowlanders now that Falcon and Cougar were gone, how had White Eagle survived? I gazed down the gentle slope over all of the eknos. They talked, they laughed, every fire ring had people gathered around it. The eknos seemed strong, with full numbers. I'd have to ask that question ere I finished my tale.

Niall made a most pleasant dining partner. He spoke of simple things, shared his bowl, tried to get me to laugh but not in a way that shamed me when I could no more than smile. He eased some of the anxiety that grew in me: my tale, Na's Calling had such great import for these kind people! But I'd failed with Gaunt and I couldn't fail with White Eagle. I've always been far more content to listen to tales than to tell them. I felt Niall's hand on my arm, his concerned gaze. I smiled, setting aside the future for the present, and asked him some diverting question.

He wasn't fooled in the least. But he answered all the same.

And then the feast ended and the moment was upon me. At the ekma's invitation, I stood. "For all that what I will share with you may sound like a tale of old, alas, it is not. Perhaps my plain speech will convince you, for what I have to say is full of dark forebodings, danger, and death." I ran my hand across my scalp and then grimaced at the brush of hair. Moving my hands to my side, I looked up, noting as I did that those around the fires – *all* of the fires – had fallen silent. Even the children. I lowered my voice in the stillness and continued. "Ask as you will, but there's much that's beyond my understanding. As I have an answer, so shall you have it."

I pulled the Calling medallion from my tunic and held it up for all to see and began my tale. I told them of the Calling dream that wracked our sleep and the death of Sleikin. When I related his story, the taking of my mother Selwe and the hunter Grainna, Niall gasped and looked over to where his own mother sat. Fiona shook her head when I explained how I had taken it upon myself to do as Na Bid me even as the elders still debated the correct course of action. All gasped at Gaunt's attempted treachery and nodded when I explained that her name was to be forgotten and that we'd left her body unburned. Dáiri wiped tears away at the untimely death of Kiri, and I saw her reach out to cover her own daughter's hand.

My tale finally passed through the old Falcon lands and reached us here upon this hill. "I have questions of White Eagle eknos when I may." I took the cup that Niall handed to me and eased the dryness in my throat. I'd not spoken so many words at once in most of a season. "But I'll answer your questions first."

The questions came fast and hard and I answered them as I could. I didn't know what actions my eknos took after I left, but the very question divided White Eagle as it had my own eknos. My decision to go alone met with frowns and nods in nearly equal portion. That Lynx eknos had so few hunters dismayed them nearly as much as to the reason why. I saw Fiona's eyes grow hard and calculating at that news. "And the nosmoot yet two years off," she muttered.

When the same questions began to repeat, as if the answers were hard-met the first time, Fiona held up her hand and silence fell. "You have questions for us as well, child," she said. "Ask."

I looked to Dáiri: "Can you tell me more of this 'Prophet' that my mother asked you about when she traded you for that moonhart skin? More than perhaps you told my mother?"

"I know little," Dáiri said. "The Prophet seems to me to be much like any other shaman but the lowlanders hold him in awe as if he were the God Himself come to live in Anacarra. He – the prophet, not the God – lives in Kairclavan, a monastery southeast of here, about two days' walk."

She shook her head and sipped from her cup of mead. "Since the Prophet has been spoken of in Kairclavan, the city surrounding the monastery has grown tremendously, like a poplar on a southern slope. We've not been able to get close to it in several years."

"Have the sowers taken from White Eagle?" I asked.

Dáiri shook her head, her smile grim and smug at the same time. "They try."

Fiona looked fondly on her daughter and then turned to me. "Indeed, they try, the lowlanders. Twice I've received word that they wished to parley, inviting us into Kairclavan where we aren't welcome otherwise. Twice I've rebuffed them, at the counsel of my shaman." At this point she nodded to a grizzled old man sitting well down the circle from her. His long hair and ancient features had hidden his sex from me. I'd taken him to be sister to the old woman next to him but I learned instead that they were mated. I bowed my head to him and he smiled a toothless grin. The man was ancient! If I'd been asked to describe how one of the Old Ones looked, my description would have been of him.

"I'm Pendal. Welcome to White Eagle." His voice, despite his frail frame, sounded loud and clear amidst the gathering, as if I heard it with more than just my ears.

"I thank you, grandfather," I told him.

"Pendal foretold of the actions of the lowlanders," Fiona said. "He —" but the old man stopped her by angrily pounding on the plate in front of him.

"I did no such thing, young woman, as I've told you any number of times." He turned to me, his pale eyes intense. "I don't foresee the future. No one can, for Na does not give such sight to humanity, despite what the foolish sowers say of this Prophet of theirs."

"And yet, shaman, your ... insights ... have always helped us to avoid calamity."

He shook his head. "No magic there, child. If one but looks, and listens, and pays attention to all things, one can determine the course of a stream from a drop of water."

I nodded, hearing in his words his spiritual kinship with Feanna, my own shaman. "Like how, from scat and broken twigs, one can anticipate where a hart might be found."

"Just so, and no more than that. I see many things – none of them the future – but from those things I see we may have some idea where this path will take us."

I looked around at the others in this smaller circle. Niall beamed at the old man while Dáiri shook her head. Fiona laughed at her rebuke and turned to a woman next to her and whispered. I glanced back at Pendal and asked him: "What do you see, grandfather?"

"I see the lowlanders falling under the sway of this one they call the Prophet. I see them giving over their own inherent decency for the empty promise of something greater. I see danger all around, but especially in that monastery of theirs, Kairclavan." He sighed. "I see that no place will be safe for eknos for long, should this rain keep falling."

He fell silent and gazed deep into the flames of our fire as if to divine the answers there, as if Na spoke to him through the flames She'd given the Old Ones long ago.

A thought occurred to me, a memory of Gaunt staring into a fire just that way. "What do you dream, shaman of White Eagle?"

He turned his keen gaze my way. "I dream of a pack of fierce wolves clambering up as if from sleep and it seems we're just now seeing the prey that these wolves stalk." His answer stilled much of the talk around the fire. He stood up, turned unsteadily to face those downslope. But when he spoke, his steady voiced reached even to the furthest fire. "I dream of fear that overwhelms all sense, and I dream of Na." He shook his head at the murmurs this provoked. "No, my children. I've had no Calling dream as this moonhart fawn has for I dream of Na as if She were a demon threatening all I know. I dream...." He shook his head. "My mind can make no sense of these dreams, for they aren't my own."

"How can you dream another's dream?" Fiona asked.

He shrugged and sat down. "Ask our Moonhart friend, here. She did as I've done, and it enabled her to outwit the one she calls Gaunt. Let us hope I can use these dreams as well."

Fiona reached out and touched my arm, turning my attention to her. "We've seen things that we didn't understand. Our hunters, at Pendal's urging, have kept an eye on this Kairclavan. Twice since the snows melted, we've seen wagons carry a human crop into the Prophet's monastery."

I waited, waited for them to tell me more, tell me what happened after the women arrived at this monastery of the lowlanders. I turned back to Pendal and the questions must have been in my eyes. "I have to see the scat on the forest floor before I can know that an elk has gone down the trail." He shrugged. "We've heard nothing from Lynx or eknos north and your tale tells me why. We know they've taken eknos as captives, but not all in those wagons are eknos. We know they go into Kairclavan, bound or drugged. We've not seen them come out again."

Dáiri spoke up. "We hunted that eastern slope in the last hand of days. We've seen no more captives arrive, so perhaps you're ahead of this latest outrage."

Pendal caught my attention and looked me full in the eye. "There's another dream I'd tell to you. I dream of fire, Rhia, Na's Favorite. Fire that devours the past and licks at the present. Packs of wolves in full throated roar at prey brought to bay. And a hunter, alone, standing against the pack."

My heart froze within me, even though I'd long feared as much. My old fear at the lowlands shook me and I found my arms wrapped about my middle.

"There is a goodly-sized town, downstream from Kairclavan," Dáiri said. "The lowlanders call it Kairill. Two days ago, we watched from a ridge more than a mile away, as many men robed all in black, rode in and out of that town. It may be the best place for you to seek the abducted eknos. We've not gone into that city for some years. We didn't have a reason to. Then."

"Nor do we now!" The ekma stood, glaring first at her daughter, then at me. Her glance softened when she looked at me but her hands on her full hips and the set of her shoulders told me all I needed to know. "Your tale is one to frighten all of us. It makes me even more certain that we should have nothing to do with the lowlanders. Any

267

attempts made on our territory will be met with force but we will not take the fight to them. I'll send a hunting party to Lynx, help them to stay strong in the face of this new danger. This I can do."

She turned to me and took my hands in hers. "But as for you...." She shook her head. "I'll offer you what comfort this eknos can provide. Food and other supplies. Time in which to rest and heal what hurts you may have that don't show. Our knowledge of the lowlander terrain. But I'll not send my hunters into the lowlands and I'll ask that you not go either, though it means the sure death of your mother. We've lived closer to the sowers than most, surrounded as we are. We don't fear those in the west and even trade with them. Those to the east, this Prophet ... he we fear."

I nodded but could think of nothing else to say. I looked to the shaman who gazed past me, towards the east, as if his rheumy eyes could see through the darkness to the running of the Bainrill. "Yours is a most perilous path, child. You must both avoid the black-cloaked wolves and seek them out. They're the warriors of the Prophet and as such hate our kind. But as his men – for his warriors are always male – they're the ones who hold your mother and the others. Find where they gather and you may find what you seek. Or your own capture."

He fell silent then, and with that the feast ended. I stood and bowed to both ekma and shaman and offered my thanks to the eknos before walking by myself to the botha set aside for me, disturbing one of the cats who'd made it her home. I picked up the cat and set her on my lap, the quiet purr soothing me. The walls around me felt both protective and confining at the same time. I find I missed the unmuffled sound of the woods at night. What would they think of the wild Moonhart if I took my pack and slept beside their cooking fire? As I lay in the dark, I heard a scratching at the doorway.

"Are you still awake, Rhia?" Niall asked. "May I come in?"

"Aye, Niall. I'm awake." I put aside the cat and sat up on the bench as he pushed aside the leather hanging and entered the botha. "And much likely to stay up, although I'm tired to the bone."

"The Mother gave you much to think about, didn't she?"

"And nothing to do! I can't just sit here —"

He took my hands, startling me. "Tonight, there's nothing you can do but rest." It surprised me to realize how I longed for touch. Better it were Sarae, but she sleeps warm in Goban' arms tonight, hundreds of miles away. *I'm alone, and I've been alone for so long. In danger when alone and worse danger when surrounded by others.* The hospitality of White Eagle had shaken me, taken away the wall of defenses I'd laid about myself from my first day out of Moonhart.

Something of my thoughts must have shown in my expression. Niall's eyes grew soft with compassion. "Do you want me to call for the hetairi, Rhia? You've been alone so long, have suffered so much. Let me call someone to attend to your comfort."

I surprised us both when I reached for him, kissed him. "I'd share Na's boon with you tonight, if you're willing. If you aren't, I'd still ask you to share the botha with me."

"And I thought Moonhart were cautious, skittish creatures." He tilted his head and peered at me. "Are you sure, Rhia? I'm no hetairi to know what you need."

"I know I don't want to be alone."

He smiled, nodded, and kissed me again. I did not sleep alone that night.

Twenty

Dughal

The bane of Players: A crafty carrinanen, a cheating innkeeper, or a bad playwright.

- Actor's proverb

For three days we sequestered ourselves in either our rooms or in the stable that held our wagon. We put costumes and properties together: the easiest part. We blocked out the scenes on the wagon's stage. We memorized the lines. Our Players' pride refused to allow this poor play to make of us poor performers. A handful of times I went to Neacal with requests to change a word or a line. I never sought to change the sense of it: I knew that for a fool's errand. But for the sake of a better rhyme, a more mellifluous phrase, a better transition, a more profound conclusion I reminded him that Bardeelin had the best wordsmith of any troupe. That angered him: "The plow does not suggest which field to turn," he'd say, or words equally foul, to remind me of how he saw me and mine.

After one such request, Neacal raked me with a look of utter disgust. He strode forward into me, forcing me to dodge out of his way and then follow at his heels. "I won't waste more time, Player. I'll see the play tomorrow and tomorrow will your fate be judged. I will be your audience, along with Fachtnel and His Own. If we remain unmoved by the end, Bardeelin will end as well."

I scurried ahead and placed myself in front of him, my hands clasped before me, my eyes downcast, just as I'd seen my father enact Valir in the Bard's greatest play. "One thing only, then, I beg of you. Let us have more than just His Own for audience. If you want to see how we'd play this to common folk, then let us play to common folk. If you dislike either our playing or their reaction, then you have your answer and we'll answer for it. If we move the audience as you hope, then we'll move on to the next town." I inhaled slowly as if forcing the air past a great block in my chest. "Playing your play," I finished, looking up at him.

I waited. I had scarce hope he would grant me even this small request. He looked at me, and then looked off at Fachtnel arguing with Eimhen over some small matter (they argued thus constantly). Then Neacal turned his attention back to me.

"Agreed, Player. Tell Eimhen and tell it in the common room. Whatsoever crowd gathers tomorrow at the midday you will play to. They, along with His Own here in Beldann, will decide if you are a meet tool for the Prophet's purpose."

I hoped for rain, such chilling and torrential rain that we'd be forced to cancel our performance. Perhaps I wished as well for lightning or a sweeping tempest, although I couldn't have said were it me or Neacal I wished into oblivion. As it was, the day dawned blue and clear, the warmest day so far this season. Our play would be outside where the maximum number would see our shame, see once-proud players brought to heel.

We rolled the wagon out in the late morning and began to set up, dropping the right side down to create the stage and opening the front and back to create wings from which we might make entrances and exits. The wagon's roof became the arch under which we performed while the left side became the backdrop for our scenes, somberly painted as a new-shorn field after harvest, the season in which the play was set. All this happened with a strange solemnity, with none of my players joking or laughing. Normally, lines of the new play would be tossed back and forth, proclaimed with odd inflections and rhythms, and it was through this that I would understand that my men knew the play well enough to make sport of it. With this silence, I knew not what to expect.

By the time we finished preparing the wagon, a good sized crowd had gathered. I didn't know whether to be pleased or not for all that I had requested our audience be expanded from simply His Own. Of course, at least two hands of His Own attended as well, as grim a flock of crows as I've ever seen. While most of the town came to treat our presence here and this play as a holiday of sorts, the black-cloaked righteous glowered at us as if ready to take us into custody simply on principle. Eimhen and his boys wandered through the gathering crowd, chatting and laughing (and avoiding His Own), selling oat cakes and the Clavan beer.

Neacal and Fachtnel came into the yard from the common room. After their breakfast, I suppose. Fachtnel glanced at the gathering group, his eyes going wide and his grizzled eyebrows arching upwards as if silver moths in flight. He tugged at Neacal's arm and whispered an urgent message into his ear. For his part, the leader of His Own glanced about the courtyard in a most casual way and he laughed at Fachtnel's words. Then Neacal's gaze met mine and he smiled his mocking smile, bowing his head in a most ironic fashion before roughly shaking Fachtnel's hand from his arm. He turned, then, and re-entered the inn.

When next I looked up from my work, I found Neacal directing two of Eimhen's boys in placing one of the common room benches directly in front of the stage, nudging aside several men who already stood in that spot. Neacal paid no attention to the glares this earned him but Fachtnel stared at those who grumbled against His Own taking precedence over common folk, no doubt making a mental mark against their names.

They sat themselves on the bench and looked up at us on our cart. "When do you begin, Player? I'd be gone before nightfall," Neacal asked. I noted with some chagrin that the groundlings flowed wide around the bench whereon His Own sat, only to find themselves washing against the rocks of the rest of His Own standing by the walls of the courtyard.

"It's not yet midday, Goodman. We'll begin in good time." I turned back to my preparations.

"See that in time you finish well," Neacal sallied, "for the matter you play is of great import."

I was not in the mood for word games. The ham-fisted pounding of the doggerel still rankled my senses, leaving nothing for clever ripostes. "That's for you to say, Goodman."

"Is it?" He laughed.

Beathen, as Chorus, walked upon the stage, the backdrop being a bright sun on stage left overlooking a field in the pale blush of spring. Dressed simply in an archaic style of robe, Beathen presented the matter best he could. Within a few lines, twitters broke out at the bad verse, but Beathen's somber delivery and the baleful glares of His Own crushed the humor right quick. Beathen's Chorus set up the matter well enough and he was joined on stage by Sionn and Oean. A quick change while screened by the other two provided Beathen a chance to become one of the Townsfolk who then spoke amongst themselves – for nearly the rest of the act – about the portents that heralded a golden age of Anacarra. We'd decided to have much movement and as many different levels of excitement as possible to deliver the lines Neacal had given us. I'd even had Oean create some music so that one rather long speech of Beathen's became a hymn. It lent some action to an act that otherwise had nothing but dialog.

The first act ended with the news of the death of the old Anaric and the ascension of Nabryhtric. Beathen proclaimed the words in such an excited tone that it ran perilously close to mockery. That he managed to run along that edge without falling afoul of that trap is testament to his great skill.

I led off the second act. The backdrop had changed to one of a field at full growth and the sun at its height. I strode to the center of the stage, braced my staff against the boards, my mind full of the bad verse I was to speak.

Upon my head the God has set
A crown of gold and jewels
Within my heart I feel His debt
To those whom I will rule
To guide them well is my desire
To the God I'll them bring
I'll cleanse An'cara in the fires
A praise to the God I sing

Camran, as Priest, joined me on stage after that. We'd dusted his beard again and he walked with a deliberate pace and regal bearing, the long archaic robe flowing behind him. I'd taken liberties with the script at this point. The scenes as Neacal had written them for this act existed as discrete and wholly disconnected elements. Nothing joined them together save as examples of the greatness of Nabryhtric as Anaric. As written, my character would have finished a scene with the Priest only to turn to the other wing and commence a conversation with an Official. Finish that, turn again, and have a scene with the next Official. I hadn't changed a line or a character, but I had moved many entrances and exits. A simple thing, to have characters enter together, vie for attention from the great and Divine Anaric, and have their scenes in their time. It allowed for those on stage to react to what others were saying, giving a clue to the

275

audiences. We hadn't heard any sniggers since the opening scene but I hadn't dared look to judge reactions.

For all my doubts, the act went well. Camran's Priest praised the great works to the God Nabryhtric was creating, Oean's Good Official nodding while Sionn's Corrupt Official scowled. Then the Good Official could (silently) remonstrate against the bad advice that Sionn's Corrupt Official gave, and so on. The dance the four of us wove gave some structure to the disjointed scenes and brought the flow of the argument together in one direction.

I chanced, then, to look out over the audience. I saw rapt attention, mostly. Some puzzlement, some frowns, but mostly engagement with our actions on the stage. Neacal's expression held great self-satisfaction while Fachtnel's habitual scowl had not much abated. Then, my cue came again and I spoke the words all-too-present in my mind.

The final act came. A backdrop of new-shorn field and the sun low, to stage right. I'd had the sun painted as if it were about to set. Placed as it was, none saw the slit cut in the center of the sun, or if they did, no one would remark upon the bit of stage craft. After all of the dialog of the previous two acts, now it seemed that Neacal had thought to make of this an action play. I would not have called Neacal unsubtle, but in this act he left nothing to chance. Fistfights amongst the Townsfolk. Swordplay between the Officials. Even the Priest and Nabryhtric nearly come to blows (Neacal may have intended Nabryhtric to kill the Priest for the lines suggested that very thing. I had them take the argument off stage and Nabryhtric enter again by himself. Let any draw their own conclusions, but I'd not be part to such blasphemy).

The final scene opened on a stage strewn with bodies: Camran took Beathen's place as one of the Townsfolk while Sionn and Oean had two death scenes each, with much red cloth draped across their prone bodies. Standing amidst the carnage, my Nabryhtric and Beathen's Chorus gave a final speech each. I moved from stage left to right as I spoke my lines, ending to kneel in front of the low sun. Beathen's strong voice from the other side of the stage stole the attention from me, and I slipped through the slit in the Sun backdrop. I heard gasps when Beathen spoke his lines and pointed to where I'd been:

Taken up from this place, Anaric
Divine, to us someday
He will return. Bold Nabryhtric
His heir to us will say:
Remove all stain and cleanse our land
Of blight and harm and woe
This the God our fealty demands.
We end now this our show.

For good or ill, the thing was done.

After the performance, I had Barrol return to the cart and sent Beathen, Oean, and Camran out to pass the hat. Fachtnel tried to stop them. "You will *not* take gratuities for praising the Lonely God! How dare you think to use the God and the Prophet for your own selfish gain?"

"If we don't eat, we'll not play your play," Oean said.

"Let them be, Fachtnel," Neacal said. "If the good folk of Beldann wish to show their appreciation for the performance, all the better."

When Neacal motioned me to join him, my stomach knotted and I could hardly pull a full breath into my lungs. I masked my fear as I do my stage fright, striding to his side as if every confidence strode with me. That he allowed my players to collect our due seemed promising. What need we of coins if we're to be arrested? "Do you think your performance to be sufficient, Dughal?"

I shook my head, forcing the snarl to stay behind my teeth. "No, Goodman. I do not."

He turned to me, his eyebrows raised. "No?"

"No. Indeed, I think our performance surpassed 'sufficient' as a mule is surpassed by a racehorse. You can have no complaint of us, for no one could have done better to present the matter we were given in such flattering light."

"Can't I? You sound very sure of yourself."

"I know my craft. Do you?"

He laughed, reaching out to clasp my shoulder in a comradely grip and I stood statue still as if a poisonous spider crawled upon my cloak. "There are many kinds of performers, Dughal, and many types of performances. You and yours are but one. Think you that priests and the God's Own do not know how to perform for an audience?" Suiting action to words, Neacal took my arm and walked us around the courtyard as if we were the closest of friends. Throughout his next speech, his mien never changed from hearty hail-fellow-well-met. And yet, his grip brought him close to me and he pitched his tenor voice low so that even those milling about might not hear what he said. "Today you've earned your lives, Dughal. Make no mistake, you'll have to continue earning them every day you walk the fields of Bainellen, even as you earn your bread."

I nearly bowed to him in appreciation of his performance, even as I shuddered at the cruelty of his words. He stopped walking and perforce, I stopped too. He faced me and smiled a benevolent smile, much as a priest might look when bestowing his blessing after the twilight service. And with such an expression upon his face, Neacal's words were far from benevolent. "From now until you present yourselves to the First who – the lonely God willing – be the Prophet himself, you'll play this play in every hamlet, town, and city – yea even the smallest crossroads inn. If I hear that you've shirked this sacred duty – even once – I'll have His Own beat you and your players, burn your wagon and all that you have, shackle you, and drag you to Kairclavan to face the Prophet. His wrath is a glory to behold, Dughal, but one I very much doubt you'd survive."

I opened my mouth to haggle with him, to argue against the implicit instruction that we play nothing else, nor tell tales, nor sing, nor pass along news as is our duty and our right. But Camran arrived then, carrying two bags, jingling with coin.

"We were well received, Dughal," he said, holding up the bags.

"Were you?" Neacal's dark eyes grew wide and then narrowed in calculation. He snatched one of the bags from Camran's hand. "As playwright, I'll take my fee as well. See to it that you set aside such a portion of each day's take and donate it to the local clavan. Tell them it is for me and I will hear of it." He turned away, secreting the bag beneath his cloak. "You best be on your way, Dughal. A farmer plows his fields by daylight, you know."

With that he turned and walked away, leaving me dumbstruck in outraged fury. My shoulders tensed and I wished my staff were to hand. I turned slowly to Camran and noticed a faint glimmer of amusement. "You laugh? Do you know how much that villain took from us?"

"Yes, Dughal. To the penny: two silver pieces, fifteen coppers, and love notes from Sionn to a mistress in Maukellen province." Camran chuckled at my expression. "Do close your mouth, Dughal. You look like one of the less bright His Own."

I snapped my mouth shut. The angry tension that in my chest whooshed out of me with what very nearly became a laugh. It wouldn't do to sound pleased when His Own could hear. "Come," I said. "Let us to the cart, get it loaded and on our way. I would hear this story of yours."

"Would you?" Camran asked, and laughed again as I growled at him.

Eimhen refunded to us the cost of our lodgings over the last few days and refused to change his mind, folding his arms very resolutely above his generous middle. "I follow the old ways and never have

Players paid a fee at my inn when they do their duty, performing for my guests and telling the news of the realm." He shook his bald head. "No, you've done what you're Sealed to do, and so do I." With that handful of silver and the greater part of our take from the performance, we came near to having what we had after Lechsede. We've lost some days of performing but at least we can continue to present a play. *Such as it is.*

"I would give you something to fortify you on the road." As my host brought a pitcher of beer with him, I realized he'd waited until Neacal was away to seek me out for some private conversation. He smiled as he poured me a mug. What a pleasant surprise it was to see a thick white head foam up above the rim of the glass.

"By the Bargain, I'll say you'll find this a bit more to your liking." His dark eyes twinkled with mischief. "Not all grain goes to the Clavs, despite their insistence on tithes and duty."

I drank deep and sighed in real pleasure. A single sip did much to improve my mood. "This is fine indeed. While I see the benefit of the Prophet's scheme to cure hunger and thirst, the fruit of such efforts seems ... bitter."

"Indeed, that's the truth of it. A wonder it is, for the Clavs had long done some of the best brewing in the area. But in order to ship the barrels further than before, more and more bittering goes into the beer."

He sighed and drank deep of his own ale and I matched him, savoring the sweet and creamy draft. After a few moments of enjoying our beer in silence, he set his mug down and folded his hands on the table. *Ah, now we come to it.*

"You travel south? To Kairclavan?" he asked.

"Well, at least as far as Kairill. I'm not convinced that the seat of the Prophet who instructs His Own is the best destination for Players."

The innkeeper shook his head in agreement. I continued: "This is our year to renew our Seal and so we will travel the whole of

Bainellen before we'll take the southernmost route around the crags and back up north to the capitol. We should arrive just before the new First among Five is chosen at the next equinox."

"If you'll listen," he told me, "I've some words of advice. Cross over the crag before you reach Kairill and forsake the rest of Bainellen. In a season's time the Prophet hopes to make himself Aric of this province. Should he succeed, he'll then seek to become First, claiming that the God demands it. Do you take my meaning?"

I did. To fill the dropping sense of my belly I drank more of the fine ale. *It didn't help.* I now understood Neacal's certainty and his insistence that we play his *Heir.* Amassing the fee for the Seal wasn't the only impediment to our continuation. Cleirach the Prophet could very well deny our application no matter how much gold we acquired.

"You grow pale, dear histrion. I see you understand. Don't tarry in Bainellen. It's possible, of course, that the Prophet will neither gain the position of Aric, let alone First. However—"

"Howsoever it may be that he succeed in both and in so doing, spell the end of the Players."

He nodded. "And perhaps, much else."

I drank down my cup and rejoined my men who had completed our packing and the wagon's walls were upright and locked. Each took his place: Camran atop to drive, Oean on the right side and I on the left. Barrol walked behind the cart with Sionn on the left and Beathen on the right. Unlike our entrance into Beldann, we wore our new colors, played our flutes and pipes, juggled and tumbled. Those gathered to see us off were a motley bunch: we were cheered and jeered both as we left. I felt resigned that we'd meet such mixed reactions throughout Bainellen province for as long as we should play here.

Once we were well away from Beldann I called my men around me. I looked to Barrol: "Tell what you heard as you wandered among the groundlings."

He nodded and began his tale. "It surprised me, the size of the crowd, for we'd given hardly any notice. I suppose, it were no secret we were at the inn, but even so, the groundlings seemed awful glad to have entertainment."

"No doubt they were," Sionn said, "if Fachtnel denied any and all players and entertainments from them."

"You have the right of it." Barrol nodded with such vigor that his blond hair swirled about. "When His Own brought the bench out and nudged aside those who'd stood there for some while, I heard grumbling from the groundlings."

I hid a smile at his word play. "What did they say, boy?"

"They said," (and here his voice took on the inflection and patterns of a much older man with such skill I had no doubt I could pick out the man by this speech should I ever hear him speak) "'Lookit that, will ye Fonn! Them black cloaks takes the best spots, the best o' the beer, an' the best cuts of the kine for the'selves. And what does that leave us, I ask you?' And his companion said: 'Hush, yi big oaf. Them 'ill take yer tongue too, should they catch ye back talking.'"

"So," Oean said with a note of satisfaction. "His Own are not so well loved as all that."

"Most folks want to live their lives as they will, taking what comforts they can," Beathen suggested. And then his words became bittered with personal experience. "His Own offer little more than condemnation for trying to find pleasure while we live, endeavoring instead to teach us that hardship is virtue and struggle noble. Should we but follow their lead, of course."

"Even as they 'takes the best spots, the best o' the beer, an' the best cuts of the kine for the'selves.'" Sionn's voice echoed the cadences Barrol had given the words. "Strange sort of struggle, that."

Barrol nodded, eager to continue his tale. "Once the play began, there were some who groused at the bad versifying. There were some confused by the matter, for it sounded not at all like the history they'd learned. A bare handful realized right away what we were about and found the matter uplifting." Here his enthusiasm for his craft, and us his fellows, could no longer be contained. "But your performances were most excellent! As the play moved from scene to scene, the grousing stopped and people listened. Not all liked what they heard but they all seemed to love the hearing of it and many were moved by the performance." Here he stopped and looked down for a moment. "I expect one or two will even join His Own, given how well you played the Prophet, Dughal, for none were so confused or ill-learned that they didn't know who you were supposed to be."

"So well as that?" Despair mixed with pride in my heart. "Thank you, Barrol. I'll tell you what passed between me and Neacal, then." I proceeded to do so, that we were instructed to present this play at ever town and inn we stopped at.

"But did he say we could play nothing else?" Oean asked.

"No, he did not," I answered. "I was about to ask when Camran arrived with the day's take."

"And well I did when I did, Dughal." Camran cleared his throat. "No use in asking for permission from one such as him. He'd delight in the denying of it. As he didn't expressly forbid it, then I say we play his play and then do as we're asked to do by those in the towns and inns." Camran smiled, his beard spreading wide and the grin lighting his eyes, before he placed a very affected solemnity upon his visage. "It is, after all, our duty."

"So it is!" I laughed at his ability to navigate the strictures placed upon us. "But tell me, what happened when Neacal took one of the sacks." I heard exclamations, for not all had realized that Neacal had cut into our take.

Camran shrugged. "Simplest thing in the world, Dughal. I'm surprised you don't remember. About a score of years ago, Bardeelin played Varranellen and one carrinanen insisted that all fees paid to us must be shared with him. As a tax, you know."

To tax Players was forbidden, but some carrinanen lived far enough from any other authority that they ruled as they would.

Camran continued: "Fortin saw that we had two choices, either leave and play no more or deal with him in such a way as to leave him unable to complain, but not much richer. When I heard Neacal chide Fachtnel to let us pass the hat, I saw in him a man similar to the landholder in Varranellen. So, I did what your father did."

"I remember the landowner, but not the trick."

Camran smiled. "Say rather, you remember the landowner's daughter, for I believe you were far more focused on her than on your trade."

The others laughed at my expense, and I felt my face turn red. "I was but a few years older than Barrol here...! Ach, never mind," I growled amidst the teasing. "What did Fortin do?"

"He divided the take into three sacks, leaving the one with the bulk of our coin behind in the cart. The other two he added just enough coins to tinkle ever so musically and a bit of paper to fill things out." He turned to Sionn. "I thank you again for the use of your verses. I'm sure Neacal will profit from them most excellently."

"It was my pleasure. As he seemed to delight so in trite doggerel, I thought mine own verses of love to Benvi would inspire him."

"Surely," Oean said. "Inspire him to truly awful depths. Those poems caused me pain to read!" He stood proud, hand upon his chest and declaimed:

Benvi, with hair of black and teeth of white
Pray my love be with me tonight.
My love for you no bonds can contain
Meet me in the shed, it just may rain.

Sionn laughed, as did we all, and clapped Oean on the back. "Indeed. A grand gift to His Own, don't you think?"

Camran continued: "Indeed, the sacks sang with some bits of coin and bulged with verse. We might have come off worse if'n Neacal thought to count or ask for a specific percentage, but I thought in this he may act impulsively. You may have noticed, Dughal, but as I presented the sacks, one of them I held out just a bit in front of the other. True to my estimation, that was the sack he took. With the poem 'On My Ladie's Hair' as an especial gift."

We laughed and I turned to Sionn. "Be sure to include a verse of your own making in each of our payments to Neacal. For we are to offer a 'donation' to the local temple or clavan, in Neacal's name, of each day's take. Since he seemed so eager for the portion he snatched from Camran, I think that should be the amount of each offering, don't you?"

Oean laughed. "He is over paid!"

"Do we go to Kairclavan, Dughal?" Beathen asked.

"No! Bringing *Nabryhtric's Heir* to Kairclavan would be taking an awful chance. Despite Neacal wrote it himself, I've no doubts that some within the walls of that monastery would take offense simply because Players played it. "

"I hear the city has straggled out beyond its original walls, ungainly as a colt and just as young," Beathen said. "Those drawn to such a place are no doubt among the most fanatical."

I shuddered. "An entire city of Fachtnels and Firchars."

Sionn spoke up. "We could pass west, through the Falcon's Way and take ourselves to Aelfallen Province early. Leave Bainellen and *that play* altogether and seek a climate more welcoming to Players."

Camran shook his head. "We're pressed between the rock of time and the steel of funds, Dughal. We'd have to trek west through the nearly-empty Way with little chance to earn anything towards our Seal for many days. I suggest we head east, towards the sea. The plains between Kairclavan and the sea grow towns as easily as they grow wheat, giving us many opportunities to pass the hat, even offering naught but Neacal's offal. Swing east and then follow the seacoast. If time grows tight, we could use the Cougar Way through the old eknos lands in the south." He paused, his eyes far distant. "But no, I don't think we'd become so desperate as that. We'd have plenty of time to stay in lowlander territory all the way to Bierncarra."

I nodded. "Sionn, your advice is good and even our last host suggested it to me before we left. But there'll be many Players moving south through Aelfallen to be in Bierncarra before the Equinox. I'm feeling that the people may be sated ere we present our feast." I shook my head. "I don't much like either choice, it come to that. I'm not confident that our welcome will improve in Bainellen no matter what we play but I don't want to lose good Growing season days wandering through the Way. We're closer to the bustling towns of the seacoast here and the bigger cities may hold out hope that the grip of His Own is less. I agree with Camran. We'll stay within Bainellen for now. We'll move more to the east, away from Kairclavan." I smiled. "Camran! What say you we pay a visit to your niece in Kairill?"

We stopped in towns early enough in the evenings so that the spectacle of our entrance could be seen by the most people that they might talk about us that night. We ate in the common rooms of whatever inn had space for us, telling the tales and singing the songs as was asked of us (we had learned better than to offer anything else, here where His Own flocked so thickly). We ate and drank and slept in the inns according to ancient custom and even took such gratuities as those who listened saw fit to offer us. Neacal saw not one copper of that money.

By midmorn the day following our entrance into a town, whatever crowd had gathered would see us perform the play as we'd been told to do. We settled our two silver pieces, fifteen coppers, and Sionn's love notes upon local His Own or the nearest clavan whenever we played with strict words of caution but that it be opened by Neacal alone. But not one penny more would I give to that black-hearted wolf. I had no doubt that Neacal would react poorly to the joke for he seemed to have been shriven of a sense of humor. In truth, sometimes the amount we paid him equaled nearly half of our take for that day. But my contemplation on Neacal's fit of pique when he encountered bag after bag of small coins and meager verse made the expense worth more than gold.

There came days when I no longer saw her face, that unnamed woman of eknos dead in the woods. Days where I ignored troubles of the wider world and thought only of mine own: our one cart and the stretch of road we trod upon, our small troubles carried along on our backs. Until the larger troubles of the world intruded themselves upon us again, of course.

We were but a day out of Kairill, trudging along one such a stretch of road, when we heard the pounding of horses, many of them, riding up from the south, from the direction of Kairclavan. We hurried to move our ungainly wagon to the side of the road before a flock of His Own rode past us, spraying us with clods of dirt. We shared looks, us players, but nothing much was said. We moved back onto the road and continued on our way.

Late that afternoon we again heard horses and some shouts, but this time they came from behind us. Again we moved off of the road to our right, for those so moving would take it ill to find as large a wagon as ours blocking their way. Again, a flock of black clad His Own gained fast upon us but this time they escorted two tall and swaying wagons, such as a farmer bringing in hay from the fields might use. The sides of both carts consisted of tall staves placed less than a foot apart, but instead of straw these wagons carried a crop of people.

Mostly women we saw, but not all. Some of the captives clutched hard at the staves, their expressions open with terror and despair. Some captives huddled together, clutching shreds of clothing around themselves along with the remains of their modesty. The clothing was torn, tattered, open to expose breast and bruise and dried blood. Some captives lay insensate upon the bed of the wagon, jolted and jostled by every rut the road offered up, every bump bringing piteous moans and sharp cries. I gasped to see them, to see their abused state, to be given the proof (as if such were still needed) of the truth of the unnamed uplander's words. My guts clenched and I hefted my staff and began to step forward, and stopped as if a wall had grown between me and the carts.

Two hands of the captives were plainly eknos and mostly women: once-shaved heads now covered in stubble or else long graying braids knotted about with leather and beading. But these people stood up straight, unbowed by their own set of bruises, the mottling of dried blood did nothing to reduce the sheen of their pride. Or their hate. More than one fixed her eyes upon me and mine as we stood by, just stood there, watching the carts with their human cargo rattling and swaying into the distance.

Gah, their anger and justifiable hate cut me. My knees grew weak as if I should fall down and beg forgiveness. I nearly dropped the staff in my hand, clutching at my heart in guilt and pity, my share of their anger at their abuse not even one tenth of their own.

A snap and a cry stole my attention from their wagons to mine own. Sionn had fallen to the ground, a hand to his face, while above him one of His Own sat his horse, his riding crop still raised. I rushed to Sionn's aid, my staff in hand. I'd sweep that smug villain from his horse, should he swing again. Beathen, too, came up and I called to the others to stand their places. As I approached the horse, the black cloak looked to me and seemed to realize we would not be easily cowed.

"Get back, Player," he spat at me, although it was he who sidled his horse some feet from where Sionn lay, putting distance between us. "As I reminded your catamite there, you've seen nothing today. Don't interfere and it'll go better for you."

Beathen knelt next to Sionn while I moved between them and the rider. "As you say, *Goodman*," I said, (using the same degree of scorn that Neacal had put into the word 'learnéd'). "Who are we to interfere with such a holy mission as yours? Tell me, though, if you would spare the time: wherein the scrolls of the lonely God will I find His adjuration that His Own might kidnap, torture, and rape? I don't think I've heard those verses from the priests."

I'd meant to use my words to cut him, to show him his shame. Instead, he laughed at me, a bit too loudly, his eyes wide in his flushed face. "Shrewd, Player. But all know that Players are liars and clannish and heretics who hate the God. Say what you will. No one will heed you." He turned his horse and galloped away from us, to catch up with his fellows.

Beathen had helped Sionn to his feet, and as the last of His Own had ridden out of sight, the rest of the Players left their positions to gather around our comrade.

"What, by the God of Sheaves, was that?" Barrol demanded. I feared I knew the answer even before Oean supplied it.

"Don't you remember what the Hunter had said before she died?" Oean asked. "'We are starved and beaten,' she said, 'forced to lie beneath men who beat us before they enter our bodies and curse us even as they cast their seed within us.' These must be those who have been taken, one such 'prisoner' that Neacal warned us about."

"Taken and raped repeatedly by the most righteous His Own." I gagged at such a thought.

"To what purpose?" Camran asked, his face pale as he struggled for understanding. "Hate?"

"Two hands," Beathen said. "Remember? She had said two hands of eknos had been taken. How many did you see in those wagons? I'd say twice two hands at least!"

"Did you note?" Camran asked. "Not all within were eknos."

"I saw!" Barrol cried. "The ones who stared ahead or who lay in the bottom of the wagon, they had once been dressed in clothing any woman would wear. And they had long hair."

"We must go after them, Dughal," Sionn argued. He pulled free from Beathen's helping hands and faced me. The welt from the riding crop marred Sionn's cheek, rising red and angry. "We must free those captives. No matter what you think of those of the uplands, this newest atrocity can't stand! That," he shouted, pointing to the cloud of dust drifting away ahead of us, "is not right!"

"No," I agreed, even though my heart beat in fear. "*That* is wrong and most foul."

"But what will we do?" Barrol asked, looking from one to the other of us and then down the road. Nearly a man's height but still a boy's concept of fairness.

"You fools," Camran said. "Dughal said it. 'Who are we to interfere?'"

"I didn't mean...!" I stopped, lowered my voice in painful realization. "No, what I said in anger is the simple, awful truth. We're but six of us, unmounted and unarmed. What *can* we do?" I looked up, into the eyes of each of my men in turn. My guts twisted within me with fear and anger both, but outrage at what I'd just witnessed strongest of all. "Tell me that, tell me what *we* can do, and by the lonely God we'll do it!"

Sionn opened his mouth to speak, but then an anguished astonishment arose in his eyes and he closed it again. He saw the way of it. Cursing, he turned and stomped off the road. Beathen looked as sick as I felt, Barrol looked bewildered. Oean stood next to the rail of the wagon conversing with Camran. When Camran glanced at me I looked him a question. He simply shook his head and faced down the road, towards that dwindling dust cloud.

I gave them all a few minutes, myself not the least. At last I motioned to Camran who clicked to the horses and started them on their way.

Twenty-One

Epistle the Third

10ʰ Aililnaian, In Kairill

To Cleirach durMiach, Prophet and Voice of the Lonely God, and my great good Friend, I send you both my Greetings and greetings from the fellowship of His Own, in the town of Kairill.

All is in readiness. Tomorrow, at the height of His glory, Bainellen shall see the Power of the only God and the Wisdom of you, His Prophet. Justice and Mercy will be done, turning the multitudes to His worship.

Yours, in the Peace and Love of the God of the Plow,

Neacal durCleirach

Twenty-Two

Rhia

For every death, a life. For every life, a death. For eknos must not over run the Uplands as the sowers do the Low, but must be as one among the many of My creatures.

- Ealdranna Proverb

The White Eagle ekma allowed Niall to accompany me on my journey from the ekarra to the edges of the lowlands once he promised he wouldn't leave the safety of the woods: Fiona would not risk any of her own. "If Na wants us, She can Call on us easily enough." Together we loped east, following the flow of the Bainrill towards the edge of the uplander territory. We stood for a few moments at the edge of the crags, watching the small stream tumble hundreds of feet down to the lowlands. I took Niall's hand in mine and spent a moment, just a small moment, to enjoy the beauty of the uplands. We kissed. Then I let go of his hand, turned away, and began traveling again.

We couldn't follow the stream in it's path to the lowlands, we had to follow our own. Our course took us north a bit, and then east, following a gentler path down the steep side of the crags towards the lowlands. When the brush became thick and tangled, when thorny bushes prevailed and paths disappeared, I knew we'd entered the briarwood. Even so, Niall traveled with me, pushing at the edges of his ekma's command. He stayed within the wooded lands but we were well into that space that was no longer uplands and not quite lowlands.

I said good bye to Niall then. He was willing to defy his ekma, but I told him no. I stopped his protests with a kiss, followed by another. We shared pleasure once more. I took him with a desperate passion, pulling him into me as if I sought to take the uplands with me.

And after we had eaten our evening meal, I kissed him deeply one more time and turned away. Just as when I had crossed the old Falcon territory, I thought it best to travel by night, dashing across the fields by the light of the waning moon. Just below the crags and for some acres, I ran through a natural prairie, land reclaimed from sowers' fields years before, teeming with a variety of grasses and scrub and flowers just coming to life with the start of the Gathering season.

By morning the next day, I decided to cover the last few miles in ever-brightening daylight. I feared discovery, yes, but I feared blundering through some strange sower city in the dark more. The land sloped away from me so that I ran downhill, the light from the morning sun winking off the tumbling river, reappeared off to my right. I ran eastward across the eradicated prairie, turned into exposed black dirt speckled with the shoots of all the same plant, stride after stride of sameness.

Soon enough, I knew I'd intercept the stream – nay, now a river – and approach the city from the west, for the river formed the town's southeastern limits. The Bainrill had taken a circuitous route from where we'd left it tumbling off the crag: through the foothills for several miles before flowing into the Prophet's city of Kairclavan, and then wandering again through the lower hills, oftentimes turning north or south as the slope of the land dictated during it's journey towards the sea far to the east. I paused to catch my breath from a vantage point a mile or more distant and some several hundred feet above the town. This must be the same spot where Dáiri watched the city from and I wondered if the ekma her mother knew just how close her daughter approached Kairill.

My first sight of a sower city caught my breath in my throat. *Dearest Na, what are you asking of me?* I closed my eyes and crouched down upon the ground, letting the city fall out of view. Just for a moment, just until my heart stilled and my breath resumed.

When I finally stood up to look again, I managed a semblance of calm. Pendal had told me what he could of the layout of the town, for in his younger years he'd journeyed often into the lowlands. Unfortunately, it took me some time to match his description to what I saw before me. What he had described fell short by half and I realized why Dáiri's description and his had differed. The city had grown. When I spotted the wall he'd told me surrounded the place, I counted myself lucky that the original town looked much as he had described it. Unfortunately, the center lay near to a mile from where the last of the houses and buildings sprang up.

In the original section of the town – the part that Pendal had described to me – roads radiated out from a center point nearest the river like spokes on one of their wagons. Several spots of green marked where buildings gave way to something growing, but from such a distance I couldn't tell what. Two landmarks Pendal told me to seek: one he called an "amphitheater," a place where a great many people might gather to hear a special sort of story told, called a play. From his description, the place sounded much like my ekarra back home, with the central space at the bottom where the elders presided and the ranks of fires stretching up the hillside. And there it lay, just north of the center of the old town, and I marked it in my memory.

The other landmark he had called an "inn" and it provided yet another place where sowers gathered to hear stories and music and to eat, and where travelers might rest. Less obvious than the amphitheater, for it was just a larger building amongst many other buildings. But he'd told me it would be west and south of the amphitheater, so I believe I found it as well. With that as my destination, I approached Kairill.

Pendal had also told me something of what to expect from the sowers themselves, but his knowledge did not reassure me much. My dread of the lowlands sat like a rock in my belly and it grew more, not less, the closer I got to the sprawling place before me. Empty fields, stripped of trees and brush and covered in the merest blush of green from whatever plant the sowers had seeded there, described most of the land surrounding Kairill. However, not all land had yet been cleared. One of their ubiquitous fieldstone walls delineated cleared land from that left to grow wild, and I scurried from shadow to shadow, aware of how bright the sun shown upon my face. At this rate, I should indeed wait for dark to cover my entrance to the town, but the thought of going blind into the wolf's den pressed me to continue.

I ducked below the wall when I heard a commotion to my left. A family exited their home, father and mother and two children, all laughing and happy and oblivious to the Hunter hiding nearby with a knife in her hand. I chanced to peek above the wall, needing to know if they'd seen me and would give the alarm. But no. After picking up a bundle left by their back door, the family turned and went around the house and away from me. I relaxed for a moment until I realized that the danger had not passed. Pendal had reminded me that my speech would set me apart from the sowers and so I'd resolved not to speak if possible or else, speak only a little. The words used by Anacarrans – eknos and sower both – were the same for the most part, but inflection and tone were not. Best to keep quiet.

But seeing the clothing on the family showed me my true danger. The woman and girl wore the most ridiculous outfits: cumbersome and bulky tunics that fell to their ankles and swirled around their legs as they walked. Their sleeves draped so low and full I could smuggle one of their sheep within so much cloth! The clothing must be hot, awkward to move in, with quick movement impossible. The tunics of the man and boy were shorter, coming to about mid-thigh and they wore leggings even in this mild weather. Shoes, too, despite the smoothness of the streets.

No matter. If I were to move out from the shadows in search of my prey I must blend in with my surroundings. My dark leather tunic, cut short to just the tops of my legs and sleeveless, gave me great movement and little problem passing through the well maintained woodlands of my home. Here it marked me as much as torch on a dark night. I was nearly of a size with the boy in that family and hidden within that mass of cloth no one would notice my small breasts or slim hips. Since I had no desire – nay, nor saw no need – to wear the bulky and cumbersome clothing of a lowland woman, I resolved to steal myself some boy's clothing. As Na had dressed herself in the pelt of an otter so She could share in their play, so I'd borrow the "pelt" of one of these sowers.

I closed my eyes, took a deep breath, and bade my heart to slow its pounding. I hadn't slept since the day before and might not sleep again for many hours, but I couldn't let that interfere, not when I was so close! When I opened my eyes again, my breathing back to normal, I spied in the yard clothing hung from a tall pole. I realized that they used the pole instead of a bush to place their clothing out to dry in the heat of the day. *Huh. Ingenious. I should thank them for their naive trust.*

Creeping closer, I sidled right up to the wall that partitioned off this house from its neighbors (it seems that sowers very much like their walls). I heard nothing from the house itself, although the stones that made up the lower level would muffle most sounds from inside, so I couldn't be sure that the house was empty. Examining the suits of clothing hanging there, I saw what I wanted: a tunic, trews, and belt for the boy. No one approached the house from the street and no one moved passed the open windows inside.

I needed to capture this prey and be gone. A lane crossed on the far side of the house, beyond the twin to the wall I stood against and beyond that lay a copse. If I made it through the yard and across the lane without being seen, then the copse would give me a place to go to ground. I checked my pack and my weapons, making sure the straps were tight.

I sprang over the wall and dashed across the yard, pulling at the various bits of clothing as I ran past. Small wooden clips held the items onto lines of cord strung around the clothes tree, but these sprang free as I yanked. I leapt the far wall in a bound, hit the lane at speed, and was into the copse before a mourning dove had finished her song.

No pursuit. Or at least, no shouts, no cries of alarm. I shrugged out of my tunic and pulled the damp lowlander clothes on, wriggling about as quietly as I could. It felt as if the entire day would pass before I'd get the wet cloth up over my skin, shivering at the clammy feel of it. I stuffed my uplander tunic into my very obviously uplander pack, covered it and my bow with leaves and small branches I cut from the lower limbs of the trees. After some time, dressed as a lowlander boy, I stepped from the copse and walked directly up the lane towards the center of town.

I no doubt wore the manner of the lowlanders as awkwardly as I wore their clothes but to skulk and sneak would be to draw more attention to myself. The road ran straight as one of their walls, wide enough for a wagon but obviously not a main trail as few people walked the road with me. I watched those that did as closely as I could, adjusting my stride or the lift of my shoulders as I tried to mimic their movements, even adjusting the belt that went around my waist for I had tied it differently from the boys near me. The very uncertainty of it kept me pulled taut as a bowstring.

Even here the sowers planted crops. Some houses such as those I'd passed earlier each had their own garden. These didn't, but then I noticed a much larger common plot that seemed to have many families working in it. I turned away, onto a different lane that ran at right angles to the one I'd been on, walking away from the dozen lowlanders farming right where they lived.

Some while later I turned again towards the west, towards the heart of the town. This road carried much more traffic, but I was beyond knowing if that would help or hinder me. I walked as I'd seen their young boys do, hands clasping onto the rope knotted about my waist, elbows out, and eyes towards the ground, taking great plodding steps. Despite sharing the road with a hand or two of sowers, no one seemed to notice me and soon enough I spotted the city wall ahead. Like the others, I simply trudged through the open gates and entered the original city of Kairill.

The buildings clustered thickly on this side of the wall, the plots next to the houses smaller and strewn with lattices of withes leaning every which way. I took a breath and nearly choked: everything stank, from middens heaped with rotting meat and vegetables to cesspools aswirl with human waste. *How can they abide to live in such a noisome place all their days?* Noisome and noisy both, with sowers all around me. More people joined me on the road while some stood outside their homes calling to those inside, and still others idled beside their walls and talked over them to their neighbors. I breathed shallowly to avoid the worst of the stench and peered about me as intently as possible, relying on my eyes since my ears were near to overwhelmed by the din. I kept my head down but my eyes lifted up: seeming to watch the lane instead I watched all around me.

An odd rhythmic clopping noise caught my attention and I lifted my head to look about, avoiding the eyes of those with whom I shared the road. Some distance behind me, but catching up quickly, a hand of men sat atop giant beasts, larger than elk, with a great boles for chests and long flowing manes. Twas the clatter of the beasts' hooves upon the road that I'd heard. The men all dressed in the same fashion and I felt the blood drain from my face. Black tunics and trews, black cloaks and black hats. I'd found my prey. *Or had they found me?*

I faced forward and began to edge towards the side of the road, ready to run and leap the nearest fence should these men seek to give chase. Many on the road moved aside, some of them touching the brims of their hats in what I took to be a kind of greeting. Others, I noted, merely nodded, while a very few tried to ignore the raucous clamor of the men and their great beasts, which must be the horses I've only ever seen at a distance. As we proceeded into the town, more men passed by, also dressed in black and riding. The dampness of the clothes I wore hid the sweat that had sprung out upon my back and beneath my arms, but I strove to be as still within my movements as if I faced down a call of skittish moonhart.

More hoof beats behind me and more shouts from this group to those ahead. I chanced to lift my eyes from the ground as we crested a hill. A few score yards ahead of me I saw a great open space and it was filled with black cloaked men. I stumbled to a stop and a woman behind collided with me.

"Stupid boy!" She cuffed me on the back of the head. "Watch where you're going." She seemed to be waiting for some sort of response so I mumbled what I hoped sounded like an apology.

"Where are your parents, boy?"

I didn't like how closely she began to look at me. To my right, a road ran off at right angles to the road I was on. Seeing the great pack of wolves so close at hand made me realize I needed a better plan. *So many of them!* I mumbled my apology again and pointed down the road we crossed, making haste to get beyond her inquisitive eyes.

"Well, then, you get yourself home," she called out, and began walking again, muttering to the man beside her. I bent my head down, doing my best to look chastened even as I hurried away. Others joined me on this road but I didn't dare look at them. And then that distinctive clopping sounded behind me. I peered about me, looking for whatever could be used as a route for escape.

"You there!"

Twenty-Three

Rhia

Greet those you meet with gladness: men and women all, from the youngest toddling about on unsteady legs to the oldest leaning upon oaken staves. Greet even the beasts of the field, for the God's emissaries may be present.

- The Seventeenth Sacred Scroll, verses 5-6

A pair of women came up beside me even as the man shouted from down the street. They didn't seem to be hurrying at all and yet they matched my pace stride for stride, one on either side of me. Both of them carried baskets heaped with what must be foodstuffs, although it all looked strange. They chatted over me, as if I were part of the conversation. Before I'd gone a hand of paces in their company, I realized that their voices had been pitched to reach my ears and one of them spoke directly to me!

"Don't turn around, my young friend," said the older of the two women. She smiled at me in a most congenial way, lifting one hand to brush her long, mousy brown hair behind her ear. "It seems that you may have attracted the notice of His Own."

"Should we get involved, Catha?" the other woman asked. If Catha owned half again as many years as I, then this other one may have been only a few years younger, her hair falling long and loose to her waist in jet-black waves. But when she turned towards me, I nearly started to see the piercing blue of her eyes. Few in eknos had eyes that color. Twas very striking.

"You'd ask that of me?" Catha's voice was merry. "I've taken in strays for many years, Kyna."

"This one's a stray?"

Catha peered at me but I looked straight ahead, keeping an even pace despite every instinct screaming *Run!* My plans had all been based on not attracting attention!

"Oh, yes," Catha answered.

"I said, you there!" A man's voice called out from behind. Twas the oddest thing, to hear the voice come from above me when there were no trees around. Catha reached out a hand and touched my arm but I needed no warning. I wasn't about to turn around.

"Follow Kyna. The house is just there," Catha said. Her tone of voice suggested she was commenting on the chance for rain, so at odds with her words themselves. She turned around and faced the men who had ridden up behind us. Kyna took me companionably by the arm and steered me very decisively left towards a large, two story house.

"Yes, Goodman?" Catha called out. "What can I do for you?"

"Keep walking, you," Kyna said. I hadn't been about to stop and turn around. Perhaps she was warning me not to run.

"I wish to talk to all three of you," the man said and I heard a quicker clopping of hooves and suddenly he was between us and the house.

Kyna deftly maneuvered us around his horse and she lightly skipped up the steps, forcing me to stumble behind her. By the time we'd reached the porch, Catha was there as well, again casually placing herself between us and the man.

"This is your house?" the black cloak demanded.

"Yes, Goodman. It is." Catha handed me her basket and I was so startled I took it. She then folded her hands inside the voluminous sleeves of her dress and gazed at the man. From the height of the porch she stood nearly face to face with him as he sat astride his horse. I took in every detail of the magnificent beast. *Such a one would feed half the ekarra!*

The man spoke again. "Isn't this part of the inn?"

"No, Goodman. It isn't." Catha seemed intent on leaving it there, but the look on the black cloak's face told me he wouldn't be satisfied with such an answer. She sighed quietly and continued: "At one time, this was the guest house for the inn. My barn and the inn's barn share a wall, but the house and property are mine."

"You mean, your husband's," the man pressed.

"Oh, dear. Do I mumble? My father, once innkeeper, left it to me. I have no husband."

He frowned at that and several of his men snickered. "And yet, you have a pregnant daughter? Where is *her* husband? Or have you passed on your wanton ways to her?"

Beside me, Kyna went very still, scarcely seeming not even to breathe: a rabbit wary of the hawk. Catha laughed. "Oh, my, Goodman. You are very wide of the mark. This is my uncle's girl, come to stay with me for her laying in as I've some skill in that area. Her husband sent his youngest brother along to keep her company while he's away to Bierncarra. He's a merchant, you see."

"I see." Now his men snickered again, but at his discomfort rather than ours. He pulled himself up and cast a quelling glance to his men. "My apologies, then. I mistook the situation."

"Yes. Well." Catha waited. "Is that all, Goodman? Have His Own taken to interrogating every woman they meet on the roads of Kairill? Is that why there are so many of you in town?"

"Ah. No." He shifted a bit upon the back of the horse, twisting the leather straps in his hand. I wanted to look at his face, the faces of his men, but dared not. I contented myself with gazing at the big brown eyes of his horse. *No, not for meat. Look how lovely she is!* "His Own have gathered for another purpose entirely, mistress. I've come to ask of you the use of the barn. To stable our horses."

"Did my brother Breaslain send you?"

"Well. That is, no, but — "

"You mean, you mentioned it to him and he told you not to bother, didn't he?" I chanced to look up. The rider sat very still, his mouth set firm and I knew no other answer was forthcoming. "I'm sorry, Goodman. You may not stable your horses here. You'll have to pay Breaslain what he has asked for fodder and stabling."

His face turned red and he twisted the leather straps so tightly that the horse began to sidle and dance. Releasing his hold on the poor beast, the man reached up and touched his hat. "Sorry to have bothered you, mistress." He violently pulled the horse's head around and, with his men following suit, clattered off down the road back the way we had all come.

"Let's get inside before he decides to just take from me what I won't give him." Catha opened the door to her home for us.

"That is ever their way." Kyna's voice was quiet and I'm not sure she meant for me to hear it. The young woman was, indeed, pregnant. Her small frame made it more obvious than it might be, but I took her to be at most pregnant two seasons: no, not so much as two.

Kyna caught me looking. Catha had just shut the door, the three of us standing in an entry way between two large rooms, when Kyna turned on me, her startling blue eyes narrowed in anger.

"Yes! I'm pregnant! Aren't *you* going to ask who the father is?"

"No!" I replied, startled enough to speak. "Why would I ask that?"

Kyna dropped her basket and stepped back, her eyes gone wide and her hands gone to her belly. "Uplander!"

Twas my turn to back away, but Catha stood between me and the door. While there were openings into the walls to let in sunlight, they were covered over, glinting coldly. Glass I recognized, but I boggled for a moment to see so much of it and so clear. But what I couldn't see was where to run so I held my hands open, showing the two women I had no weapon in them.

"I'm a hunter of Moonhart eknos." I smiled at a fey impulse. "Pleased to meet you."

Both Kyna and I started to hear Catha laugh. "I'm Catha darElli and this is Kyna durTornan. Pleased to meet you, young hunter."

"Catha! What if he kills us? Or rapes us?"

The memory of Sleikin lying beaten and dying rose up within me. Then Gaunt's memory of being shackled to the floor while black-cloaked wolves did this thing called rape. I shook my head, hot with outrage: both that such things were done and that someone thought me capable of it.

My expression must have shown my thoughts, for Kyna took another step back, fear plain on her face, and I regretted my anger and indignation. Males have power in their world and while my voice had identified me as eknos, my clothes still concealed a female body. It was that power, coupled with the alien experience of eknos standing in their hallway, that they feared.

Having seen what men of the lowlands can do, I understood their fright and would not add to it. "No! Eknos don't rape," I promised. "I'm grateful to be off the streets so full of black cloaks. Killing would be a poor way to express my gratitude."

My words startled another laugh out of Catha and an uncertain smile from Kyna. "Indeed," Catha said. "Such actions would be the poorest of manners."

I bowed. Kyna, still uncertain, nevertheless, knelt down to return the items to her basket.

"Come," Catha said. "Let us sit." She ushered us into the room to the left of the door we'd just entered, a room filled with so many things new to me at the time: table and chairs; sink with water pump; even plates and mugs of ceramic, hard as stone. I watched closely as Kyna pulled out a chair and sat down and then I mimicked her actions at the other end of the table. Catha set her basket on the table next to Kyna's and then pulled out a chair between us and sat down as well, her hands folded on the table in front of her. "You are a stray indeed, Moonhart hunter. There lay some hundreds of miles betwixt Kairill and Moonhart territory."

"Aye, that I know well."

She smiled at me when my tale ended there. "You don't trust us, I see. I understand. You're far from home." She sat up and leaned forward, catching my eye. "Instead of me asking questions of you, perhaps you have questions of me."

"As much can be learned from questions as from answers."

Catha nodded her head, acceding my point. "Are you hungry? I set stew to simmering this morning before we left for the market. Would you break bread with us, hunter of Moonhart eknos?"

I nodded, scratched my chin, and happened to glance down at my hands. Creeping through copses did not leave me very clean. "I'd be honored to share your bread, but may I ask for some water to wash my hands?"

"Just your hands?" Kyna asked with a sniff.

Catha slowly stood, pushing her brown hair behind her ears and glared at the young woman. "Do you forget that you, too, are a guest in my home, Kyna?" I didn't understand what that implied, but surely Kyna did. She blanched, looked away, and then took in a deep breath.

In an unconscious echo of Catha's own movements, she stood up and pushed her black hair behind her ears and then raised up her eyes to meet mine. "I apologize for my words. I meant no ... I was out of line."

I nodded, uncertain as to what to do. I had no real plan and Catha seemed ready to give me food at the very least. Since my pack and all my food with it lay buried on the outskirts of town, I wouldn't pass up the opportunity. "I accept your apology. I present you much strangeness and I, I am out of my depth. I'd be grateful for any kindness."

Kyna nodded and began to turn away but I stopped her with a smile. "I took no offense, you see. I would indeed like to wash more than my hands, given the opportunity."

Catha tilted her head to the side as if seeing me in a new light. Then she stepped up to me and moved me into the light, indeed, for she had me stand near one of the windows. "These clothes are stolen, are they not?"

I felt my cheeks heat. "Indeed, and to my shame. But I knew that what I wore in the uplands would not suit me well in your town."

"No, you're right. But you choose very poorly when you stole these. See, Kyna?"

Kyna moved closer to me and turned me about in the light. "Oh, yes! I see. Made by dirKirken do you think?"

"I'm sure of it." Catha turned to me. "Large wooden house on the edge of town with a stone fence? Ah," she said with a nod. "And the clothes tree right in the middle of the backyard."

I nodded. "'Tis the same place, surely."

"We need to get you other clothes. Goodwife dirKirken has a distinctive hand with her embroidery, see here? On the yoke, the cuffs, and the collar. She'd spot you as a thief and send her husband after you." She paused before adding: "A deacon of His Own."

I repressed a shudder. "Then I should get out of these quickly, although I don't know what I'd replace them with."

"You are not the first stray I've taken in," Catha said, giving Kyna a pointed look.

"Why?"

"Why do I take in strays?" Catha asked. I nodded.

"Therein lies a tale," Catha said. "In short, it's because I must. Used to be that a woman like me, alone with no man, could still have respect, a voice." She shook her head. "Instead, more and more women are silenced, pushed out to become 'strays.' So I do what I can: I remind the people in town that a woman on her own still can be respectable and I can do something, a little, to keep some of us from getting lost." She turned away and I hastened to follow. "Come, I have clothes that should fit you better than what you have on. Kyna, would you bring up some warm water to the spare bedroom? Our guest can wash and change clothes and then we can have lunch."

"Yes, Catha." Kyna turned to push a metal pot over the fire in the hearth while Catha showed me the stairs leading up to the second floor. We walked up three steps onto a landing and then a turn to the left and more stairs. At the top of the stairs were doors on both my right and left. Catha took me through the door on the left while a third room lay towards the front of the house.

The cluttered room contained a pair of wooden chests, a small bed, and several wooden frames filled with odd, square items that served no purpose that I could see. Catha flung back the curtains from the window and then knelt down near one of the chests, opened it, and began rummaging inside. I stood near the window and looked out, careful not to let myself be seen from below. I'd gotten turned around inside the wooden walls and so I started to see that this window looked out over the back of the house. The barn the leader of His Own wanted to use filled most of the large yard. A fence ran across most of the property, with half of the barn on this side of the fence and half on the other. Beyond the fence....

"His Own flock most thickly today, do they not?" Catha asked. She'd joined me at the window, looking over the fence to the large set of buildings beyond it. "That's the Inn my brother – well, my father's son – runs. And that's where the most important His Own are staying. They've something planned, I hear."

So many of the black wolves roamed about the building just across the way! *What can I do against so many? Alone? Dear Na, what have you set for me?*

Catha sighed and turned away. "As long as they leave me and mine alone, let them have their rituals and worship. I'll none of it."

"They leave you alone?"

Catha frowned, gathered her long hair and tossed it over her shoulder, standing a bit slouched. "Not enough, no." She looked more closely at me. "Have they done something to you, Moonhart hunter? Are they why you are here?"

I shrugged. "You've asked to be left alone. I'll not repay your kindness by denying you that wish." I crossed to the bed where she'd laid out some clothing. "Is this what you have for me?"

"Yes, I think it should fit well enough, and what doesn't I can mend to suit."

Kyna came in at that moment, warm water in a basin which she set down into a wooden frame that must have been designed for that very purpose. She hung a cloth over the arm of the frame and set a clay jar on the rim of the basin.

"Ah, water and something to clean myself with. Thank you, Kyna." I untied the cord at my waist and pulled off the tunic and draped it across the end of the bed.

"What are you...?" Kyna spluttered. I'd not given thought to my actions and had already dropped the trews to the ground. That's when she cried: "Why, you're a girl!"

I turned towards them wearing nothing but my Calling medallion. A blush warmed my cheeks despite I saw no reason for embarrassment. "I'd named myself as Hunter. I thought you knew.... Eknos hunters are female." I turned from one to the other. Kyna stared at me and then flinched away, before looking back again. Catha, while pink warmed her face, smiled at me, her eyes locked upon my own.

"We tend to bathe or change in privacy, that's all. I take it that's not the eknos way?"

I shook my head and turned to the water to use it before it got cold. I splashed some on my face and arms and then sniffed at the jar. It contained a soft substance that smelled subtly of some flower and I turned a questioning glance to Catha.

"Yes. That's soap. It'll help you get clean."

The soap felt harsh, abrasive on my skin, but it cleaned me well enough. I washed my hands and face and used the towel to wipe down the rest of me. Save my feet. They were dirty indeed, stained with the muck of the town, and I didn't want to ruin the towel.

"Why do you wear boys clothes since you're not a boy?" Kyna asked.

"My own clothes marked me too plainly as eknos. Your clothes seemed to be too ... cumbersome to move in properly. The clothes of a male sower seemed to offer me both concealment and freedom of action."

"But a girl can't wear a boy's clothes!" Kyna protested.

"'Can't?'" Catha asked. "'Doesn't,' I agree, but I'm not even sure about 'shouldn't.'" She shook her head. "You saw her walk, heard her voice. Does she act like a farmer girl acts? Her size, too, wouldn't give lie to the charade, I believe. A boy's clothes and manner fits her well enough. And thus we dispense with 'can't,' 'doesn't,' and 'shouldn't,' all in a go."

Regardless of clothing, one other thing set me apart from all the lowlander women I'd encountered that morning. I smiled at Kyna and drew my hand across the inch of stubble on my scalp. "You have lovely hair, full and long. Both of you wear your hair long and unbound. I've noted that not all men have hair as short as mine, but no woman did. That, as much as clothing, marks me as not the same as other women. I don't think it is safe for me to be so marked."

"You're right in that," Catha said.

"We can say it was cut because of the lice," Kyna said with a sniff.

Catha ignored her, saying to me: "Ah, now I see why you were reluctant to give us a name. May I have it now?"

"I'm Rhia darSelwe."

"And she's standing there in her skin, Catha. Can we get her dressed?"

"Of course, Kyna. You had brothers. Can you help her into these?"

She sighed as if the weight of the world had fallen upon her shoulders. "I can try."

"Thank you. I'll leave you to it while I get our lunch prepared." Catha nodded to me as she left the room. Kyna watched her go with something akin to fear in her eyes. I admired her then: for when she turned to me, I saw no trepidation in her.

"Come. It looks like Catha has it all laid out for you already."

She turned to the bed and named off the articles of clothing: tunic with full sleeves, longer by only a hand or two than an eknos tunic. Trews. Socks, which she called stockings, I recognized, although ours are thicker and worn only in the winter. Then she handed me something that made no sense: they were like another pair of trews with the legs cut off. "What are these?" I held them up.

"Why, those are smallclothes. You use them to cover your, ah, parts."

"My 'parts.' Perhaps I misunderstand your use of the word. Which parts?"

"You know! You're just playing with me." Kyna's most expressive eyes opened wide when she realized I truly didn't understand. "Your *saedrow* and buttocks, that's what." She spoke the words in a rush, as if afraid of them.

"How in the world do you piss or shit when you need to?"

She gasped. "What a savage you are! Don't you cover your sex?"

"Why should I hide that which every woman has?"

"So men don't see it, that's why!"

"Under these?" I held up the long trews. "Never mind," I said when she looked ready to argue. "I don't care why sowers do as you do. I just have to look enough like a lowlander to pass unnoticed." And then a thought struck me. "Ah. This is like the dressing and bathing in private, is it not? Do sowers always keep their 'parts' hidden from one another?"

She nodded, her face bright red and her breath shallow. "Yes. Mostly."

And yet there are so many of you! Outwardly, I nodded, and stepped into the small clothes and pulled them up. The fabric was softer than that of the trews, which may have provided another reason to wear them. I sat on the edge of the bed and reached for the stockings and then remembered my feet and reached for the wash cloth and began to scrub.

"Did you really run hundreds of miles? Did you wear out your shoes that you're barefoot now? Where did you stay when night fell? Who protected you?"

I smiled at her barrage of questions. "Yes, I suppose I did run for hundreds of miles. I slept in the most likely spot, beneath the stars or clouds or in the rain. I rather like the last very little. I ran alone, for I'm the one who received the whole of the Calling dream."

"Your feet must be hard as old leather." Kyna's lip curled and her eyes grew wide with fascinated dread.

I couldn't fathom why Hunting capable feet should be a bad thing. "Why yes, I should hope so! Running on rough ground can be quite painful else." I vividly remembered the escarpment in Lynx territory but was glad to see that the wounds from that trek had healed well. With my feet clean I reached again for the stockings.

"No man will want you with feet such as that," she said with an air of authority.

"No?" I smiled as I thought of Niall's warm hands holding my feet in the air as I lay upon my back that last night in White Eagle ekarra. "If you speak of lowlander men, I'll not dispute you."

Kyna opened her mouth as if to answer and then shook her head.

I put on the light trews and picked up the tunic. Kyna reached out, hesitated, and then touched my left arm.

"What's this?" She traced a finger across the raised and colored flesh.

"That's my eksig. It shows I'm part of Moonhart eknos."

"How many eknos are there?"

"There used to be nine, but sowers wiped out two of them before either you or I were born."

"And all the marks are different?"

"Aye. Different marks and in different places." I turned to face her and placed my hand between my breasts, high on my chest. "Lynx eknos has theirs here. White Eagle wears theirs on the arm opposite of Moonhart."

"You're all over scars!" Her lip curled again and she wrapped her arms about herself, reaching out with one hesitant hand to point at the scar beneath my breast. "What caused this?"

"Ah, that was from the moonhart buck I took down during my *stealna kir*." To her blank look I simply shrugged. "An accident while hunting." She didn't reply but she looked thoughtful indeed. I pulled the tunic over my head and, to my astonishment, she tied the tunic to the trews using dangling thongs she called "points."

I laughed. "How to piss indeed. I'll have to plan well ahead, won't I?"

"If you're truly male you'd just pull your *saedgar* out from within your small clothes." She snorted in disgust. "Tis your choice to wear trews."

Then she handed me a pair of shoes. Not unlike the schoh worn by Lynx and I managed them well enough. I stood while Kyna stepped back and looked me over.

"Catha's right, you act nothing like a real girl. You stand like a boy and in those clothes you look like a boy. Your voice is low and not at all womanly. Speak little and even what they hear won't tell them you're not what you seem."

I thought back over our conversation, about how Kyna shaped her words and inflected her phrases. Even though her words held scorn for me not acting like she thought a woman should act, I wanted her to see me as less of a threat. "I thank you, Kyna durTornan." I tried to mold my words as I thought a lowlander would do.

Kyna's eyes grew wide. She left the room and I followed, back downstairs to the kitchen.

Catha had prepared a hearty Gathering season stew. Kyna began to set out bowls and utensils. Catha sat at the head of the table and I sat on one side, giving Kyna room on the other.

"Do you know how to use these?" Kyna held up a knife and spoon. I nodded and she placed the utensils in front of me. She also placed a mug of something dark and foamy before me as well as a loaf round as a ball. I reached out and tapped it tentatively.

"You don't know what bread is?" Kyna demanded. "What kind of ignorant —?"

"Kyna! That's enough. Uplanders don't grow their own wheat, now do they?"

"Tis true," I said. "We do not, although we do gather the grains that grow in the meadows."

Catha nodded. "Bread is made from gains like that, ground and mixed with water and allowed to rise, then baked. Surely, you have bread in the uplands."

"Bread, yes," I said, uncertain. And then Catha ripped the loaf apart and I saw, not dense grains, but light and airy. "But not like that!"

"Like what, then?" Catha asked, true curiosity in her voice.

"Flat and dense. Very chewy and, if not eaten right away, unbreakable unless it's soaked first." I smiled at the memory. "But soak it well in mead and serve with fresh Gathering season berries and it's a wonderful thing."

Catha nodded. "It's the time we give to allow the bread dough to rise that makes the difference in texture." She paused and thought for a moment, and then pointed at the mug in front of me. "In fact, beer and bread are much the same that way."

"You don't know what beer is, either?" Kyna scoffed. She folded her arms across her chest.

"No." I pitched my voice quietly as if I'd spook a wild creature with too loud a voice.

"Well, it's what *we* drink," she declared.

"Kyna!" Catha's voice spoke of her growing exasperation. "It doesn't surprise me that Rhia doesn't know beer if the eknos don't eat leavened bread. You do know how to make beer, don't you?" Catha demanded of Kyna.

"Of course! Every goodwife knows that. It's made from barley!"

"And other ingredients *sown* as *crops*." Catha turned back to me. "Be sure to drink it slowly or water it well. I wouldn't want your wits muddled."

I nodded and carefully tasted the beer. The effervescence reminded me of well-stored mead long in the jar but beyond that it tasted nothing like mead. Dark in both taste and complexion, slightly sweet but with a bitter bite to it that was nonetheless refreshing. "Thank you," I said to Kyna, again in a soft voice. "This beer is pleasant."

She sniffed and took the seat across from me. Catha served out the stew and I watched as each ripped a piece of bread from the loaf. I copied them, near as I could, committing the movements and the rituals to memory.

We sat in silence for a bit, eating the stew, delicious and strange. I found the bread to be good, chewy yet soft, quite different from the flat loaves of baked grains we ate in the ekarra. With my belly becoming full, I turned my thoughts to what should happen next. My quest wasn't near complete. I couldn't just sit and wait. "Earlier, outside. The man on the...."

Kyna rolled her eyes and responded to my unasked question. "Horse."

"The horse, yes." I replied to her and then turned to Catha. "You sent him away."

"His Own do not welcome me, so I give them no welcome." She glanced at Kyna, a quick flick of the eyes. "Especially now."

"You don't like the black cloaks." It wasn't a question, but she nodded. "Who are they?"

"Ah, that's a long tale indeed. Finish your meal and I'll tell you a story. I'm no Player, but this tale would be ill served told prettily." Catha stopped, took a drink of her beer as she seemed to gather her thoughts. "I don't know how uplanders worship the God and Goddess, or even if they do, so forgive me if I tell you what you may already know. Once the Five of the lowlands followed God and Goddess in equal measure."

"Seven," I said.

"Sorry?"

"Before the Two that become the eknos we are now, they were part of the Seven of the lowlands. At that time, our stories tell us, we followed AnA, the joined aspect of both An and Na."

"Indeed? Yes, I suppose they did. In that time, we were taught that the world is all in balance: God with Goddess, day with night, male with female, good with evil. Not like separate ends of a stick, but like a circle, every gradation between dark to twilight to full day back to dusk again and the dark. We were taught in the temples during services held in the twilight hours between night and the day by priests who encouraged us all to find the balances within our own lives and among the lives of those with whom we lived."

She sighed and took several bites of her stew before she continued. "But for nigh on most of your young life, those who call themselves His Own have gained strength and influence. They now tell the priests and people how to worship and they outright deny the worship of the Goddess."

I shrugged my shoulders. "The eknos don't worship Na, at least, not as I think you mean it. I've always been taught Na is most pleased when we take delight in all that She's given us: the forests, the streams, the plants. Each other. Take of her bounty and yet leave enough so that more can be taken later."

"Huh," Kyna said, her voice full of surprised wonder. "That makes a lot of sense."

"Yes. Eminently sensible," Catha said, while her voice implied danger. "Such sense makes it imperative we keep you from the hands of His Own." She tore off a chunk of bread and used it to wipe up the last of her stew. I did the same. "His Own have declared what and who and how to worship. They tell the priests to hold services at noon, during the height of His day and His power. They change the fabric of my world and through this, they've gained much in strength and power." She shrugged, but I could see the issue struck her deep. "They are one of the reasons I open my home to strays."

"I know something of the reach of their power." I stopped from saying more and instead asked my next question: "Have you seen others of my kind? Uplanders held captive by these black cloaks?"

"Eknos? Here? Why?"

I held out empty hands, then made up my mind to tell all. "Over three score days ago, my mother fell in amongst those you call His Own. She and another woman plus two men went to meet with sowers who live near my eknos. The lowlanders murdered both men and took the women captive." Now it was my turn to drink of the beer and collect my thoughts. "While we don't worship the Goddess as you do the God, still, She looks after us. When those of my eknos were captured, She sent to Moonhart a Calling dream. You've not heard of such a thing?" When they both shook their heads, I pulled out my medallion. "That's what this signifies. The dream was sent to all of Moonhart, allowing us to share different parts of the dream. I, alone, was given the whole of it, and with it, a quest to fulfill." I tucked the medallion back inside the tunic. "I've been running since then to find and rescue my mother and the others if I can. To end their lives if aught else fails."

"You've run hundreds of miles in just over a season? Amazing!" Catha looked past me to the window behind Kyna as if she could see Selwe from her home. "You think she was brought here?"

"A few times since the Burning season, we know that captives have been taken south through Bainellen to Kairclavan by His Own. It's possible they stop here first."

Catha pushed her bowl away, her face stricken. "In answer, I've seen nothing, heard nothing.... Save that His Own flock most thickly." She shook her head and turned away from me.

"What will you do?" Kyna asked me.

"She'll do nothing, at least for the moment." Catha turned back. "She can't be wandering out in the town, not with the place so full of His Own."

She stood up and walked to the window and Kyna and I fell silent. Catha stood there some while watching, but what she saw I know not. In the silence I heard the oddest sound, a far-off melody, much muffled, but music nonetheless. I wondered what it might be, but before I could ask Catha tuned back towards us, a look of determination on her face.

"You must do nothing, for the moment. But there might be something I can do. I'll venture over to the Inn, see what can be seen. Hear what might be heard." She turned back to me. "If there's anything to learn, I'll learn it there." She brushed crumbs from her sleeve and then picked up the empty basket to take with her.

"When will you return?" Kyna asked.

"When I can. Watch for me. Clean the dishes and keep quiet, inside. I'm unsure of what I'll find. It makes me anxious. Be ready to hide in the rooms above, if needs be." She touched Kyna on the shoulder and nodded at me and then walked out the door. Kyna turned to me and I smiled.

"If she gets hurt, I'll kill you." With that, Kyna turned away from me, the long skirts and sleeves of her clothing swirling with the movement, and took the dishes to the sink.

Twenty-Four

Dughal

Attempts to tie any troupe of Unencumbered Players to a single theater, town, or even province, will prove impossible. From the days of Ailil'naric, Players have seen all of Anacarra as their especial duty, their own demesne. As such, God's children spring up behind a Player's cart as it rolls across the lanes like almond trees in a midden pile. Acknowledged more often than not, these children force the Players to see all provinces as family.

- Letter to Siod'aric from the Old Poet, Year 422

Our slow pace, with six sullen men and one Player's huge cart pulled by two old horses, allowed those of His Own with their awful wagons to pull further and further ahead. At each cross-roads I asked the lonely God if He'd be so kind as to call those men down some other path. My prayers became most earnest when we reached the point where the road split, with one branch leading into the foothills and the monastery of Kairclavan while we took the other into Kairill. I resolutely did not think about the fate that awaited those taken by His Own. I don't think I could bear knowing and knowing that I'd been powerless to do anything about it.

Kairill had grown large since last we'd been here. New homes sprouted up well outside the original walls, with merchant's homes sitting upon fields once tilled, an odd crop indeed. When we'd traveled far enough into the town as to reach the original walls, I had us stop and take out our entrance clothes and prepare a spectacle. The garish and gaudy clothes chafed upon our shoulders, but there was a crowd to entertain. Although my Players, to a man, simmered in their anger – towards me, towards His Own, perhaps towards the two-faced Godhead itself – still the men performed well in our noisy entrance into Kairill. Within some minutes the rage and anger, the frustrated impotence, quieted beneath the roar of the spectacle. As it should be.

Oean today chose a horn to play us in, it's metal voice cutting through the other sounds. Sionn may have muttered something about wishing the knives he juggled might be sharper should he meet the black cloak who had struck him, still he and Beathen exchanged their passes without flaw. That Sionn had to focus on the mirrors affixed to the back of the wagon and couldn't scan the crowd for crows allowed him to set aside such concerns and be a Player again. With the roads being somewhat narrow in the old town, I had Barrol do his tumbling and acrobatics behind our jugglers.

As he spent much of the journey into town walking upon his hands, Barrol may not have noticed the large numbers of black cloaks watching us pass. Being just a day's long walk downhill from Kairclavan, it didn't surprise me that His Own were numerous here, too. Even so, many of those so cloaked were not actually part of the brotherhood of His Own, but aped them in dress and manners and speech. I'd seen this more and more as we'd traveled south. I despaired that one day we'd see no more color in the world, only somber suits of deepest black, black like night, like death.

We discovered as we reached the center of Kairill another reason for all the crow-colors: the band of His Own that had near run us down had not taken the road to Kairclavan after all, and had, in fact, taken our preferred inn. Granted, it was the largest inn that Kairill had to offer: the oldest and the best situated, being but a few minutes walk from both the town baths and the amphitheater. It looked as if we'd find no welcome here.

"Let's go, Dughal," Sionn said. "I'd not stay here knowing that the man who gave me *this* walked about and me no chance to throw even." He pointed to the welt on his face, still red and angry these hours later.

"I'm inclined to agree," Beathen said. "Although I have additional reasons, you understand."

"But Dughal!" Barrol grabbed my tunic. "What if the captives are here?"

"We've seen nothing, remember?" Bitterness twisted my words more than I'd intended. "As was pointed out to me not so long ago, we can't turn tail every time His Own appear before us. While this inn is full, and over full, there are other inns within Kairill. We'll find someplace else and give these folks something other than dour sermons to listen to."

My men nodded and I called up to Camran, still sitting on the high seat. "Since you met your dear Avrea in this town, perhaps you can suggest someplace else."

Camran shook his head. "Not I. Avrea grew up not far from this very spot. But here's our erstwhile hosteller. He may have something to tell us." Camran easily leapt down from the wagon. I remembered then that Avrea's brother had owned the inn back when Camran had met her. He certainly greeted the man walking towards us as family.

"Breaslain!" Camran reached and gathered the rather surprised hosteller into his arms.

"Camran? Is that you?" He stepped back and held my Player at arm's length. "By the Bargain, it is you!"

"Indeed. And while you knew well of the Bardeelin that was, let me introduce you to the Bardeelin that is."

321

Breaslain allowed himself to be guided towards us, but then he stopped. "Why, it's a day for reunions. Catha! Came here, sister, and see what the winds have blown into my courtyard."

I looked around for whom he hailed, then I saw her appear out of the several groups scattered about the courtyard and move towards us. Catha was much as I remembered from when last the troupe had visited Kairill, a decade or so ago. She walked with purpose and precision, her head held high, and I was struck by the simple strength of her carriage. When she reached Camran's side, she laughed, her eyes wide in surprise.

"Uncle Camran?" She shook her head, nonplussed. "I heard the horn, but hadn't dared to hope it might be your troupe."

Camran shared an embrace with her before turning towards the rest of us. Breaslain had changed little. His deep brown eyes seemed lit from within and I deemed he missed little of what transpired at his inn or in his town for that matter, and his bearing spoke of both ease and energy as so many keepers of inns have. Camran introduced him to the others as Breaslain durBreaslain, nephew to his own dear Avrea, dead these many years.

"DirAila, now." Breaslain greeted the rest of us. "I married some half dozen years past."

"And this is Catha durBreaslain." Camran turned to the woman. She may have been a few years younger than myself, with pleasant eyes, brown and kind and lively, and a fine figure within a modest tunic of simple cut. She wore her light brown hair long and loose in the style of an unwed woman, which Camran noted and asked with some irony: "Or have I given the wrong name again?"

"No, uncle. I'm durBreaslain still." Then her eyes glinted and she tapped him on the ribs. "Or, darElli, if you would."

Breaslain blushed and laughed and Camran shook his head. "Still holding those sorts of opinions are you?" he asked. "Breaslain doesn't begrudge you your father's name, does he?"

Catha grew somber and reached out to Breaslain. "No, Camran, he does not." Just then, a group of His Own sauntered past us in the courtyard, on their way to the inn. "But there are those," Catha continued, "that would seek to deny me my mother's name."

"We've become more acquainted with His Own as we've journeyed in Bainellen." I kept my voice very even. Even so, I motioned towards Sionn who turned his damaged face towards her. "As you can see."

Catha gasped and Breaslain frowned. "I wish I could assuage those hurts with beer and beds and a place to perform," Breaslain said. "But I fear I've no place fit for you to stay with us, for His Own have *taken* all my rooms."

"I'm not surprised in the least." Sionn's voice was low but laced with venom.

"We understand," I said, more loudly than Sionn. "We were just discussing what other inn might have room for us this evening, and a place wherein we might perform on the morrow. We've only ever stayed with you and yours when in Kairill and we know of no other place."

"It isn't right that family should be turned away," Breaslain said.

"That's right," Catha murmured. And then much louder she said, "You *are* family, aren't you uncle? Then I'd ask you to stay with me."

"Catha?" Breaslain asked. "You haven't put any of the inn's guests up in the old guest house since it came to you from our father."

"Ah, but these aren't guests, are they brother? They're family. In a way."

"Would that make you my mother?" Sionn asked.

"I've seen your mother," Beathen quipped. "This fine woman most decidedly is not she."

Sionn scrunched his eyes up quizzically for a moment. "If, at some point, I discover you've insulted either me or my mother, well ... then it'd be too late, wouldn't it?"

"Yes," Oean said. "It would be."

"All right then," Sionn decided.

"Hmm, yes." Breaslain looked bewildered at the exchange and went on: "You're still welcome to eat in my common room in exchange for your songs and news." His smile faded and he became most earnest. "I want no trouble but I have guests other than His Own who would welcome news and entertainment."

"We'll offer no trouble, I assure you. Catha, thank you for your hospitality. It's good to find family willing to acknowledge their connection to Players in these days. Breaslain, we'll get ourselves settled at Catha's and then be back to sing and tell our news, eat and visit the baths."

"Excellent!" Breaslain turned and hustled back to his inn.

"Poor, Breaslain," Catha remarked. "He is forever running about." She turned away. "Because of the wagon we'll take the streets to my house but when you return to the inn this evening I'll show you a way between the buildings."

I remarked about the wall that now divided the inn from what had served as both guest house and innkeeper's home. Catha nodded. "When father Breaslain died, my mother lived still and his will gave us this place. Brother Breaslain's mother lived as well, and she was the one who commanded the wall be put up."

"That sounds like a tale in itself," Beathen said.

Catha shrugged, thrust her hands into her pockets "Suffice to say, Breaslain and I had mended any rift between us, living side by side as we do, at least until he married." She grew quiet, and then turned a resolutely pleasant face towards us. "But that is not a tale I'd tell at all."

"We thank you for opening your doors to us, mistress." It had been plain that there was some hurt there, and so I made to change the subject.

"Please, call me Catha." She grinned. "No need for formality among family."

Camran snorted. "You're my deceased wife's brother's daughter."

"Nevertheless," she said, taking his arm. "I'm very glad to have this opportunity to have Players stay with me."

"You don't worry for your reputation?" Oean asked.

"No!" She laughed. "You can't stain something as muddied as that. More likely your reputation will suffer for staying with me. His Own think little of unmarried women these days." An edge honed her words, for all that they were spoken matter-of-factly. She folded her arms across her chest, the empty basket before her like a shield.

"They think less of Players." Sionn absently traced the mark on his face. She noticed the movement and stopped, turning to him.

"Let me see." She took his face in her hand and turned it this way and that in the lessening light. "This is new?"

Sionn nodded. "Some hours old."

"I have somewhat that'll help," she said. "And then, perhaps, there might be something you can assist me with."

Ah, there it is. Her ready offer had seemed too ready, for all her joking of family. Players pay in coins of many denominations and so I was ready to hear her out, when she was ready to speak.

By then we were at her door. She showed Barrol and Beathen where the horses might be fed and brushed, where the wagon might be stored inside for the night. The rest of us took our things from the cart, me and Oean carrying the packs for the two seeing to the wagon, and we followed Catha inside. She may have inherited the land, but not much wealth to go with it. Fewer pieces of furniture than one might expect in such a home left the main room feeling bare but while all was clean, none was new.

"Carrinan used to stay here many years ago, when my father ran the inn and the province still had carrinanen instead of the ancarrinanen beholding to the clavan." The wistful tone left her voice. "You'll sleep here tonight," she said and motioned to the mostly-bare front room.

"Thank you, mistress," I said.

"I've asked you to call me Catha, Player. Is your memory so poor as all that?" She smiled at me, her warm eyes sparkling at the joke. "Odd, that. In a histrion." I heard the hesitation in her voice, as if she had to remind herself how to tease.

"One would think he was the one clopped in the head today," Sionn said.

"Ach, there I go complaining of Dughal's memory. Please, lad, come here and I'll see to that welt of yours." She took Sionn by the arm and led him away from us into the large room that served as both kitchen and common room. We moved some furniture and set about getting the room ready for sleep so that, once we returned, we wouldn't be fumbling about in the dark. Barrol and Beathen returned not long after and we gathered up the things we'd need for our time at the inn, changing out of our entrance finery and into colors more plain and somber.

"Remember," I told them. "Play no song nor tell any tale not specifically asked for. And still use your best judgment, even if asked. The inn's common room will look nigh unto night with the numbers of black cloaks in it. And Sionn won't listen to me, but perhaps one of you can convince him it's best not to parley that welt of his into either a fight with His Own or a tumble with a stable girl. I feel we tread a knife's edge here and would fain not fall off it. Understood?" They nodded, even Sionn. I may not have needed to say anything, for most of them seemed as put off by the vast number of His Own in this town as I was. But one role I ever played was that of mother hen to my chicks, even though they resented me for it.

Catha showed us the route to take back to the inn. A narrow path all but concealed led alongside her barn to the inn's corral and thence to the outside wall leading to the front of the building. At that time, with the sun low in the west, the way was shadowed and dark. We marked it well for we'd be taking it again after full night fell.

We ate in the kitchen of the inn, for no table had space for us in the common room. The food was tasty and plentiful if simple, and we were soon enough done. We left the kitchen and spread out into the hall. Oean, Barrol, and Beathen stood near to the empty hearth and asked if any would have a song of them. I and Camran wandered amongst the tables, sitting when invited and telling what news we had. Sionn wandered out into the courtyard tossing his juggling clubs as he went. I worried for a moment should he get into trouble but then turned to answer the question of the man next to me.

As a Player, I've taken great pleasure in watching the work of other Players: how they move upon the stage, how they say their words, how they present their stories. Whenever we chance to come to one place – a festival or the Naming of the First – Players will watch and study and learn and denigrate all others. But through it, we come to learn how the leader of each troupe tends to arrange his sets, block his scenes.

Throughout the evening, although I neither saw him nor heard his name, I felt Neacal's hand guiding and directing all the action upon this stage of Kairill. We were questioned about incursions by eknos into Maukellen territory, concerns regarding eknos activity. We knew of no truth to any of that but our denials did little to dissuade these men. They seemed very excited by the prospect of strife with the eknos and would not listen to any word we had of peaceful relations in Maukellen between uplanders and low.

Going hand in glove with requests for martial news came also requests for martial songs. We sang the songs asked for by name and repeating loudly enough so that others could hear that we sang at the especial request. A belligerence filled the room, an urge to fight and smash and win "glory" against those who denied Neacal's image of the God. I feared that if eknos were not to be found, others closer to hand would do.

When there was time, I sent the men by pairs into the baths next door, one to bathe and one to watch, turn about. When it was their turn, I looked for Sionn to accompany Oean. He stood in the courtyard, tossing clubs and balls into the air despite the dwindling light, with a fair sized crowd around him. I moved into his line of sight and in time he noticed me and gathered in his clubs to a round of applause. A few coins landed at his feet as the crowd dispersed.

"Ye've forgone your allotted dollop of old goat's piss, young man," I said in a deep northern brogue. "Should I call the 'pothecary for ye?" It took a moment but then Sionn remembered the quip from Rillsherd and smiled. His smile often eased whatever friction lay between us.

"Ye've gone and drunk it all!" His hand clutched his heart in feigned outrage. "That's no way to treat the man who brings you tidings."

At that, I raised my eyebrow but said no more. Sionn also fell silent even as he fell into place beside me. "Go with Oean and take your bath. I'll hold onto your gear. We'll have a bit more time in the common room and then return to Catha's. Then I'll listen to your tidings."

"You won't like them," he told me over his shoulder as he trudged towards the bath.

"No," I said, although he couldn't hear me. "No doubt I won't."

Twenty-Five

Dughal

It was only later that I came to enjoy plays enacted upon the stage. As a boy, I loved streetshow most of all. The juggling and music were fine, but to have stories enacted right before me, to be part of it, the tale surrounding me. The ribaldry I loved best of all, watching my sister blush, the mothers' laugh.

- Diary of Kalen dirAila, Mayor of Rillsherd during the reign of Ailnaric I

"Neacal's here," I said when we had gathered in Catha's large kitchen.

"You're right, Dughal," Sionn said and all turned towards him. Night had long since fallen and the moon wouldn't rise until much later, so the sky outside held naught but stars shining in profusion. "The captives are here." This brought all of us sitting up on our stools.

"Captives?" Catha asked.

I glared at Sionn but it was Catha's manner that intrigued me. She sat quietly, moving only so far as to brush a strand of hair behind her ear, but her gaze was intense and intent. Sionn would tell it or she'd have it out of him. I knew him well enough to be certain of the first and suspected what I knew of her to concede the likelihood of the second. I own it surprised me that he showed some restraint and only told the latest part.

"Just this morning, a band of His Own overtook us on the road here," Sionn said. "Near on to a dozen of them, riding hard and escorting two large wagons. These wagons had sides like a hay cart but the staves ran full around to the front and back ends as well. They didn't carry hay, lady, but people. People of eknos and lowlands, too, men and women both, although the lowlanders all seemed to be women. Taken and beaten and ... we fear what else."

"It was then you got your injury?" she asked.

"Indeed, it was. The Goodman who gave me this told me, 'You have seen nothing!' and other such threats ere he rode away."

Catha leaned forward, her hands clutching the fabric in her lap. "You know these captives are held somewhere near?"

At that question, Sionn's face fell. He sighed. "In truth, no. What I know for cert is that the wagons they were carried in are stored right out there." And he pointed out that window into the darkness beyond. I couldn't fathom his meaning, but Catha did.

"They're stored in the inn's barn?"

"Even so," Sionn said.

Catha looked to me. "What are you going to do?" Her voice flowed smooth and easy, as if asking the plans for a holiday, but her brown eyes narrowed, her gaze hard and urgent. If she hadn't directed that gaze at me, I mightn't have seen that below her calm demeanor roiled a swift and implacable current.

"What can we do, Catha? So, the barn is there, part of the inn. It'll be guarded at every opening, especially if the prisoners are held there as well."

Catha shook her head. "Not every opening." She laughed at our amazed looks. "These buildings used to be part of a whole, the inn and this house. My barn, where you stored your wagon, abuts to the barn of the inn. There's no longer a door on the main floor and never was on the second. But on the third? As children, Breaslain and I would play in the hayloft. The wall there is low, open, more of a delineation than a barrier. I can tell you where it is."

I slowly closed my mouth against the swarm of arguments, cautions, denials that crawled up my throat. The knife's edge trembled beneath me. My players all started speaking at once.

"Here's something we can do! We can go at once and free them all!" Sionn said it but Barrol's head nodded in agreement.

"We don't know they're there," Beathen countered. "Yes someone should look and see what can be seen. But blundering about will get no prisoners released and you added to their numbers."

"Or dead," Camran added. "And over what? A bunch of savages."

"You forget, Camran," Oean said. "Not only eknos huddled in those wagons we saw today."

"This is a chance to finally do something, Dughal!" Sionn glared at me, all the frustration of youth at the world's injustice filled his voice.

"Yes, it's a chance to do something," I admitted. I wouldn't admit that the prospect revitalized as much as it terrified me. Torn between risking – not only the troupe, but our very lives – I wavered and fell silent.

"I'll go." I, sitting next to Barrol, heard him speak and it froze my heart. This dear lad, my spry sweet tumbler, lifted up his head and spoke again, louder. "I said, I'll go." More heard him this time, including Sionn who stopped his arguments. "I'm small enough, still. I can climb up there and through to the other side and tell you what can be seen."

"Good, lad," Sionn said and then shook his head. "But it would be too dangerous. I'm sure I'm not so large that —"

"So, you admit there's danger?" I demanded. "Good of you to acknowledge that, for all you've accused me of cowardice."

"Of course it's dangerous! Doesn't mean we shouldn't make the attempt. If it were you so abused you'd hope for someone to make the attempt, wouldn't you?"

I nodded. "You're right. If he's willing, Barrol should go. Tonight." I breathed deep. "Now."

I exhaled that breath and with it that knot of dread that had sat within my belly ever since we'd found the dying Hunter. Ah, it felt good to act instead of waiting to be acted upon! Having made up my mind I then made up a plan, planning the actions as if I blocked them on the stage. I turned to Barrol. "You, my boy. Are you sure of this?"

He nodded and I watched as he physically put aside his fear. Standing from his stool he faced me. "I am. I want to help."

"Good lad. Then take a strip of cloth and bind it over one eye. See to it that it's well and truly dark on that side. After you've had that across the eye for some while, we'll send you off." Barrol raced away ere I'd finished my instructions to get just such a cloth. This was an old trick of players working the playhouses of the largest cities to keep their eyesight ready to traverse darkened passageways in safety, moving from dark wings to bright stage without being blinded between.

"Sionn and Oean, you two will go with him when he returns. Bring plenty of light with you, so that should any chink be open in that wall you'll be seen. And heard. Sionn, you are to tell the most ribald story you can think of. Make it your own and tell it to a most enthusiastic and appreciative Oean, who'll then tell his own tale in turn. I want it known that you're there and any of His Own will be either entranced or scandalized by your stories, drawing their attention." Oean smiled and nodded while Sionn laughed outright.

When Barrol reappeared with the cloth around his head, Catha took the three of them aside and explained to them what they would find. To Barrol she explained how the inn's barn differed from her own and where carts or captives most likely would be kept. After some while, the four of them departed, led by Catha, carrying lanterns aplenty to provide bright light down below and drawing attention there. She returned some moments later and set out cups and produced a mug of good beer she brewed herself. She excused herself and went upstairs for some moments while the rest of us sat down to wait.

Patience.... At times, I'm master of the wait, finding much or nothing to occupy my mind in the meantime, as most pleases me. Contemplating a new way to perform an old favorite play, or reminiscing about the last time I'd been with a woman for more than one night, or just letting the sun shine upon my face. All are ways one might wait until some anointed hour is come. None served this evening.

Patience visited none of us. While I feigned a relaxed manner, I found that my thumb returned to rubbing the scar I have on my left hand, an accident from a time when I'd been younger that Barrol. For his part, Beathen sat upright upon Catha's hard wooden chairs, pulling at the hem of his tunic as if to smooth out the wrinkles to my plan. Camran, perhaps seeing in Catha somewhat of his long-lost Avrea, focused most successfully upon our hostess. But even his eyes and attention wandered away to look out of the darkened window to the barn beyond.

For her part, Catha told us stories of her growing up in this town on the crossroads to places elsewhere, filling the empty waiting with words. She'd worked at the inn as a stable girl in her youth, about the time when women and girls were no longer welcome in the inn itself. "I was old enough to realize that something had changed, but not so old to know why."

Camran nodded, looking off into the distance as if he could see his beloved Avrea there, alive and well before the birth that was her death. "I remember those times. Women weren't welcome to eat in the common room and then they weren't welcome to even serve there."

"I remember being told that, 'One girl among so many men would be unseemly,'" Catha said. "Of course, those doing the telling ignored the fact that had they not ostracized the women from the room, one serving girl would not be alone."

"'Unseemly'?" Beathen asked, rubbing at his beard. "Who did they fear, I wonder? Did they fear their own lusts, or did they fear on your behalf for seeing men as they are?"

Catha shook her head. "I've no idea. Nor, I suspect, do they. It didn't matter the reason given, only that women would find no welcome outside their own homes."

"About the same time as you were being moved out to the stable," I said, "Players were told no women might act, despite most of the oldest companies were operated by women."

"'Despite,' Dughal?" Catha asked. She pulled her long brown hair off of her shoulder and then placed her hands flat upon the table as if, on their own, they'd turn into fists. "Say rather, 'because' and I think you'd have the right of it."

Her words struck me as revelation and I opened my mouth to pursue the thought further. But Barrol, Oean, and Sionn returned then and I sprang from my stool, hurrying to open the door. None seemed the worse for whatever transpired, yet I stepped outside the door to hear any pursuit or commotion. Frogs and the sighing of wind in the trees met my questing attention and soon enough I returned inside. Catha had given all three mugs of the good beer – Barrol's well watered – and they drank easily enough. I couldn't decipher their manner at all. "Tell us. What did you find? Did you manage the route through the hay loft?"

"Well enough, Dughal," Barrol replied. "Although —"

"Wait!" Sionn grinned, his dimple beaming. "Tell this tale proper, in full and as a piece."

"Tell, then." Camran's patience with Sionn less even than mine own.

Sionn didn't roll his eyes at Camran, although I suspect it was a close thing. "We found a spot where the walls between the two barns fit not as well as they once may have and we set ourselves down and the lanterns before us. We would of occasion bang upon the cart, fixing that which wasn't broken, and I'd curse you, Dughal dear, for

334

making us be out here in the cool of the night. Oean replied you were a right rogue and as tight fisted a man as ever walked the world."

At that, Camran laughed. "So, you told falsehoods from beginning to end."

Sionn smiled. "If you say so, but I warrant anyone listening wouldn't believe it! We talked directly into the side of our cart to bounce our words back over the shoulder, our shadows dancing with our words. Any eye placed against a gap in the boards would have a view of our backs and the sounds of our voices."

"You didn't shout, did you?" Beathen asked.

While Oean has never been comfortable with the actor's art, still his pride at his hard-won skill felt the criticism. "Of course not! We wanted to be heard, but not without effort. Then Sionn started telling tales of Benvi." I do believe I saw a blush begin upon Oean's cheek. "I daresay she'd either be heartily offended at having her name so used or quite pleased with herself at the glowing tales of amorous love Sionn proffered to me and any unwary listener."

"Both, if I know Benvi," Sionn said.

"Which I begin to doubt myself," I replied. "But please, continue. So, you two who have the lessor task have set yourself in place and Barrol has ascended to the hayloft. Is that the way of it?"

Barrol picked up the tale, nearly bouncing from his chair with the effort. "Yes, Dughal. The route was just as mistress Catha told me. Once I climbed above the brightness of the lanterns, I uncovered my eye and found myself quite able to see my route. I passed between the two barns with no more rustling or noise than a mouse in the hay."

"Good lad!" I exclaimed. "You've returned, and that's what's important. Did you see anything untoward?"

Barrol's energetic bouncing ceased and he looked down into his mug. "I don't know, Dughal. The top of the barn was as dark as below stage at the Lechsede amphitheater. I moved, quiet as I may, through the straw stored there until I got to the edge. Looking down, I could see men standing below, as well as a handful of His Own sprawled and sleeping. A pair of them, who I guess should have been guarding opposite doors, crouched near to the wall by which Sionn told his tales, so that part of your plan worked perfectly."

"Glad I am to hear it,"

"The captives, boy!" Catha exclaimed. She tried to cover her exasperated exclamation with a forced laugh. In a quieter voice she asked: "Did you find them?"

"I can't say, mistress!" His cry of frustration echoed in the room. "I couldn't see below me so I crawled down, to the second floor along the ladder affixed there for the purpose —"

"But lad! That put you in full view of those below!" Camran exclaimed.

"Well, yes." Barrol's piping voice fell into despondency. "And yet, it wasn't enough. As I bestrode the ladder I saw, directly below me, another pair of His Own standing as if to guard ... something. I couldn't see what."

"That side of the barn has neither windows nor doors," Catha said. "Unless I'm much mistaken, Breaslain made of that section a single large room, intending it to have a lock so as to store more valuable items for guests."

"It may be he's done just that," I said.

Barrol continued: "Despite I put my eyes to the chink in the wood below me, I saw nothing of note. I heard breathing, yes, but the barn was full of sleepers." He turned to me, his eyes troubled. "But Dughal, one other thing I thought I heard."

"Yes, boy?" I asked. "What is it?"

"It might be I heard crying, Dughal."

At that I felt my stomach drop within me, fear and anger and greatest desperation.

"That's it!" Sionn exclaimed. "They *are* there. Now we can rescue them."

"Can we?" I asked. "No, give me not your glares, Sionn. Give me, instead, a plan. The rescue of sleepers who may or may not be whimpering in their innocent slumber. I've heard you of late. You, too, have cried out in your sleep. Would you risk all of our lives on the strength of that?"

"Come, come, Dughal. You know full well why I may cry in my sleep!" He stood and faced me, his fists again ready at his sides. "That you don't says more about you, I think."

"Go, go, Sionn. Don't presume to know what tears I've shed over her."

Catha stood at my shoulder. I'd so forgot myself that I hadn't noticed her move from her chair. "Who, Dughal? Over whom do you weep?" Her voice was tight, demanding and fearful both.

I stepped back, from her and Sionn both. "It's best I don't say."

"Best for whom, Dughal?" Sionn shouted at me. "Best for the unmourned woman of eknos we left dead in the woods?"

"Hush, boy!" I cried, afraid of what might follow such an outburst. And yet, what did follow was beyond my wildest imaginings.

We heard a commotion: a door flung against the wall and then slamming shut again, feet hard upon the stairs. Scarcely had I gathered myself when a boy burst into the room. With unerring speed he moved to me and I found a cold steel knife at my throat. A slim boy, perhaps Barrol's age but with a certainty of movement that Barrol in his growing body no longer had. And stronger. I looked up into pale green eyes narrowed in blazing anger. *And desperation?*

"Tell me!" cried the boy. "Tell me about the eknos you left for dead! Did you kill her?"

"Rhian!" Catha shouted. My gaze stayed fixed on the boy in front of me. With a visible effort she lowered her voice, her hands held open and out before her. "Let go of him, Rhian. He's been willing to help so far, but if you cut him further he may become somewhat disinclined!"

The boy eased back from me but the knife stayed up and ready. When he stood far enough from me, I slowly lifted my hand to my throat and felt the warmth of hot blood.

"Tis but a scratch," the boy said. Something sounded odd about his words but I was too distracted to place what it might be. At that moment, yet another person burst down the stairs: a young woman, her hair unbound and yet obviously pregnant.

"I'm sorry, Catha. Rhia —"

"Yes, Kyna." Catha interrupted. "Rhian decided to make his presence known." She motioned to Kyna to sit at the far end of the table and I indicated that my much amazed men should sit as well. Rhian could not be persuaded to move far from me and so I sat with him next to me in Barrol's chair, hastily vacated. Couldn't be persuaded to relinquish the knife either, for that matter. In seeing that, Catha sat on his other side.

"Now, Dughal. I think you have a story to tell." Catha's calm surprised me, for her tone sounded for all the world as if my turn at tale telling by the fireside had come around again.

I nodded. Looking to my men I saw relief in their expressions. I own, I desired to dredge this story up from the depths where I'd long and unsuccessfully tried to smother it. We, all, had kept this tale too long secret. I took a deep drink of my beer, exhaled, and spoke: "More than two score days past, we left a village called Rillsherd, north of here by some 300 miles and traveled the road through Craobac woods. Deep in the night, a commotion sounded near to us and out of the woods stepped a woman of eknos." I turned to Rhian and spoke directly to him. "She was much hurt, lad, though not by our doing. Naked, cut and bruised, she fell right at our feet."

"Did she speak, sower?" the lad asked. *This was a uplander boy!* My gaze narrowed. In the excitement of having a cold knife cutting into my skin, I hadn't noticed the ill-worn clothes, the nearly bald scalp. The color of his eyes, a green like shoots new in the fields, was common in Maukellen, and he spoke our inflection well enough, but it was an accent new-learned for all that. Camran realized the truth at the same moment I did. He lurched out of his chair, stepping back.

I nodded to Rhian's question. "Indeed. She did. She told how she had been abducted by His Own, beaten nigh unto death." I sucked in a deep breath. "Raped. She told us little else before her life expired."

"Did she give a name? An eknos? How say you she looked?" Catha placed a restraining hand on the boy's arm at this last outburst, but didn't silence him.

"A name she didn't give us, uplander," Oean said. No one contradicted his appellation. "She was perhaps 40 or more years of age, strong and lean. Of Moonhart eknos, she said."

At Beathen's words, Rhian shouted, thrust his knife hard into the wooden table top. He pounded his fists and raked his hands across his close-shorn scalp. Catha moved as if to comfort him, but he kicked back from the table with such force that his chair crashed to the floor. Camran picked up a firewood log as if to defend himself while the rest of us tensed.

Catha looked to me and said: "You may have met Rhian's mother in those woods, Dughal. She's dead, you say?"

I became aware of the flute in my pouch as much as if it had sounded sweet notes just then. I pulled it out and stood up. "Yes. Dead of her wounds at the hands of His Own. I'm sorry." I held out the bone flute to Rhian, all that was left of the woman dead in the forest. "She gave me this, so that others might know her and her eknos. It should go to you, I think."

Rhian took the flute as cautiously as if I held out a serpent. "She gave you this?"

"Even that. Said that we'd know by this flute that she was a Hunter of Moonhart eknos."

I confess it, the relief that showed on Rhian's face at that moment much perplexed me. He uttered this strange noise, between a laugh and a cry and clutched the bone flute to his chest. "Grainna," he said. Then his eyes turned shrewd and he looked up at me again. "Tell me her appearance. Was her hair long, braided, color of moonclouds at night?"

Sionn answered. "No. Her head was shaved, even as yours is."

Rhian nodded, lifted the flute to his lips, and kissed it before putting it inside his own belt pouch. "You bring me sore tidings, true enough. But the one who is dead was the other woman taken along with my mother. Grainna was her name, and if you would tell the tale again, tell it true. She who you found is not my mother."

Twenty-Six

Rhia

It is said that on that day did the troupe perform upon the amphitheater's fine stage, and before some 15,000 of the good citizens of Bierncarra, the play by him that came to be called The Old Poet. The play, then called The Care of the Carrinanen *(and afterward* Siodaric's Delight*) brought such consternation to the Anaric that he leaped up onto his bench and shouted epithets of a most rude and specific nature to the Players below, but most specifically to their wordsmith. In his wrath, the Anaric stormed from the theater, half of his household and retainers following him.*

But his wife stayed behind and bade the good Poet to continue his play, for she found it to be most delightful.

- The Life and Times of the Old Poet

With Grainna's flute tucked safely in my belt pouch, my intention became the rescue of my mother and the other captives. But I had only the knife in my belt and the sling on my wrist for weapons. My bow and arrows lay safely and impotently hidden within a copse near the outskirts of town. Catha, already angry with me for prematurely showing myself to those she called Players before she could enlist their aid on my behalf, discouraged any other actions that night. Not that she had any claim over my actions, of course, but I couldn't deny the wisdom of her words. Ultimately, I had no certain knowledge of what might be in the barn across the way. I would do better to eat, rest, gain strength and more information on the morrow.

For the second time that day, I shared meat with sowers. Or more properly, lowlanders, for neither Catha nor these Players tilled the soil themselves. I learned the names of these men and learned that, while Grainna was unburned she was not unmourned, for both grief and outrage I saw in their eyes. The Players learned a form of my name but both Catha and Kyna kept knowledge of my true sex from them for reasons they didn't explain. Catha told them that Kyna was her uncle's daughter and I was – if asked – her husband's brother. The men, casting somber glances among themselves, nodded in agreement, as if at a tale well told.

"That seems wise, Catha, if I may say so," the one called Dughal said, in a voice smooth and subtle. His dark hair lay charmingly mussed upon his head even as his dark eyes scanned those of us at table. That gaze came to rest upon me and his voice took on a pointed resonance. "If your upland guest here stays silent, it should go well enough."

"And being your uncle indeed, His Own will hear no different from me," said the one called Camran. He was the oldest of those here, black hair turning gray. He may have had a handsome face, for a lowlander, but whenever he turned his countenance my way, I saw disgust, fear, and animosity such that he didn't seem fair to me.

Animus towards me, but he smiled as he held out his hand in greeting to Kyna. "Pleased to meet you, niece." She blushed and looked to Catha who nodded, and then took Camran's hand.

I wondered at the words. I felt as if I saw only the sliver of the moon: what is seen is limned brightly, but it doesn't reveal the whole. I know I missed much of what passed between these people. I knew I wasn't Kyna's husband's brother, and from how it was said, I surmised that Camran was not truly Catha's uncle, or perhaps Kyna's. Or neither's? I'd deal with the black cloaks on the morrow and lowlanders and their ways could remain mysterious. I needed no understanding.

I awoke before dawn, before any others in the household, or even most of the town. I crept out passed the Players, sprawled and snoring in their sleep upon the floor of the front room. I envied them that, for the bed Catha had put me in near to suffocated me in the night. Never had I thought to sleep so smothered in softness and hoped never to do so again. I took a large, coarse-woven sack from a hook by the door and quickly passed through the streets to the edge of town. I feigned retying the points on my tunic when a family loitered near the copse where I'd stashed my pack. Within moments they resumed their way and were far enough distant that I could duck inside. To my relief, all was as I'd left it. I left the clothes I'd stolen upon the stone fence surrounding the dirKirken home and then I waited for some while as group after group sauntered by on the lane. No one paid me any mind and I followed at a leisurely pace, a large bundle upon my back but not one that looked eknos in origin, and returned to Catha's. I trotted up the stairs and through the front door, only to be greeted with hostility.

"By the dark Bargain, I thought we were rid of you." Camran's brown eyes narrowed in disgust. "Why did you come back, eh? Neither my niece nor my 'niece' need the danger you bring."

"Uncle!" Catha strode to my side. She wiped her hands upon a towel and then placed those hands on her hips. "I'll thank you to remember you are my uncle in courtesy only and have no right to abuse another guest in my home." Catha reached out for me but I pivoted away to stand with my back to the wall. Both a window and a door could be reached within a few strides should I need quick escape. My heart beat hard and I felt as I did when Gaunt first threatened me. *Would I never learn? Kind words and a fair face can still bring danger.*

343

Catha opened her hands in a calming motion and began to speak very slowly and quietly, as if I were quail to be lulled to her snare. "Rhian, I'm sorry for Camran's words—"

"Don't offer that savage anything on my behalf!"

"He doesn't speak for me, I assure you. I've opened my home to you and I've not withdrawn that hospitality."

"I thank you, Catha," I said, equally slowly and quietly. "I'd avail myself of that hospitality only a short while longer. I returned the clothing that I'd stolen from dirKirken," (the mention of which drew a "Ha!" from Camran) "and retrieved some things of my own. If you have something that I can break my fast with, I'd be obliged."

"You could repay the obligation by leaving," Camran said.

"Oh, leave it you old fool," the one called Sionn said. He was about my own age and he rolled his eyes at Camran and shared a crooked smile with me. Despite myself, I began to relax.

The one named Oean looked up from the table where he sat with paper and pen in hand. He wiped at the ink staining his fingers. "Whatever harm you think eknos bring, surely this one has brought no harm to you. 'Judge a man by his actions, for that tells you more than the place of his birth. The one is chosen and in the choosing declares itself.'" He shrugged and turned back to his pages. "As he's a guest, so are you."

Camran blushed to be so shamed but he glared at me as if his outbursts had been my fault. He turned away to march out the door I'd just entered. The other men started to chatter amongst themselves when Dughal gave a short whistle. They fell silent and he turned to Catha.

"We'll be leaving now, Catha. Thank you for your hospitality."

"You won't have breakfast?" she asked.

"Oh, no," Dughal said. He seemed flustered by the question. "We go to the inn and will eat there. Your brother follows the laws: he'll feed us and we'll entertain his customers."

They started to gather their things when Camran burst through the door again. He spared me not a glance as he called out: "Neacal is here!"

"Where?" Dughal asked.

"At the door." The clatter in the yard announced both horses and men, and then footsteps sounded upon the porch outside.

A tall, powerful man strode confidently into the room and I shuddered before holding myself very still. In silence and stealth, my hand inched towards the knife at my belt and only when the haft was in my hand did I dare to look up. He took some pains with his appearance for all that he dressed only in black: black trews with a black tunic above, and even his hat was black. Red cord splashed like blood upon the cuffs of his tunic and the brim of his hat and I felt a frisson of recognition when he turned his eyes towards me, seeking and yet not seeing me. He swept off his hat and saw Dughal. His eyes widened even as the corners of his mouth tightened as if he'd just bitten into something sour. For a moment he said nothing, then he scratched at his belly and smiled an unconvincing smile. "Greetings, Player! Why am I not surprised to see you in ... this house?"

"Perhaps because the hosteller informed you of the arrangement?" I marveled at how calm Dughal seemed in the face of this black wolf. "This house used to be part of the inn. Catha agreed to host as you've taken all the rooms there, you see."

"Have I? Well, I suppose that's true." The black wolf turned to Catha. "Ah, good morrow, Goodwife. This is your house, so I'm told."

Catha frowned. "Do I know you, Goodman?"

"Ah, where are my manners?" Dughal moved to stand between Catha and this Neacal. From my position I could see his fingers drained white by their tight grip upon the staff in his hand. "Allow me to make the introduction. Catha durBreaslain, I would have you meet Neacal durCleirach. I believe I may have mentioned him in our discussions yesterevening."

The welcoming smile on Catha's face became rigid and cold. Where her manner had been joking with His Own in the street, she seemed to realize such would not work with this one. "You are welcome in my home, Goodman Neacal."

"Am I?" He peered about the simple room. "And yet, my men and horses were not welcomed last night. Why is that?"

Catha shrugged and wiped her hands on her apron before hiding her hands within her enormous sleeves. "You have other resources and I have few. Your men did not offer fees to corral their horses, only demands. Had they offered payment, well...."

"And this one offered payment?" Neacal raised a leering eyebrow at Dughal.

It surprised me that Dughal did no more than stiffen ever so slightly, the expression on his face still as if twere a mask instead of human skin. For his part, Sionn bristled, rising up and would have spoken, but Catha defended them all. "The proper payment of all Players. The ancient fee. I've heard news from them and they've told me ... tales."

"Did they?" Neacal smirked. "Well, I've entertainment more fitting than anything you will get from even half a dozen Players." Dismissing Catha, Neacal faced Dughal. "As much as I'd enjoy seeing you perform *Nabryhtric's Heir* again, today you're invited to a far different spectacle. Very edifying, I assure you."

"Do you?" Dughal stopped just short of mockery but the distance twas small indeed.

Neacal laughed. His mirth set the hairs on the back of my neck to rise. "I do, indeed. At the height of the day, we will hold a spectacle in the amphitheater. Don't be late. My men are out rousing the whole town so I suspect the amphitheater will be quite full."

"And you came to invite us yourself?" Camran asked. "How ... kind."

"Think nothing of it." Neacal put on his hat and moved to the door. I suppressed a shudder as I saw the red upon it. "Remember,

346

when the God's day is at His height, in the amphitheater." With that, he strode through the doorway, not bothering to close it behind him.

"I don't like that man." Kyna blushed as if surprised to have spoken aloud. She rose from where she had sat on the stairs next to Beathen and walked to Catha, whispering in her ear: "He has met with my father."

"Then we'll make sure he does not meet you." Catha held Kyna close. "I think you should stay here and miss whatever 'spectacle' that man has planned."

Camran nodded. "I agree. I'd add, Niece" he said, hesitating over the words, "that you might consider not going as well."

Catha shook her head. "This is my town. I'd see what these men plan for it."

Beathen was a large bear of a man and he reminded me of Hrothar, although much more fastidious in appearance. He'd been sitting next to Kyna on the stairs, in effect blocking her from the casual glance of Neacal and the others of His Own. *That had been well done and subtle, too. No one could have accused her of hiding and yet she hid as well as a hare behind a boulder.* "Do *we* need to see what these men plan, Dughal? I can guess at some of it and am fairly sure I've no wish to know the rest."

"Beathen's right, Dughal." Oean stood and joined him at the window. "There'll be no playing for us here, even if His Own intend nothing more threatening than a sermon spoken from the amphitheater instead of the Priest's Spiral."

"And do you really think they would have such benign intentions?" Camran asked.

Dughal nodded. "Sionn? What say you?"

The man so addressed looked quite surprised to be asked. "I think I don't like knowing what I know." He looked up at me. "I don't like knowing that I might have done somewhat to help Rhian's mother and the other captives." He stood up straight and resolute. "Which I might remind you were not eknos only." He shrugged then, slumping

347

a bit. "We *must* know what happens in the towns we visit, Dughal, if we are to tell the news which is our duty and right."

Dughal rubbed at his hand and glanced over at Barrol. The youngster's eyes grew wide and he looked from man to man before shrugging. Dughal nodded again and then drew his shoulders back. "To be absent would be to mark ourselves more in Neacal's eyes than if we attended. I think it safest, insofar as anything Neacal has a hand in could be termed 'safe,' that we go and see this spectacle." He looked at me and Catha. "But I don't think that all must attend. I could leave some of my men here, protect you and yours, Catha. We'll report back faithfully, I assure you."

Catha shook her head even as I drew breath to protest. "No, Dughal, although I thank you. We will all go, save Kyna who needs no more of His Own's attention than she's had already."

I wondered at the blush that rose hot on Kyna's cheek. Camran cleared his throat then. We looked at him and he spoke, slowly but with no heat. "What about Catha's other, erm, guest?"

All eyes looked to me. I ran my hand over my scalp, both chagrined and comforted by the hair growing there. "If these are the men who've taken my mother and others, those of uplands and low, then I need to hear them, see them." I paused again, looked between Camran and Dughal. "Fight them, if needs be."

Sionn smiled, Beathen blanched. Camran and Dughal both began arguing with me but with different aims, I think. Barrol's eyes grew wide and Oean looked concerned but said nothing. Into that tumult, Catha interrupted, her voice loud and certain in her own home. "If you're going to the inn, Players, then you should go." The voices fell silent and, as a one, they looked at her. "We'll eat and join you there."

With only a few more words, more uttered than declaimed, the men departed some few minutes later. Catha put food out upon the table for us three and we ate in silence. afterward, Catha and Kyna had gone about doing whatever it is that sowers do in their home. I took my pack, my bow and other weapons, out onto the back porch, away from the street. I checked the stringing of my bow, the fletching on the arrows, the edge of my knife when I heard feet pound hard upon the stairs of the front porch and the echoes of the front door banging open. I tucked a pouch and my knife into my belt and adjusted the tunic such that it concealed both. The bow I hid below the porch and the sling went around my wrist, all this done in just moments, since I didn't know who had arrived. I'd only just finished when the back door opened and Barrol's head poked out.

"Are you ready? Dughal feels that those who'll be at the spectacle should be there, marking what's said and how it's said. As important before as after, he says."

"I'm ready." I came inside where Catha found a simple hat for me to wear and placed another, quite different type, upon her own head. Catha walked over to Kyna and murmured something and then kissed her forehead. Kyna nodded and rose, glared dire warnings over Catha's safety at me before climbing the stairs. I heard the snick of the door falling shut and knew that Kyna hid safely within her bedroom.

As we walked out onto the road, Barrol rushed a bit ahead and then would come back, something he repeated at least twice. With great restraint he eventually fell into step at my side, matching my stride and even my movements. He was a fine mimic. I realized I'd need to mimic the mimic if I wished to stalk a sower herd without it turning on me.

"How old are you?" he asked me.

I shrugged as I'd seen him do. "How old think you?"

"I don't know." He peered up at me. "You act as if you're at least as old as Oean and yet you're nearly a size with me. And even less beard!"

"Give me a guess," I asked him.

"My own age? Fifteen?"

"Good enough," Catha interjected. "Late enough for some maturity and soon enough not to have a beard." She nodded to herself and then turned to me. "But, my 15 year old boy, don't speak. We don't wish any untoward attention. And you, Barrol." He turned towards her. "You don't know Rhian as anything other than a boy from the town. Right?"

Barrol nodded and then smiled. "Well, he don't seem to know much. Perhaps the country and not the town."

"Leave it to a Player to understand the power of seeming," Catha said, a remark which I didn't understand but at which Barrol beamed a proud smile.

"Nearest the truth is oft the best lie," Barrol agreed.

We turned and turned again and I found myself on a much larger road, thronging with people. Not since the last nosmoot, when all the eknos come together in one place, have I seen so many people. I found myself walking closer to Catha even as Barrol, our destination sighted, scurried off, dodging through the crowd as easily as I ran through the forest. I held up my head, walked as if I belonged in that town, and kept my mouth closed fast.

Not that I might have been heard had I tried to say anything! The tumult of so many people closed the world down around me: I felt as if I'd lost use of my senses. I suppose I had. We walked a bit further to the east, the crowd growing all the while but at least we moved with it. Entering a large open space, Catha sighted Dughal and Camran. We then walked, sidled, shoved, and otherwise moved through the crowd to join them.

Before us opened up an amazing space. Much akin in shape to the gathering place in my own ekarra, this 'amphitheater' had been dug into the side of a hill, creating row upon row of benches on which to sit. Most of the bowl had been filled already and I felt my stomach grip at the thought of going amongst so many sowers packed so tightly together. I breathed a relieved sigh when I learned that Dughal had a different intent.

A large circular space lay before the rows of seats and within that space, three poles had been set up. Behind this, across the open space from the seats, was a long, low building. "See there?" he said, pointing to the building. "That's called the 'tent' although it's been centuries since it was anything but a building such as you see before you. They'll make their entrance and exit from there. Passageways exist on both sides as well as from within and behind the building." He nodded as if in thought, taking in the crowds upon the seats, the men of His Own standing at the ends of the passageways on both sides of the stage and even on top of what Dughal had called the tent. "But what those posts are for, I don't even want to guess."

"Where are your men, Player?" Catha asked.

"I have them working the crowd, scattered throughout."

"Playing at townsfolk."

"Indeed. I'd hear more than I can from here and see more, too. I suspect foul mischief." The last he said with anger and fear both, but quietly so that the sowers who came in high spirits as one would expect at a celebration, might not hear him.

If the amphitheater was a bowl – or half of one – then we stood upon the rim facing the center of what Dughal had called the stage. Below us, going down in tiers, were the seats that had filled with thousands of lowlanders. Close to where we stood a small, squat building rose up a hand or so above my head. Dughal brought Barrol and me together. "That building usually serves as seating for carrinanen or other worthies, so that their august heads might not feel the sun or rain. It's empty today, so up you go lads. You can watch from on high. Best seat around."

"Watch and yet not be seen, is that it?" I asked and in imitation of Barrol's own round tones.

Dughal nodded. "That's it exactly. Now, up you go."

Barrol and I pulled and hauled ourselves up onto the roof and then laid down flat, out of notice of all but the most curious. We'd been laying there in companionable silence for some minutes when Barrol nudged me. Neacal, the man who had come to Catha's that morning, strode out from the tent and stood beside the three wooden posts.

351

"Who is that man?" I asked Barrol.

"He's a bad one, he is." Barrol's voice held equal parts anger and fear. "Some little while ago, he told us we had to perform *his* play the way he told us or he'd kill us!"

"He's one of those you call His Own, correct?"

"Leader of them, more like." Barrol nodded, his long blond hair falling across his eyes. "If His Own are doing it, Neacal's the one that told them to."

"This pack of black cloaks is his?"

Barrol paused in thought before speaking. "Maybe, but not for himself. He's right hand to the one they call the Prophet. He who lives in Kairclavan." He nodded as if reaching a conclusion himself and looked back towards the bottom of the bowl, the stage. "If Neacal orders His Own around, it's the Prophet that orders Neacal around."

At that moment, a great clamor went up, the raucous noise of thousands of voices pummeling my senses. Two hands of black cloaks filed out of the "tent," one group moving to the left of the building and one to the right, forming lines that bordered the three tall poles. The men then all shouted together: if there were words in the rhythmic shouts, I couldn't distinguish them but all those in the amphitheater fell silent. Neacal strode from the tent to the front of the stage, stepping around the poles as if they weren't there. At his first words, those in the seats leaned forward as if eager to hear more even though his words carried easily over the assembled crowd all the way up the hill to where Barrol and I lay.

"Good people of Kairill! I bring you words of peace from the Prophet of the God of sheaves. Kairill, being so close to the monastery at Kairclavan, is much in the Prophet's thoughts these days. He tells me of his great and abiding affection for this humble town, that in the past, had always been right with the lonely God. He hopes that you will remember him as fondly, for he has done much from Kairclavan to the benefit of the people of Kairill. He wants you to be the first to know that it is his intention to become Aric of the province, so that the blessings he has bestowed upon Kairclavan and Kairill might be seen throughout the land."

The people cheered even as Dughal and Camran exchanged a look between them. I don't know what the look portended, but surprise was not part of it.

Neacal waited for some moments, his manner slowly changing. I've seen that expression, that posture and slow shaking of the head before, most often when my own ekma wanted to express her disappointment in something I'd done. The cheering died raggedly away in confusion. "But that was in the past. The God of the plow has shown to the great Prophet the sum of Kairill's iniquities. He has shown to Cleirach the secret places, the hidden foulness at the heart of this once-righteous community." Shouts of No! and angry glares followed these words, spoken with such quiet resignation. *He plays this crowd as Grainna played her flute. I fear the tune will not be to my liking.*

"The lonely God sees all but, unlike men, He is not put off by appearances. You are like a boychild covered in mud: the foulness is there to be seen but underneath is hope for righteousness and strength. You need to cleanse yourselves, Kairill!"

Growls and cheers were intermixed. The crowd was angry and ashamed in nearly equal measure. *Why, he tells them a tale that they long to hear! Like Skiem regaling the nosmoot in "Skiem's Wager," I don't doubt this Neacal is as crooked and devious. Why do they suffer this man to stand before them, proclaim them all to be dirty and then wait for him to show them how to be clean again?*

Neacal held up his hands. "In order to move forward, in order to cleanse Kairill first and then all of Anacarra we have to be strong! We have to be vigilant! Even now, dread hunters from the eknos have infiltrated Anacarra. Both Maukellen and even Bainellen provinces have seen vile depredation by these savage and barbaric killers. Whole families have been murdered, virgins raped in defiance of the ancient prohibitions, men tortured unto death. The evil eknos come in the night, spreading disease and death where ever they go!" The crowd began to growl like a pack of wolves with the scent of an interloper in their midst. Camran turned my way with a calculating glance.

"Keep strong, Kairill! Drive out the unwholesome influences in your midst. Cleanse yourselves of all taint and you will find the peace of the God on your families, your homes, your town."

Neacal turned then and motioned towards the open doors of the tent. Three of His Own came out leading three women, bound and hobbled. One looked to be over three score years of age, her long gray hair loose and disheveled and blowing about her face. Her long, lowlander tunic was stained and dirty, and she limped and shuffled upon unsteady feet. When they placed her against the pole she looked about her with a piteous, bewildered gaze, unaware of what was happening or why.

The next woman was not so old, perhaps of an age with my mother. I gasped and nearly sprang forward: Eknos! Her shaved head marked her from the others as did her bearing. She strode unbowed and stood unbending as the black cloaks roughly jerked her arms behind her to tie her to the pole, the sudden movement causing her short tunic to gape and ride up. I searched the exposed skin for sign of her eksig but from my perch I couldn't tell what eknos she might be from. I didn't think to search within.

The last woman was within a year or three of my own age. She pulled at the men, pleaded and cursed them both. Screaming No! at the top of her lungs, one of the men cuffed her into silence before tying her arms behind her. Such a position thrust her belly forward against her lowlander tunic, making it very apparent that the youngest woman was also big with child. At the sight of these bruised and battered women, the growling from the townsfolk grew louder and more vicious.

"See here, Kairill? These wantons, these evil harlots, stain your town with their very presence! These, these are the embodiment of that which drives the lonely God from your side." He grabbed onto the old woman. "This one practiced vile arts in her village, cursing a man to death, a good husband and devout follower of the lonely God!" The crowd booed and the poor old woman looked about in terror and confusion, crying something that none could hear over the mob.

"And this," Neacal grabbed onto the pregnant woman by the hair, "this one seduced a good father away from his family, tricked him into lying with her so that she could claim what he had as her own. Look, even now her body swells with the proof of her trespass, a bastard child tainted with lust and debauchery and carnality!" I heard shouts of "Whore!" and "Harlot!" and "Slut!" from the crowd. I longed to ask Barrol what those words meant. The sense of them was wrong and the gathered crowd built up strength in their fury like a thunder head massing on the horizon.

Neacal grabbed onto the eknos last. I can't say he intended it, but by how yanked at the back of her clothing, as if to hold her up to the crowd, ripped the torn tunic asunder. Neacal flicked the shreds of the tunic off of her as if he'd discovered offal in his hands, exposing her nakedness to all. She flinched, at first, and then she stood up tall again, resolute. A growl went up at the sight of her nakedness – or perhaps at the sight of a naked woman not ashamed. "See here, good people, that which you should fear most. A woman of eknos in your very midst! Down she came from her mountain demesne to spread her lies and her filth amongst the men and...." here he paused, his last word hanging like a promise. "And the women! Lying in unnatural lust with women and seducing the men, polluting that which should be held most dear on behalf of the God of sheaves. She was caught not five miles from here. She may have rutted with your very neighbors in defiance of the ancient laws, spreading her disease within this very town!"

The rabble roared at that. I gazed at her closely. In her exposed flesh I saw deep, old bruises, welts and open wounds. Her scalp bled and I wondered if, perhaps, someone had shaved her head for her, and that ungently. Worst of all, the tops of her thighs were stained with old blood. That she could stand surprised me, but that she would stand as defiantly as she could, made me proud of eknos even as I despised these sowers shouting for her blood.

The mob screamed and surged to their feet. Neacal stood off to one side, watching intently. I saw no such rage in him as roiled the throng. No hate, but simple calculation. He shouted, his voice barely intelligible over the tumult. "Cleanse your town, Kairill! Cleanse it of all pernicious influences and get right with the God!"

I didn't see the first stones fly. I'd looked down to see what Dughal and his men would do. What Catha might do. Bewildered, they stood rooted to the ground like young hunters facing their first angry boar. The ten His Own that had flanked the stage at the beginning of the spectacle, now stood in the aisles of the audience, passing out bags to men in the crowd. Those men reached into the bags like presents and pulled from them fist-sized rocks. In blind fury, the men stood and began hurling the stones. The captive's screams could be heard, then.

I stood and pulled the sling from my wrist and my pouch from my waist, reaching in and pulling out the stones kept there for hunting. The hiss of the sling over my head went unnoticed before the screams, the shouting, the hate boiling below me. Long ago I'd taught myself this trick: I let fly the stone and it sailed true, striking Neacal, but before that first one had even hit its mark, a second was on it's way. Then a third and fourth in quick succession at those passing out the sacks. I couldn't tell where Neacal was struck, but struck he was, driving him back into the "tent." I let go two more stones and the black cloaks scattered from the aisles, dropping their bags of rocks, their task accomplished. I wrapped my sling around my wrist and scrambled down from my perch. I grabbed Dughal by the tunic, twisting him to face me.

"You would allow this?"

"How would we stop it?" His eyes expressed his shock and impotent sower dismay.

"Bah!" I pushed him away and leapt onto the back tier of seats and began to hop down, one row to the next. I slipped and twisted and dodged through people much as Barrol had done earlier, but I didn't scruple to shove anyone to the ground who barred my way.

I'd never seen such fury, such a storm of rage as filled those farmers then, hurling stones at women bowed and cowed. Even so, the tumult raged higher as I reached the bottom, for all those that I'd knocked or shoved on the way down added a sharper note to the frenzied song the mob sang. Hands grabbed at me, hands which I slipped, or twisted, or broke as needed, but the long lowlander tunic and leggings confused my movements. Dodges or jumps which would have been simple in my own clothes became uncertain now.

I pushed hard against one large farmer, kicked him behind the knees and he toppled, knocking two of his fellows aside as well. In that I got my first glimpse of the captives and I staggered to a halt. All three women – the crone, the mother, and the huntress – sagged against their bonds, their bodies bloodied and torn from the hundreds of rocks pelting them. Yet they lived, for they cried and winced with each new strike upon their flesh. I realized in that moment that none would survive.

In that same moment, I recognized the eknos tied to the pole, close enough now that I could see the thin scar on her upper thigh, there since before I'd been born. But now, bloodied and broken by the rocks, she was dying in the lowlands she'd spent so much time studying.

"Mother!" I shouted, but not even those closest could have heard me. In that moment I opened myself up and instantly felt Selwe's familiar presence. She felt like home, but through the ties that bind all eknos, I also felt her agony. She looked up at me, her dark eyes that had gazed at me in love and kindness, now glazed and narrowed in anguish and fear. I started to move forward, but that large farmer surged to his feet and grabbed a hold of my long sleeve, growling at me. If I didn't move soon, I might not survive either.

I twisted out of his grasp and used the motion to plant an elbow square upon his jaw. I stepped around his sagging body and reached the space before the poles. When I stepped between the mob and their prey, at first they hesitated, waiting. Then, when I provided no new sport, the fury rose even higher. Hatred and inhuman rage boiled from that howling mass. A stone buffeted me and I hurried, my time short. The full clothing of the Sowers helped me then, for the layers of cloth lessened the impacts of rocks upon my skin.

I knelt before my mother. "Rhia?" she asked, then shuddered as a rock struck her leg. I hurled it towards an approaching black cloak, striking him true on the brow. He dropped, hard, and his confederate went to his aid, hauling him out of the way. Other black cloaks hovered nearby. I hoped they feared me, but it may have been the bestial mob they'd loosed that they feared more.

"Aye, mother. I'm here." I pulled my knife and began to hack and saw at the rope binding her. "I'll have you free soon."

She shook her head. "No, dearest daughter." She coughed then, blood frothing her lips. Blood also streamed from a gash in her forehead, another on her jaw. I began to count the new-made cuts on her face, her chest, her arms, her body, and quickly quailed at the tally.

Greatest Na, you treat your favorites cruelly. I freed her arms and gathered her to me.

"Tis time I start a new course, ealdra." She must have felt my outrage, for she pulled back and smiled at me. But blood streaked her teeth and her once kind eyes had begun to swell shut. "By your love for me, Rhia." Her uncertain gaze noted the Calling medallion hanging at the collar of my tunic. "I knew Na would Bid you come here, Rhia. Even from my captivity. Na has indeed favored us. Tell your father so, when you meet him."

"My father?" Selwe had always been unmated and had shared pleasure as she would. Which man who might have sired me had made no difference before. That she'd mention him now struck me as the height of absurdity. I would've laughed if not for the stones striking the both of us.

But Selwe only said, "My days beneath the forest are done."

Black despair twisted my guts within me. I wanted to deny her words, to know she erred. But I couldn't, I heard the truth in her voice. As I loved her, I had to end her suffering, this moonhart doe amidst carnage.

"Through your sacrifice of blood, you bring life to Eknos. I thank you, mother."

She smiled in benediction and tilted back her head, barring her neck. My blade ended her suffering and robbed this mob of its prey. And me of my mother.

I would've aided the other two women as I had my mother, giving them release from this world and it's agonies. But the crone was dead already and the young woman screamed invective at me when I would have moved towards her. She clutched at her torn tunic but that couldn't hide the horrific gashes in her skin, the bruises blooming on her body. She'd been branded not that long ago, the burns raw and a different red than the blood covering her. Each of us may choose our own course and she wanted nothing from eknos even as her own people murdered her.

I turned towards the tent, wondering if other prisoners might be held within. A few of the mob fell back at my approach, my bloody knife held before me. I'd taken no more than a step when stones that might have been thrown at the crone or the eknos sought me instead. I felt half a dozen land in good order, one buckling my leg, one bruising a rib. The one that landed against my skull I felt for only the briefest moment.

Twenty-Seven

Dughal

The God in His wrath is a terrible thing. Mountains crumble, seas rise, and humanity must tremble. Humanity in its wrath is more terrible still. Mountains remain, seas disdain, and the God weeps.

- Hereric

When that fool boy shook me and I could offer no good answer, the disgust in his eyes matched the disgust in mine own heart. That good townspeople could act so savagely! When he jumped into the howling mob, slipping, dodging, and pushing his way down the tiers of the amphitheater towards those hapless, helpless, women, I felt my fear collapse into a hard, angry, rock deep in my gut. Not gone, not that, not then. But no longer robbing me of movement or thought.

Catha grabbed onto my arm. "You've got to help her, Dughal!"

"Her? The woman of eknos? I think your boy's gone to do just that."

"And one of yours, too," she said. "Look there!"

"Sionn! You fool!" Camran shouted.

"Sionn would imperil us all," I whispered. Again, the impetuous boy did what I'd been afraid to do. He'd made it around the His Own guarding the aisles and entry ways to the tent. I hated to think what he might have discovered there in the dark but he now stood up on the stage. I clenched my fists: should he survive, I'll spend much time chiding him for his rashness.

As the audience-turned-mob began spilling up out of their seats, I realized that this scene had many actors and not all were upon the stage below. "Bardeelin! To me!" I called and all my men (save Sionn) converged on my spot. We pushed Catha into a center formed of the five of us, our staffs threatening whenever the mob got too close.

When Rhian's knife drank the blood of the Hunter lashed to the pole, then did the mob roar. Stones flew in earnest, striking Rhian and sending him to the ground. He crawled behind the first post but then stopped moving. As if this additional violence removed some impediment I'd not realized existed, the mob's bloodlust scaled even more frenzied heights. I spared a final glimpse for Sionn. He'd left the shadows of the tent and rushed to Rhian, applying his staff with right good will. I hoped he'd make his way back to us.

Violence began to spill out from the courtyard as if the death of the three unfortunates pulled a cork upon a bottle too long in storage. More converged on our spot and I could spare no more attention to Sionn. "Beathen! Get us out of here!"

"And leave Sionn?" Beathen shouted to me over his shoulder. Unlike our positions around the wagon, powerful Beathen had the lead, the edge of our plow in a field filled with riotous weeds.

"He'll bring Rhian to Catha's, if he can. We'll meet them there."

"If not for that damned uplander, Sionn'd be with us and we could be gone straightaway, out of this madhouse." Camran shouted over Catha to me. But he pushed his way forward.

Barrol, young and unpracticed, took up Sionn's neglected spot and rained heavy hits upon any who came too close. After a dozen or so paces we broke through the front of the mob and I saw the extent of the hatred unleashed by the most holy His Own. Houses nearest the amphitheater sported gaping holes where windows or doors should have been. "Cleansing Kairill" seemed to be just another way of saying "steal from your neighbors." I smelled smoke from the marketplace as some righteous citizens set fire to the stalls there.

I led us at a run, out of the town's center, down the side street and back. We moved quickly as we could, the way ahead being clear. With some of the God's own luck, the riot would either stay contained within the marketplace, or surge towards the eastern, poorer, section of town. We reached Catha's door without further incident. Save for being winded and a bruise or two that I'd most likely feel in full later, we were unscathed. Oean sat down in the street, breathing heavily. Beathen's tunic had torn and he bent over with his hands on his knees. Poor Barrol looked terrified.

"Good lad," I told our youngest. "You did well."

"By the God's *saedgar*, Dughal!" the lad cried. "What happened?"

"Hate." I turned to follow Catha who had already run into her home.

"Do we make a stand here, Dughal? Do we *have* to make a stand?" Camran looked shaken. He brushed back hair from his face and looked down in surprise to find blood there.

I turned away, looking up street and down. Smoke rose to the east but the riot raged distant enough that I heard nothing but a confused rumble on the edge of perception. "The mob seems no longer so keen on seeing us as elements to be cleansed. Get the wagon loaded and see that the horses have water and plentiful feed. I don't know when they'll be put in their traces nor how long they'll have to stay in them once there." I shook my head but couldn't clear it of what I'd just seen.

"We should leave now. This is their town, not ours." Camran pointed at Catha's house. "Let's get Sionn and get out while the way is clear and the sun is high."

"Camran!" Oean heaved himself to his feet. He squeezed and opened his hand, looking down at it. Shook it. "We can't leave them."

363

"Don't forget yourself!" Camran said. "We're not the mighty warriors of old from your stories, playwright. Staying here too long will get us killed. And for what?"

"Do what I've bade you. Also, treat what hurts you all have taken. We'll leave in good time." I left him and the others to do what needed doing and rushed into the house in search of Sionn and that fool boy of Catha's. Once I entered the house I heard voices raised and I rushed up the stairs. I burst into one of the bedrooms and breathed a sigh of thanks: Sionn stood next to the bed wherein lay the lad, Rhian.

No, not a lad! Her torn tunic exposed her secret, as well as massive bruising and cuts from the stones. When I saw the skin of her face and temple, scraped raw, welted and bruising deep, I feared for her life.

"Does she live?"

Sionn glared at me, consternation and contempt equally mixed in his gaze. "Sure and no thanks to you!" He snorted and rolled his eyes. "I, too live, if you care a whit."

The knot in my gut relaxed a bit at the sight of him. He had knuckles scraped raw, the uplander's blood upon his tunic, and his trews were dirty and torn, but I saw nothing worse. "That you yet live is plain. For her there may still be doubt. What other hurts does she have but those so clear writ upon her skin?"

He mollified a bit, shook his head. "I don't know. She's not awakened since I reached her in the amphitheater. I put her upon my back, escaped into the tent. Between her and the mob, His Own had already quit the place, their filthy deeds done. Backstage has its own entrance onto a different street, so I fled ahead of the riot. With Kyna's help, I carried her up here. Kyna went to get Catha and I began to seek what hurt the lad had." To my surprise, Sionn blushed. "I stopped once I realized it wasn't a lad I touched."

Catha snorted and pushed both of us aside. "Such scruples are of poor comfort when one's bleeding. Please give no such thought to my modesty should I be in such straits. Kyna, come help me with Rhia." With easy confidence, Catha felt along all of the girl's limbs, her ribs, her skull, hips, and belly. Catha frowned at the old scar beneath the girl's right breast. "I think Rhia's Goddess watches over her, for I can sense nothing worse than you can see, although the ribs feel tender."

Being pushed away from Rhia's side I took my chance to look over Sionn. "Damn you, Sionn. Play the hero only on the stage. I'd not lose you to uncouth townsfolk." I took his face in my hands and searched for signs of hurt before I held him close. "You did well, boy. Good staff work."

He held me, too. I think he'd been more scared than he'd admit, even to himself. Soon enough he pushed me away. He grinned, his dimple plain. "But, I *was* on stage, Dughal!" And then the dimple disappeared into a grim glower. "Two women of eknos we've watched meet bloody and painful deaths. I'd always been taught *they* were the savages, Dughal."

By the bed, Catha bent low over Rhia, who'd begun to stir. "Rhia? Can you hear me?"

"Aye." Rhia nodded, and then winced. She brought a hand up to touch the wound on her scalp, still oozing blood. "I hardly felt that one at the time." A faint smile curved her lips. "Now, the one to my ribs ... that I felt."

I laughed, startled. "You're either very brave or very foolish, Huntress of the eknos."

She looked up at me, her eyes squinting a bit in an effort to focus. "Ah, Dughal. I think you'd find my ekma saying tis both and not one or tother."

"Indeed, they oft come together as bosom as brothers." I laughed again. "Or perhaps, in this case, sisters."

Rhia smiled, and then the smile faded from her face like the dying of a sunflower. "I found my mother, Catha. All but too late, I found her."

"By the dire Bargain!" As I realized what the hunter told us, heat washed over my body in a wave of despair. And fury. *That her tale should bring her so far for such an ending!*

"Oh, Rhia." Catha reached for her hand, but Rhia reached up instead and clasped a ceramic medallion that lay upon her chest. Catha looked at me, then at Kyna. For her part, Catha's pregnant friend stood still as a statue upon the town's square, the cloths and bowl of hot water in her hands. I wondered at what would have driven the young woman so far from her own mother. Did Kyna hear in this tale a memory of her own mother's death? Or the fear that she may no longer ever know should her mother yet die?

"I'm so sorry, Rhia. More sorry than you can know that my neighbors could cause this."

Rhia relaxed her grip upon the medallion and turned towards Catha. "Your neighbors were but the arrow, loosed. His Own pulled the bow."

And where are they now? "You're right, Hunter. We need to find out what His Own intend before such an arrow is loosed against us."

Catha nodded. She stood and motioned to Kyna to bring the bowl and cloths. "Indeed. Rhia, Kyna will remove the rest of your clothes and tend your wounds while I talk to Dughal."

"No," Rhia replied, her voice stronger than I expected. "I'll hear what you discuss. If you talk of black cloaks then I need to hear." She laid back in the bed and motioned for Kyna to begin. "He can turn away if sight of my nakedness so offends him, but if you'd be talking about me, I'd have what you do and say be in my presence."

I held up my hand, stopping her rising anger and distrust. "You have that right, Rhia, but I wouldn't interfere with the tending of your wounds. I need to find my men and see what's towards. When you're patched as may be, then we'll all meet and discuss what roads are next to be taken." She nodded and Sionn and I left them there, Catha and Kyna both. The wounds upon Rhia's body I had no doubt they could tend as well as may be. But there are deeper wounds than those we see and I had no idea if those could be healed.

I called the rest of the men into Catha's kitchen. None had escaped hurt, but all had escaped true injury. They brightened mightily to see Sionn.

"I saw some and you've told me more," I said to Sionn. "But I'd know it all. How did you get the uplander away?"

"I'd been working the crowd on the western side of the amphitheater —"

"There's a tavern on that side, isn't there?" Beathen said, his tone shrewd. "You wanted to be sure the ale was close to hand!"

We all laughed then, a good cleansing laugh all out of proportion to the worth of the joke. I touched Beathen upon his shoulder in thanks.

Sionn smiled and continued: "Be that as it may, I was there when the black hearts began their performance. I saw Rhian move through the crowd and realized her intent —"

"Her?" Oean asked.

"Indeed," I replied. "Seems Catha's uplander 'boy' is an uplander Huntress. Her secret was revealed in the tending of her wounds."

"Are the wounds grievous?" Barrol asked.

"I wouldn't wish to suffer so, but she makes jokes with one breath and demands with the next. Her life isn't in danger, I think."

"Might I finish?" Sionn asked. "Before another steps upon my lines?"

"Tell, do," I said.

"Rhia, as she's called in truth, had all eyes upon her. Her descent down the tiers of benches took so much of the attention that no one noticed as I moved around back stage. When the stones started falling, His Own fell back." He looked down and I imagined I saw a blush on his cheek. "I may have met one of them in the dark of the tent."

"Tell me that he didn't meet you."

"No Dughal," Sionn said, a hint of a smile on his lips. "He met only the business end of my staff. And too quickly to cry out."

"Thank the lonely God," Camran said. And then, almost despite himself, he asked, "What happened then?"

"It was a pleasure to see the consternation on the faces of His Own when Rhia started throwing their own rocks back at them! That scattered them in truth."

"I think, having inflamed the mob, their task was done," Oean said.

"*That* task was done," I said.

"How did you get him, I mean her, away?" Barrol asked Sionn.

"The backstage has an entrance out to its own street, empty of both His Own and 'righteous' townsfolk. After she gave her mother the release, I gathered Rhia upon my back and moved without detection to here."

As understanding of Rhia's loss bloomed, Beathen blanched white and clasped his hands together. Oean cursed most inventively, leaping out of his chair to pace about the room. Barrol, whose own mother died while he was still too young, looked riven to the core. I could only imagine what memories arose in the poor boy. Even Camran looked stricken, all invective against uplanders washed away in shared grief.

I clapped Sionn upon the shoulder and waited while my men came to themselves. "Yes, she found her mother, bound and killed by His Own, even if she died by Rhia's own hand." The men sat back down, words gone for the moment. I continued: "But there are other stories in this town and we need to know what they are. Does the riot continue? If so, do the rioters head this way? Where are His Own and what might they be planning?"

"How safe are we, is that it?" Oean asked.

"We, and the women. Yes."

"What do you want us to do, Dughal?" Sionn asked.

"You stay here. I'm not convinced that you didn't take greater hurt in your time upon the stage." He scowled, rose up as if to contend with me, and then winced, his hand going to his thigh.

Beathen shook his head, a mocking smile for Sionn on his lips. "Well, Dughal. You cast Sionn's role a-right. Do you have parts in mind for the rest of us?"

I nodded. "I'd have you follow the riot itself. See what's driving them and in which direction."

"Yes, Dughal. I can do that."

"Oean, scout the middle distance, no further than the amphitheater and surrounding marketplace. The riot burned most hotly there, so be careful."

"I will, Dughal."

"Camran, old friend. Take Barrol and visit your kinfolk Breaslain at the inn. See what he knows. See also what food or other supplies we might buy and bring it back."

"We'll leave immediately, Dughal. The sooner done, the sooner we can quit this town."

An hour or more passed. I fretted, making several trips out to check on wagon, on horses, on sounds in the street or someone who might come too close. For his part, Sionn disappeared upstairs to give what assistance he could to Catha and to get his own hurts tended.

Camran and Barrol returned first but with hands empty of supplies. I refrained from asking any questions so we would all tell and hear but the once. When Beathen straggled in last, then I sought to hear what they would tell.

"You were out furthest and gone the longest," I said to him. "What's about?"

"The riot continues, Dughal. I've followed some mobs at a distance, climbed a tree or two to see what might be seen."

"Which was?"

"Death." Beathen brushed at his tunic, but the mud and other dark stains would not be coming off. "I've seen bodies aplenty, struck down and left where they fell. Mostly women, but it would appear the good folks of Kairill are using the riot to settle old scores. Houses have been sacked and looted, rioters fight amongst themselves. Chaos." He stopped and wiped his brow before continuing. "Although the tide has receded to more easterly parts of Kairill, I fear should the tide turn and rise against us."

"What of the inn? Breaslain wouldn't part with food for us?"

Camran slumped upon his chair, his expression troubled. He cleared his throat and sat straighter on his chair. "No Breaslain, more to the point. We couldn't get near him. Nor near the inn for that matter. His Own have forced everyone out, sent all others away. We watched for some while, as those carrion birds swooped in and out of the place. I can only hope that they're doing no worse than seeing where the riot has gone and protecting their own."

"I have no such hope," Beathen said.

Camran shook his head, looked down again at his hands clasping and unclasping in his lap. "No," he said softly. "Nor do I."

"The marketplace is nigh destroyed," Oean reported next. "'The God in His wrath....'" He stopped and shook his head. "I saw shops ransacked, carts overturned. A huge fire burns in the amphitheater, burns with wood taken from the very tavern Sionn would have visited."

"You went as far as the amphitheater?" I asked.

"Yes." He looked down and away, gulping a bit. "Gagh! My gorge rises ... the three women are not only dead, but mutilated. Raped, even in death." At our gasps he looked up and nodded. "Yes, all of them: mother, eknos, and crone, stripped naked and dishonored in death. The damned men of this town took turns shoving their pox-ridden *saedgars* into those now-fallow furrows."

I heard a sound, soft and quickly stifled, and turned to our youngest Player. "It's a terrible thing, Barrol," I told him. "In time we'll all grieve for what happened here."

"If only I'd seen last night for certain!" cried the poor lad, muffled tears making his voice harsh. He stared about himself, his hands clasping his arms, his legs. He stood up and began to pace. "This is my fault. If I'd seen more, if I'd gotten closer, this mightn't have happened!" He gasped, sat down hard upon the chair, eyes wide. "It's my fault Rhia's mother is dead!"

Beathen knelt down by Barrol and took his hand. "Hush, now. This is no fault of yours, none of it! No, by the lonely God, it's not!" Beathen forced Barrol to look at him and the big man smiled in reassurance. "The only fault lies in the hatred of His Own and the gullibility of men. You saw all there could be to be seen, make no mistake."

"And we chose to do nothing," Oean said. "Chose to ignore the lessons of Anacarra's own bloody past. How many plays, gentlemen, have told of chaos instigated by the evil designs of men for their own purposes? How many tell of sects that rise to power upon the twisting of scripture?" He shook his head and slumped in his chair. "We saw and chose to believe that what had been written down before our births could not be played out during our lives." He knelt on the other side of Barrol and took the boy into a hug. "How could you, my young lad, have seen what we old Players failed to see? Take not this fault unto yourself. It belongs wholly with Neacal and His Own."

Twenty-Eight

Rhia

The God takes note of the Makers of exceptional deeds.

- The Fourteenth Sacred Scroll, verse 65

A deed done well is its own punishment.

- The Old Poet

After Catha and Kyna washed and dressed my wounds, they asked if I wanted something to eat, if I felt like leaving that too-soft bed, clothing myself in their cumbersome costumes, and joining them in the kitchen.

I did not.

I turned away, mumbling thanks, and faced the wall. Catha whispered something to Kyna who whispered back, and they left the room. Sighing my relief, I closed my eyes, hoping to block out this sower house and all the terror and pain that sowers bring. But I couldn't block out the pain brought to my own body, and with my eyes closed, I saw again and again the terror done to my mother. And those two other women who, I'm sure, had committed no crime worse than Selwe's: be something that His Own feared. I may have slept then, despite all, for when I next opened my eyes, the shadows upon the wall had moved.

"My own mother died but three years ago." I spun in the bed, too fast: my head throbbed and Skiem's own sheets tangled about my body. Sionn sat and looked at his hands, his empty hands. "I'll not pretend it was anything so awful as what has happened to you and yours. Oh, no. Although it was by mischance and sudden."

He said all of this while looking down and then I remembered the lowlander men's aversion to the sight of a naked woman. Once I untangled the cursed sheets, I pulled them up to my neck. Only then did Sionn raise up his head and meet my eyes.

"I'm sorry, Rhia. So very sorry."

"You've done nothing."

He laughed, a short bark devoid of mirth, and again looked away. "Ah, yes. Exactly." He rubbed a welt that marred his cheek. The injury could be not more than a day or two old.

The throbbing in my skull kept understanding at bay for some while, but finally I realized what he said. "Yet, you risked yourself to save me." I swallowed against sudden nausea. *This, this sower, seeks my forgiveness! After what sowers have done to my people, my family, to me!* I closed my eyes and breathed in deep, but all I got was the cloying air of the too-close room, the stink of animal shit and middens and the dust of the roadway. *I can say no more to him.*

"Yes, well," he said. "I thought you should know. The men have returned and they bring news. If you feel well enough, would you dress and come downstairs? If not, Dughal says that we'll all come upstairs." He took in a deep breath, as if reveling in the morning scent arising off a mountain meadow. "And all come into this room. Around this bed. Between you and the door."

I groaned and then saw the glint in his eye. "You'd threaten a woman, injured such as I?" I turned my head and regarded him anew. "Are all Players so unsubtle?"

He held up tunic and trews, cleaned of my blood and mended of the tears caused by thrown rocks. "In my case, Dughal would say yes."

I smiled, pushed aside the covers, and reached for the tunic. I hadn't thought of it, but when the blush arose on Sionn's cheeks I had to laugh, despite the pain it brought to my ribs.

"Are all uplanders so unsubtle?" he asked.

"Say rather 'practical,' and I'd agree." Although his face flamed red the entire time, Sionn helped me dress, showing me better ways to tie the points so that I might undo them much faster. The pain had become an over-all ache and I took the shoulder Sionn offered and went downstairs.

Catha had set the table with sliced meats and cheeses, hunks of bread and pitchers of ale. Sionn pulled out a chair for me and I sat, gratefully. The blow to my leg and ribs pained me more than I'd let show and my head swam with every too-hasty movement. I kept my motions even and certain as I partook of the meal, hiding the extent of my injuries from the lowlanders.

The western window showed just how late the day had gotten. *A whole day spent in wrath and ruin.* For the moment, the street showed few people upon it and those that did walk by hurried quickly, their heads down.

None of the Players had escaped the day's events without some hurt. Barrol, although I didn't see any bruise, looked haunted by what he'd seen. *As well he should.* Beathen, Oean, even Dughal himself all sported new bruises and cuts, though none had taken hurts worse than mine. Catha, too, looked haunted, staring out at the street with eyes filled with dread. Of all of us, only Kyna had no hurts and energy to bustle about the kitchen.

I heard from Dughal's men the way of it, the track of the mob and the damage to the town. While the others chewed over this information, I had another question entirely. "Why would they kill a breeding woman?" I asked. "Set aside Selwe my mother or even the crone for the nonce, why that? A woman large with child should be congratulated, given the richest food and the softest places to sit. Instead, your people murder her and the unborn with her. Why?"

Oean spread his hands on the table, empty. "She wasn't married," was his answer.

"Wasn't what?" The word sounded familiar to me but wasn't one we used.

"You don't know what married is?" Barrol asked. Like all younglings, he was happy when someone knew less than he.

"Indeed, I don't."

"Of course not." Camran's voice slathered with disgust. "Uplanders rut like rabbits, breeding will-he nill-she, bringing fatherless children into the world to breed more just like them." Dughal and Oean both started to remonstrate with him but he continued. "In civilized lands, a father bestows a lass to a man who'll take her to wife, and she him to husband. Together, they have children with the blessing of the lonely God."

His smug condescension stung, his lies needed correcting. "Aye, rut we do, with great passion and in all pleasure. But breed? Tis the lowlands that fill up with people, rising to flood even the uplands." My words brought to mind my Calling dream. *Is that the flood that threatens my home?* I rubbed my face as if to clear that thought. "So, you say that the lass doesn't chose her own mate? How could any man chose aright for a girl child in such a matter?"

Dughal interrupted whatever Camran might have said. "When I was a boy, fathers chose for their sons and mothers for their daughters. Always, though, have parents in the lowlands selected mates for their children, to ensure inheritance, property, alliances. But in the last score of years, mother's voices have grown quieter and fathers have made all the decisions."

I shook my head. Winced. Said, more carefully lest my head throb with pain, "You breed your children like you breed your cattle: so be it. Why, then, murder one who's mated?"

This time Kyna spoke up, facing the counter, the knife she used on the meats still in her hand. "She mated but was not *married*. Her father hadn't given his consent to the union." She shrugged, a painful posturing that hid her hurt from no one. "Even *she* may not have consented to the union, for all of that. Perhaps the man was older, powerful? Charming and kind where her father was not." She laughed. "Cruel in ways not even her father had been. What if the man took her, laid with her, told her it was the God's will and his that she should open herself to him?" Kyna's hand fell to her burgeoning belly. "In their coupling a child was conceived. What if she'd believed the lies, that he'd set aside his wife for her? But he didn't. He laughed when she reminded him of that promise. Cuffed her when she pleaded with him. Then he went to her father with a tale."

Camran half rose from his chair. "You mean you ... er, she was raped? By her father's friend?"

Kyna began to shake her head and then stopped with a shrug of her shoulders. "No knife was used, no threats of violence." She set the knife upon the sideboard. "Just ... persuasion."

"Even in *civilized* lands, a woman must be free to say yay or nay to taking a man into her body, surely!" I looked around and the downcast eyes of the men, the eyes streaming outraged tears on Catha. "But a father, or even more so, a mother would defend her child. Wouldn't she?"

Kyna shook her head and turned to face me. "Her *father's* authority had been usurped. *He* was shamed before all his neighbors. *His* property had been taken from him and used without any gain to *himself.*" She turned away again. "He punched her full in the belly when he found out."

Catha wiped at her eyes. "Kyna, you don't —"

But Kyna continued, her words as relentless as rocks rolling down a mountainside. "He disowned her, claiming his daughter was dead. He summoned the priest and a date was set to punish the unfathered girl, for she'd stolen the value of her virginity from the rightful owner, her father, and displeased the God in the doing of it."

"Punished? For *being* raped, while he who rapes goes free?"

Kyna nodded, pulling aside the top of her tunic to expose part of her breast. "A brand would be applied, here, so that all would know of her shame. She'd be carted off to the brothels, for what better place for a wanton, a whore? The bastard child of the union, should she come to term and deliver it, would be put out on the hillsides, exposed to the weather and the wolves. The daughter would be gone, the child would be dead, and so would the *father's* shame be erased."

Rage burned like a brand in my belly, my own hurts forgotten. "But what of the man? If the woman would be treated so, surely the man would be punished most severely."

Kyna's words, which should have roared to the heavens, fell like scalding tears upon my ears. "Oh, yes. *Severely.* He paid his fine and stood his penance in the market place before going back to his wife, properly chastened. He has been forgiven, so he may continue his life as he had always lived it."

My horror must have been writ full on my face. Each and every man there avoided my gaze even as I demanded: "You mean to tell me...? How is it that...? Gah!" I spat upon the floor in disgust and fell silent, pushing my plate away from me. "Oh, yes. I'm truly traveling within civilized lands. And you call uplanders barbarian!"

"I'm sure that even Kyna doesn't know the whole of the tale...." Camran's confused voice trailed away. He then turned to me and shouted: "Don't mock what you don't understand!"

"This ..." I waived my hand to encompass all the town, "is easy enough to understand."

Dughal slapped his hand upon the table. "Enough." He stood up and would've moved to comfort Kyna but she flinched away, her hand reaching for the knife. Dughal held up empty hands and turned towards Catha. I rubbed my head, hating the stubble that grew there and wished that I might shave it in defiance of His Own and even

Camran. I looked up to see Dughal staring at me. His eyes grew wide as he looked again to Catha and then to Kyna. "Ah, me." He stopped, looked out to his wagon and back to the three of us. "We should all leave this place. Tonight."

His Players sounded as much surprised as Catha did, for they all started arguing at once. Dughal held up his hands, urging silence. "I don't suggest this rashly! While you are certainly no crone, still you're under no man's protection. You three are too, too much like those who died in the amphitheater today: single woman, pregnant woman, woman of eknos. When we leave, you should all come with us."

I scoffed at that. "I will not! My hunt is my own, lowlander, and I doubt we seek the same prey. Aye, my mother is dead because of these vile wolves, but she isn't the only eknos held captive. I'll continue what I've begun until it's finished. Or I am."

I'd no sooner fell silent when Catha began arguing loudly with Dughal on what a rash and silly idea it was, for this was her home and she'd be damned by God and Goddess both before she'd leave it. His Players, too, had words enough to share and no fear of doing so. The tumult rose in the kitchen, resounding in my aching head.

I rose and walked with great care to where Kyna stood at the counter. "What is your choice?"

She shrugged. "Choice? If I don't stay with Catha, why then I've nowhere to live. It was only by luck that a friend knew a friend who knew that Catha might help me." Her eyes brimmed with pain and anger both. "My father is one of His Own and powerful. Now that I've further defied him by running away, he may decide I should be dead, just like her out there in the amphitheater." She sighed and looked down at the carving knife still in her hand. "Perhaps that would be better."

"These men sought to arrange your life to their benefit, and you'd give to them your death?" I hissed. "No man owns another, not even lowlander fathers." Then I thought of how the Lowlanders name themselves as child of the male parent. "What's your mother's name, Kyna?"

It may have been the strangeness of the request but she looked up at me and answered: "Scothe."

"Then listen to me, Kyna darScothe. You are no man's property: not a bitch to be bred to a hound of his choosing."

"Don't call me that!" she yelled. "I'm no uplander fatherless whore's get like you are!"

I closed my mouth, realizing it had fallen open in amazement. "As you will." I stood directly in front of her, meeting her glare with one of my own. She stood a few inches taller than me and not all of it was piled dark hair. "Be *civilized* and die at a man's word!" I turned away, only to find Catha standing beside me.

"Until His Own grew thick as fleas on a dog I called myself Catha darElli. Perhaps you could call me a 'fatherless whore's get' and not be too far wrong. But you've eaten my food and called me friend. I think that despite my parentage you might be glad that my mother didn't expose me at birth nor kill herself with me still heavy in her womb."

Kyna gasped and stepped back. I, disgusted with all of this needless talk of fathers, pushed passed them all and limped to the door. At Dughal's call I turned and said: "My counsel is neither needed nor heeded. I'm none of yours to follow your commands, sower. I need to be out of doors. These walls suffocate me."

"Understood, Rhia. But please. Don't go far. Not even a huntress of eknos can fend off an entire mob."

I closed the noise of argument behind me but found my hoped-for fresh air to be smoky and thick with ash. I choked and coughed and then wrapped my arms about my tender ribs. I bent to squat upon the boards of the porch until the pain in my leg sent me upright again. Gingerly, I righted one of the chairs just outside Catha's door and sat down. If I'd not felt the sun full on my face as it set in the west I might have thought the sun set also in the east, for the horizon glowed red and fierce with fire.

The door opened and Sionn stepped out, closing it softly behind him. He sat upon the steps at my feet and said nothing for some moments. "You've lost your voice, Player, that you don't add it to the noise inside?"

"I've said my piece and, as usual, Dughal ignores me." He turned and looked up at me, his brown eyes concerned and kind. "You've lost more than your voice, Rhia. How fare you?"

"I would mourn," I answered. "But there's no time, is there?"

"Precious little," he agreed. "But to have come so far, *run* so far. Ach, Rhia, your tale trembles the heart. Oean would make of it a lovely poem, I've no doubt." He leaned back, facing away again. "If you would, tell me, dread hunter," he asked, his voice wry and kind, "what kind of woman was your mother?" He forestalled my indignant snarl with a raised hand and a devastating dimple. "I ask only so that Oean will have material for his poem. You understand."

I found myself growing warm towards this young man and a smile tried to form on my lips. "Ah, Selwe. Unlike most my other age mates, I shared a botha with my mother. It gave me time to myself, for she traveled often."

"Really? I know the traveling life well." He pulled his long dark hair back from where the gentle breeze had tossed it. "I didn't think eknos traveled at all, but then, I never thought to actually meet one, let alone hold pleasant conversation with her."

"Selwe traveled often, mostly to the lowland villages to the west, but sometimes to the east of the crags. She, too, had been Bid by Na to some task before I was born and it left her restless."

He tilted his head, which allowed his long dark hair to fall most charmingly across one eye. "'Bid by Na,' Rhia? What's that?"

"Doesn't your God send Callings to anyone in the lowlands?"

He shook his head. "I've never heard of such nor read it in any of our plays, although Oean might have."

They don't know An's will! They smother the silence with their own shouting voices. "Well, then. Sometimes, though not often, Na sends into our sleep a Call for one of us to do Her Bidding. Everyone in Moonhart eknos experienced parts of the same dream. I, alone, dreamt the whole of the dream. That meant Na Bid me to Her service. This folly, this run from the uplands to here, is what I thought She wanted me to do." I wiped my face and nose, looking away. I attributed the sudden tears to my aches and fatigue.

Perhaps he noticed my distress, for he asked no more about Callings. "Will you be restless for the lowlands when you return to the crags?"

"No." His face fell at my blunt word, and then, as I'd seen on Dughal, his expression became a mask: too rigid, too *expected*, as if the face he wore was Kindness and not his own. "I mean, I no longer believe I'll return home. I fear Na's service will end in my death."

He reached up and took my hand in his. So unassuming was the gesture, so like Niall's in its attempt at comfort only, that I found no objection in it. And then he turned my hand over and ran his fingers across the pad of my hand and the tips of my fingers. At that, I snatched my hand back.

"Your pardon," he said, "but your hand reminds me of my own mother's. No, really! She'd married a blacksmith, my father, and so for many years had helped him in the forge. She worked with her hands, as you do yourself: hard work. Not for a 'lady' but for life." He smiled again and I found myself smiling back. Then did his smile glow even brighter. "In other ways, you are not at all like my mother." He laughed and a blush rose upon his cheeks, and he held his hands out in front of his chest as if lifting very large breasts. "She could have never played the role of a lad."

"Given what has transpired today, you find mirth in my decision to hide who I am?"

His smile fell and he shook his head. "That? No, not at all."

"What then? Come now," I said, when he hesitated. "I never thought to meet a sower – your pardon, a Player – and here I am in pleasant conversation with him—"

"By the Bargain," he laughed. "You tell me my own words and in my own voice!"

"I've seen today that to be found out will be my death." I paused and took a deep breath, willing the sight of the enraged mob from my mind's eye. "Tell me, I'll be thankful, not wroth."

"Since I came of age, I've been a Player. I don't suppose you know what that really means, but depending on the story being enacted, I'm often given to playing the parts of women or girls for no women are allowed upon the stage anymore and I have little beard and a slim build." He shrugged. "It never crossed my mind until now that a woman could play the part of a boy just as easily. And yet here you are, doing so with skill enough to fool, well, all of us."

I smiled then. "You Players are not like other lowlanders are you?"

"Indeed not, Rhia. Oftimes, we're greeted and feted and hosted as if we're long lost brothers newly returned home. But lately, in the east, we're reviled. Cheated and scorned and forced to flee, as if we're worse than common cutpurses or vagabonds."

"Last season I thought of myself as simply another Hunter of Moonhart eknos." Thoughts of Sarae made me smile and long for those days. I thought everything I'd ever wanted had been mine. Until it ended. "And then black cloaks took my mother and others captive and Na Called me. So I ran from the Midcrag to the Kaircrag in chase, to find my mother and lose her again, this time to death. Now I no longer know what She Bids me do. Besides, no doubt the wolves have all fled the riots, taking the rest of the captives to Kairclavan and the one you people call the Prophet."

He didn't respond but looked towards the barn beyond Catha's barn, hidden by a high, separating wall. Then Sionn jumped up and smacked himself in the forehead. "I'm as foolish as Dughal thinks me."

"What?" I stood with him. "Tell me, I implore you."

He turned to me, all attempts to charm forgotten in his anxious haste. "Upon the road coming here His Own escorted two wagons filled with captives. Camran said His Own still flock heavily about the inn." He stopped and grasped my shoulders. "Would they guard an *empty* barn?"

I, too, turned towards that building so close. "Would they indeed?" My mind began to whirl with possibilities. "Can you show me where Barrol climbed up into the loft? I'd know if the other captives were so close to me as that." I pointed to the shadow of the stable.

"Better yet, I'll go with you." Sionn, all easy manner gone, implored me earnestly.

"Tis your choice. But first, I need my knife, which I left in the room upstairs. And my bow, but that's only just under the porch in back."

"I'll get your knife." He turned to the door, adjusted his tunic and paused a moment, lips moving. In a blink, all signs of eagerness or anxiety left his face, replaced by a markedly neutral expression. He opened the door and strode in, neither slinking nor hiding, but still very much unobtrusive. I heard no question or exclamation from within and left him to his task. For my part, I moved as quietly as if game had been sighted, crouching low so as not to be seen through the windows by those inside. Each step hurt my leg, each breath strained my ribs, each sudden movement made my head swim. But my spirits had risen: I had purpose again and an end to my quest lay just there, beyond that wall.

When Sionn met me by the back door, he handed me my knife in its sheath. He'd tied his hair back out of his eyes, the cuffs of his tunic and trews also tied down. I nodded: with clothing as ridiculous as this, to move in stealth required extra effort. I wanted my own tunic back but had to settle for kicking off the shoes and shucking the trews entirely, tearing the points in my haste.

Each movement hurt, but I did what I could to hide my hurts from Sionn so that he wouldn't decide against our hunt. As it was, he hardly blushed throughout this process. I'm sure Dughal would have been shocked and Camran disgusted. From the lack of noise inside, I guessed Sionn chose not to tell the others and for that I thanked him.

The setting sun shone full into the open barn and we stepped quickly into the darkness nearest the stalls so that our shadows wouldn't be seen should any be looking from the other side. Sionn glided through the darkness to the ladder and, with remarkable silence, began to scale the heights. Such motion brought fresh pain to my ribs and leg, a wave of red agony lashing my left side with every step. I tried to keep my breaths shallow as possible but my exertions called for more. I fought for a balance between pain and need. Need won out.

We passed the first level of the barn and up to the highest. Filled as it was with mounds of straw, moving through that mass without sound was like tracking ptarmigan through hunting season grasses. The dried straw threatened to rattle with every movement, and while I found the smell oddly comforting, the dust of it threatened to make me cough or sneeze. At the opening between the two buildings, Sionn made to go forward ahead of me. I pulled him back, held him close to me and whispered in his ear: "No! This is my battle with the black cloaks. Stay here. Watch. Be safe. I'd not have Dughal wroth with you."

He shook his head and flashed me a smile, his dimple at it's most charming. "Too late for that, Rhia. Let me go with you!"

I shook my head. "I require you here, watching and guarding my escape. If I need you, you'll know." I slipped passed him, pushing my bow ahead of me into the darkness and following with all the stealth needed for a hunt of such dangerous prey.

The hay loft was dark but three stories below I could see well enough, for His Own had torches lighting the center of the barn. A dozen men at least surrounded two carts while another pair set horses into their traces. At least ten people, mostly women, stood or lay within each cart, high walls caging them there. From what I could see of clothing, the wolves held both eknos and lowlanders.

385

I pulled arrows from my quiver and placed them in the straw before me, quick to hand. Bracing myself against the low rail that ran along the open side of the loft, I fitted an arrow to the string and pulled it back, ignoring the tearing pain in my side. I sighted down to one of the men outlined by the open doors and let fly the first arrow. By the time it had buried itself in his chest, I had loosed another towards one of the torchbearers and he, too fell.

By this time, the other black cloaks had begun shouting in alarm. To their confusion, and to let the captives know that rescue was at hand, I cried out a high, ululating cry, a hunting call of Moonhart eknos. The men below turned, looked up, searched the deadly darkness for me but two more men fell to my silent arrows ere they spotted me.

From below me strode the same man as had harangued the mob this morning. He shouted instructions to his men and they quickened their pace, getting the horses tied to the cart and moving them out the doors.

"Cowards!" I cried to them. "Craven lack-stones!" I taunted. My next arrow took another of the torchbearers full in the chest, his arms flying up and his torch falling into a pile of straw. Before I could aim again, the others had thrown their torches into barrels, extinguishing them and my aim, for the light from the doors had continued to fade. I shrieked out my call again and then startled to hear it taken up behind me. Sionn! Our two voices gave more resonance to my cry, making it echo within the barn. I heard answering cries from the wagon until one of the black cloaks thrust a spear within the bars of the cart.

"Go!" the leader called. "Get them out of here. The Prophet has need of them in Bierncarra."

Two more arrows I let fly but they fell without finding targets. I scrambled from my perch and raced for the ladder, heedless of noise or even the pain in my leg, my ribs, my head. Down the ladder to the second floor but most of the vile black cloaks had fled. The light of the new fire had grown, but the foul straw smoked as much as it flamed, obscuring my sight even further.

One more arrow did I set to string just as the last cart cleared the doorway of the barn. Their leader took that moment to turn and look back. I saw his face, the last of the evening sun falling full upon it. He laughed. I pulled my bow taut and let fly the last arrow. Alas, my bruised body, used beyond endurance, failed me. When agony spiked inside my battered skull, my eyesight blurred. I loosed the arrow anyway, but it flew wild. I fell.

I'd lost consciousness for a moment, for as I came to I looked up into the eyes of one of His Own. Alas, not the leader. His glance traveled from my shaved scalp to my lowlander tunic and my bare legs and feet. "What are you?"

The air around me burst into straw as Sionn lifted great handfuls of the stuff and rained it down upon me and the black cloak both. The flames began to lick and writhe with all the fresh fuel and the man took a step back, waving the smoke from his face.

Sionn scrambled over the railing of the loft and jumped the last few feet onto the back of the wolf. I struggled to rise, found the pain in ribs and leg even greater than before I had climbed the loft. Sionn had found some farm implement and began laying about himself as if with his staff. The black cloak fell back and drew a long knife. Sionn cried out the Moonhart cry again and leaped at the man.

The world turned dark as I managed to gain my feet and pull my own knife from my belt. Sionn held his own well, his staff work hampered by the shovel end. The black cloak began to retreat now that he faced both of us.

"No you don't!" Sionn cried. "I *see* you, blackguard!" He lunged. Sionn's foot slipped on a pile of fouled straw and he went down to one knee. The black cloak took his chance and stabbed at Sionn with the knife. Sionn twisted away, falling to his side. Again the black wolf stabbed. This time the knife found its mark.

"No!" I shouted. Sionn's hands grasped the knife, keeping the man from standing upright. I picked up Sionn's shovel and swept the man's legs with it, feeling the impact in my own ribs. He landed with a satisfying thump and I drove the blade of the shovel into his throat, the soggy-sharp sound of torn flesh and crushed spine echoed in the stillness of the barn. The blood drained out of him even as awareness dimmed from his eyes.

Unlike any animal I've ever killed, I didn't ask his forgiveness nor thank him for his sacrifice. Instead, I tossed the shovel aside, the bloody blade covered in gore and I turned away, gasping for breath and knelt beside Sionn. Seeing what had been done to him nearly brought me to tears but twas better than focusing on what I'd just done. "Damn you, lowlander. This wasn't your fight."

He reached up and touched the welt on his face. "Not true, Moonhart. I've been waiting three score days for that fight." Sionn's breath caught and he writhed upon the ground. "Damn me, but I'm dead, Rhia."

"No, Player. Tis simply my turn to carry you to the house."

He shook his head. "The fires grow around us, Rhia. Is it true that eknos burn their dead? Well then, I'll die with your cries upon my lips and find my new course through eknos."

"You talk too much." I bent down to lift him. *Ah! I don't know if I can. The pain takes all my breath.* I waited a moment for the world to come back up from the darkness but realized Sionn's words were correct. The fires grew, spreading even faster by all the straw Sionn had dumped on the floor. Smoke now filled the barn and rising heat prompted me to make haste.

"I can't carry you with that knife in," I told him. "This is going to hurt."

I yanked the knife from his chest.

"Aiee!" And then he smiled, blood on his teeth. "You tell no pretty lies, I'll give you that, Rhia."

"Press your hand upon the wound and I'll take us to Catha's." I lifted him then and carried him out of the barn, every step an agony for both of us.

Twenty-Nine

Dughal

I remember....

The argument within Catha's kitchen continued for some time. Sionn's words still hung most clearly in the air. Oean took up the part of our departed uplander. Beathen took the part of the silent Kyna. Catha had no trouble speaking for herself. Camran seemed to want to speak for all of the lowlands together. After some moments I fell silent and just listened to the dialog play out like a badly written script. After I'd heard enough, I raised my hand. It took some while, but silence fell.

"After what we've seen today, there's no question that we should leave Kairill as soon as we might deem it safe. This is no town for Players." I turned to the woman whose home we stood in. "Catha, I'm not proposing your abduction. It has proven too hot for Players, and I think, unmarried women, especially one with child. Simply tell us if there is family nearby with whom you will stay."

I turned to the oldest member of Bardeelin: "Yes, Camran, old friend, the uplander can – and no doubt will – choose her own path. We've done precious little to give succor to eknos wronged by His Own and offering her our protection and concealment is a small enough thing. I think we could hide her within the wagon and get her out of Kairill without further harm." I sighed and stood up from my chair. "If we're lucky, the worst of the storm has passed us and we can sleep here tonight, and make our final choices in the morn."

I helped myself to some of Catha's fine ale and walked to the door. Just as I lifted the latch, the door burst open and Rhia struggled into the room carrying a wounded Sionn.

"What did you do to him!" Camran moved as if to block her while Rhia struggled simply to hold Sionn aloft. Catha followed in Camran's wake and, more perceptive or less suspicious, assisted Rhia in laying her burden down upon a hastily cleared table. When Rhia's strength failed and she set him down heavily, his woof of air and gasp of pain told us he lived yet. Rhia staggered backwards and fell onto a chair, gasping, her arms wrapped around her ribs, her head bowed.

"Thank the God, you're alive," I told Sionn. Soot stained his clothes, smudged his face black where the blood hadn't made it red. Fear gripped my belly as the boy shook his head.

"No, Dughal dear." The boy's voice rose scarcely louder than a whisper. "Neither old goat's piss nor an 'pothecary can help me now. That black-cloaked bastard's knife took me in the lung."

"I'm sure we can —"

"Dughal." Catha's voice cut through my nonsense and I stopped. Blood frothed with every breath he took. Out, and it frothed his lips. In, and it bubbled from his chest.

"Now you've done it, Sionn," Oean said. "You'll be late for rehearsal."

Tear's rolled down Sionn's face but he managed a blood-stained smile. "Indeed, I'll be a grave Player now."

Catha roughly moved us aside and offered a drink to Sionn. I turned to the uplander crouching on the chair. "Tell the tale, eknos. What happened?" Soot stained her too but gore covered her as well. "By the Bargain, Rhia! Have you taken more hurts?"

She looked up at me, her face ashen, her pale green eyes shadowed with pain and more. She looked at the blood and matter dripping from the ruined tunic and her bare legs. "No, Dughal, I've no more injuries than before, although I fear I've made many of those much worse."

"I don't care about *her* hurts!" Camran cried. "What did she do to Sionn?"

"Saved me, you old fool." Sionn's burbling voice commanded our every attention.

"Ha!" Rhia cried out, her voice stricken. "Twas other way 'round, you fool."

"Twas turn and about," Sionn gasped.

"Hush, lad," I said. "Save your breath."

"No, Dughal. I'd say my last speech ere I leave this stage." His voice lacked all its usual vigor and volume. Not even the groundlings in the first row would have heard him and yet we all hung upon his every word. He told of Rhia's shot at Neacal but couldn't say if it landed. He told of her fall from the second story and his own rush down the ladder to her side, despite her admonition that he stay in Catha's barn. The fight with His Own he allowed Rhia to tell: she cursed the fouled straw with right good breath and, as if in passing, mentioned that she'd taken the life of the black cloak who'd murdered Sionn.

Catha strode to her window, then, and turned with a worried look. "Dughal! I see flames in the dark of the barn!"

"Are the animals still in there?" Camran asked.

"We need to put it out!" Beathen and Barrol rushed to the door.

"Hold!"

"All will burn, Dughal! Why do you call us to wait?"

"Hush! There, do you hear it? List!"

"To what?"

Oean opened the door and let in the sound of the riot. It raged, still. It raged closer.

"They come," I said. "The rioters come this way."

I began to appoint roles extempore, a macabre and most earnest streetshow. "Barrol! You and Oean take Sionn and Rhia direct to our wagon and secrete them inside for neither are in shape for another fight. Camran, Beathen, get to the wagon and make it ready. Take all the food you can from Catha's larder. We ride I know not how far nor how long before we might stop again. Catha, I'll help you and Kyna carry what belongings we can out to the wagon. We leave. All of us. Tonight." I stopped and the sound of the mob grew closer.

"Say rather within these ten minutes," Catha whispered.

"I hope we have that much time." I turned to the men. "Go!"

For all that they argue with me in the quiet times, my Players move with a will when times call for it. I followed the women up the stairs. This scene, Catha became the director and me just a bit player. She commanded us to gather what things she would, piled into various trunks.

"How much space do we have in that wagon of yours?" she asked.

"Not as much as I'd like so take only what is essential. If you have anything saying this house and land are yours, any deeds or copies of your father's will, take them as well. I don't know if you'll ever be able to return but I'd have the way made easier should it be your path."

She nodded and directed me to a wooden chest at the foot of her bed. We filled it with clothing for her and Kyna. Another chest we filled with bedding while into a third went papers, journals, mementos, and objects Catha couldn't bear to part with. A small enough amount and yet I resented the time it took to move it all.

Finally we loaded the three chests atop the wagon, lashed down beneath an oiled tarp. The women entered the wagon to find Sionn upon one of the four bunks built into the front wall, his breath harsh, faint, but present still. Rhia huddled upon the floor, her arms around her ribs but quiet as a mouse hiding from the cat. No choice but to leave them in there, hoping they might care for themselves and each other, as I closed the door and turned to face the mob.

Torches proclaimed their approach, for the twilight had given way to night. Clouds and smoke obscured the sky, leaving our path lit by the fire even now consuming the barns behind the house. Any animals that had been in that barn before the fire were dead or already escaped, for no ghastly screams pierced the night. I own I took solace in such a little thing, the absence of screaming.

Like an ocean whose tides were commanded by hate instead of the moon, the fell wave of rioters washed ever closer. Camran pushed the horses as fast as he dared. Navigating around piles of burning refuse athwart our path, Camran piloted our wagon like a float boat crew navigates sandbars on the lower Bainrill. I ran ahead, clearing what debris I could.

A black cloak rose up out of the spreading smoke, a cudgel raised high against me. I expected hate, a frenzied bashing at every thing in his path, but this man didn't hate. He marked me and lunged, his first blow scarcely missing.

I spun aside to escape his second blow and used that momentum to swing my staff hard against the backs of his legs. The meaty shock vibrated up my arm, but the black cloak fell to land with a whoof and a thud upon the paving stones. Surprise marred his features then, especially when I brought my staff down again, this time at his head. I had only a moment more to shove his unconscious body out of the way of our horses' charging hooves.

Did my face hold the frenzy that the carrion crow's had not?

Barrol and Beathen engaged a knot of rioters behind me. Beathen's strong arms propelled his staff – easily twice as thick and heavy as mine own – with painful accuracy. Crack! against the skull of one and thud! into the ribs of the second. Young Barrol fended off a third, a glancing blow that raked the man's face. The man cried out, dropping his club to clutch at his nose.

I ran to take his place, but Beathen, grim and focused, told me he could do best at the back, where the fighting was heaviest. I took Oean's place, leaving Beathen and Barrol to work as a team. Oean nodded, turned, and shouted. I heard the thwack of wood striking wood, and saw Oean engaged with another of His Own. This one had put aside his black cloak, but he still wore the midnight tunic and trews. More than that, I noted his expression. Similar to Beathen's in its grim determination to play his part.

Oean shouted again, this time in surprise. Quicker than ever I'd seen him, he flicked his staff against his attacker's wrist, followed by a fast reversal, bringing the heel of the staff up into the black cloak's jaw. Metal rang on cobbles: Oean had struck a bladed weapon from the hand of His Own.

"My thanks!" I called to him. At Camran's shout, Oean sprinted towards our horses.

The dire task of those behind the wagon tired me faster than what lay ahead of us. All through that first hour we rotated duties, fore and aft, Oean and I, as Beathen and Barrol worked as a team to keep rioters from overturning the cart.

Our staff work surprised them, a surprise I found myself pleased to offer. Townsfolk turning on Sealed Players!? No better than brigands from the days of story and I treated them as they deserved. I took joy in swinging hard at their heads. I reveled in the sounds of bones cracking as I lashed out at knees and elbows. Let them remember Bardeelin for our prowess if not for our poetry.

Given our resistance, given weaker targets on either side of us, I expected our way would clear soon enough. But the rioters followed us; down the streets, past the inn, through the gates, and out into the fields beyond the town, their voices shrieking vile invective. The same faces I saw again and again. No mere rioters these. They'd been sent to take us of a purpose, their black cloaks laid aside for the moment, their black hearts on full display.

Finally, more than half a league outside the town, the pursuit ended, the last "rioters" racing back for the town's limits. "Camran! I think you can slow down and save the horses."

"Yes, Dughal. Of course."

"Barrol, you and I will take first watch if you please. Run ahead and I'll walk behind. Call out if you see aught amiss and I'll do the same. Beathen and Oean, one of you climb upon the high seat with Camran and the other upon the tail of the cart. Catch your breath for we'll need spelling soon enough, but keep your eyes open. I'd not be taken unawares."

"What course, Dughal?"

"Away. We're heading west, let's keep to it. There should be few farms as we approach the Crags." I hawked and spat on the ground. "I've not much desire for the company of others at the moment."

I spared neither us nor the horses over much, knowing we could rest on the morrow should we get far enough away that night. A dark and harrowing journey it was. The clouds never did part, the moon never looked down to see our reckless flight. Just at daybreak, the full and humid air finally gave up its burden and it began to rain. Mist at first, then drops. When it began to rain in torrents we pulled off of the road for a sodden campsite.

In a small clearing, with a screen of trees, we might be seen if sought. I only had strength enough left to hope we weren't sought. The women had kept quiet within the wagon the entire journey and I finally opened the door to see how Sionn and they fared.

Catha stood, smoothed the fall of her tunic and walked to me. "I'm sorry, Dughal."

It took me a moment, I confess it. I couldn't understand why this woman, whose home had just been abandoned to the mob's most untender mercies, might be apologizing to me. And then a sensation like a great blow struck my gut.

"Ah, Sionn!" Beathen's hand reached out for me and I gathered the big man to myself. "I told the boy not to play the hero, didn't I?"

"Not that he ever listened, Dughal," Beathen said. "Sionn took great delight in vexing you."

"Not enough that he vexed me in life, he vexes me with his death."

Camran roared his grief and charged into the wagon. I thought he'd simply fall down upon Sionn. No. He shoved Rhia from the wagon to fall sprawling upon the grass.

"You! You caused this. Eknos bring nothing but pain and destruction!"

"You dare!?" Oean stepped between Rhia and Camran. "Put the blame where it's deserved, Camran. The lowlanders that gave us such sore hurts hurt her as well. No uplander placed good women against poles as sport for the mob. No woman of eknos shoved a knife into Sionn's chest, nor burned Catha's home!"

"Easy, Oean," I said. "We're all overwrought. Seek not to continue the destruction His Own began."

Oean nodded and turned away, wracked by his own grief. I, too, faced the trees and stood in the rain, all unknowing. Not until some time later did I realize that Catha and Kyna had taken Sionn's body from the wagon, wrapped it tightly against the weather in an old blanket, and moved it to lie upon the wagon's roof, beneath the tarp that covered the trunks. There would he stay until we could find him a final resting spot.

Catha touched my arm and gently began moving me and the others into the wagon and out of the rain. It would be tight inside the wagon with all eight of us but I saw nothing for it. My weariness threatened to pull me under at near every step. Only when Camran again began shouting at Rhia did I rise above the fog in my mind.

"I'll not sleep with her in the wagon!"

I took him by the arm. "Camran! That's enough —"

"No, Dughal." Rhia's voice cut through the anger and the raging grief. "I've had enough of wooden walls and violent lowlanders." She grabbed her pack and made for herself a place beneath the wagon, sheltered from the rain but open to the winds. I'd no will left to insist upon one choice or another. All my choices had proven ill, any wise, so I left her there, me as heartless as His Own.

Sleep first. My dreams were full of heat and flames, the faces of women stoned to death, the bodies of women and men, too, that we'd passed on our way out of town. When I awoke I felt worse than before I'd lain down to sleep but I could no longer face the terror awaiting me in my dreams. I pushed the blankets aside and stood up to face a sodden day.

Thirty

Rhia

Make my final bed
A planting long not shallow.
Place me in the cold dark bed
Sow me in the fallow.

- Maira's Lament, Song

The night of the riot, the pain and exhaustion have won out. I awoke at one point by being tossed around within the black belly of the swaying and lurching wagon, with no memory of how I'd gotten there. No knowledge, either, of how I'd been dressed again in my own uplander tunic, but grateful that I no longer wore the twice-bloodied one that Catha had loaned to me. Kyna cried out when the shuddering escalated to such a degree I thought the wagon would tip, so I knew she shared my confinement with me. Sionn, too, for his breathing resounded harsh in the darkness, even over the shouts from all around us and the crunch of the wagon wheels below us.

After some while, the shouting grew less and I felt a change in the motion of the wagon. "Ah," Catha said. "We must be outside the town. The wagon slows."

She lit a lamp then. She must have left it dark during the worst, in case the swaying upset the lamp, spilling oil to burn the wagon or one of us. I shuddered. I needed no more fire just then.

Even after two days in Kairill and a day in Catha's home, the interior of the Player's wagon stood out as the space most alien to me I can ever recall. The two narrow walls, front and back, held four bunks each, one atop the other. I'd crawled into one at the rear while Sionn had been placed in the lowest at the front. Curtains could be closed over the bunks and another curtain covered the left hand wall. Behind it piled boxes and odd, assorted clothing folded into baskets. For as crowded as the left hand wall seemed to be, the right hand wall had nothing, not even a curtain across it, save for what looked like the outline of a double door just about half way between the two ends, yet five feet or more up the wall.

Catha and Kyna moved to where Sionn lay, bathing his brow and doing what they could to comfort him. I could tell by their murmured responses that Sionn still lived and even shared japes with them. Kyna laughed more than once, her hand going to her mouth as if to stop the noise, and then Sionn would say something else. I could well imagine him smiling that charming smile, his dimple breaching even Kyna's guarded heart.

Then Sionn's laughter bubbled into coughing and a final "Ah!" and no more.

Kyna turned away, Catha bowed her head, and I laid back upon the bunk, and allowed the curtain to fall over me. I didn't know what customs lowlanders have for their dead. I could only give them space and a semblance of privacy in which to perform their rituals. In my thoughts I wished Sionn well upon his new journey, and thanked him for his thoughtfulness towards me and mine.

The dark and the constant sound of the wagon's motion lulled me back to sleep, for I heard nothing until the motion stopped. Catha opened the doors and let down the stairs. I heard cries outside and my stomach knotted in shared anguish. I bowed my head, my own grief being given voice in the loud cries of the Players.

Camran burst upon me, flinging open the curtains and shouting incoherent words. He pulled me from the wagon, dragged me down the steps, and tossed me sprawling upon the ground, pain ringing out from every limb, bruise, and cut.

"You! You caused this. Eknos bring nothing but pain and destruction!"

I shook my head, as much to deny as to clear it. Camran's rough treatment had re-awakened all my injuries: the pain in my ribs kept my breath from me, the leg ached so that I couldn't stand, and a red agony shot through my head. The shouting between the Players blurred and I feared I'd lose consciousness again, this time with enemies at hand. Sometime later, when Oean knelt down next to me, I didn't know if he meant me harm or not. Then he helped me to my feet, gave me his shoulder to lean against, and assisted me into the wagon. I'd just reached the bunk when Camran again started shouting at me. I turned ready to yell in turn, defend myself against his baseless claims.

I saw his face.

The lines had deepened, in weariness and grief, his rain wet hair lay dark and curled upon his scalp. Twas the expression in his eyes that stopped the words in my mouth, for I knew those eyes. I'd looked out of them earlier that day when I cried for the death of my mother. Sionn may have been Camran's son, of kin or kith it didn't matter. He roared his grief and anger at me, for Sionn lay beyond his hearing.

"I'll not sleep with her in the wagon!"

Dughal reached out to chastise Camran and I raised my hand. "No, Dughal. I've had enough of wooden walls and violent lowlanders."

I slept little, that night beneath the wagon. Lightning flashed, thunder rolled down from the crags, and as much rain blew in below the wagon as fell above it. Sodden and aching, I sat up, wrapped in what blankets I had, and leaned against one of the wagon's wheels to await the daylight.

The storm faded with the morn, although the clouds still massed thickly to the east and no sunrise greeted me. Dughal came out first and I doubt he slept any more than I had. His eyes, as he looked upon me, were haunted by all that had occurred in the last span of days.

"We travel again today, since the rain is holding off for now. I'd find a better place to lay Sionn to his final rest: better for him and us."

I didn't know what his words meant and took no time to ask. The others came out of the wagon talking and arguing amongst themselves and Dughal left to join them. Catha touched me on the shoulder and then handed me some food. "You've had my bread before, Rhia," she reminded me. "The other is cheese."

Kyna scoffed at my ignorance and rolled her eyes at me before she turned away. I nibbled at the cheese. It had a creamy texture and an almost nutty flavor. It filled me up. I couldn't remember when last I'd eaten. Before the fight in the barn, surely.

"Can you walk?" Catha asked.

I nodded. "Yes." And then I stood. "No. Not far, at least."

She nodded and signaled to Dughal. He wasn't surprised by the news and actually looked somewhat relieved. He glanced but once at my short uplander tunic and then said: "Into the wagon with you, then. You too, Kyna. We walk as far and as fast as we can, before either black clouds or black cloaks descend upon us again."

And so I spent another day within that wagon, sleeping when I could, clutching at walls and bunk when the swaying got to be too much. Kyna took the bunk above where Sionn had died, the entire length of the wagon from me, so we shared no conversation. No matter. Sleep served me best: I'd not be spending any longer amongst these sowers than I must.

Sleep I did, waking only long enough to note the stillness of the wagon and to consider getting out, smelling air that didn't reek of wet wool, blood, and seething hatred. Before the thought even finished, I fell asleep for the rest of the day.

Dughal's entry into the wagon woke me. He went to Kyna's bunk and whispered in her ear. She nodded, glanced once at me, and nodded again, climbing out of the bunk where she lay. Dughal then came over to me.

"Dughal?" I asked. "What's happening?"

He looked haggard still but now even more weary with a day spent walking. Mud stained his clothes and hands and he rubbed at his thumb when he spoke with me.

"The grave is dug. We bury Sionn as the sun sets." His voice caught on the last and he closed his eyes, his chin quivering but no sound did he make.

"Bury?" O, by Na's warm breath! They plant even their dead!" My revulsion at this perversion caught my breath in my throat. But then I fought to push aside my own feelings. The ekma would be proud if I've learned just how much I have to learn, about the world and about myself, too. If these folk bury their dead, then I'll honor that. Even though the very thought of it raises pebbleflesh on my arms. I'll show to these distrustful Players that eknos recognizes honor and courage.

I breathed deep and said: "I'd be present at the, the ... burying, if I may."

He nodded but said no more, all but fleeing the wagon. Kyna had turned away from me, or perhaps Dughal, and had begun to change into different clothing. I crawled slowly out of the bunk and began to search for my pack that had a change of clothes, the same tunic I'd worn for the feast with White Eagle.

"Kyna? Do you know where my pack might have gone to? I, too, would change into cleaner clothing to honor Sionn."

"Honor? How can you not understand?" She sat down upon one of the trunks. "It's your fault Sionn's dead! No one wants you there, savage and unrepentant for his murder."

I gasped and sat down heavily. As if she'd struck me again in the tender ribs, I couldn't find my breath. "Murder? How can you say that to me, when my own mother lies dead and unburned, her body defiled? You speak to me of murder when you and yours would do such as that?"

"I had nothing to do with that!" She leapt to her feet and brandished the stockings clutched in her hands as she would a weapon. "Liar!"

The shouting, my own and hers, hurt my head. I held up my hand asking for peace, or at least silence. "I know, Kyna. I can tell the difference between those that would kill both you and me, and those who have offered kindness and assistance. Even sacrifice." I sighed and struggled to stand upright. "Can you?"

She paled but was too far gone in grieving over her many losses to heed any words of mine. "He sought to help you! And now Dughal and all his Players run for their very lives into the trackless wilderness."

"Did you hear me ask for their help? Lay not their decisions – not Dughal's, nay nor Sionn's neither – to my charge. I asked for none of it."

"You may as well have, you lack-father! The Players have to bury one of their own. Me, I'm running again with no hoped-for hiding place at the end and my condition grows ever more plain. Catha's home burned, did you know that?" Before she'd even finished buttoning the many buttons on her tunic, she stormed from the wagon. "I'm done with you!"

I sat down again since I still didn't know where my pack was. *My own mother lies dead and unburned.* A knot of grief welled up within me and I bent over, not sure if I sought the release of tears or made effort to push them back. The pain in my ribs and head had redoubled, pushing me back upright, back from the edge of mourning. "Now what am I to do?"

After some minutes, the door opened and Catha slipped inside. I couldn't see her features, backlit as she was from the open door. "By the lonely God, Rhia. Those bruises make you look as mottled as a Harvest season moonhart." She closed the door and stepped inside, shrugging out of her tunic as she did so. While making a great show of being very casual in her nakedness in front me of, she too, put on fresh clothing.

"Catha, I'm told that the Players honor Sionn tonight. I'd join them, but I can't find my pack. I have a clean tunic and I'd wear it so as to not dishonor...."

To my dismay, my words ended in tears.

Catha quickly knelt by my side as the sobs wracked my body. As if a dam had burst against the season's melt, tears poured out of me: tears for Sionn and my mother both. I clung to Catha as a swimmer clings to a branch in the torrent. She murmured sweet words I didn't hear and held me close, waiting with all the patience of a mother. Which only made me cry the harder.

By Na, what have I done? In my pride, perhaps I didn't understand Her Calling after all. Every step I've taken has been taken wrong. Kiri would still be alive if not for me entering Lynx territory alone. Sionn would be alive as well, not dead to some black wolf's fang. These foul wolves still have every captive, save those they've murdered. Now my mother lies dead and cold and I can't even give her a daughter's duty by putting her to the pyre.

I think some of what went through my head I also mumbled aloud but with no more clarity than Catha's own murmured words as she tried to soothe me. When the sobs faded, when I found myself able to breathe without gasping, she took my hands and looked me in the eyes.

"Sionn's death is no fault of yours. I've heard little today but reminiscences of Sionn and he was ever one to set his own course, damning advice from all others. Dughal and he even came to blows over such a thing and while I'm sure that was terrible at the time, now the Players laugh at it as example of Sionn being the most himself." She handed me a square of cloth and motioned that I should wipe my eyes and nose. "You'll find little opposition to your desire to honor him. And in so doing, perhaps we can honor your mother as well."

Catha found my pack and helped me into a clean tunic. I took some moments to wash the tears from my face and, on impulse, took Grainna's flute in case sowers honor their dead with music. "What happens at a ... burial?" I asked. "You truly bury your dead? In the ground?"

Catha's smile was kind. "Yes, indeed we do, returning to the soil even as we take from the soil our food."

"Seems so *cold*."

"For one who burns her dead, I can imagine you'd think so. But it's what we expect and what Sionn would've wanted." I didn't tell her of his desire to be burned in the flames of the barn fire. Perhaps he hadn't really meant it after all.

She helped me from the wagon. Camran turned away when he saw me, but Dughal took my arm and helped me walk the short distance to where they'd dug a deep pit, deeper than a standing woman is tall and long as Sionn's body. They'd wrapped his corpse in a dark green blanket and tied it closed across the chest and the ankles. The others stood with the grave between him and them, as if his death were something that could reach out and touch them.

Catha spoke to Dughal for a moment, glancing at both me and Sionn's body as she did so.

"Yes, you well may be right." He motioned to the others, gathering them close.

As Catha came over to stand next to me, with Kyna on the other side of her, the younger men sprang away, all save Camran who glowered at me again but said nothing. I looked an inquiry at Catha but she just smiled a reassuring smile. "Just wait, Rhia, and all will be clear." And with that I had to be content.

We'd stopped in a clearing full of young trees, lands that hadn't seen the plow within my lifetime. The uplands of White Eagle lay still some distance to our west, while to the northeast a butte rose up out of the lowland plains. The sun, low in the sky, illuminated the butte and I caught my breath at the beauty, the ruddy light setting the pale green leaves afire.

The men came back, each carrying dead fall, branches, and any brush they could find in such a short while. They piled it high at the foot of the grave, nearer to where I stood. "Rhia?" Dughal moved to my side. "I can't say as I know anything about eknos customs for the dead, save that you burn instead of bury. To my shame, we don't have your mother's body here, but we'd light a pyre to her." He held up his hand quickly, mistaking my shock. "Only if you feel that it'd be to her honor." He blushed, his face even more ruddy in the sunset. "As I said, I don't know the custom."

It took me several tries. I opened my mouth but no words could be found, so I shut it, only to try again. My eyes turned hot and something felt large in my throat, stopping all speech. Finally, after some moments wherein Dughal began to look most uncomfortable, I managed a nod. His relief came so rapidly that it broke the dam in my throat. "I would be most honored, Dughal, if you and yours would sit vigil for my mother."

"And Grainna," Oean said, earning him a smile of thanks from me.

"Do we just light it?" Dughal asked. "Are there words to be said?"

I shook my head. "She isn't here to heed our words. We stay in silence when the pyre is lit, for at the end there is no breath for tales. After it has begun to burn down, then we tell tales. But you know of no tales of my mother." I wiped my face and stood as tall as my painful leg would allow. "A few moments, while the pyre takes flame, within our own thoughts. I'd ask nothing more."

"So be it." Dughal motioned to Barrol who poured oil over the damp wood and to Beathen who carried a bucket of hot coals from their cooking fire. Soon, the makeshift bonfire began to burn, smoking mightily. Rightly enough, the smoke blew west, into the woods and up the crags.

Once it had caught as well as it might, I nodded to Dughal. The sun's edge had just touched the horizon when Dughal went to stand next to Sionn's corpse. "From night arises the day, and falls into night yet again. From the soil we take our food, upon the soil we live our lives..." and here his voice caught and he closed his eyes as he said: "...howsoever long or short. We return to the soil at our death and thus are all things kept in balance."

Dughal and Camran placed a length of rope beneath Sionn's shoulders while Oean and Beathen did the same at his feet. Together, they lifted Sionn up and slowly lowered his body into the ground, pulling the ropes free at the end. They bowed their heads, their thoughts to themselves. I followed their lead, my memories of the brief time I'd known the Player all too quickly done.

After some moments, Dughal turned to us. His red-rimmed eyes were dry for the nonce and he stood tall as he declaimed: "I remember Sionn: when he petitioned to join Bardeelin, he promised most earnestly to do all that I told him to do with neither complaint nor demur." The others laughed and sobbed (twas often difficult to tell between the two) while Dughal raised a skin and drank from it. He handed the wineskin to Catha and then picked up the shovel stuck into the mound of earth that lay next to the grave. With a grimace upon his face, he threw down dirt upon Sionn's body. I looked away but couldn't close my ears to the wet thud as soil fell upon the canvas wrapped corpse. I shuddered and listened to the flames of my mother's pyre. *And Grainna's.*

Catha waited until Dughal had returned the shovel to the pile. Like myself, she'd only just met the man whose body they now threw dirt upon. Her shoulders slumped and she seemed lost in thought, grieving for other things lost than just new acquaintance. She stood up tall and brushed her hair back behind her ears. Her voice sounded steady and she smiled gently. "I remember Sionn: his passionate desire to help all those taken by His Own and held unjustly." She drank and the others nodded. While she tossed in a scoop of soil, Camran glanced at me and then away.

Oean took the wineskin next. He looked down into the hole and then up at us, his hands clenching and unclenching. "I remember Sionn: When he first began learning the plays of Bardeelin he'd often say the lines aloud, for his reading wasn't strong. His smile when he found a well-wrought phrase or particularly apt image could light a room. And did light my heart, I do confess it." His tears ran freely down his face as he drank of the wineskin. "'In the end, your words are but dust.'" He reached for the shovel and tossed dirt down into the grave.

Beathen held the wineskin. He stood tall, shoulders straight, his tunic clean and without a wrinkle. "I remember Sionn," he said, his light voice rough with emotion. "Juggling with him was both a pleasure and a challenge. He strove to push both himself and me to our utmost." And then Beathen slumped down with a shuddering laugh. "Well, push me at least."

"To distraction!" Oean called out to great, cleansing laughter.

Beathen looked at me a moment and raised an eyebrow. I nodded and he handed me the wine before going to the grave side and tossing down the dirt.

I looked to my mother's pyre, burning well despite the rain of the last few days, and then I turned to face that cold hole in the ground. "I remember Sionn: during the fight in the barn, he struck down the man who had struck him in the road outside of Kairill. In that way, Sionn found a measure of justice." I drank and Barrol took the skin from me, his eyes bright. When I picked up the shovel, I realized my strength wouldn't allow me to dig very deep. Still, I honored their custom and dropped the heavy clods down upon Sionn's still form. *Forgive me, my too-soon lost friend. Your last sleep will be cold indeed.*

411

Barrol wiped his nose with the sleeve of his tunic and then stood up straight, flipping his head so that his long hair fell back, over his shoulder. "I remember Sionn: in rehearsal—"

"When he wasn't late!" Beathen called out.

Barrol choked back a sob. "When he wasn't late, he'd chide my performance something awful. Even when it wasn't my fault! But afterward, he joked with me and helped me with my lines." Barrol finished in a rush and all but threw the wineskin to Kyna before grabbing the shovel.

For her part, Kyna looked startled to have the wineskin in her hand. "I remember Sionn," she said, drank, and handed the skin to Camran. She took the shovel from Barrol and heaved in a large clot of dirt, much more than I had managed.

Camran's hair looked more gray in the flickering light of the bonfire and his beard looked patchy and rough. He turned towards everyone but his eyes never sought mine. I bowed my head, trying to give him the space to grieve. "I remember Sionn: when he first joined Bardeelin, I argued with Dughal over letting him in. Too unlettered, too uncouth, I said. Well," Camran drawled the word out. "I was right! And so very, very wrong. Now I've lost a second son, even if he wasn't of my body." He drank, handed the skin to Dughal, and threw down a large scoop of soil.

And so it went, turn and about, for as long as there was a pile of dirt beside the grave. When next the skin came my way, Beathen handed it to me without hesitation. "I remember Sionn: he seemed most bemused that, while he'd often played the woman's role, never had he met a woman who would play a man's role." I shook my head, glancing at each of the Players. "I don't understand all of that, but I'm glad that I gave him a small amount of pleasure in something new." I drank and I shoveled and so it went.

It takes a long while to fill a hole so deep. Stories and remembrances were shared and even laughter amidst the tears. I had glanced at Dughal when his laughter choked off after one such jest.

The sad joy of such sharing became eclipsed in his eyes. With each passing round of the wine skin, with each shovel full of dirt mounded upon Sionn's cold body, his jaw became more set, his eyes more hard. At last, the wineskin came back to him and he stepped forward one last time.

"I remember Sionn." Dughal paused as he stared at the mound below which his Player lay. He turned to us and, in the light of my mother's pyre, his eyes sparkled like wet granite. "I remember Sionn telling us we should do more: to burn Grainna as she'd asked. To resist Neacal's insidious machinations. To rescue the women held by His Own. He was my conscience and I ignored him." Dughal wiped his nose on his sleeve and stood up tall. "Now, he has no more to give. Beside Sionn's grave and by the light of Selwe's fire, I tell you now. Sionn had the right of it. There's nothing for us in Bainellen, God-bothered and benighted land! We head back north and then west to the Falcon Way."

Beathen's laugh choked off at the end. "He would've been delighted to hear you've heeded his words, Dughal."

"Would that I could tell him so. But what we will do is tell all of Anacarra what we've seen here. Sionn's death will make a tale worth telling throughout the west. No more will we be yoked to Neacal's plow. If tools we are, then we'll be a firebreak, doing what we can to stop what we've seen in Bainellen from spreading." Dughal poured the last of the wine upon the mound of Sionn's grave and picked up the shovel. With nary a pause he marched past his men and towards the wagon.

The lowlanders then turned from the grave to follow Dughal back to the wagon. "Rhia?" Catha asked. "Do you need help walking back?"

"I thank you, but no. I have sought to honor your friend Sionn and now I seek to honor my mother. It's our way. I'll sit here in vigil beside the pyre until dawn."

Oean had hung behind and he looked from me to the other players and back to me. "Do you wish, that is, should we keep vigil with you?"

I shook my head. "You never met my mother, met Grainna only at the last, and are not of Moonhart." I smiled at him, warmed by his offer no matter how uncomfortable it had been for him to make it. "There is no obligation."

The others had already gone back to the wagon, led by Camran and Kyna. Oean looked again at me and then Catha. She said to me: "Do you wish to be alone, Rhia?"

I nodded, not trusting my words would be heard. *I wish to be with my mother.*

They left me then, Oean with relief, Catha after she squeezed my shoulder. Standing, I moved closer to the bonfire for the night was cold and placed myself between the fire and the grave. There had been too many vigils this year, and the year yet young: Sleikin, Kiri, and now Grainna and my mother. Since the night of Na's Calling, how many more eknos had died and been left unburned? "I remember Sorchen and Grainna, Gellae and Treassa," I whispered to Na or the night, it didn't much matter. "And of the 'two hands of us' Grainna had told Dughal had been held with her, how many still lived? Is there any yet for me to save?"

I shut my mouth. I had no tales to tell. Or more rightly, no one to tell them with. Not even my mother's body was near to hand, despite that her pyre was. So I took up Grainna's flute and began to play. She'd fashioned it differently than my mother had her wooden one, but I could still manage to place my fingers upon the holes and play wordless songs, to rise up into the woods with the smoke.

The long night stretched ahead of me and a longer road stretched behind. I was so tired. Tired unto death. So tired I'd share an earthen bed with Sionn or a warm blanket of ash with my mother. *Nothing more can be asked of me. I've failed. I'm finished.*

I will say I didn't fall asleep that night, although the hurts my body had suffered over the last hand of days perhaps robs me of credence. But Na has no need of even sought after sleep when She wills it. Before dawn, the Calling dream came upon me again.

Upon the Crags, wolves still threaten the glaring of lynx, the convocation of eagles, and the call of moonhart: rending and tearing and harrowing. But the animals begin to move, to react to the danger in their midst, and hope arises in me. Alas, the flood threatening the lowlands churns and roils, cascading down from the walls of the Kaircrag in violent torrents, forcing the Bainrill from its bed to inundate the land, rising higher and faster than before. My hope dashes like water upon rocks. Fear and pain and despair fills the emptiness within me. The flood seems poised to cover all of Bainellen and flow through the lowest places in the Crags to cover all of Anacarra.

The urge to flee overcomes me, to run and bound like a deer seeking any bit of higher ground in the face of the flood. But then I feel Her presence stilling those fears, transmuting them into something else. Not flight but escape. Then a final, awful image, of a single moonhart doe, caged upon a huge wagon, surrounded by threatening men. *No, that's not right! That poor doe is dead, I sit before her pyre!* But the image persists, blurring and resolving again. A doe upon a wagon, yes. And while I see no cage, she still isn't free. The men around the cage throw about knives and clubs and stones. I feel no threat from the weapons but neither do I feel protected by them. The wagon, the men, and the moonhart doe, all travel into the west, to a destination I can't discern.

I awoke to sounds of the lowlanders milling about: eating breakfast, packing the wagon, readying the camp for departure. I arose, stiff and sore, sharp pains in my side and leg. I limped to the fireside to take my share of food. I had to rebuild my strength. My mother was dead, but eknos are still held and threatened by His Own.

Na wasn't done with me yet.

Thirty-One

Epistle the Fourth

15th Ailinaian, Near Kairill

To Cleirach durMiach, Prophet and Voice of the Lonely God: I bring you greetings from the fellowship of His Own, south of Kairill.

Thank you, ancari'ni, for your kinds words regarding the successes of the Spectacle in Kairill on Tudae last. Evil elements within Kairill were Purged in a fire that consumed near half of the oldest and most disreputable parts of the town and utterly destroyed the amphitheater.

As always, your generosity astounds me. My seconds will meet up with your hand-picked company of architects and workmen. Having them direct the rebuilding of Kairill into a shining example of Na's power and might will allow all to see your Benevolent hand. The local carrinanen will come to see the wisdom of your guidance. The Lesson displayed in the amphitheater has not been lost on the old leadership, decadent and degenerate though they may be.

Bardeelin has since disappeared but another troupe of Players has been reported in the south of Bainellen, one called Siodaric's Pride. I suspect they'll cross my path as I journey to Gerramer. I'll offer them the same option as I did Bardeelin: play *Nabryhtric's Heir* or be destroyed. So will all Players be yoked to the God's Plow or become nothing more than manure spread upon the fields.

I also bring you word of great successes, my ancari'ni. The demonstrations continue throughout Bainellen. In each village and town we've seen a great uprising of devotion for the Will of the Lonely God. The old order trembles to see the Glorious fervor: many have sought me out and given unto me tokens of their intentions to follow you in all ways. Others have fled, their carrins left untended. Ah, my most Beloved Cleirach, the ground, hard packed and long fallow, is being turned by the God of the Plow, broken anew so that your words may sow a new beginning, for Bainellen and all of Anacarra.

In addition to the great, the lowly have begun showing renewed Reverence for the proper way of things. Good men in these towns have delivered unto us the names of evil or depraved Harlots living in their midst. We add these to our number of captives.

I gift the most healthy of the eknos to the most devout of His Own for their use for a handful of days, spreading the Blessing of the God of Seed. We're more careful in this use of the uplanders than we have heretofore, so I anticipate half a dozen or more will still be for use at your discretion upon your arrival in Bierncarra at the end of the season.

But, mistakes do happen. For any uplander that comes to conceive or suffer any other unfortunate damage, I'll use them in a spectacle. The Harlots we've taken can be used in various ways, of course. If we're fortunate enough that the eknos stay healthy, why then we'll shave the head of some Whore and present her as Savage Uplander somewhere down the road. The seeming is what matters. That, and that the townsfolk develop a taste for shedding uplander Blood.

Yours, in the service of the God of Sheaves, Commander of His Own,

Neacal durCleirach

Miscellany

Glossary

Ainaricin   Favored Player troupe of the First

Anaric   Male ruler of the Rici. The later lords were called Aric

Anaricu   Female ruler of the Rici. The later women who ran the estates were called (sometimes derisively) Aricu.

Aric   Lords who command the provinces during the Republic

Bardeelin   Player troupe of which Dughal is the leader

Botha   A structure made of woven branches covered in bark that the uplanders sleep in. They leave them in place and go to the next ekarra where another botha waits. Some of the bark panels can be removed for increased air flow in the summer.

Carrinani   How one would refer to a carrinan or carrinanen. Often shortened to carri'ni.

Carrin   Small land holder. Most people outside of villages are small holders or "carrins." These lands can be any sized plot from an eighth of an acre to several dozen acres and are held by grant from the larger land owner.

Carrinan   Moderate land holder. Could be a carrin that acquired enough land to subdivide it into plots

	that other carrins hold lease.
Carrinanen	Large land holder. Enough acreage that the land holder can grant land to both carrinans and carrins.
Clav	The term given to a religious house.
Clavan	The term given to a female religious house
Crofters	landless tenants on another's property
Dar	Means child of a female parent.
Dir	Means mate/spouse of. Can be a prefix for either the male or female
Dur	Means child of male parent.
Ekarra	The gathering place of the eknos. Each eknos has four primary ekarras, one for each of the different seasons. Can be used to denote any camping or collection of dwelling places.
Ekma	The title given to the woman who leads each of the different eknos of uplanders
Eknos	The word used to describe the culture of the uplanders. Can denote both the people and the tribes
Eksig	The marks that each of the eknos wear that distinguish them from the other eknos.
	Moonhart's mark is on the upper right arm
	Lynx's mark is on upper chest, on the breastbone
	White Eagle's is on their upper left arm
	Elk's mark is on their right upper thigh
	Hawk's mark is on their forehead
	Bear's mark is on their left upper thigh
	Cougar's mark is on the back of their neck
	Serpent's mark is on their face/cheeks
	Falcon's mark is on their lower left forearm
Goddess' Touch	A sexually transmitted disease that affects pretty much everyone in the uplands to the point where

they consider it to be part of becoming sexually active. The virus becomes active or present in both mucus and the mucus membranes (mouth, vagina, anus) and other bodily fluids. It is absorbed easily by the skin, particularly the thin skin of the vagina, penis, rectum, or mouth. It does not require penetrative intercourse to be spread, but is not likely to be spread simply by deep kissing.

Symptoms:
Sense of well-being, euphoria
High fever and mania
Disorientation, light sensitivity, hallucinations
Sexual symptoms include lust/desire, insatiability, inability to orgasm and/or multiple orgasms (male and female).

His Own   Fundamental religious group founded by Cleirach of Kairnaclav monastery, also known as The Prophet. They become a force imposing a kind of orthodoxy on the population of the lowlands.

Lifros   uplander word for the vulva

Lifthorne   uplander word for the penis

Moonhart   An elk sized deer that changes hide from deep brown, almost black in summer to fit in the deep woods, to a shade of white/gray in winter. The name references the phases of the moon going from dark to light and back again.

Also the name of one of the eknos.

Nacarri'ni or **Ancarri'ni**   How one would refer to a nacarrinan/ancarrinan or nacarrinanen/ancarrinanen in speech.

Nacarrin or **Ancarrin**	Small holder of land held by a religious house. Prefix is determined by whether the house is male (naclav) of female (clavan)
Nacarrinan or **Ancarrinan**	Moderate land holder. Could be a carrin that acquired enough land to subdivide it into plots that other carrins hold lease. Prefix is determined by whether the house is male (naclav) of female (clavan)
Nacarrinanen or **Ancarrinanen**	The clav itself, such as Karinaclav, that grants lands to others. Prefix is determined by whether the house is male (naclav) of female (clavan)
Naclav	The term given to a male religious house
Nawroth	"God's Wrath." A plague brought about initially by a spore that infected a clavan that had sought to enlarge its domain by cutting down some of the uplands. This is a very virulent plague and spreads rapidly. In the initial out break in the reign of Unrad'naric the Unready over 45% of the population died off within a few months. This lead to the destabilization of the Rici, the ascent of the Two to become the Nine in the uplands, and the creation of the Five Republics.

Symptoms:
Sense of well-being, euphoria
High fever and lethargy
Disorientation, light sensitivity, hallucinations
Intense headache pain and spasms leading to unconsciousness and death

Nosmoot	Gathering of all of the eknos every three years.
Rici	Non gendered "Kingdom"
Saedgar	Lowlander word for the penis
Saedrow	Lowlander word for the vagina

Siodaric's Pride	Player troupe that was destroyed by His Own in Bainellen
Stealna kir	A female hunter's rite of passage that happens shortly after menarche. Alone, they must go out and hunt, returning with food for their eknos. It is part of their belief in the stages of life: "Begun in blood, sustained by blood, ending in blood."

At the time of the story, most of eknos simply take their bows and slings and go hunt something, the only difference is that they have to do it by themselves. Rhia distinguished herself by following the oldest traditions: she left for her hunt naked and carrying only an obsidian blade. Despite this, she brought home a full grown moonhart buck.

Te-ana	The "goddess" tea. This is drunk in combination with the *te-an* and *te-na* by the couple who wish to procreate.

A woman who finds herself pregnant and wishes to terminate the pregnancy drinks *te-ana* by itself. This needs to be done early or the risk to the woman becomes very high.

Te-na	The tea a man takes to prevent conception. Works in conjunction with the tea the woman drinks. If one is missing, it may not be as effective.

To combine the teas along with *te-ana* into one drink aids in conception. The drinking of the combined tea is a big ritual/party. Less than a wedding in that it promises only a child not a

	"family."
Te-an	The tea a woman takes to prevent conception. Works in conjunction with the tea the man drinks. If one is missing, it may not be as effective.
	To combine the teas into one drink along with *te-ana* aids in conception. The drinking of the combined tea is a big ritual/party. Less than a wedding in that it promises only a child not a "family."

Months

Each month is 45 days long and matches the lunar cycles. Equinox and Solstice days are not counted in the month totals

Aethenian	Marks the time after the Winter solstice until the beginning of Tilling / Burning season
Eabian	Marks the beginning of Tilling/ Burning season and runs until vernal equinox
Nabryhtian	Marks the time after the vernal equinox until Growing / Gathering season begins
Aililnaian	Marks the beginning of the Growing / Gathering season and runs until the solstice
Aelfanian	Marks the time after the solstice until the beginning of Harvest / Hunting season
Yffian	Marks the beginning of the Harvest / Hunting season until the autumnal equinox
Siodian	Marks the time after the equinox to beginning of Fallow / Singing season
Cathairnian	Marks the beginning of the Fallow / Singing until the solstice

Seasons

	Lowlander	Uplander
Winter	Fallow	Singing
Spring	Tilling	Burning
Summer	Growing	Gathering
Autumn	Harvest	Hunting

Counting

Lowlander Term	Uplander Term
Ondae	Wuda
Tudae	Tuda
Tredae	Thrada
Firdae	Furda
Fidae	Fivda
Sidae	Sekda
Sevdae	Seda
Adae	Aeda
Nidae	Needa
Tedae	Tinda

Plays Performed or Referenced

Nabryhtric's Heir: Play written by Neacal about the spiritual heir of the last of the "divine Rici."

The Last Days of Aelfanaricu: A History play that tells the tale of Aelfanaricu, the last female ruler of the Rici to rule in her own right.

Arminaric V: A History Play that tells the tale of the end of Golden Age of the Rici.

Tale of Immin and Aelfwynne: A Pastoral Comedy

The Tragical Tale of Raffe the Lover. A farcical play about finding and losing love in all its forms.

Current Day Arics

Oeric	of Aethellen (named First)
Ricberat	of Maukellen
Elias	of Aelfallen
Gabrel	of Varranellen
Cleiarach	of Bainellen

List of Anarics

Name	Reign	Notable accomplishments
Aeth'anaric	-12 to 18	Founded the Rici after having been the ruler of Aethellen province for twelve years previously.
Irm'anaric	18 to 35	Long reign kept things stable. Put down a few minor rebellions, but most notable for not being a warrior first
Aethanaric II	35 to 42	
Aethanaric III	42 to 62	Long, prosperous reign. Great patron to the arts. Many of the first Players began at this time.
Ald'anaric	62 to 68	Lost the throne to his half sister which began a hundred years of female rule. Once they lost the rulership, women began to be moved to second class position. The time was used as a myth

Name	Reign	Notable accomplishments
		and, because how it ended, used as an example of why women can't rule, themselves or others.
Ceol'anaricu	68 to 102	Young to the throne, she ruled a very long time. The prosperity of the reign of Aethanaric III continued and expanded.
Cwan'aricu	102 to 115	
Ceolanaricu II	115 to 117	Death in childbirth. Became a "matron saint" of women in labor
Cwanaricu II	118 to 145	Sister to Ceolanaricu. Won brief skirmish with brother to regain throne
Aelf'anaricu	145 to 161	She was a very sensual woman who used sex as statecraft, sharing pleasure with pretty much everybody who was around her. She had five living children. The prosperity, power, and plenty were near its height. Decadent and very sensual court. Deposed by rival house of Aelfellen Province
Arminaric II	161 to 165	Barely got his power solidified when died of sepsis
Nabryht'ric	165 to 193	Beginning of a cult of royalty. The next few rulers claimed a kind of divine right and a heavenly descent. Some claimed that they were the offspring of An and Na mating, but this was only whispered.
Nabert'ric	193 to 214	
Nabryhtric II	214 to 215	Killed in winter skirmish
Nawynd'ric	216 to 232	Sailor king
Nabrihtric III	232 to 253	
Nabertric II	253 to 268	
Naldanaric II	269 to 273	Died by a commoner's hand. Ended the

Name	Reign	Notable accomplishments
		divine royalty cult. "Bad luck" name never used again
Ailil'naric	273 to 301	Cousin to Naldanaric II
Aililnaric II & Aelfanaricu II	301 to 315/345	He died early in the reign and she took over "in his name." Made great gains amongst the original Eknos and was first to claim Rulership over the Old Ones. "Ruler of lands Low and High." The true golden period of the High Kingdom.
Ain'aric	345 to 363	
Ainaric II	363 to 399	
Arminaric III	399 to 415	
Siod'aric	415 to 442	
Ainaric II	442 to 442	
Arminaric IV	443 to 450	
Ailnaric II	450 to 471	
Ailnaric III	471 to 495	
Siodaric II	495 to 499	Complained upon his deathbed that Ana punished him by not letting him live until the year 500
Arminaric V	499 to 505	End of "Golden Age" of Anacarra. His early death was seen in retrospect as a bad omen
Dall'anaric	505 to 512	Increased trade, both between the provinces and with other countries
Dallanaric II	512 to 517	Died of ague
Siodaric III	517 to 529	
Nawindric II	529 to 537	Attempted increase in worship to appease the bad things going on
Nawindric III	537 to 559	Carried on frenzy of worship as the answer to the changes in climate and prosperity

Name	Reign	Notable accomplishments
Cathair'naric	560 to 601	Clan Killer
Cathairnaric II	601 to 611	
Iar'naric	611 to 623	
Cathairnaric III	623 to 648	Also called Clan Killer
Iarnaric II	648 to 649	
Og'naric	649 to 655	
Goba'naric	655 to 668	
Unrad'naric	668 to 679	Loss of the "Two" The Unready

Author's Notes and Acknowledgements

This novel grew from more seeds than found in a Sower's field. I wasn't searching for my next book to write when I picked up *Guns, Germs, and Steel* by Jared M. Diamond but I struggled with the seeming inevitability of that choice and wondered *What if we'd chosen differently?* When I read *1491* by Charles C. Mann the how of it became much more clear and my gatherers had a way to eat and live and tell their stories.

For the lowlanders, two ideas persisted from the very earliest efforts: a group of actors dragged into the political conflicts of their day despite themselves and a woman masquerading as a man playing women's roles on stage. Then the conflicts implicit in Diamond's work became clear and more story took form.

The self-righteous and implacable religious zealots have too many precedents to count.

After that, it was dogged determination and the assistance of many people that got this book created. My sweetie Stef listened to me as every new idea blossomed and her feedback – and patience – was vital in determining which of those blossoms should see the light of day.

The members of Smokey Wizard Bacon – Kat Beyer, Brendan Day, Carrie Feguson, David Gallay, and Kelly Janda – tore my book in half and gave me the tools I needed to build it up again, better than it was.

And last, but not least, is you, dear reader. You've chosen to give my novel a try and for that I thank you.

ABOUT THE AUTHOR

David has always been curious. "What if...?" was his favorite question as a child. In high school that curiosity got him into trouble, in college it ... well it got him into college! But all of the history, philosophy, literature, theater, language, economics, anthropology, and political science classes combined didn't assuage that curiosity, they honed it. He thought more schooling might finally get him answers but his Master's degree mostly means he just asks more troubling questions.

He also discovered early on that writing novels and lyrics and short stories and articles and anything at least gives him the excuse to pursue those questions. And the answers he has found would fill a book! Well, more than one, actually.

www.ingramcontent.com/pod-product-compliance
Lightning Source LLC
Chambersburg PA
CBHW070859260626
47162CB00007B/2511